Acclaim for Charlotte Bingham:

'Compulsively readable'
Options

'Irresistible . . . A treat that's not to be missed'
Prima

'A rip-roaring combination of high romance
and breathless excitement'
Mail on Sunday

'Compelling'
Woman and Home

'Heartwarming and full of period charm'
Daily Express

'Her imagination is thoroughly original'
Daily Mail

'Charlotte Bingham's devotees will recognize
her supreme skill as a storyteller'
Independent on Sunday

'As comforting and nourishing as a hot milky
drink on a stormy night. Her legions of
fans will not be disappointed'
Daily Express

Also by Charlotte Bingham:

CORONET AMONG THE WEEDS
LUCINDA
CORONET AMONG THE GRASS
BELGRAVIA
COUNTRY LIFE
AT HOME
BY INVITATION
TO HEAR A NIGHTINGALE
THE BUSINESS
IN SUNSHINE OR IN SHADOW
STARDUST
NANNY
CHANGE OF HEART
DEBUTANTES
THE NIGHTINGALE SINGS
GRAND AFFAIR
LOVE SONG
THE KISSING GARDEN
THE LOVE KNOT
THE BLUE NOTE
THE SEASON
SUMMERTIME
DISTANT MUSIC
THE CHESTNUT TREE
THE WIND OFF THE SEA
THE MOON AT MIDNIGHT
DAUGHTERS OF EDEN
THE HOUSE OF FLOWERS
THE MAGIC HOUR
FRIDAY'S GIRL
OUT OF THE BLUE
IN DISTANT FIELDS
THE WHITE MARRIAGE
GOODNIGHT SWEETHEART
THE ENCHANTED
THE LAND OF SUMMER

THE DAISY CLUB

Charlotte Bingham

BANTAM BOOKS

LONDON · TORONTO · SYDNEY · AUCKLAND · JOHANNESBURG

TRANSWORLD PUBLISHERS
61–63 Uxbridge Road, London W5 5SA
A Random House Group Company
www.rbooks.co.uk

THE DAISY CLUB
A BANTAM BOOK: 9780553819939

First published in Great Britain
in 2009 by Bantam Press
a division of Transworld Publishers
Bantam edition published 2009

Addresses for Random House Group Ltd companies outside the
UK can be found at: www.randomhouse.co.uk
The Random House Group Ltd Reg. No. 954009

The Random House Group Ltd supports The Forest Stewardship
Council (FSC), the leading international forest certification
organization. All our titles that are printed on Greenpeace
approved FSC certified paper carry the FSC logo.
Our paper procurement policy can be found at
www.rbooks.co.uk/environment

Typeset in 11/13pt Palatino by
Kestrel Data, Exeter, Devon.
Printed in the UK by
CPI Cox & Wyman, Reading RG1 8EX.

2 4 6 8 10 9 7 5 3 1

*This book is dedicated to those joyous,
life-enhancing beings who value friendship and
loyalty. May their shadows never grow less
and flowers grow beneath their feet.*

THIS NOVEL BEGINS IN ENGLAND
IN THE AUTUMN OF 1938

Prologue

The sea can still be heard in the distance, and the wind of course, howling; sometimes in despair at what had happened in that much loved place, sometimes murmuring quietly, perhaps whispering about the past, stories and secrets that only those who had been there would know. Occasionally a door can be heard banging, not noisily so much as a little hopelessly, an intermittent sound, as if it is calling to someone to come and shut it, as a child might call in the dark of the night: *'Is anyone there?'*

There is no one there. There are no eyes looking or ears listening behind their brave stone walls, although there is some flowered material at one window, and one still has a faded blue front door, and another some broken flowerpots beside the back door, and further along there are the heads of flowers among the swaying grass, perhaps sown there long ago, in the hope of better times to come.

Now it seems that with the warmer weather that optimism might not be misplaced, that the wind from the sea, having moved to a soft warming zephyr, is at last welcoming; and the wild flowers in the meadows, having overtaken the last signs of spring, are bending their heads towards the calm of the barely moving blue sea that lies between the two cliffs ahead.

Someone appears at the foot of the meadows, standing at first quite still, seemingly immovable, framed by the view, perhaps watching intently, then all of a sudden he waves and beckons to the figures he can begin to see arriving above him, figures which appear at first only as dots of colour among the long grass, until at last they become people, laughing and talking, the men in jerseys and jackets struggling with rugs and picnic baskets, the women walking ahead of them, their headscarves fluttering in the warm breeze.

Once they arrive by his side it rapidly becomes apparent that this is to be a joyous day of laughter and chatter, as picnic rugs are spread out, and food and drink produced from a mix of old-fashioned leather picnic sets, and straw baskets made pale by time and use. A day full of gaiety, but gradually lessening in volume as the talk subsides, and finally only one voice is heard – and with it comes the certainty of victory.

PART ONE

Chapter One

The silence in the dining room was such that a piece of thistledown falling on to the carpet would have created a stir. Finally, and at last, a maid moved away from the sideboard, her tight-laced walking shoes squeaking as she moved over the dark polished floorboards. Daisy waited for her to refill Aunt Maude's elegant flowered breakfast teacup.

'You're going over to the Court this morning, did you say?'

'Yes, Aunt Maude, to help with the sand-bagging.'

Aunt Maude gave a small sigh, and frowned.

'*Sand*bagging—' She followed this word with yet another silence. '*Sand*bagging. It does not seem possible, after all we have already been through, that there is more to come.'

Daisy tried not to look or sound excited.

'And then a gas lecture, I think, or is it an ARP lecture, something like that,' Daisy went on, still far too cheerfully, she realised, far too late.

'Hmm.'

Aunt Maude's 'hmm' was any other human being's 'humph', except in her case it had a more than adequate dose of bitterness added to it, not unlike the bitter aloes with which she had once insisted that Daisy's fingers should be painted before she went to sleep at night.

The front of Daisy's knees started to hurt, as they always did at mealtimes at Twistleton Hall. She thought with envy of the jolly times she knew the rest of her friends would be having at breakfast at Twistleton Court, only a few miles away. It had always been the same, Daisy locked up in the grandeur of the Hall, surrounded by portraits of the family ancestors, suits of armour and, not least, the ghosts of Aunt Maude's four brothers, three of whom had been lost in the Great War, while Freddie and the rest of them enjoyed jolly times with Freddie's Aunt Jessica.

'Does Jessica Valentyne still have those ridiculous servants of hers, do you know?'

The front of Daisy's knees stopped aching, and she started to cross and uncross her legs beneath the heavy linen breakfast cloth, twisting them into tortuous shapes, and untwisting them again. It just so happened that Freddie's Aunt Jessica was one of Daisy's heroines, and with good reason, for a certain Miss Warmington had persuaded Aunt Maude Beresford to let Jessica Valentyne take Daisy on when she opened the Court as a finishing school. Up until then it had been governesses, governesses, and more governesses.

Being all alone with a governess had become

Daisy's nightmare, resenting, as she had, the slowness of their brains as they waded on through dull subject after dull subject. The whole week of solitary schooling would only be relieved by the arrival of Miss Warmington to take English and History, both of which she somehow managed to persuade Aunt Maude were better taken in the open air, or as Miss Warmington briskly called it, 'on the hoof'.

'Why do angels fly, Daisy?'

'Because they take themselves so lightly!'

Quotations from the works of great men such as G. K. Chesterton were learned not from a dusty book, but while striding through the woods around the house, before setting up their easels and starting to try and paint the sun coming through the trees. History was learned from walking around houses and castles, villages and towns, no blackboard or chalk needed.

'You will understand Henry VIII and the Reformation much better when you stand in an old village church, and see the desecration done in the name of the deity, dear.'

By the time she was sixteen, Freddie's aunt, Jessica Valentyne, and Miss Warmington finally managed to obtain Daisy's release from what seemed to her to be the tomb of Aunt Maude's unbending way of life, and set her free to go to the Court, to get to know girls of her own age and generation. Which was probably why Aunt Maude still disapproved of Jessica Valentyne, her servants, her gas lectures, and possibly even the Air Raid

17

Precautions. Quite apart from anything else Aunt Maude did not think a war *was* coming. She still thought it could be prevented, which meant that, in her opinion, people like Jessica Valentyne were actually warmongers.

'I suppose it is quite necessary for you to go to the Court today?'

'Oh yes, I am afraid so. I am quite promised to help out, and, besides, Aurelia Smith-Jones and Laura Hambleton are arriving, and they want to see me.'

Aunt Maude sighed, and looked around for another cup of tea, which was always a device of hers when she wanted to delay Daisy escaping from her sight. To Daisy's delight the maids had cleared all the breakfast dishes into the food lift, and it was even now hurtling down to the sculleries below the dining room.

'*Hu-blooming-ray!*'

Daisy exhaled quietly, waiting for Aunt Maude to give another sigh and rise to her feet, her upright stance, stiff back and proud head-carriage a warning to all that, unmarried though Miss Maude might be, nevertheless the sole chatelaine of Twistleton Hall was someone whom everyone was forced to respect.

'You are staying the night at the Court, I understand?'

Daisy, who had shot to her feet and was now feeling like a horse who sees the field gate opening, and the bliss of endless meadows in front, said 'yes', and then promptly felt guilty as she realised that this meant that her aunt would be on her own at both luncheon and dinner.

'I can come back to the Hall for dinner, if that is what you would like?' she asked, hoping against hope that the answer would be in the negative, which it thankfully was.

'As it happens I have various people coming to dinner. We will be talking agricultural matters, so it is quite convenient if you stay with Jessica Valentyne for the night.'

Daisy walked slowly behind Aunt Maude across the great hall, and then up the shallow wooden staircase to the first floor, and then just as slowly down the corridor, where they both parted at their different bedroom doors.

Once inside the bedroom, with its mix of eighteenth-century and later, heavier, Victorian furniture, its flower paintings and narrow four-poster bed hung with faded silk hangings, Daisy flung her few night things, a couple of changes of clothes, and some highly frowned-upon (at the Hall, particularly) lipstick and a small powder bowl into a knapsack, and herself into a pair of dungarees, and without more ado, bolted back down the corridor, shoes in hand, to the hall once more, where, shoes back on, she ran out into the drive, and from there across to her trusty ladies' bicycle with its more than useful basket on the front. She jumped on board and started to cycle ferociously out of the back entrance, and down on to the open road that led in splendidly zigzag fashion past the old farms still belonging to the estate, to Twistleton Court, which did not belong, and never had, to any but the Valentynes since that same English Reformation upon which her old teacher, Miss Warmington, had frowned so particularly.

'Heigh ho for the open road,' Daisy sang as she bicycled. 'Heigh ho for the jolly times! Heigh ho for the Valentynes!'

So childish, but she had been singing that since she was sixteen, and now she was eighteen, she still liked to sing it. And oh, the bliss of getting away from the funereal atmosphere with which Aunt Maude seemed to surround herself, away from the servants of whom Aunt Maude silently disapproved, however devoted or efficient – because they were females. Before the Great War, only males – footmen and butlers, under-footmen and under-butlers – had worked at the Hall, whereas now, apart from Pattern and Bowles, the old place was forced to depend on goodly ladies who came in from the surrounding villages to help out, before hurrying thankfully back to their families.

Long before she cycled up the short carriage drive that led to the Court, Daisy imagined that she could see all her friends, already in their dungarees, spades over their shoulders, possibly singing some silly, childish song, as she had just been doing, or something from a musical they had just seen. Oh, the bliss of it all, compared to sharing the home life of Maude Augusta Katherine Anne Victoria Beresford, known to Daisy alone as *Aunt Maude*.

*   *   *

Branscombe adjusted his eyepatch and frowned. He was not in the best of moods, but when he rounded the corner and saw Miss Freddie and her recently arrived guests at Twistleton Court digging enthusiastically at piles of sand, filling the bags with childish enthusiasm, he could not help smiling. The three young women, all wearing dungarees, their long hair tied back into ribbons and combs, were carrying on more as if they were on the beach making a sandcastle, rather than preparing for the war everyone knew was coming.

'Miss Freddie, Miss Laura, Miss Daisy, it is time for luncheon, and if you do not come soon there won't be any, and that is for certain, for Miss Blossom's dogs will have been sure to have eaten it all in your absence.'

'The dogs' digestions are much better suited to Blossom's cooking,' Freddie muttered, pulling a face as Branscombe turned away, making once more for the house.

'I heard that, Miss Freddie, and that was not you at your best, if I may say so, for even should it be true, it is not something that should be said in front of guests. Fill them with dread, that will, and what will that do for their digestions then, may I ask?'

Branscombe continued on his way, while the girls simultaneously threw down their spades and made for their lodgings in the old stables.

'I remember this old place as if it was my own

family home,' Laura Hambleton stated, as they passed under the archway into the great square cobbled yard that had once housed as many as fifty horses.

A small section of the yard, with the grooms' quarters above it, had long ago been converted into smart little cottage-type flats for the use of Aunt Jessica's finishing-school pupils, but with the closing of the school some few months before, they were now only used for occasional guests. Each flat that the girls had been given had its own stamp of originality, not least the one that Daisy had used.

Over her cottage-type door with its up-and-down black enamel latch was a notice that she had painted what now seemed to be aeons ago: *THE DAISY CLUB – MEMBERS ONLY!'*

Daisy stared up at it, remembering the excitement of those early days, kitting out the flat with rugs and lamps, and things brought from the Hall. Putting, tongue in cheek, a visitors' book with *'The Daisy Club – please sign in'*, at the door, and how everyone, even Branscombe, had done as directed. She smiled and pushed open the door, somehow knowing that the innocence of those days had already gone, the magic-carpet moments that bridge childhood into adulthood, the excitement, most of all the freshness, they were there, locked in her memory, too dear to think about too much, but also, gone.

The girls quickly changed into the cotton dresses and cardigans, and white peep-toed sandals that for some reason were the required uniform at Jessica's country lunches, and having brushed out their hair and powdered their noses, they crossed to the main house, all of them filled with a pleasant feeling that they had done their patriotic duty by their country by filling so many sandbags.

'Oh, Laura, sorry!' Freddie stopped suddenly, and taking out a handkerchief from her sleeve she pushed it at her friend. 'No lipstick to be worn in the country.'

'For heaven's sakes, I'm not still at school here!' Laura protested, but she wiped her lips clean nevertheless.

'Have you forgotten that Miss Valentyne thinks it looks tarty to wear lipstick in the country?' Daisy asked, surprised. 'The unwritten rule, my deah.'

'Well now, there's a thing!' Laura laughed. 'I do believe, my dear, that I had forgot.'

'Even so, Aunt Jessica would have excused you, because you are one of her favourite old pupils,' Freddie murmured.

'Oh my, people who live in the country seem to have rules for everything. Is there a rule for breathing?'

'As a matter of fact there is,' Freddie told her old friend cheerfully. 'It must be done quietly, or not at all.'

The library at Twistleton Court had a low ceiling in keeping with its ancient origins, and had been built long before the Valentynes acquired the estate as part of some heiress's dowry. Once upon a time the library's ancient walls had been lined with books, now they were merely lined with shelves, some of which bore family photographs, others of which were dotted with silver cups of all shapes and sizes, perhaps won at local agricultural shows.

'Ah there you are, girls, good, good, good. Glass of sherry before luncheon? How many sandbags did you fill this morning?'

It was inevitable that Aunt Jessica should take a proprietary interest in the filling of the sandbags, for the very good reason that she was one of the founding members of the Air Raid Precautions committee, and as such, providing sandbags was one of the many items on her list of things to do, in the event of an all-too-inevitable aerial attack.

Laura gladly accepted a glass of sherry, lit a cigarette, blew a smoke ring, and watched its progress across the room with lazily appreciative eyes. It was all so dear, being back in the library with its low ceilings and its ancient, faded Persian rugs, watching Aunt Jessie pouring a glass of lunchtime sherry, and everyone lighting up cigarettes with accomplished grace, because smoking prettily from holders was what Freddie called 'one of Aunt Jessie's *things*'.

Twistleton Court had been the scene of some of Laura's happiest days, a so-called finishing school for young ladies, started by Freddie's aunt, purely for the purpose of trying to make the old place pay for itself. Laura's father, Arthur Hambleton, was typical of so many parents. He had been in the diplomatic service, finally coming to live in England after his wife had died suddenly of a fever when they were in Singapore, and bringing with him his only daughter.

Not deeming it suitable to share his life with a lively young girl, he had sent Laura to be 'finished' at Twistleton Court. Despite being still in mourning for her mother, the moment she had arrived outside its mellowed exterior, and started to climb its shallow stone steps, the old place had caught Laura up in its magic, and now, it was no surprise to find that hardly had she returned when it did so all over again. And now it seemed it needed her, but more than that, she knew she needed it. Twistleton could be her way out of the endlessly dreary social scene into which her father and godmother had insisted on plunging her for the last few months.

It was not only the fact that Laura was just not suited to becoming a leading society figure, or that she didn't enjoy endlessly repeating the same languid dialogue every night as she sat at dinner, turning first to her right and then to her left, or equally endlessly circling some dance floor – it was that a never-ending diet of socialising was beginning to make her feel as if she was losing her mind. Besides which, the sight of her father openly flirting with ladies of every age was, to say the least, nauseating.

The fact was that Laura's father had become a continuing embarrassment to his only child, which made it a positive pleasure to answer

Freddie's invitation to go to Twistleton Court, and help prepare for the war. The moment she had read her old friend's letter Laura had known that doing whatever was needed would give her life a purpose, which just at that moment she was only too aware it sadly needed.

The glasses of sherry drained, they all filed behind Aunt Jessica to the dining room, which at Twistleton Court was so far away from the kitchen that food had to be sent up on an internal lift, clanking and heaving its way up to the ground floor from the basement, where Blossom Valentyne, Aunt Jessie's eccentric cousin, who acted as housekeeper in return for the use of a cottage on the small estate, would be standing ready to receive it.

She turned when she saw the luncheon guests coming into the room with Jessica.

'Miss Laura, how very nice to see you. Miss Freddie, the same,' she bellowed, raising her voice above the sound of two dachshunds barking. 'Algy and Bertie are pleased to see you, too,' she added, moving towards the table, but since both Algy and Bertie were attached to either side of her waist on pieces of string, her progress, it seemed to Laura, was distinctly reminiscent of a barge moving along a canal.

'Don't you trouble yourself, Blossom, we can help ourselves, thank you,' Jessica called down the room.

Blossom hesitated, but seeing the logic of this, and since Algy and Bertie's well-being always came before everything, she turned back to the sideboard.

'I'll just wait here, while you all help yourselves; as you said – better that way.'

She settled herself comfortably to the side of the serving table, the dogs doing the same by her stoutly shod feet.

Inwardly Laura sighed with delight. Nothing much had changed at Twistleton Court, in fact nothing at all had changed, and that was before she helped herself to the haddock-strewn rice from the old silver dish.

After lunch they retreated back to their cottage, where Laura could not wait to light up her first cigarette after lunch, if only to suppress the memory of the food. After this she leant back against the cushions on the chintz-covered sofa.

'Miss Valentyne's not selling Twistleton, is she, Freddie?'

'Aunt Jessica selling Twistleton? Good gracious, no. I mean, she should, of course. But you know how it is, the Valentynes have been here since fifteen hundred and eight – no, sorry, fifteen hundred and *twenty*-eight.'

'So rather newly arrived as far as the village is concerned?'

'And, as you know, Aunt Jessica will never, ever leave, and that is a fact. Two of her brothers were killed in the Great War, as well as her fiancé; and then both my father – her second youngest brother – and my mother were killed in a motoring

27

accident in Egypt when I was only a baby, so she has been landed with Twistleton Court, and me, for far too long to be able or want to budge, poor soul. And then there's Branscombe, and Blossom, not to mention Algy and Bertie, who because of the growing anti-German feeling are now permanently attached to Blossom's belt, because for some reason best known to themselves there are people, would you believe, who think kicking dachshunds is patriotic, even though we are not yet at war, either with Hitler, or dachshunds.'

'So what should be our plan to help Miss Valentyne, may I enquire, Freddie, dear?' She looked round at Daisy. 'Really and truly, that is why you asked us down here, is it not? To put our shoulders to the wheel?'

'Partly,' Freddie agreed. 'And partly not. But,' she paused, 'I don't know whether I should burden you with this. Perhaps I should let Aurelia tell you when she arrives. In fact, I am sure I should.'

Laura gave Freddie her best 'come on, tell us all' look.

Freddie pulled a face. It did not enhance her strangely ancestral, unfashionable looks, but nevertheless Laura remembered the expression with affection. Freddie usually made it when someone or other found them being somewhere, or doing something, they were not meant to, and, it had to be said, enjoying themselves all the more because it was against the rules.

'Very well, I will tell you, to save Aurelia having to tell you herself. She is pregnant—'

For the first time in years Laura could think of absolutely nothing to say.

'That is just *awful*,' she finally volunteered, after what seemed a very long silence, but was actually only a very small one.

'You are quite right, too awful for words, really,' Daisy nodded in agreement, following which she and Freddie both reached for Laura's cigarettes, and lit one.

'Who did she fall for?'

'Some married man, not knowing, I mean she didn't know the wretch was married, of course.'

'Married, you say?'

'Yes, married, and much older, and not wanting to become unmarried, either.'

'But, I mean to say, what is she going to do?'

'I think that what she was thinking of doing was coming down here to Aunt Jessica and me, and having the baby, at Twistleton Court, because we are so very out of the way. I mean, the Post Office have only just *heard* of Twisters.'

'But, I mean to say, Freddie, that's all very well, but does Aunt Jessica know any of this?'

Freddie's number one distraught expression came into play once more.

'Er, no, at least not yet.'

'So who is going, er, um, going to tell her?'

'Er, um – we are, I think.'

'Is that why you asked us all down here, Freddie?'

'Sort of, yes, Daisy, and – and sort of not. Also, because of the war, I thought we should have a few days down here, before our world comes to an end, and we are wiped out.'

'The world won't come to an end, Freddie. We might, but not the world, you can be sure of that.'

'She's only seventeen and a half,' Freddie went on, appearing not to hear Laura. 'Blossom says that is a very dangerous age to have a baby.'

'Miss Blossom knows?'

'Of course. She reads all my letters, always has.'

'Why don't you stop her?'

'Probably because if I did, she might leave. She enjoys them more than the wireless.'

They were all silent, suddenly. There was nothing to say about Aurelia's state. It was a disaster of such magnitude that it could only be fully appreciated in silence. A girl of any class getting herself into what Aunt Jessie always called 'an interesting state' was bad enough, but for someone like Aurelia it was the end.

'Poor Relia, what a to-do, what a to-do.'

It was teatime of a still tranquil autumn afternoon when Relia, as she was always known to the other three, finally stepped out of the evening train at Twistleton Meads Station, but despite the fact that Daisy, Freddie and Laura were all devastated about her news, they did their best to pretend everything was normal, and to prove this Freddie drove far too fast all the way home. And neither did it stop Laura from opening some champagne she had bought to celebrate their reunion, not to mention lighting up so many cigarettes in swift succession she actually started to feel vaguely sick. Finally, however, the consumption of drink and the forced laughter stopped.

'What are you all staring at?' Aurelia stubbed out her cigarette, before promptly pushing another one into her black holder and lighting it.

'We are all staring at you, ducks.' Freddie leant forward to pluck the cigarette from the holder in her friend's hand. 'Because you shouldn't be smoking so much, not in your state.'

Aurelia stared from one face to another.

'My state?' she asked, frowning.

'Yes, your state. Remember you wrote to me?'

'Yes, you wrote to Freddie, and told her you were in an interesting condition as a result of falling in love with a married man.'

'Oh, *him*. Oh yes, of course. Yes, well, he was a so-and-so, of that there was no doubt, but—' Aurelia stopped, and re-lit her cigarette. 'But as it happens, I am not in an interesting state after all.'

'*What?*'

Freddie felt instantly indignant, as if she had been smoking and getting anxious for nothing, which led her to stub out her cigarette in the small silver ashtray.

'Why did you write and say that you *were*, then? That you were in an interesting state?'

'Because I thought I *was*, Freddie.'

Laura also leaned forward, but it was to pour herself another glass of champagne.

'We could all willingly strangle you, do you know that, Relia? We have been sitting here in

31

the cottage worrying and worrying, and trying to think how to help you. Freddie here had already started to plan how to get the ancient wooden family crib down from the attics, and I had begun to plan how to save from my dress allowance to help with paying for the nursing home. You are a pest, and a pill, Aurelia, and please never tell me otherwise.'

'Well, I am very sorry, but so would you be, if you were me, because—' Aurelia said, assuming a half-apologetic and half-sulky expression. 'Well, because you would, I promise you, you would.'

'What happened? Why did you think you *were*—' Freddie asked, trying to ignore the fact that she found she was feeling a sudden and quite keen disappointment that she and Aunt Jessica were *not* going to be asked to bring Aurelia's baby up at Twistleton Court.

'Well, it was like this.' Aurelia looked around at the three faces all keenly watching her, and felt the sudden enjoyable power of the storyteller. 'It was like this,' she repeated. 'I made the mistake of saying I would go for a drink with this chap, and after we'd had a few, which I admit was a mistake, he took me home to my parents' house, but they were away. Well, they're always away at the moment, and he pushed his way into the house the moment I turned the key in the lock. Of course, there were no maids anywhere in sight, which is just so typical – anyway, he started to kiss me, very roughly, and it was all so horrible I fainted, and, well, when I woke up I was quite sure

I must be pregnant, because I know that kissing like that *can* make you pregnant. But anyway, as it turned out, I wasn't, so that was that.'

'Oh God, how awful, you must have had a horrible few days.'

'More than a few days. So that was why I wrote to Freddie here, because by then I was quite sure I must be, really I was. I mean girls are meant to know, aren't they? And I was sure that I knew, but obviously I was just lucky. Still, serve me right, don't you think? I mean I should have known he was married all along.'

'Why? Why should you have known?' Daisy leaned forward, looking and feeling more riveted than indignant, despite the fact that it was so typical of Aurelia to get herself in a muddle after drinking too much and being kissed; but still, they all knew that kissing could lead to anything.

'Because he was so polite, you know, all that opening doors, and being terribly, terribly, terribly nice about listening to you, and being frightfully, frightfully interested. Well, only men who are pretending not to be married, or men who are wild flowers and so on, are like that, aren't they? They are the only men who are really polite to you about door-opening, and flowers and chocolates and so on, Mummy says.'

Laura nodded slowly and sadly in agreement.

'Your mother is right. I know she's right, because my father's like that.'

'Not quite fair on your father, Laura. I mean, he's not married any more. I mean, he is a widower.'

'He's a disgrace,' Laura burst out suddenly. 'Really, he is a disgrace. Honestly, if there wasn't a war coming, I think he would be the talk of London, instead of just what Miss Valentyne calls a social nuisance. Not that any of the other older men are any better, from what I hear, but this is not getting us any further with the matter under discussion.' She went to the desk, and taking up a pen and pad, she sat down again. 'I started to make a list of things to do in the run-up to the war, starting with helping with Relia's baby, but now we can cross off her interesting condition and get down to the business of helping Aunt Jessica and Freddie stay at Twistleton Court.'

Freddie held up her hand.

'Correction, Laura, I don't want to stay at Twistleton—'

'You don't?'

'No, I want to join up. I am a romantic, I want to fight for everything we hold dear, for everything here, I am as—'

'Mad as that—' Laura put in.

'You don't need to join up, Freddie, really you don't, none of us need to join up.'

'*You* may not need to join up, Relia, but *I* do.'

'Mummy believes Mr Chamberlain and Lord Halifax. She thinks that we won't need to join up or anything like that, that everyone is just panicking needlessly, and people like Churchill are trying to get attention by making dramas where there shouldn't be any,' Aurelia told her, assuming a superior expression because her father was a Tory MP.

'Oh really, well, send one of these to Mummy dear, Relia, and tell her to make sure to wear it at all times.'

Freddie threw her one of the boxes that Branscombe had given out to them after lunch. Aurelia opened it, perhaps expecting some sort of nice present, something pretty for her mother, only to find it was a gas mask. She covered her face and started to cry.

'People like you are just warmongers,' she moaned.

'No, Relia, it's people who let Hitler stroll across Czechoslovakia unhindered who are the warmongers, just too lily-livered to recognise a tyrant. Now, come on, everyone, it's off to the Golf Club for a bit of practice.'

'What sort of practice—'

'First aid, gas masks, anything you care to name, apparently.'

Aurelia sniffed.

'I wish I'd never come down, now. I thought we were going to have fun.'

'I know, dear, and you're not the only one,' Laura told her affectionately. 'Now belt up, buckle up, and look on the bright side, it's something to do when you get back to London. You can practise bandaging Mummy and Daddy.'

'I wish you weren't always so horrid to me, Laura, truly I do. It makes me feel sick when you are horrid.'

'At least you're not pregnant,' Freddie said, putting an arm round Aurelia in a vaguely patronising manner.

'Now you've only gone and reminded me of that awful man—'

Aurelia shook her head, looking tearful once more.

Laura walked ahead with Daisy.

'Oh well, at least we have our very own secret weapon—'

Daisy nodded.

'Yes, if Relia doesn't get Herr Hitler down, no one will,' she agreed. 'Five minutes with her, and Hitler will turn tail and flee back to Germany.'

Chapter Two

The party from Twistleton Court could walk round
to the golf club, where the ARP meeting was being
held, because the club backed on to Twistleton
land. Laura appreciated that they must make a
strange-looking party. First, leading the way at
a brisk pace, was Aunt Jessica, her head a little
forward, her brogue shoes supporting surprisingly
elegant legs, her tweed skirt and twinset of pale
blue, and her single string of pearls all looking as
they should in the countryside setting. Next came
Branscombe in eyepatch and his faded butler's
jacket and trousers, looking brave because he was
walking beside Blossom and the dachshunds,
and then the four of them, Laura, Freddie, Daisy
and Aurelia, all wearing expressions of solemnity,
as if they were going to church, while sporting
rather less countrified clothes than Aunt Jessica.
Laura was once more wearing lipstick, which she
knew was just not done in the country, but about
which she cared less, since she always thought she
looked fawn without a dash of red on the mouth,
and looking fawn was not something that suited

her, it made her *feel* fawn – so too bad about the proper rules of how to look in the country.

They were all so busy chatting that they walked past a notice on the open gate. As always Branscombe was the only person to stop and bother to read it.

'Oh dear.'

Aunt Jessica, having rattled the door handle on the thin wooden golf-club door, stepped back, and turned to the others.

'They must have forgotten we were coming.'

Branscombe hurried up.

'There's a notice on the gate, Miss Jessica, says all ARP meetings are to be held at the village hall.'

Jessica stared at her beloved general factotum of many years, and then at the gate, as if it was a badly behaved visitor.

'It says what, Branscombe?'

Branscombe sighed.

'I told you, Miss Jessica, the gentlemen of the club would not countenance anyone of the opposite sex—'

Jessica turned towards the door of the golf club and rattled the handle.

'This is a disgrace, Branscombe,' she protested, quietly. 'Quite, quite disgraceful.'

'They've never yet allowed a woman into Twistleton Golf Club, Miss Jessica, not even though Miss Manningham won that cup off of them, disguised as a man.'

'Oh yes, dear Dorelia Manningham, dear well-named lady.' Jessica sighed nostalgically, momentarily distracted. 'Was that before or after she won the Wychford pipe-smoking competition, Branscombe?'

'As you may remember, Miss Manningham attracted so much publicity for that particular incident, it put paid to her sporting exploits. Whereupon she retired to Scotland and took up whaling, only to return here after an unhappy incident involving some nets, a grand Scottish lady, and a dozen lobsters found hidden in a suitcase. Chutney-making is now the order of the day at Needles House, I believe.'

'Good gracious, Branscombe, you are a walking encyclopedia of Twistleton news, truly you are,' Jessica told him in a distracted, yet admiring voice, before nodding towards the distant church spire of St Mary. 'Well, I suppose the only thing we can now do is to redirect our efforts to the village hall, as per the instructions on the gate.'

The elegant man took out a gold cigarette case and, having extended it to his companion opposite, took a cigarette from it himself, and lit it.

'Hosting a dinner party this weekend,' he said, as they both watched the smoke from their cigarettes drift out of the open window over the London rooftops. 'Might well get a handle on the two of them, they're coming over, bringing George Arletti, and *un tel*.'

'I think you'll find it is *une telle*, one Gloria Martine. We've been tagging her since 1934, much good it has done us.'

His elegant friend gave a short humourless laugh.

'Much good any of this has done us, my dear chap, but we must soldier on, keep going, nothing else we can do.'

'It would be easier if we knew just a little of what was going through Chamberlain's mind.'

'My dear fellow, the answer to that is truly – nothing. Nothing goes through the mind of a ditherer. No defined principles means that you go in all directions at once, spread yourself thin, and fall through the middle – all at the same time.'

His companion gave a genuine laugh at this.

'An apt description of an appeaser, if I may say so. What have you arranged for the weekend?'

'Apparently Jessica Valentyne is sending me over a quantity of debutantes to dress up as waitresses, who might, now I come to think of it, report back to me, and after that we shall just have to see. The moment the balloon goes up, that little clutch of Fascists, otherwise known as my neighbours, will be thrown into jug, or else I shall want to know the reason why.'

The speaker stubbed out his cigarette, shook his companion by the hand, and walked with a quick light step from the small sitting room of the nondescript flat, and so out into the summer sunshine. As he walked along he felt, as he always did after such meetings with his contacts in the ever-growing, colossally chaotic security service, distinctly frustrated. The feeling of treading eternal water, of being a greyhound left

40

in the traps, the sheer helplessness of it all, of not quite knowing what could be done, or whether the little they were doing would do any good at all, would sweep over him – and only throwing himself into his motor car, and driving down to his country house just a little too fast, cleared the depression.

Today he drove if anything even faster, putting it all from him just for that time, and finally arrived at his house feeling better. He had, after all, sought and finally been given a role: that at least was something.

To her immense surprise, by the time they reached the village hall Jessica found herself and her little party edging past the best crowd that they had yet seen. There must have been thirty or forty villagers, of all ages. Jessica immediately felt heartened. Blossom, understandably cautious, picked up the two dachshunds, and the whole party from the Court made its way up to the front of the hall, where Jessica then took her place at a pre-set table.

'As you all must now realise, this meeting was meant to be at Twistleton Golf Club, but looking round I see you were all commendably more realistic than I was, and redirected yourselves here, knowing as you obviously do that the members of Twistleton Golf Club do not recognise the existence of the opposite sex – it seems they were all born of men.'

A surge of laughter greeted this statement.

'Now, we must get on with the lecture, but first of all – gas masks.'

'Oh, dear, I think I will faint if we have to wear one of those all the time,' Aurelia moaned.

Laura stared ahead at the demonstration on the stage. Somehow, even up until this last week, despite all the talk in previous years – perhaps because of it – war had seemed really quite remote. A little like a thunderstorm raging fifteen or twenty miles away, but which still might miss where you happened to be living. But now, seeing the goodly people on the stage with their gas masks on, it was a dreadful reality for the first time, although thankfully very far away from the ballrooms and elegant townhouses she had left behind in London, where everyone seemed to be still pretending that war would never, ever happen, and nothing would come between them and their social lives.

Even so, surely something would happen to prevent it? Surely someone would put up a hand, or blow a whistle, and cry, 'Enough of this dangerous carry-on! Of course we are not all going to kill each other again when hardly twenty years have gone by since we were all burying our dear ones? Please, please, please not.'

At that moment the door of the hall was flung open, and everyone turned.

Jessica looked down the room, and smiled, albeit a little wearily.

'Good evening, Jean . . .'

The tall young girl with a mass of shining dark

curly hair and strangely cat-like green eyes limped up the side of the hall, her progress followed with great interest by the rest of the gathering.

'I'm so sorry, Miss Valentyne, I didn't realise that the brakes on my bicycle were completely bished.' She turned first one grazed elbow round, and then the other, and stared at them with detached interest. 'But I do now.'

'Obviously, Jean, but just so long as you are all right.' Jessica frowned. 'As a matter of fact you can come up to the stage, if you would, because seeing that you are so conveniently covered in cuts and bruises, I think we will find we can put you to jolly good use.'

To the sound of appreciative laughter Jean limped up on to the stage, and proceeded to stare with some interest at the array of gas masks on the table.

'Do you want me to put one of these on, Miss Valentyne?'

Jessica shook her head.

'No, dear, we want you to lie down so we can bandage you.'

Without more ado Jean prepared to lie down on the floor.

'Shouldn't we put some sort of sheeting underneath her—' Blossom demanded from the side of the stage, raising her voice above the sound of the dogs yapping at Jean.

'No point now, Miss Blossom,' Jean called to her cheerfully. 'My clothes are wrecked anyway.'

She promptly lay down on the floor, putting

her arms under her head, smiling up at Jessica.

For her part Jessica stared down at the long-limbed girl with her wild dark curls. Of course, and it was only natural, this was just a game to Jean, but to Jessica it was reality. Here was yet another generation, another set of young people, going gaily into war, as if it was some sort of a game. All of a sudden an unwanted memory came back to her. She remembered writing teasingly to Esmond in about 1915, *'I bet you are all having a grand time of it in France!'*

How could she have written that? What a fool, what a silly, silly fool.

But they didn't know, they just didn't know, not until much later. They knew nothing of the stinking trenches, the men blinded by the gas, the horror of men being led over the top, the hundreds of young officers dead within a few days of their arrival at the Front. Three-quarters of those sent off with their hand-knitted socks and their home-bred hunters, and their picnic sets – oh, dear heaven, did they really get sent off with picnic sets? – were, like Esmond, never to return, so that even though they hadn't been married, nevertheless Jessica had been allowed to join the 'little democracy of valour' at the Cenotaph on that special day of national mourning after the Great War.

In those few seconds, too, she remembered the desolation of the empty rooms, and the clothes that would never again be worn by their owners. The suddenness of coming across them unexpectedly, in cupboards and cloakrooms, in tack rooms and attics – their shape retained, the outline of a foot in a boot still visible, the collar of a coat still turned up. It was almost as if the clothes themselves were constantly turning towards the door, expecting the loved one, the owner of the cap or the riding boots, the thickly lined overcoat, to walk in and claim them.

It took very little effort for her to remember Jean Shaw being born at Number Three, The Cottages, Twistleton. In fact she would never forget it. Why should she? She had helped to deliver her. The first time she had ever seen the reality of childbirth, but not the last. Doctor Blackie had been delayed by the storm, and so Jessica, and Doctor Blackie's wife – who, thank heavens, was actually a nurse – had delivered the baby. But though the little girl's arrival had been most welcome to the two impromptu midwives, it had not been to Jean's mother, Mrs Shaw.

'Take it away, take it away!'

Well, of course they hadn't taken 'it' away, they had left 'it' instead in the hands of Mrs Shaw's mother-in-law, who fed 'it' with bottled milk, and more or less brought 'it' up next door at Number Four, The Cottages.

Old Mrs Shaw had only just passed, the previous winter, of pneumonia, and to the fury of her daughter-in-law was found to have left her cottage not to Jean's parents, as expected, but to her first, and as it had transpired, only granddaughter, Jean.

Jessica turned away from the memories, which for some dreary reason were far too busy crowding themselves into her head, positively queueing up to be in the forefront of her mind. There was soon going to be a war again, and because she had known one did not mean she should weaken at the thought of another. She must not, simply must not, go back on determinations already made. This war had to be fought. They had to win it, just had to, or else everything, all that had gone before it, would be for nothing, nothing at all. She was convinced of it, and had been for a long, long time, and now that she could see how crowded her first lecture was, it seemed that at long, long last, she was not alone.

Since the invasion of Czechoslovakia, local people had stopped calling her a *'warmonger'*, sometimes even to her face, had stopped sneering at her convictions, long ago aired, that there would one day be attacks on the population, gas attacks at that, and that everyone, all of Twistleton, should be arming themselves, preparing themselves. Since the last few days, since Hitler walking into Czechoslovakia, even the village had come to realise that it was actually going to happen, that Hitler and the Nazis were not just a rumour helping to sell more English newspapers.

'Very well, now who would like to be the first to come up and practise bandaging on Miss Shaw, please?'

A hand shot up instantly, a bronzed masculine hand. Jessica thought that she must know that

46

hand, those hands, all too well, just as she knew the handsome smiling face of the owner. Joe Huggett looked like a grown-up blond cherub, if such a thing was possible, all pink and white skin, blue eyes, and the open expression of a boy who had always been loved. Dear Joe, like all his brothers, born and bred at Holly House in Twistleton. His father was the local solicitor, the son of a barrister, the grandson of a lawyer, and the family had connections with the village going back over a hundred years.

Joe now walked up to the stage and mounted the few steps that brought him up to their level, smiling with all the proud assurance of a young man in an obviously very, very new Royal Air Force uniform.

Just the sight of Joe in uniform for the first time seemed to give the Twistleton audience a shock, and to add the necessary authenticity to the scene that was about to take place, a scene that suddenly seemed more to be part of some play that they were all re-enacting for the benefit of, say, the renewing of the church roof, or new gymnasium equipment for the school hall, rather than real life. Joe Huggett in his ill-fitting RAF uniform was so very real.

A question rose instantly in everyone's minds, and they all started to shift uneasily in their seats, and look around at each other. If Joe was in uniform why not Tom, or Alan over there, or Doctor Blackie's son Richard Blackie? Why not all of them, come to that? Very well, Joe was young and fit, and the rest of his brothers were already away in the army, but even so? Even so. No state of emergency had been declared as yet, surely? Or hadn't they heard? Had they not been told? Was there something they should know? Then they stared at the stage in front of them, and started to laugh as Joe made a hash of trying to bandage one of Jean Shaw's ankles, blushing to the roots of his blond hair as he did so, while Jean – always a bit of an actress was Jean – acted up no end, pretending he was hurting her.

'Any more volunteers, please?'

Laura and Freddie both stood up, if only to help out Aunt Jessica, but once on stage Freddie looked back at Laura suddenly, and Laura knew at once what that look meant: 'Oh Lord, will this really be necessary? Surely not.'

Laura's expression set. Who knew? Perhaps not? Perhaps something would happen to save them from a war?

But first it seemed they had all been corralled into helping out at a local dinner party.

'Who is the poor soul who owns this house where we are expected to disport ourselves as waitresses?'

'One Guy Athlone. You may have heard of him?'

'Heard of him? I worship him, and his plays!' Aurelia sighed. 'It can't be true. Are we really going to his house?'

'Yes, dear, but not to socialise. We have to help

him out, not as guests, as waitresses! He telephoned Aunt Jessica. Been let down. They've even sent over the uniforms. Here, they're here, in this basket.'

Freddie undid the laundry hamper and started to hand out the statutory black uniform dresses, together with the white aprons, and white cotton headdresses.

'How do you wear these awful hats without looking like something brought in by the cat?' asked Laura.

They took it in turn to cavort in front of the mirror, putting the hats on at comic angles, before finally settling, amid gales of laughter, for putting them at what they imagined to be at an attractive angle, at the back of their heads.

Aunt Jessica greeted them in the hall.

'No, no, Freddie, no, Laura, no, Aurelia, no, Daisy, waitresses wear their caps at the *front*, not the back. At the front, to disguise and cover the hair.'

'We don't look very pretty with them at the front, though.'

'That,' said Jessica, 'is, I think, the point. If you look too pretty no one will pay attention to the food and drink, or their fellow guests. As it is, I would advise reinforcement to your derrières: men often see waitresses as fair game – the black stockings, you know, reminds them of their mothers' maids, I always think.'

Daisy promptly tied her hat forward, low on her forehead, shortly followed, all too reluctantly, by the other three.

Jessica gave Daisy an affectionate look. Out of the four of them, Daisy always had been the most amenable, the first to volunteer for everything, the first to put a log on the fire, or rush out into the winter weather and help dig up vegetables with Branscombe.

'There, now off you all go, and be good enough to remember that you are waitresses, not debutantes. Keep your lips buttoned, and if anything untoward occurs, or you hear anything of interest, I beg you to report straight back to Mr Athlone, no one else.'

A frisson of excitement ran through the four of them before they bolted through the hall doors and out to Freddie's car, where they all squashed in.

Jessica stared at them through the half-glassed doors. God help poor Guy with that lot in his house, but then, when it came to Guy Athlone, God did seem always to put in at least one oar to help him out of whatever corner he might have been backed into.

She turned away, feeling glad that she was not going to the dinner, that she had been able to step aside from it, although sorry for Guy who had yet again been let down by caterers, alas, an all-too-frequent occurrence for bachelors who only spent Friday to Monday in the country.

Jessica was so fond of Guy that if she had not been so busy in so many other directions she would have rolled up her sleeves and gone over to help him with his dinner party herself, but since the invasion of Czechoslovakia, Jessica, along with so many of her friends, had realised that the time had come to put into practice many of the contingency plans that they had only talked about up until then. ARP committee work took up all her free time.

Besides, if she went over there to help out, or even as a guest, she knew that sure as eggs were eggs once the guests had gone, Guy would want to talk about a mutual friend of theirs. He would fulminate. He would be beside himself with pent-up fury over recent events, and who could blame him? Along with Guy, Jessica had known for some time now – and sometimes she wished to goodness that she had *not* known – that the friend, whom they naturally could not name, had reported back to the security services a conversation he had had with a leading member of Hitler's government, a conversation which had made it quite clear that if Britain joined forces with Czechoslovakia, they could, together, defeat German ambitions. This, then, had been the time to act against Herr Hitler, but the benighted British government, in their infinite wisdom, had done nothing except bury their heads in their own weaselly ambitions, and pretend that the German threat would go away. And now, look! Shakespeare's sceptred isle set in a silver sea was no longer a precious stone – more a blancmange wobbling on a plate. Why could not the few, the very few, who were not appeasers, why could they not have made their mark better? And why could only a few of them see what *had* to be done to prevent another war?

She turned, sighing inwardly, enjoying a strange relief in going back to her lists, back to organising what to do in the event of an invasion. And then she sat down to write, personally, to each head of a household in Twistleton to ask, in the event of a declaration of war, how many evacuee families they thought they might be able to receive in their homes.

Maude Beresford might once have had a secretary to open all her correspondence, but no longer. It was not just that taxes, the failure of farming, and many other monetary constrictions, had limited the number of servants that she could take on, but also that she was single, lived deep in the countryside, and hardly ever left home, all of which meant that she received very few letters, and no invitations, except occasionally to Scotland. The family still owned a lodge in the Scottish Highlands, where, sometimes, a distant relative, about to marry, would suddenly remember that Aunt Maude was their great-aunt, or their second cousin, or some such, and in the hopes of receiving a present by return, would send her an invitation.

With Daisy gone for the evening, Maude felt quite able to enjoy herself in her own special way, taking on her lap the old photograph albums, all that she had left of her innocent youth, of the days before the Great War, when the eldest of her brothers was such a very keen photographer, and they were all made to dress up in fancy clothes, so that he could pose them in all sorts of amusing ways.

Three of her four brothers had died in the Great War, and with the mix-ups that war brings, none of them were brought home to be buried in the family churchyard at Twistleton, the war memorial by the village crossroads being the only place where their names were recorded, together with their decorations. The last, poor Daisy's father, had been killed in an aeroplane crash in 1920.

She'd been the eldest in the family, and her favourite brother had inevitably been the youngest, Roderick.

Ah, yes, there he was.

So bonny always, so good, and so sweet-mannered, never a cross word, never a bad temper, he had been special to everyone. No one had wanted him to go to war, the last of the four boys. With two sons already dead, and one still fighting, their mother had done everything to prevent it, but he had gone, if only to prove to everyone that he, too, was a man. And he was killed on his first day – in the last week of the war.

Of course it was no exaggeration to say that receiving that final telegram had effectively killed their mother.

She had become like a walking graven image, until finally, in the winter of 1919, she had succumbed to pneumonia. And it had seemed to her only daughter that she had passed away with a sigh of something like contentment, to be buried alongside her husband in the grounds of the Hall.

So it was that Maude – who had once been the merriest of children, only too willing to dash between one brother and the next, loving to be teased, the first to fall off her pony, or out of a tree, the first to start a bonfire, the first to learn to bicycle, to lead the way with buckets of water and hoses, jostling happily with the firemen, when a wing of the laundry house caught fire – had been left with one surviving brother, Raymond, who had married Daisy's mother, only for both of them to be killed, not in a motor accident, but in an aeroplane flying to Deauville for the Friday to Monday, details of which she had carefully kept hidden from their surviving daughter, her only niece, Daisy.

Between the two houses, Twistleton Hall and Twistleton Court, two single women had been left to bring up two little girls. With so much in common, it might have been expected that Maude Beresford and Jessica Valentyne would have had every reason to become firm friends, and yet they had barely been known to speak. It was as if, under the weight of such mutual sorrow, the two of them had been unable to face each other, dreading not the sharing of their burdens, but the doubling of them.

Maude had a recurring dream of before the Great War. It was always the same. She was in a white dress, ribbons in her long, curly waist-length hair, and she was dashing round a corner, trying to get away from being chased by her brothers. She was always laughing, running ahead of them, before stopping and looking around her, whereupon she would see the landscape devoid of everything, of trees and shrubs, of flowers and fields, and then, turning to remark on it to her brothers, she would find no one there, and only the sound of the wind from the sea, that sea that was always so close, murmuring, threatening, howling, eventually drowning out the sound of the sobs that would finally wake her up.

She set aside the photograph album, and looked around at her drawing room, with its faded Knole sofas, its large oil paintings, and its rugs of a hue that could barely now be made out. Her chair was always placed at a certain angle to the fire, which burnt winter and summer, for such was the height of the ceilings, there was much need of warmth. Once upon a time the room would have been filled with chatter, and laughter, and someone would have been playing the piano very softly, while someone else turned the pages. After dinner there would have been a recital of classical music, some talented guest, usually a girl, sitting down and playing; while at other times there would have been singing, too, and old eyes would have filled with discreet tears as a delicate young soprano voice sang about the last rose of summer fading away.

When she was alone, it seemed to Maude that what had gone – everything – could come back again. She could fill the rooms with her family and friends, and have them back at her side, imagine what they were saying, hear their voices just as they had been – and just as they would still be now if they were alive – mellifluous and kind, sometimes anxious, but only for someone else, never for themselves. It was simply not done to think of oneself, which was why one said 'one' and not 'I'. In those days the ego was so frowned upon, any form of boasting so shocking, that she honestly couldn't remember any of her brothers even touching lightly on such facts as that they had just achieved a First at Oxford, or been picked for a rowing eight, or some such.

Of course when it came to the horses it was something quite other, as it should be. Pride in one's horses and their achievements was perfectly permissible, as was pride in breeding a winner, or a spanking pair of matching greys for going around the countryside. Dogs too, bred at the Hall, were a source of constant delight, and although nominally barred from nursery and bedroom, the sound of dogs' paws scrabbling up the back stairs was a constant of every evening, and blind eyes were turned to lumps under eiderdowns, or the sound of pugs snoring less than discreetly beneath the blankets on the children's beds.

'I suppose it is wrong of one to think back in this way?' Maude asked silently, as she stroked the head of her oldest pug, and stared into the still hot fire, her face turning a delicate pink.

'I suppose it is, Trump?' she asked yet another of her pugs, despite the fact that he was fast asleep. 'But somehow I doubt it. After all I have no one else with whom to share memories, no one else to think about, no one else who would not be bored by such meanderings and reminiscences. No one would be interested, least of all our poor Daisy. She feels it terribly, living here, all alone with me. She does her best, but really, she is as absent when she is here, as she is absent tonight when she is not here at all.'

Maude picked up another album. Quite her most precious and favourite of them all. A beautiful leather volume containing photographs of a certain young man whom she had loved with all her heart. Dearest Harry, how handsome he had been!

Long before Aunt Maude had opened the first of her beloved photograph albums, Freddie and her guests had duly arrived, correctly attired as waitresses, at Longbridge Farm, the country home of Guy Athlone.

Freddie, knowing the form, for she had once before had to stand in for a missing waitress at one of Mr Athlone's dinner parties, went straight to the tradesmen's entrance, and walked in, smartly followed by Daisy and Laura, with Aurelia tagging along last, because she had a horrid feeling that it was all going to be a bit what her mother always called *infra dig*, and she was terrified that one of her parents' friends might be at the dinner, and recognise her, and it would get back to her parents that she was spending Friday to Monday, not, as she had told them, at a country ball, but dressed up as a waitress.

The farmhouse kitchen was dauntingly empty, occupied only by a desultory-looking kitchen maid, and an old man who was flapping a tea towel at the smoke coming from the open fire, upon which was a spit turning, roasting what looked like half a cow. Freddie, who was used to just such primitive conditions at the Court, where she had helped out Aunt Jessica since she was tiny, and where the water was still drawn from a well, did not turn a hair, but went straight up to the old chap in his leather apron.

'Hallo, Bob. I hear you're in a bit of trouble, so we have come across to help out. Is Mr Athlone here, do you think?'

'He's through there,' the old man told her, pushing a large carving fork into the side of the beef to see the colour of the juices that ran out, for despite the fact that the vast joint looked blackened to a cinder, it smelt wonderful. 'In the Big Room, as they call it. You can have a gander at the placings in the dining room on your way. Twelve tonight, and eight tomorrow night, and Cook passed out in the wing from doing too little during the week, Mr Athlone says, and the caterers gone to help the Duchess of Who Knows Where, so it's all ends to the middle, and no mistake.'

Freddie paused, looking back at the others,

eyebrows raised. Laura looked past her, interested only in seeing more of the house, which seemed to be long and rambling and made up of many previous buildings, not quite a proper house the way the Court, or the Hall, were, but nevertheless atmospheric, intriguing, with meandering corridors and uneven floors, the whole painted in warm colours. They passed, as instructed, through the dining room, which was beautifully laid with glass and silver, linen and lace, all placed upon long lace-edged cloths, in the French style. No formal portraits, though, only large silver-framed mirrors, perhaps to increase its proportions? Or perhaps, Laura suddenly thought, for some other reason? She frowned. Why would she think that?

She did not have time to question herself before she was following Freddie down three or four steps into the largest, whitest room she had ever been in, filled with the largest whitest furniture she had ever seen – it must surely have been specially made for the room? At the farthest end, dominating the whole, on a raised platform, stood two very, very large shining pianos, placed back to back.

All in all it was a room befitting a famous playwright, song-writer, and actor, and undoubtedly a room that would be greatly enhanced by other brilliant people, or even people who might find that they rapidly changed once they were in it, their conversation becoming faster and wittier, as befitted the place they were in – just as those who walk in hallowed places, churches and museums, find their voices dropping along with their eyes, taking on an awed demeanour in keeping with their surroundings.

Guy Athlone, tall, elegant, dark-haired, arose from behind one of the pianos, and walked with what Freddie observed was almost self-conscious precision towards the new arrivals, while for her part Daisy could not help noting that his shoes were made of fine, black suede, which was so soigné, and that they looked really rather perfect as they moved – almost floated – across the thick white carpet.

As he advanced towards his improvised wait-resses for the evening, Guy himself found he was having a pretty hard time of it not to burst out laughing. Happily both his good manners, and his stage training, prevented his being so unkind, and yet gracious though it had been of Jessica Valentyne to offer him help, to be quite truthful, a less authentic gaggle of young waitresses he had yet to see.

First of all there was, necessarily, because of their backgrounds, a general air of innocent amazement about them, so they looked a little like a bunch of startled fawns staring out from under their awkwardly tied waitresses' hats. And then there was their air of sophisticated appreciation as they looked from him to their surroundings, their quick surreptitious glances appreciating everything around them in a way that professional waitresses would not, professionals finding, as they always did, one rich man's house really very little different from another, the only thing of interest being their pay cheques.

'Is that a Boudin, sir?' one of them asked, after he had introduced himself to them.

'I believe it is,' he agreed. 'Very much so. Do you like it?'

Laura smiled.

'Oh yes, very much. We have one at home rather the same,' she told him, and immediately coloured as she realised, too late, from his look of mild astonishment, that she must have stepped out of turn talking about a painting, that this was not what was expected of a waitress.

'Now, let me see, I must remember you correctly. So I will start again. Freddie Valentyne, I know, of course.' Guy nodded at Freddie, and she smiled. 'But – but you are Laura Hambleton? And you, Daisy Beresford? And finally, Aurelia Smith-Jones. Please correct me if I am wrong.' After they had affirmed that he had remembered their names correctly, he continued. 'Freddie here can show you the ropes, of course, since she has served at dinner before, but tonight we have an added excitement, I am afraid, and no, it is not royalty. Cook has done a vanishing act, fallen into a bottle and disappeared, so we only have old Mr Bob in the kitchen, and Edie who is only partially here, and by that I mean on this planet, and from Friday to Monday even less. So who is good at knowing what sauces go with what, and what plates go where, and not to serve the meat before the fish? If we can find any, that is,' he concluded gaily.

'We all are, Mr Athlone,' Freddie told him, raising her head a little. 'And what is more, we felt jolly sorry for you when we heard that you had been so let down by the catering people, and that they had absconded to help out at the Duchess of Charlbury's masked ball.'

'How very charming of you, but I am happy to tell you that revenge is indeed a dish best eaten cold – I happen to know that the dear Duchess never pays her bills, so, little do they know it, but the benighted caterers will be working for her tonight, not for shillings, not for pennies, but for nothing. Ah me, it is just a little bit sad, but as I understand it, nowadays everyone is let down by caterers. Caterers, like hairdressers and couturiers, and, well, just about everyone in power, know when to flex their muscles. Life is only really tolerable if one does everything oneself. Unfortunately, giving a dinner for a dozen people, and being the terribly famous Guy Athlone at one and the same time, is impossible, so when Miss Valentyne's aunt, Jessica Valentyne, heard of my misfortune and offered me your services, I could hardly believe my luck. The only trouble being that at that precise moment I did at least think I had a cook in residence, but no.' He lit a cigarette, took out a small aide-memoire from his inside pocket, and started to flick through it before reading out. 'First course was, rumour has it, to be quails' eggs in pastry baskets, followed by fillet of sole and asparagus in a prawn-flavoured sauce. The entrée is beef, with all the usual ghastly over-cooked English vegetables, and then Queen of Puddings.' He looked up. 'Has anyone here by any utterly brilliant chance ever made the lovely Queen of Puddings?'

Freddie put her hand up.

'Yes, many times for Aunt Jessica at the Court—'

Guy lowered his gaze and stared at Freddie. It was the look he always gave terrified actors at auditions.

'Recipe, please?'

'For twelve? Let me see, three pints of milk, twelve ounces of white breadcrumbs, one and a half of butter, six of sugar, six eggs—'

'"*The Mole could only hold up both fore-paws and gasp, 'Oh my! Oh my! Oh my!'*"' Guy raised both his hands in delight. 'To the kitchen, my girl, and a bonus is yours tonight if you can deliver the goods. The very moment when the last dessert spoon is lowered, the pumpkin in the vegetable basket will turn into a coach, and the rats in the larder into high-stepping ponies, and you will go to the ball – although not here! Off you go to your tasks. I know you will defeat the evil caterers and send all home singing!'

They all turned and fled after Freddie, and Guy watched them for a moment, feeling both amused and grateful.

Once in the kitchen Freddie hurried out to the cold larder, followed by Laura and Daisy, leaving Aurelia standing wordlessly in the kitchen, which was where they found her as they all turned back to fetch forgotten trays to carry the necessary dinner ingredients.

'Come on, Relia, come on, we are in a bit of a tight squeeze, you know. White sauce with prawns for the fish, but clean the asparagus first.' Freddie stared at the still-frozen Aurelia. 'You *are* up to helping Laura here do that course, aren't you? You do remember Aunt Jessica's rudimentary cooking lessons at the Court, don't you?'

Aurelia nodded silently at Freddie. Daisy shoved a tray at Aurelia. Aurelia took it, and followed her friend to the cold larder, where she obediently loaded up with the necessary ingredients for the fish course.

'Something wrong, Relia?' Daisy demanded. 'You're looking more than a little grey about the gills. In fact, now I come to look at you, you seem to have taken on the same colour as the fish.'

Aurelia remained silent, hurrying back to the kitchen. She could say nothing, she would say nothing, she would tell no one. It was only too lucky that she had not made a fool of herself already, and passed out. She half-closed her eyes at the thought of how terrible that would be, even more terrible than what had just happened to her.

She started to shave the asparagus stalks, and to curl up the tender pieces of fish, whose skin, thankfully, had already been removed, before buttering a large dish and placing the fish and the asparagus in it. White sauce made with stock boiled from fish bones and skin, prawns to scatter in the white sauce. If anything went wrong with *her* course she was quite, quite sure she would commit suicide.

'I wonder who is coming to the dinner. Did you manage to have a peek at the *placement* – see who is next to whom?'

Daisy looked up from chopping vegetables, and raised her eyebrows in anticipation of hearing some famous names. As far as she was concerned it had been heady enough meeting the famous Guy Athlone, and now it seemed she would be placing food in front of people who had their names up in footlights outside theatres in Shaftesbury Avenue, whose names appeared regularly in the gossip columns of the *Daily Mail* and the *Daily Express*, people who were friends of the most famous English playwright of the time – Guy Athlone.

She waited for Freddie, who had popped out of the dining room to give them all the exciting news, eyes wide.

'*Well?*'

It seemed that everyone was looking at Freddie, even as they could all hear the guests arriving and being let in by Mr Athlone's secretary, who they understood was posing as a stand-in butler for the evening.

Freddie made a little moue with her mouth, before twisting it into a silly shape.

'Well, dears,' she said, acting up like mad. 'If I said George Arletti and that well-known enter-tainer Azure La Monte, not to mention Miss Gloria Martine herself, would you be satisfied that you are about to serve the crème de la crème, not to mention the Vere de Veres, and many another? Of course the under-secretary to the foreign secretary, too, will be here, and other such members of His Majesty's government, but they will not be of the least interest to all of you *Tatler* readers and theatre snobs, I know. Nevertheless try very hard not to drop asparagus and roast beef in their laps, because, with the coming emergency, we might well all find ourselves behind bars.'

This last was greeted with nervous laughter, because, as they all knew, there was a dreadful truth behind the jokes. A state of emergency meant that anything could happen, and might.

As it transpired, nothing untoward, at least as far as the dinner and the serving of its courses went, did occur that evening, at least nothing of which the girls could have, or would have, been aware.

The dinner party went swiftly through all the usual motions that, Daisy noted, dinner parties held at English country houses always do. People drank wine, they ate, they turned first to the right, and then to the left, they conversed, they aired their opinions, they agreed with each other, and after dinner they strolled in the evening air in their host's garden, before coming back in and listening to him playing some of his frightfully amusing songs.

'That all went like clockwork, then,' Guy's secretary, Clive Montfort, murmured, as the last of the guests' motor cars drove away into the darkness.

'Oh yes,' Guy agreed, lighting up a cigarette as he watched the tail lights of the cars disappearing, and a strange silence fell in the Big Room, broken only by the distant sound of the young waitresses and old Bob in the dining room and kitchen clearing up, their murmured conversations rising in a late-night chorus of sporadic chatter above the sound of boiling kettles and doors banging as water was brought in from the well in the yard. 'Yes, it all went just like rusty old clockwork, all right. And not one guest trustworthy, all appeasers to their lily-white cowardly gills.' Guy drew more strongly on his cigarette. 'All still clinging to the idea that Mr Hitler will back down this side of Christmas, that the poor Czechs could not have been saved whatever we did, and that now Herr Hitler has what he wanted all along, he will be a good little boy and toddle along when he is told.'

He threw his half-finished cigarette into the fire, went over to the piano and closed the lid – then to his own and his secretary's surprise, he locked it – before going to the sister piano, and locking that too. 'Mark my words, by this time next year, Clive, this will all be in storage, and you and I God knows where. Write that down, Mr Secretary: I said it here, at one o'clock in the morning of a September night in 1938.'

Freddie drove the girls home at a much slower pace than earlier in the evening, first of all because it was dark, and second because they had all been given a glass of sherry by old Bob, who, being well-pleased with their work, had toasted their health in front of the great kitchen fire.

It was early in the morning, and dark, but the

stars above them had never seemed brighter to them all, most of all Aurelia. She knew now that she had met the love of her life; that she had seen and fallen in love with someone who could and would never love her did not seem to matter. She knew she had to do something to get close to Mr Athlone.

Daisy, too, had fallen in love, but not with Guy Athlone. She had fallen in love with the heady aura of danger that he seemed to have about him. The fact that he was so different from anyone else she had ever met was hardly surprising – since she had rarely been allowed out of Twistleton, and even being allowed to stay at the Court with Freddie and the rest had been, from Aunt Maude's point of view, a huge concession. Daisy perfectly understood this, and indeed, if Aunt Maude felt over-protective of her niece, Daisy felt quite the same about her aunt.

Even leaving the old darling for twenty-four hours was a wrench, in the sense that she knew that Aunt Maude would be alone, and lonely, with only the pugs to keep her distracted from her state of being a single woman in a vast house filled with unused rooms, the rooms themselves for the most part filled with furniture covered in dust sheets. Indeed, so much of the Hall was protected by dust sheets, it would not have surprised Daisy to return and find Aunt Maude in the same state as most of the furniture.

By the time Daisy and the others rolled into their beds above the stables at the Court, she was filled with a sense of excitement. She had heard Gloria Martine talking about flying with a friend to Deauville, and what fun they had had. If Daisy could fly, as her father had done in the Great War, she would get away from everything that tied her to Twistleton.

She shut her eyes, imagining just what it would be like to be flying high above Twistleton. From hundreds of feet up Twistleton would be only a small dot, just one of many small dots. By flying above it, she would have left behind its sad history, which clung to her like a great lumbering monster, every hour of every day. The only trouble was – how could she actually do it? That was not just *a* question that needed answering, it was *the* only question that needed answering. Aunt Maude would not even hear of her going to London! She would need help. The others were already fast asleep when she realised, as always, just whose help she could call on.

Chapter Three

Well, there it was, the dinner was over.

Guy lit a cigarette before walking, still in his embroidered silk dressing gown and plain silk pyjamas, around his garden, normally a delight, even on an autumn morning, but, alas, not today. Today he was smoking furiously, and thinking even faster.

He was thinking about the bunch of fellow-travellers, Fascists and, God help him, appeasers, that he had had to entertain the previous night. Very well, it was his patriotic duty to listen to their twaddle, silently note the names of their friends, their foreign friends in particular – perhaps fiends would be a better word for some of them – and report back to George at 'the office', as George's headquarters were currently, and really very euphemistically, known. But the truth of the matter was that it was a beastly feeling, afterwards, knowing that you were in the company of people who were gaily delivering innocent men, women, and children into the hands of the Nazis. Handing them over without a thought or a care, as if they were stuffed toys in a shop window, not human beings. He threw his cigarette into a flower bed, and watched its tiny light burning until it was finally extinguished, although a small spiral of smoke still rose from it for a few seconds.

Guy turned, ready to go back into the house, but not before having a last look round at everything that he normally so loved to appreciate. The sunshine on the lawn left uneven shadows; above him the September sky had assumed that particular pale blue that autumn brings even on its sunniest days. He reluctantly turned to go in, sighing, realising that without his even being aware of it, the beauty of his English garden had had a calming effect.

As he was about to reach out a hand to open the French windows that led into the Big Room, he heard a voice coming behind him making the silliest sound.

'Psst!'

He turned, frowning lightly. What a perfectly ridiculous sound! No one surely said 'psst' except on stage, or in a movie?

'Psst to you, too!' he said, walking back to the centre of the lawn, while at the same time looking around him, still seeing no one.

'Psst!' the sound came again, this time more insistently.

Guy stood stock still, knowing that in his silk Sulka dressing gown, plain dark-blue silk pyjamas, and hand-stitched slippers with G.A. embroidered on them, perhaps because it was already ten o'clock of an autumn morning, he must look every inch the decadent West End playwright.

'Look, whoever you are, wherever you are, I am not going to ruin my new hand-stitched slippers tramping through the undergrowth to find you, so psst or not, I suggest you come out and, one way or another, face the music.'

From out of one of the far bushes a figure emerged. With the expertise of a man who was used to summing up everyone, instantly, whether at auditions or interviews, Guy turned a critical eye on the newcomer.

What he saw emerging from behind his really rather beautiful shrubs was the figure of a slender young girl, a young girl possessed of unruly long blonde hair, more than a little Pre-Raphaelite in style, with a figure that was thin, almost too thin, a heart-shaped face, blue-grey eyes, or were they grey-blue eyes? At any rate, pale eyes – not brilliant brown, as his were. He stared at her as she trod across the lawn.

'You do realise you are trespassing?' he asked her in a lightly sarcastic voice.

She nodded.

'Yes, and I am very sorry, but I was here last night, so it is more of a revisit, rather than an actual trespass, if you understand what I mean?'

Guy leaned forward, frowning.

'Well, yes, I suppose I might.' He moved closer. 'Ah yes, of course, of course, you were one of the debutante waitresses. I remember you now.'

'No, I was *not* a debutante waitress,' Aurelia told

him, suddenly indignant. 'No, I was a *fake* waitress, not a debutante. I'm not in the least bit that kind of social person. As a matter of fact, I am so far from being like that, I am actually quite common,' she told him, pride in her voice.

Guy managed to keep a straight face.

'Well, that makes two of us,' he said, changing the tone of his voice to chatty and interested, instead of vague and suspicious. 'How common are you, though? I myself am dreadfully proud of being common, wouldn't want to be anything else. My mother worked in a laundry, and my father was a no-good layabout sometime-brush-salesman, so beat that, Gunga Din!'

'Oh, I'm not quite as common as that. I am afraid you win, really you do,' Aurelia told him in a grave voice, and she gave a small sigh of admiration. 'Just one generation into the middle of the upper-middle-classes, that's all I am. But that is not why I am here. I am not here because I am common.'

Guy sat down on a nearby bench and crossed his silk-clad legs, for given the really rather *Alice in Wonderland* conversation he was having, it seemed to be a good idea. He patted the seat beside him.

'Why don't you sit down and tell me why you *are* here, dear?'

'I don't think I'd better sit down, really not.'

'Why not?'

'It doesn't seem quite right, seeing that I was only asked here as a waitress. I think I'd better stand.'

'How about a compromise? Pull up a chair?'

73

Aurelia sat down opposite Guy, determined not to show how nervous she was, and in many ways, over the next few minutes of their conversation – she thought afterwards, with some accuracy – she actually succeeded.

'Let us begin again, now that we understand we are both common, although not vulgar, I trust. Why *are* you here?' Guy asked her.

The expression on Aurelia's face was solemn to the point of being almost tragic, her eyes unblinking.

'Because I want to be near you.'

'Ah.'

Guy was all too used to people wanting to be near him. He had always had star quality, and what was more, and this had been vital to his success, he had always known it. Nevertheless, seeing that the young girl seated on the garden chair opposite him was totally uninvited, and he knew nothing about her at all, he found himself having the sense quickly to look her over, making sure that she had nothing about her that was suspicious, or strange, nothing on her slender young person of which he should be wary.

He was reassured at once: her cotton dress was thin enough to reveal anything untoward that she might be concealing, and she did not seem to have brought with her any kind of handbag wherein she might have hidden an unfriendly knife, or a ladies' pistol.

'You want to be near me?' he repeated. 'Well – Miss?'

'Smith-Jones.'

'Well, that is very flattering, I am sure, but although I don't wish to disillusion you, my country house, as you doubtless found out last night, is not nearly big enough to accommodate all the people who feel as you do, and nor, I am sorry to tell you, is my London house. I have rather too many admirers, and a great deal too many fans, and although I am delighted to include you in their number, I am quite unable to accommodate you. So how about if I gave you a signed photograph, and promised to let you know the date of my next country dinner party, so that you could come and make another grand fist of being a waitress?'

Aurelia stared at him. He did not realise, could not realise, and she must not let him know, that she was in love with him. She must act casual, but determined. He must be made to realise that she would do anything, but anything, for him – now, or in the future – but at the same time she had to be very, very careful not to appear ordinary.

'I could not possibly take a signed photograph from you.'

'Why not?'

'Because,' she hesitated, and then came up with what she imagined was a trump card, 'because it is such an everyday-ish, common thing to do.'

Yet again Guy found himself struggling not to laugh.

'Well, I must admit it might be just a little, particularly given that you know me already,' he agreed. 'Signed photographs are really for fans, and for royal personages to put on their pianos. So you are right, it might be the wrong thing for you to accept a photograph, now I come to think of it—' he laughed in a lightly amused way.

'But I will come and waitress at any of your dinner parties, from now until the earth closes over me.'

Guy looked at her, startled.

'I don't give that many dinner parties, I truly do not,' he protested. 'My publicity may have given you to understand that I endlessly socialise, but actually, if the truth be known, my favourite day is spent working, having a good lunch, going for a walk or a swim, and then early to bed with supper on a tray! Hardly the imagined day of a successful West End playwright and actor, you must agree. In fact I never give dinner parties unless I can help it, although you might not believe that.'

'Even so, whenever you do, wherever you are, I will always come and help you out,' Aurelia stated, her expression solemn. 'But that is how devoted I am to you. I will do whatever you want, until the earth closes over me.'

'That sounds just a little too Emily Brontë, *Wuthering Heights*, for my taste, dear Miss Smith-Jones. Could you take it again? Perhaps think of re-phrasing, making it a tiny bit lighter?'

Aurelia frowned.

'Well, I could, now I have made how I feel clear to you,' she agreed. 'So, to put it another way.' She hesitated, before beginning again. 'If I said I will always be loyal to you to the end of my days, would that be better?'

'Yes, a great deal better, but not I hope, for your sake, true. Now it is time you went, and time I went in.'

Aurelia stood up, and held out a slim hand.

'Thank you very much for seeing me—'

'Don't you mean spotting you, as in – in the bushes?'

'I daresay,' Aurelia agreed, turning and making her way across the lawn to the bushes once more.

'No, no need to go back that way, dear girl. I will call Clive and he can run you back to Twistleton.'

'I can walk. I walked here.'

'It is the least I can do after such a declaration of faith, and I think we can both agree that it will not be at all *common*.'

He laughed lightly once more, before disappearing in a really rather magical manner through the French windows into the Big Room.

Aurelia sat back in the smart car that Guy's secretary Clive had brought round to the front, and stared ahead of her. She could not believe her own audacity, she could not believe what she had just done, and she certainly could not believe that Guy Athlone's secretary, Clive Montfort, was running her back to Twistleton Court.

'Who was that?'

'Mr Athlone's secretary. He just ran me back.'

Daisy stared at Aurelia in growing admiration.

'Still waters run deep. Whatever was he running you back *from*?'

'His house,' Aurelia said, waving to the retreating car.

'He was running you back from his house, for the reason of?'

'Getting rid of me, really, that was the reason. He just didn't want me around any more. He was in his dressing gown,' she added, absently. 'So he had to go in to change, although I think he had had breakfast, because the dining room was cleared.'

Daisy sped after Aurelia, and turned her round.

'No, you don't, young lady,' she murmured. 'You tell all, or Daisy will give you a Chinese burn.'

They both laughed.

'I went over to the farmhouse early this morning, and I told Guy Athlone – I found him in the garden smoking a cigarette – that I would devote my life to him.'

Daisy stared at Aurelia. She knew that Relia had always had a streak of hysteria in her, but really this was the kind of thing that you read about in newspapers, young girls with a 'pash' on famous men breaking into their houses and swearing everlasting devotion to them – one of them even did it to Hitler, for heaven's sake.

'Aren't we a tiny bit old for crushes and pashes, Relia darling?' Daisy asked her in as kind a voice as she could muster.

'Yes, of course, but this is neither a crush nor a pash,' Aurelia assured her, using just as kindly a tone as Daisy had used on her, and improving on it at the same time by putting out a hand and patting Daisy in a gentle and slightly patronising manner on the arm. 'No, no, this is the real thing, and I really mean it. You will see, I will devote my life to Guy Athlone, in one way or another.'

Daisy tried not to look as she felt, which was quite appalled.

Later, when she was going in search of Miss Valentyne to tell her that, although they hadn't finished the sandbagging, she, Daisy, would have to scoot back to the Hall to have lunch with Aunt Maude, she confided what Aurelia had said to Jessica.

'I know I perhaps shouldn't, but since he is a friend of yours, I just thought I should – I mean I don't think Relia is likely to become dangerous or anything, but I do think she is very serious about Mr Athlone. Some people can become fixated, can't they? And if we think about it, what with being an only child and so often on her own, and her parents being so social that she hardly saw them when she was growing up, well, it might make sense of her condition.'

Jessica gave Daisy one of her penetrating looks, and as she did so it occurred to Daisy with a sudden sense of shock that Miss Valentyne was really very pretty, especially when she had just washed her hair, and put it up on top of her head in a rather raffish manner.

'Put by any stores for the coming bad times yet, Missy?'

Daisy shook her head.

'Aunt Maude won't hear of it – just won't.'

'Better if Aunt Maude *did* hear of it. Tell her from me, but ever so politely, of course, that now is the time to start storing everything from candles to bolts of cloth, wirelesses, cans of everything. You just must, or by this time next year there will be tears at bedtime, believe me.'

'I won't tell Aunt Maude, but I'll make sure to do it myself.'

'Good girl.' Jessica dipped the pen she was using in the bottle of ink in front of her. 'Lists, lists, lists, that is what we need for the coming evacuation of the cities. Because, believe me, without lists we shall be sunk. Whether we like it or not, we will soon have more evacuees thrust upon us any day now than even you and I have had hot dinners.'

Daisy took this in, as she was meant to, as if she, and not Aunt Maude, was head of the household at the Hall – but as Freddie was driving her back home for luncheon, and they were chatting, it occurred to Daisy that if she didn't get a car of her own soon, it would be the next century before she completed her flying lessons, or logged up the required number of hours. She needed a motor car, fast.

'Where did you buy *that*?' Laura stared at the brand-sparklingly-new motor car that stood, a few hours later, outside the stables at the Court.

'In Wychford yesterday,' Daisy told her proudly. 'Freddie helped me choose it.' She turned to the salesman who had brought it, and gave him her warmest smile. 'I say, would you be an absolute ducky and show me how to drive this lovely thing?'

Laura closed her eyes, and then quickly opened them again as Daisy hopped in beside the sales-man, and the car started to move towards the back entrance of the small estate, and so on to the open road.

'Do you think you should have encouraged Daisy to buy that motor car? I mean, she hasn't even learned to drive yet. It's really rather power-ful, isn't it?'

'Oh yes, very,' Freddie agreed cheerfully. 'But she needs a powerful motor car with what *she* has in mind.' A questioning look from Laura brought forth a further even more wide-eyed response. 'She wants to go for flying lessons at that place outside Bramsfield!'

'*Flying* lessons?'

'Flying an aeroplane is the only way she will get away from the Hall, and Aunt Maude.'

'Lord love a duck.'

'And the Lord does love his ducks, Laura,' Freddie told her in a pious voice. 'What He does not love, I wouldn't think, is war.'

'Is it always men who make war, do you think?'

'Oh yes indeed, the males of the species *will* insist on killing each other, because of wanting to be top dog. Mark my words, there would be no more war if men started having babies. Mrs

Budgie says they would die if they had to have babies, and she knows, she's had six.'

Laura stared at Freddie with something approaching admiration. She might look fifteen rather than seventeen, being small, brown-haired, freckle-faced, and still with a long braid of hair down her back, which she had the habit of tossing impatiently behind her, but she was always thoughtfully working things out. She was quite mature, as if she had an old head on her young shoulders, or as if she was used to looking out for herself, not having had parents for long, and not having been brought up by anyone but a spinster aunt and a butler . . .

'You should be a lady MP, like Nancy Astor, Freddie.'

'Apparently, Aunt Jessica says, Nancy Astor is many things, but a lady is not one of them.'

'Do you know they change the flowers in the vases at Cliveden every *two* hours?'

'Have they nothing better to do?'

'Apparently not, at least not until the war comes. Once it does, well, things will be different – for ever, won't they?' Laura asked over-brightly. The look in her eyes was sad, for to her mind things had already changed. Her mother had died so suddenly, leaving her in a world that to a young lonely girl was really rather confusing, particularly with a father going off the rails at what seemed like every and any opportunity, but then perhaps he always had, and it was only now that her mother was gone that it was noticeable.

*   *   *

Jean was perfectly well aware that Joe Huggett was following her, why shouldn't she be? He had followed her out of the ARP lecture at the village hall, assing about in the road with his gas mask on, as if it was quite a hoot to be given a gas mask, rather than a horrible shock.

'Can't you find anything else to do, Joe Huggett? Surely there must be a tank or a gun somewhere that you could go and amuse yourself with? Or in your case an RAF aeroplane.'

Jean turned briefly from staring ahead of her, waiting for the bus with every show of impatience, to look at him. Joe managed to smile his wicked smile before she turned back once again, staring ahead of her at the mackintosh of the lady in front of them, at the curve in the road where the country bus should at any minute appear.

'It just so happens that our journeys over the last twenty-four hours have taken us in the same direction.'

'Isn't that a coincidence?' Jean murmured, at the same time tossing back her mane of black curly hair.

'I, like you, am intent on – on going to Bramsfield.'

'As it happens I am going to Wychford—'

'Wychford, *then* Bramsfield.'

Jean turned back to stare at him once again.

'At this moment you are carrying on more like the village idiot than a recent recruit to His Majesty's army, but I daresay you know that?'

'I shall be gone tomorrow, to training school *somewhere in England*. Take pity, fair maiden, on a poor airman, take pity!' Joe seemed to be dancing in front of her now, his blond hair – too long for the RAF, surely – tousled, unkempt, but somehow delightful against his uniform. 'I shall be training through the snow and the ice, with no food and little sleep. Remember that in the weeks ahead.' He leant forward and whispered in her ear, 'And you will be sorry that you were not more kind to me while waiting for our bus, do you know that?'

Jean pulled her beret further on to her thick head of curls. It was true, he would be gone for some sort of training, and she would be sorry if she was not kinder to him. Although war had not yet been declared, everyone all over the country was sitting on a pin, knowing that one way or another it would be along soon. Jean knew that the village schoolteacher had long ago laid contingency plans for dealing with the evacuation of city children, and that Twistleton village school, with its eight pupils – as well as the village itself – had long ago been marked out by the authorities. She hated to admit it, but in some ways, now that poor Czechoslovakia had been thrown to the Nazi wolves, she, as well as everyone else in Twistleton, was actually impatient to be getting on with everything. All this hanging about waiting for the inevitable was as bad as hanging about waiting for the village bus, and there was not very much to be said for it.

'I'll take you to The Pantry for lunch, if you're nice to me on the bus.'

Jean turned and stared at Joe. Lunch at The Pantry was delicious, and they both knew it: chicken pie and home-grown peas, new potatoes smothered in butter and chopped parsley, lovely soft meringues filled with local cream.

'Oh, very well,' she conceded, more because she had skipped breakfast than for any other reason.

'Sit at the back and hold hands?' Joe asked, leaning forward and lowering his voice.

Jean shook her head.

'Sit at the back and keep your hands to yourself,' she murmured, above the sound of the bus arriving.

Joe smiled down at her, knowing that he was half-way there already. His eldest brother had told him there was nothing quite like seducing girls with the thought of food.

'You will be mine by the end of lunch, Miss Shaw,' he told her gaily.

Jean sat back and stared ahead. She would be no one's by the end of anything, but lunch at The Pantry would be just dandy.

Once again the silence of the dining room at the Hall seemed to be weighing down on Daisy, a heavy old eiderdown of a silence that felt as if it was smothering her. A fly was buzzing about around the window, a maid was hovering at the sideboard, and Aunt Maude was toying lightly with a piece of white fish, while all over England people were wondering *when* and *if* the war would begin. Daisy thought morosely that if Jessica Valentyne was right in her thinking, the fly could be as useless as Chamberlain's government, and the white fish on Aunt Maude's plate as lifeless as his policies.

'I see you have bought yourself a motor car, Daisy?'

Daisy nodded. It was pretty useless to deny it, since it was standing in the drive, outside the Hall's double front doors. She had intended to have the salesman hide it for her in the stables, when he helped her drive over from the Court. Only for a short time, though, time in which she had also intended to learn to drive so well, that before Aunt Maude could protest she would have had her whizzing down the drive and out on to the country road beyond, a road which would take them to Wychford, where she would have treated Aunt Maude to a triumphant lunch at The Pantry.

Daisy had become increasingly sure that Aunt Maude had not left the grounds of the Hall since about 1920, when Daisy's parents had been killed. In many ways there was no reason why she should leave the grounds of her little kingdom – after all, the place was sufficient unto itself, as Shakespeare had said about England – but even so, even so, surely there must be a world beyond the blue horizon that could arouse Aunt Maude's curiosity? Now, of course, the whole plan had blown up in Daisy's face, and she had been left not taking Aunt Maude for a surprise ride in her new motor car, but waiting for that dear little mechanic to arrive and tell her what to do to get it working.

'Spit in the petrol tank.'

Daisy looked up suddenly, shocked. In fact she almost found herself looking round to see who had spoken, except for the fact that the words had definitely been spoken in Aunt Maude's voice. She could have sworn they had come from someone else.

'I'm sorry?'

Daisy stared at her aunt.

'If she won't crank up, spit in the petrol tank, that is what my brothers used to say. They always said it worked like a dream.'

Daisy just had time to stare at Aunt Maude in some astonishment before she heard the dining-room door opening and, turning at the sound, saw a maid beckoning to her.

'Mr Russell from the garage in Wychford, here to help get the car started, as I understand it, Miss Daisy.'

Daisy stared back down the dining room. Aunt Maude flapped her napkin at her, so suddenly that all three pugs under her chair woke up and barked excitedly.

'Go, child, go. Get the thing going, for good-ness' sake, or we shall all be sitting on a pin until dinner time.'

Daisy shot out of the door, but she paused as she stood in the hall. Could this be the same aunt with whom she had been living for the past seventeen and a half years? Then a thought struck her, and it did seem literally to strike her almost dumb. Gracious, could it be possible, could it perhaps mean that Aunt Maude had once driven a motor car herself? Surely not? She made a mental note to ask her, and then ran to the front doors and down the steps, hand outstretched to greet Mr Russell.

'It's just a question of newness,' Mr Russell told Daisy in a pleasantly instructional voice.

'Oh, I see. Do all new motor cars act up in this way, Mr Russell?'

'No, not the newness of the motor car, Miss Beresford – the newness of you to the art of driving, and it is an art, believe me. Good drivers are hard to come by, and brilliant ones are even rarer.'

He looked serious, priest-like, before opening the door of the motor car and beckoning to her to sit in beside him in the passenger seat, as he went on speaking.

'She'll start all right for you, Miss Beresford, if you do what I tell you. This is what you do. First you turn on the ignition, pull out the choke, and press the starter button. When the engine fires allow it to run on half-choke until running smoothly, and then close the choke. If you wouldn't mind climbing in beside me, I can demonstrate it to you again. Depress the clutch, engage first gear, press the accelerator to generate some power, release the handbrake and at the same time let the clutch out, and then slowly drive forward.'

'Crikey, Mr Russell, I am so dim! I never realised it was all so complicated. I am afraid in the excitement I clean forgot everything you told me. Please continue.'

The motor car moved slowly and surely down the drive before Mr Russell stopped it, and reversed back to the same spot, and then he and Daisy changed positions, and Daisy started the exciting exercise known in the manual as 'Starting Your Motor Car'.

Aunt Maude had long abandoned her piece of white fish to stare out into the drive. She could not help feeling excited by the idea of a motor car being in the drive again. It reminded her of her brothers and herself before the First World War, of their father arriving with their mother sitting up beside him, wrapped in driving veils and large coats with fur collars. Those had really been the days, and perhaps they might soon return?

Lunch at Wychford with Joe was proving interesting to Jean Shaw.

She and Joe had known each other, off and on, all their lives, growing up in Twistleton, going to the same village school, until time and age parted them, and Joe was sent on somewhere else, and Jean was taken on at the Hall to help out as under-housekeeper, or that at least was how Miss Maude Beresford always described Jean, much to everyone's, including Jean's, amusement – since there was no actual housekeeper Jean could be 'under'.

But supervising herself doing the dusting, telling herself that the house was running on really rather straight lines, making sure that the maid and the under-maids – all about the same age as herself – were doing what they should do, was finally much too dull. Jean had no wish to upset Miss Beresford, but she knew that if she was not to go mad she had to give in her notice and strike out in a different direction. This new direction, however, was somewhat of a surprise to both Miss Maude, and Jean.

'You want to do what?'

'I want to farm.'

'Why? If you don't mind my enquiring, Shaw?'

Jean hesitated. She could read, and she could read fast, no putting her finger under the words or any of that nonsense. One of the perks of working for Miss Maude at the Hall was that they took all the newspapers, every day. No one who worked there had ever quite dared to ask why, and no one did, although Jean had always assumed that it had been the habit of the large, bustling, pre-Great-War household to take newspapers for everyone at the house, and that meant literally everyone, even the servants. So every morning, willy-nilly, to the house came the *Daily This* and the *Daily That*, and unlike the rest of the girls who could not wait to put them on either the fire, or the floor after washing it – as was the custom – Jean read all the newspapers, and what she read, alone by candlelight at her cottage, made her uneasy, and at the same time savvy. There was not enough food being grown at that moment in England. A great deal of it was being imported, so if there was a war and imports stopped, there would not be enough for everyone to eat. It did not make sense. Someone had to start growing more food, and quick, in however small quantities, because every last crumb was going to be needed.

'Land is what you need, my girl. Land will never let you down,' Granny Shaw used to say to her. 'If you have land you will never starve, believe me.' She used to point out of the cottage window to her own couple of acres. 'I can grow my own food, and that way I need answer to no one.'

Answering to no one became Jean's ideal. She did not want to answer to anyone, probably because she never had. She had been unfortunate in her mother, but fortunate in her grandmother, so her ill luck had been her good luck, and thinking that way had become a habit, as she was now telling Joe.

'Good comes out of bad, I am sure of it,' she stated as they finished lunch.

'No good can come of war, Jean. Look at the Great War, no good came of that. No, war is not good, Jean, no one can say that,' Joe told her in a vaguely patronising voice, sounding as if he was speaking to someone a great deal younger.

Jean considered this, and then began again, reluctant to let go.

'Some people say that had there not been the Great War we would have had a revolution in England, because of all the rich folk having too much, and all the poor folk having too little, and that there would have been a bloodbath like in

France at the end of the eighteenth century. That is what some people say.'

Joe stared at her. Jean was such a pretty girl, with her thick dark curly hair and green eyes and pale skin, such a pretty girl, and with such a heart-turning smile, why would she want to talk like that? Like some sort of politician, or suffragette, or something?

'I hope you're not going to turn out to be intelligent as well as beautiful, are you, Jean?' he asked, all innocence.

Jean put one elbow on the table, and laid her other arm across so that her hand held the crook of the first arm, and then placed her head a little lower and widened her eyes, making it her turn to look falsely innocent.

'Why, Joe Huggett, you are such a tease, truly you are. Do I look intelligent? I ask you, I mean, do I? God forbid that I should. Surely it is against the laws of nature for a woman to be beautiful *and* intelligent?'

Jean widened her eyes mockingly as Joe stared at her holding her ridiculous pose, and then he started to laugh.

'Where did you learn that little party trick, Miss Jean Shaw?'

'I didn't never learn it, Mr Huggett, what I did was observe it, when I worked in my holidays at grand houses. Before I left school and went to help Miss Beresford at the Hall, I observed that whenever the men were around, the ladies of quality always pretended to be half-daft. Never could understand the need for it, to tell you the truth, not never, no how – why would someone want someone else to be stupid?'

Joe frowned, realising all of a sudden that he couldn't understand it, either. It was a silly way of carrying on, and at the same time he realised, too, that the reason he was attracted to Jean was that she was not like that. She was, and always had been, her own person, ever since she had kicked around the playground with him and his brothers, she one of only two girls at the otherwise all-boys village school.

'I don't want a girl to pretend to be anything, I just want a girl to be a girl, not a boy, but with a mind of her own nonetheless,' Joe stated.

'Well, that is good to hear, Mr Huggett,' Jean went on, but her voice was still vaguely mocking.

Joe put his napkin down in a gesture of finality, as if he was preparing to leave.

'I don't really understand where all this is getting us, Jean. I didn't bring you to lunch here for you to make fun of me. There is a war coming, sure as your eggs are your eggs, and your chickens are your chickens,' he went on, referring to Jean's newer acquisitions. 'And all that land you have been renting from Miss Beresford for tuppence three farthings is going to be commandeered, and you are going to have to change your ways. There will be no time for mockery soon, Jean Shaw, and I have a uniform, and only one day left of my leave. We may soon all be dead, and, believe me, we will be regretting every minute that we have wasted.'

Jean stared at Joe. He was tall, and he was handsome in a pleasant even-featured way, and, which was pretty rare in Twistleton men – whose dentistry consisted only in 'having 'em all out' – he had great teeth.

'What are you trying to say, Joe Huggett?'

'Marry me, Jean. Before I go to war, marry me, and make me happy for a few days, or hours. Soon our whole world may be gone, every last bit of it, my mum's house, your cottage, the Hall, everything covered in Nazi flags. Hitler youth striding through the streets, Hitler standing on the balcony at Buckingham Palace waving to the crowds below—'

'Stop it, Joe. Stop it. You're exaggerating!'

'Am I?' Joe reached down and picked up her gas-mask case and placed it on the table. 'Is this an exaggeration?'

Jean stared at him, seeing the bleak landscape ahead of them both – the bus had already passed children playing in gas masks in the playgrounds – seeing everything as he, perhaps, was seeing it. Perhaps Joe was right? Perhaps she should marry him before everything disappeared?

'Whoosh!' Maude was sitting beside Daisy in the new motor car, holding on to her hat, despite the fact that she had secured it firmly with motoring veils. 'Whoosh!' she shouted again, her cheeks pink from the breeze. 'This is just how it used to be.'

Naturally Daisy was thrilled with herself, not

just because she was driving so well, and so fast, and after only a few lessons with Mr Russell, but because she had actually managed to persuade Aunt Maude to leave the Hall. It was a big decision for Maude, and they both knew it.

She had probably stayed at the Hall, Daisy thought, ever since Daisy had arrived, Nanny in tow; or was it Nanny arriving with Daisy in tow? It did not seem to matter much now. What had mattered was that one day Nanny had left, and with her had gone Daisy's childhood belief in the idea that everything was going to be all right.

A maid, Patty Bywater, had taken Nanny's place, for no reason that anyone ever explained, but she had proved endlessly cruel; not just painting Daisy's fingers with bitter aloes at Aunt Maude's request, but making fun of her because she was 'grand'. Every evening Patty would switch off Daisy's light, leaving her in the pitch black of countryside darkness, and make her own way down the corridor by the light of a torch. And just before, instead of reading to Daisy, she would dress up in frightening clothes, and, pretending to be a grotesque of some weird kind, would dance up and down in front of her charge, her shoulders hunched as if there was a string at the back of her, and she was a puppet. Too proud to admit, even to herself, that she was not frightened – but actually terrified – Daisy would sit bolt upright in bed staring at her, pretending to laugh at her antics, hating her all the time.

One day, as is natural to all bullies, the wretched

creature went too far, and while in the act of pretending to suffocate Daisy with a pillow, caused her to black out, upon which Patty immediately panicked, and ran screaming from the nursery. The sound alerted another of the servants, who, upon finding Daisy, brought her back to consciousness.

Aunt Maude, not a minute too soon, in her own words, 'dismissed the ghastly creature', and her replacement, Nippy – so nicknamed because rumour had it that she had once been a waitress – took her place.

Nippy was a cockney, and proud of it. On marrying a local boy, as a result of a country holiday sponsored by the vicar of her church, she had taken a daily job at the Hall. She liked Miss Maude, 'one of the old-fashioned sort' was how she described Maude to her farm-labourer husband, but she would have none of the old-fashioned sort's Victorian methods. The bottle of bitter aloes was ceremoniously emptied down Mr Thomas Crapper's brilliant Victorian invention, the water closet, and a night light installed beside Daisy's bed.

'Don't give that Patty Bywater another thought,' Nippy would say, when once or twice Daisy confided in her. 'She was just out to get yer, 'cos of you being 'ere, and she not being 'ere, and all that. My Bert, he says she was always a tyrant on account of her father spoiling her. Myself, I hope she falls down in a ditch and *no one* finds her, until it's far too late. She turned the back of your hair white,

I'm sure of it, but no matter, no one will notice once yer grown up, it'll just tie in with the rest of the blonde, yer know?'

How Nippy had known that Daisy's light mouse-coloured hair would eventually turn blonde, without any help from a bottle, neither of them would ever know.

'Just me intuition, love, that's all. Me intuition, always has been one of me main attractions for Bert, you know? Ever since I come on holiday here, and I told him he would marry a girl from another place with red hair . . .'

This was a great joke, as it might well be, since Nippy herself was indeed from another place, and had the brightest red hair imaginable. Of course she had retired now, and Daisy still missed her, but only occasionally, because she knew Nippy was happy with her Bert.

Aunt Maude climbed out of the motor car, a suddenly decorous figure, standing on the pavement outside Mrs Bradshaw's confectionery, newsagent, post office, and general grocery store, the potatoes and cabbages spilling from boxes outside the long, low sprawling shop seeming to make her look even more elegant, already a figure from another, calmer era.

'It is such a good idea, this motor car,' she said, sighing happily, and looking around and about her, as if she had just arrived from a different planet. 'We can take shopping home in it, Daisy dear. And we can come to the village more often.'

'Not if there is petrol-rationing, Aunt Maude,' Daisy murmured. 'If there is petrol-rationing I shall have to put the pony at the front and get *him* to pull it into the village!'

Aunt Maude looked away, suddenly deaf, as she was wont to become at any hint of another war to come. Daisy knew that her beloved aunt had set her heart against the idea, that she simply would not believe it, she simply could not believe it, and moreover she did not have to believe it, because, despite every possible newspaper being delivered, the truth was that Aunt Maude never paid the slightest attention to any of them, never even so much as glancing at a headline.

Nor would she countenance a wireless. It would have been ridiculous to even suggest that she should buy one, or, worse, listen to it. Daisy herself had secretly asked her godfather for one and installed it in the butler's pantry, where she sneaked off to listen to plays, and the news, and even comedy and variety shows of an evening, while Maude sat in front of the great fire with her photograph albums.

Maude stooped down and started to replace one or two of the potatoes that had strayed from their box, her gloved hand becoming marked by the dry clods of mud clinging to them, and as she did so the name on the side of the box caught her eye.

'This says these are Jean Shaw's potatoes,' she said, in a surprised voice. She turned to Daisy. 'You know I have leased some fields to her, on the advice of Mr Chittlethorpe, my farm manager?

Does this mean she is growing a potato crop, do you think, Daisy?'

At that moment a cloud moved across the sun, blocking out the warmth from the day, just as a frown came to Aunt Maude's face, and Daisy realised with a sinking heart that the warmth had gone out of her expression.

'Come, Daisy, we must drive back to the Hall, and inspect the lower fields that run down towards the sea, those that I have leased to Jean Shaw through Chittlethorpe.'

Oh, dear poor Geoff Chittlethorpe! He had suddenly lost his right to being a 'Mr'. It was as if a knighthood had been withdrawn from him.

'I daresay we could do that after luncheon, couldn't we, Aunt Maude? I mean, whatever Jean is growing on the fields will wait until we have finished our drive, surely?'

'Very well, continue on, Daisy, but after luncheon, willy-nilly, we will be driving across the estate to those leased fields. I was always a little nervous of Chittlethorpe's modernising ideas, and I only hope I am wrong.'

Of course she knew very well that she couldn't be, and that the potatoes must have come from somewhere, and that that somewhere must be her own fields. And of course, after luncheon, despite Daisy trying to deflect her attention from such a tedious matter, she insisted that Daisy drive her to the relevant fields, which were indeed planted, many acres of them, with potatoes. Daisy dropped her back at the Hall, and then shot off to the Court, only thankful that she had promised to give Laura and Aurelia driving lessons.

The next day Geoff Chittlethorpe was summoned to the Hall.

'Miss Shaw has ploughed up my ancient pastures to plant her wretched potatoes!'

Daisy, who was listening at the drawing-room door, straightened up. There was no need to put her ear to it any more, Aunt Maude had raised her voice. It was unheard-of for Aunt Maude to raise her voice, let alone shout, and what Daisy had just heard was really quite near to a shout.

'Well, Miss Maude.' Daisy heard the panic in Geoff Chittlethorpe's voice as he sought to justify himself. 'I know it must seem strange to you . . .'

'Strange! It is hideous. Potato crops! Cabbages! In fields that have been pastures since Oliver Cromwell! You should be shot at dawn, Chittlethorpe. If you knew of this, I shall personally court marshall you.'

Daisy wasn't sure that Geoff Chittlethorpe would believe even Aunt Maude had the authority to bring about her threat. Even so, she was very frightening, as people who believe absolutely in their own authority so often are.

'Miss Maude, may I explain?' Geoff Chittlethorpe had obviously taken a deep breath while pausing to think, because his voice had become a great deal firmer. 'There is a war coming, Miss Maude. We are going to need to eat – and not just meat. Potatoes and suchlike must be grown in place of so much pasture for sheep and cattle. We will need to eat cheaply, Miss Maude. Cabbages and potatoes will become our national diet.'

'From whom did you gather this?'

'From the wireless, Miss Maude, and from the newspapers. We all know there is a war coming.'

Another long silence, and then finally Aunt Maude spoke.

'I am severely disappointed in you, Chittlethorpe. However, what is done is done, and cannot now be undone. I imagine we have leased the fields to Jean Shaw for some interminable time?'

'For five years, I believe, Miss Maude, and she has never yet been late with the rent, Miss Maude. Never. Brings it herself, in cash.'

Cash or no cash, Aunt Maude was obviously not in a mood to be reasonable.

'Well, well, well, that it should come to this, Chittlethorpe. But, and I must in duty say this to you, if you are to make something of yourself, which I somehow now doubt, but if you are, you should take the advice I am now giving you. Avoid reading newspapers, avoid listening to that contraption called the wireless, read your Bible, go to church, listen to the sermons preached by the reverend – although not his locum who has some very peculiar ideas about almost everything including the creation – and above all, remember to say your prayers at night, together with your wife and children.'

Daisy knew that poor Geoff Chittlethorpe had no wife or children, so this last advice could surely and most happily be ignored? Before the wretched man could back out of the room in the manner of some crushed debutante at a royal occasion, Daisy shot down to the kitchens. When, oh when, would Aunt Maude start believing that there was going to be a war? Perhaps only when one of Hitler's cohorts was forcing her to have dinner with him?

Freddie had been counting gas masks for some time before it actually came home to her that they were real. Gas masks up to that moment had just been, well – just gas masks. Now, all of a sudden she remembered the Sargent painting of the gassed soldiers in the Great War moving slowly forward with blindfolded eyes, each with a hand on another's shoulders. Oh *dear*, that was how they could all be in a few months' time, she with a hand on Daisy's shoulder, Daisy with a hand on Relia's shoulder, Relia with a hand on . . . She stopped, and clicked her fingers sharply beside her head. No point in thinking like that, no point at all. The truth was that in a very short space of time their whole world would be turned upside down. She imagined, as she always had as a child, making a camp in the cellars below the house, Aunt Jessica, and herself, Blossom, and Branscombe and all the dogs, all of them quietened, listening, all waiting for the inevitable sound of people overhead going through the house, going through their things, searching, searching, not just for possessions, but for human beings, for anyone or anything.

Just for a second Freddie felt quite sick, imagining

trying to keep the dogs quiet, stop them yapping; but then she went to the window, sat down on the window seat, and to steady her nerves she stared out at the distant view of fields and trees. It settled her, and finally it was bracing. Whatever happened she would fight for their land, and for their right to lead their lives the way they wished, for everything that they all held dear. She'd fight for the gentle ways of Twistleton, all of which had been arrived at slowly through the centuries, so that not even the proud red letter box outside the general store in the village was allowed to be disturbed until after the young robins, who hatched there annually, had flown the nest.

Twistleton had ducks on its pond, cows that stared over the five-bar gates as you walked into the village. It had birdsong at dawn, it had night skies of such beauty that it was impossible to go to bed without believing in a greater good. It held everything that was dear about life and the countryside, and despite its sometimes irritating vagaries, Freddie loved it with all her heart.

She returned to the table where she had been unpacking the gas masks with renewed determination. Gas them, bomb them, let Hitler do what he could, they would never give in. She pulled out a child's gas mask. There *would* be another generation. The idea that there would *not* be was appalling. She clicked her fingers by her head once more, in yet another attempt to drive away thoughts of gloom.

Blossom, as always nowadays, with the two

dachshunds firmly attached to her waist with string, came in to help with the unpacking and the checking. Freddie could see from her expression that she had heard something on the wireless.

'It seems we may expect to have Christmas on our own. No evacuations from the cities yet, but we can't count on it. And there's rumours about it becoming illegal to store tins and suchlike.' She looked baleful. 'Since when is the government going to hold sway over our larders, may I ask?' She sighed. 'Since when are they going to tell us what to do at every turn? It'll be identity cards soon, mark my words. Do this, do that. Anyone would think the high-ups were better than us, instead of just people, the same as us. And people with a great deal less sense than a lot of us low-downs, I sometimes think.' She sniffed, and then sighed. 'I found myself just wishing the blessed war would get on with it. Here we all are, making plans for this, plans for that, gas masks and I know not what, and yet, blow me, not a word from Hitler now he's disporting himself in Czechoslovakia. Not a word, not a funeral note, only rumour, rumour, rumour.' She took out a handkerchief suddenly, and dabbed at her eyes. 'I sometimes think I can't stand any more of this waiting, Freddie, truly I can't. I just want to get on with it. Gas mask or no gas mask, I just want to stop the waiting, it's worse than anything, truly it is. I just want something to fight, not nothing, day after day of nothing.'

Freddie went to where the old darling was

seated, but instead of trying to comfort her, which she knew Blossom would hate, she knelt down and stroked the dogs, giving Blossom time to calm herself.

'What are you going to do once it starts, Blossom?' she asked her, eventually.

Blossom sniffed and then cleared her throat, before rearranging the combs on either side of her great bun of white hair.

'I think I must get into something. No point in hanging around Jessica here, getting on her nerves. I mean, she's been very kind, and given me a roof and a job all these years, but she won't want me around once the balloon goes up, will she? Stands to reason. I know I wouldn't want me hanging around. I'm not good for much here anyway, really, just a bit of this and a bit of that, and all that is to come to an end.'

Freddie straightened up. This piece of news was not at all welcome. *Freddie* was the one who planned to leave Twistleton Court, in the certain knowledge that Blossom would always be there to help Aunt Jessica. If Blossom left, then Freddie might be forced to stay. It was not that she didn't love Twistleton, as she kept saying to herself, nor that she would not fight for it, as she had previously assured herself while she was seated in the window, but neither did she want to *stay*. She passionately wanted to leave, to fight for what was right.

'But what if we have to take in evacuees? You will surely be needed by Aunt Jessica then?'

Blossom shook her head.

'I never was any good with city folk, or children, for that matter. One of the reasons why I could never, would never, marry. No, I must go and find some sort of work – on the land, preferably. I am still strong, and as long as they don't mind dogs, I'll find myself a place all right. I know, it won't be popular in some quarters, but I can't stay here, part-relative, part-servant. It won't do, dear, truly it won't. Neither fish nor flesh, and certainly not good red herring.'

Freddie stared at Blossom.

She had always imagined that Blossom was so happy at the Court, never really thought, she suddenly realised with a rush of beastly guilt, of Blossom as anything except, well – *Blossom*. Hadn't really thought of her as a human being, as a whole person with feelings and with any kind of independence. Good old Blossom, good old Jessica's impoverished cousin, given a cottage to live in, allowed her dogs, helping out every hour of the day, and sometimes the night, too; expected to be grateful, to be courteous, to be there, all the time. No actual feelings, though, nothing on display. The rest of them, even Branscombe, could have feelings, but not Blossom – except about the dogs, of course. She was allowed those, but even that was a kind of unspoken joke. Blossom and her dogs! Tied to her waist! Eternally frightened that they would attract anti-German feelings, people trying to kick them, as if anyone in Twistleton would do that . . . ha, ha, ha.

'Have you told Aunt Jessica of your plans to leave the Court, Blossom?'

'Of course.' Blossom stood up. 'But don't you discuss them with her, will you?'

'No, no, of course not.'

'I don't think she imagines for a second that anything will come of them—'

'But Aunt Jessica is the one who has always been convinced that war is on the cards. It's Miss *Maude* who is the one who won't even discuss it.'

Freddie knew that if there was one thing that was never spoken about in Twistleton, it was the continuing silence between the Court and the Hall, and all of a sudden she also knew she had to join up, and a great deal sooner than she had imagined. The only trouble was that she wanted to be a Wren – and they had been disbanded after the Great War.

Chapter Four

Daisy had never known any of her parents' circle, friends who might have been able to tell her a little of what the people who had given her life had been like. In fact, besides Aunt Maude, she had no connections outside Twistleton Hall, with the single exception of her godfather, Gervaise Fanshawe.

For Daisy, growing up a lone child among adults at the Hall, Gervaise was an adored figure. Adored because he was tall and handsome, funny and fun, and always and for ever – unexpected. For the simple reason that he never gave Aunt Maude or Daisy any warning when he came to visit.

Only Gervaise could get away with turning up in his elegant motor car, and hooting the horn outside the house, before running in, calling for Daisy, calling for Maude, 'Where are the women in my life?' And demanding luncheon, tea or dinner, as appropriate, or not.

Unbelievably, too, Gervaise could make Aunt Maude laugh, which was only a little more difficult than making the cow jump over the moon.

Not only could he make Aunt Maude laugh, but he could show her the latest dance steps, and exhort her to try them, which of course she never did, but nevertheless it brought colour to their lives even to hear about them, and all this before Gervaise sat down at the piano and played and sang the latest hits.

Sometimes, when she was younger, after a long abstinence from any form of gaiety, Daisy would find herself falling asleep, praying to the Lord to send her godfather to see them, if only to break the civilised monotony which was the norm at the Hall. The unbroken tenor of her life acting, as it so often did, as a burden of crushing silence, despite all the wildlife, despite all the animals around the place, despite the maids – despite, when it eventually arrived, courtesy of Gervaise, of course, the wireless – she still longed with all her heart for the kind of unexpected excitement that Gervaise brought to their lives.

But, quite unlike Aunt Maude, Gervaise had become caught up in the idea of a coming war, and had been instrumental in trying to convince the powers that be that they needed to build new and faster aeroplanes, planes that could dive out of the sky and drive away the enemy. Needless to say, the politicians could not see beyond the army and the navy, but Gervaise had persisted, and more than that, he had become convinced that with all the men fighting, the need for women to be trained as pilots would be as great as the need for women to be trained in the navy and the army. But, as he had written to Daisy a few months before, 'I sometimes think it would be easier to be the first man to fly without a plane, than to convince our dear government and all the top brass of what is so badly needed.'

Daisy herself needed no convincing. It seemed only logical, when all was said and done, that, just as there had been a dire need for women in the factories during the Great War, now there was a dire need for women not just to work in the factories, but to join up.

The subject of joining the services had often come up while they were all meant to be learning how to be beautifully brought-up young ladies at the Court. Not that Laura wanted to do any such thing, nor Relia, nor any of the other girls, except Freddie, of course. Freddie had always set her heart on something to do with the sea, which was hardly surprising, since so many of the outlying cottages and houses of Twistleton were in sight and sound of the sea. She had always had her own sailing boat, no landlubber she. But despite seeing the distant blue, or more often grey, of the sea beyond the cliffs, Daisy wanted only to fly, and the one person who could help her to do just that was Gervaise.

With the acceleration of war rumours, Daisy had started to bombard him with letters asking for information about flying lessons. Naturally, Gervaise being Gervaise, the letters remained gaily unanswered, until one day she had a brief note from him, his usual signature embellished by a caricature of himself, but also with a cheque attached behind the letter.

Have spoken to the chaps at Bramsfield about you, you minx. Cheque attached. Best of British, but do make sure to get the hours in. At least two hundred and fifty hours logged will be necessary, so go to, dear godchild . . .
Your wicked godfather, Gervaise

It was not in Daisy's nature to deceive anyone, let alone her beloved aunt, nevertheless, in between taking Aunt Maude for her now almost daily 'spin' in the new motor car, she also made sure to book up flying lessons as early as possible, taking off daily for Bramsfield aerodrome early in the morning, before Aunt Maude was about, determined on logging up the necessary hours.

It was not, she told herself, that she was actually deceiving Aunt Maude, she was just not telling her until the right moment presented itself, which it suddenly seemed to do just as she neared the necessary logged hours, only a few being left.

There was a long silence as Maude stared at Daisy, and it seemed to both of them that Daisy might be losing colour, as Maude's mouth tightened into a thin strip of suppressed fury, while at the same time the sound of the library clock ticking was a welcome distraction in the ensuing pause.

'Been going for flying lessons, did you say?'

'Yes, I have, Aunt Maude. Do love flying so much.'

Maude walked to the library window.

'You would, it is in the blood. And I suppose that bad man, your godfather Gervaise, encouraged you in this?'

'Not entirely, no. The idea actually came from me. I can't blame him, really I can't,' Daisy confessed.

Aunt Maude stared ahead of her, silent for a minute.

'I forbid you to go on with this nonsense, Daisy dear,' she finally announced.

Daisy dearly hoped that she hadn't heard her only living relative correctly.

'Why are you not keen on me flying, Aunt Maude?' Daisy finally asked. 'You don't mind me driving a motor car, and from what I have found, flying is, if anything, even a little easier than driving, once you start to get the hang of it, that is. I had hoped that you would be proud of me.'

Maude turned back to look at her.

'No flying, Daisy, do you hear? Just no flying, and that is an end to it.'

Daisy knew all too well that the Beresford manner of clamping down on any activity of which they found they could not approve was unrivalled. There was never any room for discussion. This had always been true of Aunt Maude. Once she had pronounced, as far as she was concerned, that was – always and ever would be – that.

Daisy gazed around her in silence. Aunt Maude was in front of her, her expression grim. Daisy's,

by contrast, alternated between despair and determination.

It might be an incontrovertible fact that when
a Beresford put one of their elegant feet down,
it stayed down. But what Aunt Maude did not
perhaps realise was that Daisy was also a Beresford,
and it seemed that quite soon there would be the
sound of one of Daisy's feet coming down, too – if
not both. Fly she would, fly she must, whatever
Aunt Maude said or did.

Joe only realised what a mistake it was to take
Jean to tea with his mother when it was too late.
Somehow, after their joyous bus rides to and
from Wychford, and their delicious lunch at The
Pantry, it had seemed just the right thing to do.
Perhaps he had seen too many American films, or
just too many films, full stop, but taking a girl to
tea with mother was what he thought a nice boy
did. And, of course, it was quite possible that nice
boys everywhere in the county *were* taking their
girls to tea with their mothers before kissing those
same girls goodbye, and going off to join the army
and fight the future war. But, unfortunately for
him, and Jean, his mother lived in Holly House,
a Georgian gem with Georgian furniture and
exquisite china in cabinets, and Jean was from The
Cottages, and cottagers' children, and children
from such places as Holly House, might go to the
village school together, they might play in the
village stream, and go bird-nesting, and heaven
only knew what together, but once they grew up,

things became very different, as the expression on Mrs Huggett's face, as she sat behind her silver tea service, was now making quite clear.

To give Mrs Huggett her due, once in the drawing room of Holly House, even Joe quickly realised that to an outside eye, Jean did look just a little wild, definitely beautiful, but – wild. Her dark curly hair and green eyes might be arresting, but they had about them something challenging and, worse, untamed. Besides which, her clothes, which had looked at lunch at The Pantry no more than pleasantly bohemian, now looked almost purposefully rural, which Joe happened to like, but which, next to his mother's excellently tailored light-tweed suit, pearl earrings and matching lapel brooch, made their guest look just a little like something from a country holiday poster – *'Come to Twistleton for Country Air!'*

'I gather you have taken up farming, Miss Shaw?'

Jean nodded.

'Yes, Mrs Huggett, I am renting eighty acres from Miss Maude Beresford, at the Hall, because with war coming I realised that we were not growing enough food to eat, and we were going to need to, to feed everyone.'

'And what sort of food do you have in mind?'

'Potatoes and cabbages, turnips, root vegetables in particular, since they are warming, and go a long way, and are inexpensive.'

'I see . . . turnips and, er, cabbages, you say? Gracious, how very . . . hearty.'

Mrs Huggett carefully and quietly offered Jean lump sugar from a silver sugar bowl with attached tongs. Jean gaily ignored the proffered tongs, and popped the sugar into her cup with her fingers, after which she gave everything a vigorous stir. Seeing this, Joe had to pinch himself hard under the table to stop himself from laughing, the way he used to when he was a boy, and something went awry in church. The whole Huggett family were all too aware that Joe's laugh was so infectious it could set the whole church off. Rows and rows of shaking shoulders was not what the Reverend Johnson wanted to see when he faced his congregation.

'I don't think your mother liked me very much, Joe,' Jean told him in a non-committal tone, as he walked her back to her cottage, down the hill from Holly House.

'Mother's very shy,' Joe stated in a determinedly detached voice. 'She's like that with everyone she doesn't know.'

'But she *does* know me, she's known me since I was knee-high to that grasshopper there, but now I'm a grown woman it's all different, isn't it? It's Miss Shaw this, and Miss Shaw that, and while she might have let me join your picnics when I was a child, now it seems I'm just not good enough to go to tea with her.'

Joe stopped walking, and taking both Jean's hands he forced her to face him.

'Listen, kid,' he said, putting on what he imagined was a passable American film-star voice.

'We don't have time for class warfare no more. There's going to be gas attacks, and bombs dropping, and whether or not you take the sugar with the tongs won't matter one hoot, or even two hoots, because there won't be no tongs, and there won't be no sugar.'

Jean snatched her hands away from him and started to walk quickly towards her cottage door.

'So you noticed. I thought you did!' she said, flinging her words over her shoulder. 'You noticed that I didn't take the tongs!'

Joe followed her to her door. Fleetingly, as Jean turned the heavy iron handle of the studded old oak door, he wondered if it would be hanging off its hinges in another few months.

'I thought it was marvellous, I thought you were marvellous. I never have had much time for all that silver tea service and get-out-the-best china malarkey, and never less than now. What will it all mean, what will it all matter when the jackboots are marching up the village street?'

Joe glanced up the street, and down again as Jean's front door swung open. He wanted so much to follow Jean into her cottage, but, on the other hand, he did not want to be seen by the rest of the village. It would damage her reputation, and he did not want that. Jean was too special.

'You won't want me to come in, Jean, I know that, but I just want you to know that I hate Mother being or seeming snooty, truly I do.'

The honesty in his eyes convinced her. It was not his fault that his mother was so snooty, and

116

had a silver tea service, any more than it was Jean's fault that she was from The Cottages.

'Quickly, Joe, come in, before anyone sees you.'

Joe went eagerly through the door, and Jean shut it behind him. Sunshine flooded her little sitting room with its two Staffordshire pottery dogs on the chimneypiece, and arrangement of flowers on the side table overlooking the back garden. She turned to Joe, and he put his arms around her, which he had of course been longing to do, and they started to kiss, and kiss some more, very shallow kisses, and then deeper and deeper. At one point Jean pushed him away, but then allowed him to take her back into his arms, finally giving in to his passion for her.

After all, he was going off tomorrow morning at crack of dawn, and after that they might never see each other again.

When Laura returned to London and put her key in the door of her father's Grosvenor Square apartment, she could not help hoping against hope that he would not be there. It was not that she had stopped loving him because of his amatory ways, it was just that she found the sight of him smooching on the sofa with a society lady distasteful in the extreme. Of course she knew she should feel sympathetic to his needs, to the fact that he had rebounded from the awfulness of his wife's sudden death into the arms of every and any passing fancy, but the truth of the matter was – and she had to be honest about it, there was no avoiding the reality – she felt revolted by it. Happily it seemed he was out, and only a few of the maids were in residence.

It was two days before Arthur finally caught up with her.

'Ah, there you are, Laura darling. I thought you might be back, had a feeling that you were, but you are so mouse-like quiet that neither the maids nor I ever know whether you are in or away.'

Arthur Hambleton was tall, exquisitely handsome – 'Arthur is almost too good-looking' Laura's mother had often been heard to say, laughing appreciatively – on top of which he was charming and attentive, so naturally he was irresistible to women.

'Yes, here I am, Father.'

Laura knew that her father hated being called 'Father', which was why she called him 'Father' as often as she could, especially in front of his mistresses.

'You are not at all in a good mood, are you, Laura darling?'

He put his head on one side and stared at her, a humorous look in his eyes.

'I am in a perfectly good mood, Father.' Laura turned away to pick up her handbag, determined that if he was staying in with a girlfriend, she would go out, anywhere, rather than hang around listening to alien feminine laughter coming from the drawing room. She knew the public rooms would suddenly be filled with exotic scents, some-times slyly Amber, sometimes distinctly Chanel, always deliciously feminine – like the sounds of the laughter, which always seemed to her, for some reason, to be vaguely challenging, as if the cause of the laughter was not something that she would ever be allowed to know about.

'I expect everything is a little flat here, after being at Twistleton Court?' Arthur said, attempting to look sympathetic, and failing quite singularly.

'No, it's not that,' Laura confessed, finally succumbing to his feigned look of sympathy, because she so wanted to believe that he was sincere. 'No, it's just there are so many people around and about here, in uniform, that it is making me feel really quite awkward. I really should be preparing myself for doing something useful in the war that is about to happen.'

'You will have a role to play, I am sure, darling. But for the moment, why not enjoy yourself? I saw there was a heap of invitations on the hall table for you. You are obviously very popular, and that is something, after all.'

'Being popular is not exactly going to help in the war, Father,' Laura told him in a sanctimonious voice. 'Surely even you can see that I must start to train to do something?'

'Your godmother wants you to go to luncheon with her tomorrow, I know that. She is very caught up with organising a Christmas ball for some charity or another. That will be something useful for you to get caught up in, surely?'

'A charity ball?'

Laura raised her eyebrows. Over the last year

she had realised, over and over again, just how terrible it was to be without a mother, because – possessing only a male relative – she had no one in her family who could truly sympathise or identify with her.

'Girls meet people at balls, Laura darling. I mean, I know you haven't, as yet, met anyone, but even so, I would say that you should be able to meet someone soon, and any minute now we will see you in the pages of *Country Life* – a girl in pearls, an engagement ring on your finger.'

'Yes, Father. Just as you say, Father.'

Laura's tone was so dismal, her expression so miserable, it caused even Arthur to sigh inwardly. Things were very difficult for him at that moment. Two of his mistresses were threatening to leave their husbands, and yet another, a widow, was threatening to marry him, all on account of the coming war. It seemed that the women in his life had all become infected with the same sense of amatory urgency, which was not at all convenient or attractive. He did not like women making passes at him, he did not like women threatening him, either with divorce or marriage, and yet, it had to be faced, he could do nothing about it. He had so many girlfriends now, life was getting really very complicated. He had even found the idea of being married just a little tempting, although he had no idea which of the many would be the victor.

And now, to make matters far from better, here was Laura, back from the country with an expression on her face like a wet week at Bognor. He had hoped that she would elect to stay on at Twistleton Court, despite its no longer even pretending to be a finishing school, but it seemed that lots of well-brought-up young girls were straining at the leash, making up their minds to join various armed services – be of use – although the country had yet to discover what use a gaggle of girls could possibly be.

'Very well, let us talk, Laura.'

'Not now, Father. I don't want to be a party-pooper, but I am worn to a thread paper after that journey, it seemed to take for ever.'

Arthur stared at his daughter, thinking quickly, trying to escape from her, just as he had from her mother.

'I will buy you a car, Laura, that way you won't have to endure journeys like that again. I should have done it months ago. I don't know what I was thinking.'

Laura stared at him, struggling as always to keep despair out of her eyes. It was always the same, whatever happened, whatever was about to happen, whatever *had* happened – since her mother's death, her father's solution to everything had been to put his hand in his pocket and bribe her.

'As a matter of fact, Father,' she said slowly, finding it very difficult not to relish the in-evitable twitch that saying 'Father' brought to his face. 'As a matter of fact, I would like a motor car. I think it will be most useful in the war. I have already tried driving at Twistleton Court, and enjoyed it very much. Branscombe taught us the rudiments.'

'Good. I will write you a cheque in the morning.' Arthur backed out of the room before quickly turning and haring off down the corridor, grabbing his silk-lined evening cloak, and charging to the door. He was late for his friend, he was late for that evening's ball, and worse than that, he was late for Georgiana Bassington. She would suspect that he had been dallying with Dora Hopcroft, even though it was only Laura who had held him back, creeping into the flat, avoiding him as usual. Poor Laura, poor motherless girl. To judge from her expression this evening, she could not wait for the war to begin.

He smiled at the maid who was holding the door open for him, and flung himself down the steps to his waiting car, where the chauffeur, too, was holding the door open for him. Unfortunately for both of them, Laura was the least of Arthur Hambleton's problems, and when push came to shove, she would just have to get on with it.

Laura heard the front door closing behind Arthur with her usual feeling of overwhelming relief. He was gone, gone, gone. Please God, he would not return until daybreak, and when he did, he would sleep in late, so she could leave before he woke up.

She gazed around the drawing room of the flat. It was beautifully decorated. A pretty French repeating clock on the mantelpiece told her that a whole evening of being alone stretched before her. A cigarette marked with lipstick in one of the silver ashtrays told her that one of her father's girlfriends had already called in for a drink. A little shadow of dust on one of the tables told her that the maids did not work as hard as they should, now that her mother was no longer there to bully them.

None of it now seemed to matter, now that she realised that tomorrow, or the next day, she could buy a motor car, set off to meet friends, or go to the country, do anything she liked – without her father. It was better than she could have hoped for. Above all, it was freedom.

With a sudden attack of religious fervour, she found herself blessing both Branscombe and Daisy Beresford for letting her take the wheel of Daisy's car, and bob about in the quiet countryside around Twistleton, relishing the freedom that a car could bring, her friends seated beside her, murmuring encouragement.

If Laura could drive away from Grosvenor Square, drive away from Father and his antics, she could find work! It was a dizzying thought. More than that, it was a blooming miracle that it was Father who had suggested that she have a motor car. It was actually the first time since her mother had died that he offered her any independence. Up until now, he had tied her to the masculine version of his apron strings, making sure that her allowance was so staggered that it was impossible for her to have any sort of freedom outside of buying a return ticket to Twistleton. But now he was going to buy her a motor car, and the world was suddenly flung wide open.

She started to run a bath, and to sing at the top of her voice. She would make Father give her enough money – not just for the motor car, but for the petrol, and in the event that they would burst, for tyres, and for anything else that she might need. She might even be able to have a dog now. She stopped, suddenly frowning, as she remembered how easily the suggestion had seemed to come to Arthur. Why had he suddenly decided to let go of her? She stepped into her bath. What did the reason matter?

Daisy and Freddie had arranged to meet Laura and Relia outside London again, but not at the Court this time. They were meeting for dinner and staying the night in a country hotel, the idea being to make sure all four could plan their future together.

'Where's Daisy?' Laura asked.

Freddie pulled a face.

'She's staying behind with Aunt Maude, poor thing, helping out. I nearly had to stay with Aunt Jessica, but she let me off, gave me a pink ticket, even though Blossom has already gone.'

Laura and Relia stared at Freddie, astonished.

'Blossom has left the Court?'

'She has, indeed. She seems to think she is going to be more useful in a munitions factory than hanging around Twistleton. She can't wait for the war to start. You know how it is, war is one thing, but waiting for it is worse, Blossom says.'

'But what about the *dogs*?'

'Left with Aunt Jessica—'

'*What?*'

'On strings around *her* waist, now.'

'Doesn't she *mind*?'

'Oh no, wherever a dog is concerned, Aunt Jessica doesn't mind at all. She always says it's because she's never had children. I think she sees dogs as a healthy replacement.'

They all stared at each other for a few seconds. They knew Jessica was a model of everything that a single woman should be, yet none of them wanted to be like her. They longed to be wanted by men, not left by them, as Jessica had been, what with her great love being killed in the Great War, and her never recovering. But then, being wanted was one thing – getting married and having to have babies was another.

'I will be the first to say what I feel.' Laura looked at the other two. 'I don't want to marry and have babies, out of duty to our country,' Laura announced. 'I would much prefer to join up, and have lots of men fall in love with me, but not have to marry them, which practically everyone seems to be doing. And I certainly do not want to have their babies just because there is going to be a war.'

Laura had always been the one to state her opinion first, no matter what the situation, just as she had always been the first to own up when they found themselves in a scrape. Since no one else seemed prepared to announce their future intentions, or declare their aversion to what would seem, willy-nilly, to be their predestined role of mothers to the future heirs to the empire, Laura lit a cigarette, and carried on.

'I understand, from what I have heard, that there are some good things about a war,' she confided to the other two, leaning back in her armchair, as waiters hovered to fill their glasses with stimulating alcohol, and whisked their ashtrays away to clean them before they were even half-full. 'War can free you. It freed lots of women last time. They earned their own money for the first time, they stopped being domestic slaves, and they were able to work in factories. Apparently, they felt needed in a way they had never felt before.'

'How do you know?'

'I have been reading about it, because we can't all go on being this ignorant.'

The other two gave each other a quick look, and then coloured slightly, guessing immediately that Laura was referring to them.

'Oh, shucks, Laura, you haven't been trying to read Marie Stopes's manuals again, have you? You know you couldn't make head nor tail of them last time.' Freddie leaned forward, dropping her voice.

'Well, at least I now know that babies do not *always* have to arrive!'

They all laughed a little hysterically, but the colour in Freddie and Aurelia's faces heightened.

They had heard that some girls *did* do it, but not *their* kind of girl. Their kind of girl, nice girls, remained in blissful ignorance – well, innocent anyway – until they married.

'*So?*'

Laura looked from one friend to the other, her head on one side.

'I want to have something to do with boats and the sea,' Freddie said. 'But I won't be eighteen until next month. As soon as I am, I've told Aunt Jessica, I'm off, and she, thank the Lord, has given me her blessing. As a matter of fact, I should think she can't wait to get me off her hands.'

Aurelia looked from the room in which they were seated to the white-tipped waves beyond the windows. She had hardly thought about what she wanted to do, and yet she knew she must.

'I, er . . . I, er . . .' She frowned. 'I think I will do the same as Freddie, actually, perhaps have something to do with the sea. I love the sea.'

'Well, that is jolly.' Freddie looked mildly astonished. 'We can volunteer for something together. If they bring back the Wrens, we can do jolly boating things. Such a pity they were disbanded after the Great War as being unnecessary, but I daresay we'll soon hear they are back, and then we will be in, eh?'

Aurelia nodded happily, despite not quite knowing why she was joining something that might or might not exist. Perhaps sensing her bewilderment, Freddie squeezed her hand.

'If they will not let you join the navy, why not try the army, Freddie?' Laura said.

Freddie looked mildly shocked.

'Really, Laura, I hope I didn't hear that.'

'No, but really, why not join the army?'

'Because, Laura dear, khaki is just not my colour. I look terrible in sludgy colours. It has to be dark blue or nothing.'

Aurelia gave Freddie a grateful look, feeling a rush of affection for her. She hadn't given a thought to the uniform. She, too, would look ghastly in khaki.

'So, so,' Laura said, having accepted this explanation as being entirely reasonable. 'So, that just leaves Daisy, who wants to fly aeroplanes, crazy girl.'

'If she can get away from Aunt Maude, that is, which I somehow doubt. The old lady hardly lets her out of her sight, poor soul. I don't know who to feel most sorry for, Daisy or Aunt Maude.'

The dreadful silence, usual in the dining room, had now infected the library. Aunt Maude had just spoken words that Daisy had never thought she would hear, for the simple reason that she had never considered herself anything more than Aunt Maude's niece. Certainly not her heir, or was it heiress? At any rate, the very idea of inheriting the Hall was somehow absurd.

'If you insist on going on taking flying lessons, I will disinherit you, Daisy.'

Daisy stared at her only relative, appalled, and it

was a few seconds before she could think of anything to say.

'That sounds a bit King Learish!' she joked.

Maude stared, cold-eyed, at Daisy.

'Yes, it is,' she agreed. 'But nevertheless, it is what will happen. I will not stand by and see you behave in this way. A woman flying an aeroplane! The next thing, you will be wearing trousers, or slacks as I believe some suffragettes have taken to calling them.'

Daisy was frightened by this threat. Aunt Maude was all she had. She must be aware of how horrified Daisy was at the idea of being all alone in the world, with only her godfather Gervaise to turn to. And since he was not exactly reliable, the thought of only having him was not reassuring. But since Daisy was, or fervently hoped she was, a young woman of spirit – and if she was to help win the coming war she would certainly have to be that – the very idea of Aunt Maude threatening her was enough to make her dig in her heels. She refused to be bullied. She would not be threatened.

There was a short pause while Aunt Maude turned and stared out of the library window, and Daisy caught her breath, and tried to pretend that her heart was not racing. Somewhere in the house she could hear one of the maids pounding about with the upright vacuum cleaner; somewhere in the garden a bird was singing; distantly, someone like herself was flying an aeroplane. Daisy thought of this, and started to speak – then paused. Finally, not wishing to be either angry, or emotional, or anything else, really, she turned on her heel and left the room, quietly closing the door behind her. If Aunt Maude disinherited her, so be it. She would be disinherited.

The following morning, after an uneasy day, and a much more uneasy night, she walked past Aunt Maude with a determined air.

'I think you should know I am going to Bramsfield aerodrome this morning, for another flying lesson, Aunt Maude, and I will be back in time for luncheon.'

Aunt Maude watched her walk smartly through the double front doors out on to the steps, before turning to one of the maids, who was hanging around the dining-room door with a tray, watching what was going on with some interest, before going in to clear. Maude turned to her.

'You can leave that, Bowles. Leave clearing the dining room for the moment, and follow me.'

They climbed the stairs in silence, Bowles following Miss Maude, while still for some reason carrying her large wooden tray.

Her mistress stopped outside Miss Daisy's door.

'You can put the tray down for the moment, Bowles. We have other work to do.'

Bowles stared at her in astonishment. '*We* have other work?'

'Yes, Bowles,' Maude replied to the maid's unspoken question. 'We, that is you and I, are going to pack up Miss Daisy's things, so that when she returns from Bramsfield, she will be all ready, and packed, everything just so, in order to leave the Hall before luncheon.'

Maude did not add 'for good', simply because the age-old habit of not telling servants more than they needed to know still pertained. Bowles and Pattern, and all the rest of them, would find out soon enough that Miss Daisy had been disinherited, but not from her.

Besides, knowing how fond Bowles and all the others were of Daisy, Maude did not want tears. More than that, they might beg for her to be forgiven, which could never happen. Daisy could not be forgiven for defying her.

Aurelia might have decided to join Freddie in donning naval uniform, but since the Wrens were still in abeyance, the two of them were forced to return to Twistleton Court for the weeks running up to Christmas. Freddie could not help regretting this, but Aurelia was deeply grateful, since it brought her back within Guy Athlone's divine orbit. She supposed that he must be going to entertain widely during the festive season, and would be in need of extra hands to help out at the farmhouse.

'The dachshunds do not need to be on their leashes all the time, you know,' Jessica told Freddie, almost apologetically, as the dogs rushed out to greet them on their eventual return from London, where Freddie had been staying with Aurelia. 'It was all in Blossom's mind, this great army of dachshund haters who were going to kick them to death because they were German.'

'It has happened in London—'

'It most certainly has, Aurelia, but not, I think you will find, in Twistleton. The people of Twistleton are far too kind to do such a thing to a dumb animal.'

No one would argue with Jessica on the subject of Twistleton or the kindly folk who lived there. The Valentynes had lived there even longer than the Beresfords, in fact longer than anyone, except perhaps the sheep, whose ancestors dated back to time immemorial, their faces carved with loving care by travelling craftsmen employed to decorate the ancient church stalls. Angels might gaze down with beatific expressions, but the sheep in the choir stalls looked out on the congregation with mystical expressions, or, seated close to the Virgin Mary in the crib, helped to keep the infant Jesus warm, while the cow behind the holy family gazed out with bovine content at the blessed people of Twistleton.

'You look most modish, Freddie dearest.'

Aunt Jessica's expression was not particularly disapproving, but it was cool.

Freddie saw this at once, and looked embarrassed.

'In fact you look almost soigné I would say, Freddie, and you, too, Aurelia, your coats and skirts are really quite up-to-the-minute.'

Freddie did a twirl. It was a pathetic effort to cheer up Aunt Jessica, which it singularly failed to do.

'Your hair looks very nice up,' Jessica continued.

'And yours, too, Aurelia, very nice. Very tidy.'

Both girls looked at each other, hoping against hope that, although they were not wearing lipstick, Aunt Jessica would not notice that they were wearing face powder, and that as a consequence Freddie's freckles had quite disappeared.

Of course Jessica had noticed, and straight away, but she was more concerned with how on earth Freddie had come by such a stylish coat and skirt, not to mention shoes and handbag, since on her allowance it just would not have been possible to buy such things.

'Mrs Smith-Jones took us both to her tailor just off Bond Street,' Freddie confided, after a quick reassuring glance at Aurelia. 'She has this tailor who can copy anything, and so quickly. She has only to show him something in a magazine, and that is it, he has made it up in a trice, and so she let us choose, and he made us these. She thinks it ever so important for us to get as many things together as possible – silk stockings, underwear, make— Well, scent, everything, in case the war does come off, because there won't be anything left, then.'

'Well, quite.' Jessica turned on her heel, dachshunds following her with their particular idiosyncratic waddle. 'How very farsighted of her. I must remember to send her up one of our baskets of produce, by way of thanks, Aurelia. She has obviously been very kind to you both.'

Freddie tried to feel guilty about her new clothes, about her hair having been put up by

Mrs Smith-Jones's maid, about the beautiful hair combs Mrs Smith-Jones had bought her, among so many other things, but she failed, utterly. She felt pretty, and a young woman at last, not a freckly-faced girl with a plait down her back, who only really warranted a pat on the head and an offer of a piece of chocolate.

'I am so glad you like our coats and skirts, and everything,' she finally said, when Jessica came to kiss them goodnight.

Jessica glanced towards the wardrobe in Freddie's bedroom, sensing it was now bulging with fresh purchases, while at the same time resigning herself to the fact. Well, well, nothing more to be said or done. They might as well enjoy these gifts while they could, since God knows what lay ahead of all of them – certainly not expensive presents.

The next morning they were up early, break-fasted early, and the sleep was hardly out of their eyes before they were helping Aunt Jessica roll stacks of bandages.

'In the Great War we used moss instead of cotton wool, much better to staunch the blood,' Jessica told them, conversationally, as they worked alongside her. 'They would dig it up on Dartmoor and then bring it up to the various Red Cross points to help out with the wounded. Very effective it was, too.'

Up until then Aurelia's bandages might as well have been ribbons, but now they suddenly became real bandages, covered in blood. She stared down at them, feeling vaguely sick.

'I think, if I may, I will be excused for a minute.'

She slipped out of the room, and after a while both Jessica and Freddie noticed their guest, coated and hatted, smoking a cigarette in the garden.

'Has something upset her, Freddie?' Jessica turned to her niece, a look of concern in her eyes. It wasn't like Aurelia to take French leave.

Freddie looked embarrassed.

'She's just not used to thinking about the war, because her parents are always away either in Europe, or in America. *They* still believe they can stop the war. Of course, Aurelia doesn't agree with them,' she went on hastily. 'But her father's on the side of Lord Halifax. They would do anything to be nice to Germany.'

'Not a very good idea. That kind of talk is no longer a very good idea, Freddie. I only hope that she doesn't come out with that claptrap down here. She won't find very many sympathisers.'

'Daisy's Aunt Maude thinks the same.'

'I am all too aware of Maude Beresford's attitudes. She won't even take in any evacuees, despite all those empty bedrooms, she just refuses. She will, I think, take in the wounded, which is what happened in the Great War up at the Hall – they turned it into a hospital for wounded officers – but she won't hear of anything else, just won't. The committee in charge of this area cannot persuade her otherwise. She seems to be hanging on, hoping, always hoping—'

'She's kicked Daisy out without a say-so or a say-nay . . .'

'Yes, I heard. Where is Daisy now?'

'She's dividing her time between the flying lessons at Bramsfield, and staying at a basement flat in London that her godfather has given her.'

'Poor child.'

'She can stay there just so long as she doesn't bother him. He is going mad trying to get people to listen to his ideas, but they won't. Still, he does approve of her flying lessons. She will be the first to be taken up by him when the time comes, but only so long as she keeps herself to herself. He doesn't want to know about her, otherwise.'

'I see. Well, in that case we had better ask her down for Christmas, hadn't we?'

Freddie nodded, and threw her long plait of brown hair over her shoulder. Outwardly, at least, she was back being tomboy Freddie once more, hair no longer up, freckles to the fore, no face powder. She glanced out into the garden. Aurelia was still smoking. Crikey, that must be her second cigarette. She *must* be upset.

'Oh, I forgot to tell you, Freddie. Guy Athlone wants you and whoever happens to be here to help out with a small dinner party tomorrow night. Would you be willing?'

Freddie nodded, and bolted out into the garden. This was just the thing to cheer up Aurelia, a party at her hero's house.

But the next day the party was cancelled because Guy was detained in London with a bout of flu, and Aurelia and Freddie were dragooned into helping stack tins of corned beef, and beans, and other sturdy foods in Aunt Jessica's cellar.

'I never knew cows had corns, but now I realise they must have when you see how many tins they fill,' Aurelia joked, feigning naivety.

'Come on, time to go out in the loudspeaker van that Branscombe's rigged up. We have to yell for people to join the ARP. Apparently, Aunt Jessica says only about four people have volunteered so far. We have to yell at them through the loud-speaker, and then put posters up all over the village. Actually, I don't think anyone in Twistleton really believes Hitler exists. I think they think he's just something on the wireless, a comedian on the wireless.'

Aurelia tried to look scandalised, and failed. Besides, it was fun going out in the van with a loudspeaker, particularly when she thought of how it would shock her Hitler-loving parents.

For Guy, having flu over Christmas was a positive relief. He travelled down to Longbridge still with a raging temperature, but with the glorious knowledge that he had the perfect excuse for getting out of having to entertain his neighbours, or to put up bored friends who had been busy angling for invitations since the previous Christmas. The dreary side of it was that he simply did not have the energy to go to see George at 'the office', the influenza having left him, as he said, 'as weak as Mr Chamberlain'. George therefore came to see him.

137

Under cover of darkness George drove to the farmhouse and, having parked his car, found his way to the far side of the house, where there was a private apartment that very few people knew about.

'Ah, there you are. I have been scrabbling about outside trying to find a door, any door, a handle, anything,' George complained, holding up his lighter to see Guy's face better, as what had looked like just an outline in the ivy swung open, revealing itself to be a door.

'This door is so well-hidden even I can't find it,' Guy told him proudly, opening it a little wider so that light from the self-contained apartment, that Guy had made for himself many years before, spilled on to the gravel outside. 'Actually the ivy is false. Feel it. Rather good, don't you think? I nicked it off a film set a few years ago, and very glad I am that I did, since they never paid me for my week's work, the lice.' He stopped suddenly in the doorway of his study, making George stop as suddenly behind him. 'If someone is a louse, is the plural for nasty people lice? Does one ever say 'what *lice*!'? No, one does not – strange but true.'

George said nothing, and they continued through Guy's small writing study to his large, light studio, where he could paint, and think, and make himself small meals in a tiny kitchen off the main room.

It was a perfect place for thinking, being creative, and hiding from the rest of the world – and, even better, it overlooked a lake.

'No one ever finds me here,' he told George, who had never been to the studio before, and as a consequence was looking around him in some admiration – at the paintings and the sculpture, pieces collected from all over the world. 'Here, in the studio, I can be quite alone in my little bit of paradise. I can leave poor old Guy Athlone, the famously witty playwright, in the other part of the house. So relaxing, don't you see?'

But George wasn't interested in Guy's little bit of paradise, nor in his fame, only in what information he had, which, happily, was plentiful.

'I have a list here.' Guy put his hand into his pocket and took out a very small diary. 'For obvious reasons I have noted down the names in such small characters that you will need a magnifying glass to see them.' He handed a small piece of flimsy paper to George. 'You will see that beside some names I have written a large 'A' for appeaser, and beside others 'FT', also for obvious reasons. There are, happily, far more appeasers than there are fellow-travellers. Not many of the latter around at the moment, not since the Spanish Civil War. At least not that I know of, although I might just have been lucky.'

They both knew that, being well-known, Guy was incredibly useful to 'the office', since he could mix, and always had done, with any number of different people. He had been used by Operation Z, an entirely privately funded anti-Fascist, anti-Communist organisation, without arousing suspicion, either from left or right. Whether in a crowded pub or a ballroom, everyone saw Guy Athlone as he wished them to: as a consummate lightweight, someone who could not care less about anyone other than himself and his success, and whose main interests were whether or not the Windsor knot had gone out of fashion for gentlemen's ties, or who might be having an affair with whom. As a matter of fact, that last was certainly of great interest both to Operation Z, and to himself, most especially if national security was involved, which was certainly the case with the Duke and Duchess of Windsor, and their all-too-recent visit to take tea with Herr Hitler.

'No Communists, I see,' George stated, as he carefully placed the thin slip of paper between the pages of his own diary, and closed it by sliding a small pencil back into place at the side.

'No, no Communists, at least not that I know. I have found, in artistic circles at any rate, that the hammer-and-sickle brigade went out of fashion after the Spanish Civil War, even with the younger chaps. What a nightmare to end up being killed, having fought for the wrong cause! Tucked away in some corner of a foreign field that *isn't* for ever England.'

George turned from studying a nearby sculpture of a beautifully draped woman with her hand on the neck of a stag, and gave Guy a surprised look, for although Guy's tone was, as always, light, it was also filled with disparagement.

'How many of these people will be coming here for your New Year's Day thrash?'

'Oh, I should think as many as I can keep my eye on without feeling "ick",' Guy assured him. 'Oh, and by the way, I also have a new little person in my life, who I think might be useful to us.'

George looked instantly bored. Guy's affairs had been numerous, too numerous to annotate, even on file, but since some had actually proved useful to George and the Bros at Operation Z, he was hardly in a position to disapprove.

'No, not that sort of new person, dear boy, far from it. No, this person is a very young beauty, who has taken it into her head to devote her life to me, or at least a few days, or so she told me. I shall use her at the party to listen, and report back to me. It will only seem a game to her, but she might come up with something. The trouble with operating solo, as one does at these things, is one cannot be in two places at once, but by using her, I might well have broken my duck, and you, Georgie boy, might turn out to be really happy with me, which will surely be a miracle of sorts?'

'As a matter of fact we are all happy with your work, both the Bros and myself,' George said, accepting a whisky and soda from Guy.

The Bros, as they were always and ever only known within the organisation, were the two men, brothers naturally, who had started Operation Z as long ago as 1931. The anti-Jewish feeling in Europe was such back then, that they had secretly begun to infiltrate various organisations with the sole purpose of getting as many as possible of their own faith to safety, which, to all intents and purposes, usually meant to America.

'You should be very happy with my work, George, since I never even send in my expenses. Now, let me see, on behalf of the Bros, I have been to America twice, France three times—'

'Smuggling back cheese as usual, eh?'

'And Germany, for my sins, once – although never again, not since I have found out that my great-grandmother was a Romany, and that I have an uncle who has always scrupulously avoided associating with the opposite sex. Tut, tut.'

In reality the risks that Guy had run were no joke, which was exactly why he *was* joking.

'Here's to the downfall of Mr Chamberlain, and of all the Fascists who ever lived and breathed in this great country of ours,' Guy said, after a pause, and quickly drained his own whisky and soda.

'Yes, indeed.' George drained his, and then added, quietly, 'Keep up the good work, old boy.'

'Will do, dear boy.' Guy smiled. 'You see, that's the difference between us, George. You say "*old* boy" and I say "*dear* boy"!'

He let George out of the ivy-covered door, and George free-wheeled quietly down the back drive, only starting the engine of his battered old motor car once he was well past the entrance to the main house. It wasn't exactly necessary to do this, but old habits die hard, and secrecy was now second nature to him, as it was to Guy.

*   *   *

When Guy summoned Aurelia to his study, she thought she had made a mess of laying out the canapés to go with the cocktails, or that the apron on her uniform was not as starched as it should be. Certainly, her heart sank as Clive beckoned to her to follow him, and all she could think about was what she might have done wrong. After all, they had only just arrived.

'I think Relia's in for it now,' Daisy murmured, taking over her canapé duty. 'I think Mr Athlone is going to have her washed and brought to his tent.'

Freddie and Laura laughed, but then looked at each other, nervously. Aurelia's disappointment when Guy had cancelled his Christmas party had been palpable.

Daisy had been taken in by Jessica and allowed to live at the Court until she had finished her flying lessons, and had joined them once again at the flat above the stables. But it had been noticeable that their happy festive mood had not rubbed off on Aurelia, who could frequently be found sighing, making her passion for this famous man all too evident.

'Well, at least he's not married, Daisy,' Freddie said, looking round at the other two for support. 'I mean, that is something, surely?' she went on, keeping her voice low so that the rest of the kitchen couldn't hear them.

'Hardly a comfort when you're wandering the streets all alone, pushing a pram.' Laura nudged the bottom of her maid's cap further up her head.

'Still, I don't think anyone puts waitresses on casting couches these days, do they?'

'If she's not back in half an hour, I vote we get the secretary – Mr Montfort – and torture him, until he tells us where she is.'

Unaware of the stir caused by her being hauled out of the kitchens and taken to see the boss, Aurelia grabbed her coat and followed Mr Montfort out into the garden. Much as she was determined to take everything in her stride, she was well aware that unless she was very careful she might well succumb to her nerves, and faint – and of course the secret nature of the door, the fact that she had no idea where she was being taken, or why, only added to her nervous state.

As they went through to the studio, perhaps sensing this, Clive turned back to give her a reassuring smile.

'I shan't leave you, don't worry,' he told her in a low voice. 'I'll be around and about.'

He ushered her into the studio, and then slipped into the kitchen.

'Ah, there you are, pinny all starched, and maid's shoes on, too. Commendably clumpy, I see,' Guy joked as Aurelia walked into the middle of the room, and he turned back from an easel, where he was busy drawing something which was, perhaps happily, not yet discernible. 'I always start a drawing before a party,' he said, turning back to the easel to admire his work. 'It keeps me going, you know. Either that or a new play, or a book, or a lyric, anything creative; that way I can let all the idle chatter wash over me, while thinking all the time of what I have left here. It means I can float above everything, detach my mind from the silliness, let the real me wander back here to sit beside the quiet stream of the imagination.'

By the end of this speech Aurelia's expression had gone from nervous to reverential. It was strange to think of the celebrated Guy Athlone having to employ mental tricks to get over his social boredom.

'Sit down, please.'

Aurelia looked around for a chair, but she need not have, for Clive was already behind her, chair placed.

'I shan't beat about the bush, Miss Smith-Jones – are you really called Miss Smith-Jones? It sounds so like something in a song. At any rate, I shan't, as I say, beat about the bush.' He gave her a long look. 'I need your help. At least it's not just myself, it's many people, but for the moment it is Clive here and myself who both need your help.' His expression changed to a grave one. 'There are people coming here tonight, Miss Smith-Jones, who are a positive danger to this great country of ours. They are people who can help Hitler, and help him they will, the moment he lands. What I want you to do to help us is to listen in to their conversations, as often as you can. Hover with your plate of canapés, re-fill their drinks as soon as it is perfectly possible, and generally make a jolly good fist of being over-eager, while remembering what they are talking about. Can you do that?'

145

'Yes, yes, of course, I will try.'

'No, no, Miss Smith-Jones, trying is not what is wanted. Success is.'

Aurelia wanted to say that she would eat poisoned canapés every five minutes, if that is what her idol wished.

'I will listen and report,' she affirmed, in a tone that – it seemed to both Guy and Clive – she had probably used when vowing to be loyal to God and the King when, as a little girl, she was being enrolled as a Girl Guide.

Clive cleared his throat to stop himself laughing, because, following Aurelia's words, as he turned away from her, Guy had bossed his eyes and made a bunny mouth at him, which he usually only did when he was with his accountants.

Aurelia hurried off, accompanied by Clive.

'Well, and what did the great man want from you? Did he try to get his wicked way?'

Aurelia nodded. She didn't know why she did. She couldn't help herself. Perhaps it was the secrecy thing, perhaps, dimly, she thought that this would be the best way to put the others off the scent. She was so flattered that she had been the chosen one.

'He did try to get his wicked way?'

They all turned as Aurelia nodded again.

'And?'

'And I turned him down, of course.'

The other three looked momentarily reassured.

'What is it about you, Relia, that you always seem to attract married men and unsuitables?'

146

Aurelia shook her head.

'It's OK, he perfectly understood. He's a gentle-man.'

'I should think so, too.'

Freddie gave Daisy the nearest she could manage to a grim look. Just wait until she told Aunt Jessica what she had just heard! But then she realised that if she did Jessica might stop them coming to help out at Guy's parties, and that would affect her so far all-too-meagre savings. Instead, she contented herself with the fact that Aurelia had returned within half an hour, and, it seemed, completely unscathed. Men were men, after all, particularly the older ones.

For her part, Aurelia was now quite certain that she knew what she wanted to do, and it had nothing to do with flying lessons, or joining the Wrens if they started up again, or the army, or even becoming a nurse. It was something more dangerous, and even more exciting.

Chapter Five

Jean never really found out what had happened to make Miss Beresford so angry with her, because with the rumours of war becoming more and more heated, life at The Cottages had accelerated to such a degree that she hardly had time to go to bed or wake up, before someone was knocking at the door with a new piece of news. Either about the expected gassing of civilians, or about shortages that were soon to happen, or evacuees soon to arrive.

This morning her close neighbour Dan Short had paid an unexpected and not wholly welcome visit, plagued by the idea of the coming of the 'Germs', as he called the Nazis.

'I'm told I'm going to have to paint me windows black against the Germs seeing me candlelight, but I don't use no candlelight. I go to bed with the light, and I get up with it, too,' Dan kept repeating, while staring round at the winter sky, which had barely become dawn.

Jean liked to get up early all right, but Dan's idea of early and her idea of early were, even so, just a little different.

She had long known that Dan was the salt of the earth, but seeing him so bewildered by what was happening – or, more importantly, what he thought might be going to happen – was unsettling, to say the least.

'It's all right, Dan, you just settle back, and let the others paint their windows, or put up whatever they have to when the time comes. If you don't use candles or oil lamps, there will be no need, will there?'

Dan sat down suddenly and heavily on Jean's old oak settle without being asked, which was normally all right by Jean, but not this morning, since Joe, on a glorious twenty-four-hour pass, was upstairs in her bed.

'I had such an attack of nerves in the night I 'ad to give meself a dose of bromide kept over from the last one, from the trenches. Kept it in me haversack all this time, but I never thought to have recourse to it.'

Jean had little idea of what a bromide might possibly be. She imagined it must be some sort of laxative. She therefore gave Dan an understandably nervous look.

'No, well, there is a good reason for all these things in war, I do agree, Dan, but surely you should save it up, in case you need it when the war comes, whatever it is – this medicine . . .'

'No, Jean, I need it now. Calm me down, truly it will.'

'Oh, I daresay you are calm enough, aren't you, Dan?'

Jean looked at the old man, unshaven white stubble on his chin, his striped shirt collarless, leather patches not just on the elbows of his much-worn jacket, but on the knees of his thick worsted trousers. And all of it set off by a splendid pair of clogs, which he was never without when walking through the village, or pottering in his garden.

'I can't believe we's to go through it all again, Jean, that's the trouble, when all is said and done, just can't believe it . . . S'posing they send me back to the trenches, I couldn't take that! I'd rather stay here and hang meself with me own belt, if I can find one.'

Jean patted him on the shoulder, while pointedly holding out a hand to help him to his feet again.

'There won't be any trenches this time, not to my way of thinking, Dan, no trenches this time round.'

'But gas – there'll be gas! And that gives me the collie-wobbles, see what gas did last time, Jean? What'll happen to me hens?'

'Well, yes, but that's why we have been given gas *masks* to take everywhere, Dan. We're lucky this time round, that's the way we should look at it, that we're lucky.'

Dan stopped by the door as there was a sudden sound from up the steep cottage stairs. Dan stared at the ceiling, immediately curious.

'You got company, then, Jean?'

Jean pushed him out of the door. Dan was a typical Twistleton nosy parker. She suspected he

150

wasn't frightened of being called up at all, he just wanted to poke his nose where it wasn't wanted, and next thing the news would be all round the village.

She closed the front door behind him and shot up the stairs to Joe.

'What's he doing poking his nose around my cottage door, and talking laxatives, and I know not what?'

Joe burst out laughing.

'A bromide, you silly girl, is something you put in people's tea to keep them calm, it's not a laxative!'

Jean shook her head.

'I couldn't care what it is, but you will have to slip out the back way, because sure as eggs are eggs it's going to be all round the village that I have someone staying, and then I'll be the one to need a thingamabob – bromide for my tea.'

'Come here, and let me calm you.'

'What you have in mind, Joe Huggett, is far from calming. Besides, have you seen the time? You must be on your way, soldier boy, on your way back to your barracks, while I must to my early potatoes. As it is, since you arrived at midnight you have only ten hours left before your pass runs out and your mufti turns back to khaki.'

It was all too true, and Joe, passionate though he was about his gypsy Jean, now realised that he must start for the station. As he dressed, he only hoped that no one in the village would tell his parents that he had been back on a twenty-four-hour pass – that really would mean trouble.

The party at Longbridge Farm had gone with a swing, so much so that for a short time even Guy forgot that he was meant to be keeping his eyes and ears out for George and the Bros at Operation Z, and found himself, in post-influenza form, as horridly witty as ever.

Aurelia, however, had taken her role as his 'eyes and ears' very seriously indeed. She had hovered with the canapés, she had listened as she poured wine, and she had sat up that night noting everything down in a small notebook, which she put under her pillow.

The following morning, as she slipped the same precious notebook into her handbag, she realised she was faced with a problem: how to get the information she had gathered to her new boss. Would she be able to give it to him before he went back to London? Should she telephone Clive Montfort and ask him what to do? Aurelia had always known that she was not over-imaginative, but finally it seemed to her that she would have to do the last, making some silly excuse to Jessica Valentyne, so that she could use the telephone. But then someone might be listening in. In other words, in the language of the movies – she might 'blow her cover'.

'Just going for a walk. Shan't be long,' she told Freddie, who, busy helping Jessica, hardly heard her.

Aurelia started to hurry towards the village, towards the telephone box, the change in her handbag at the ready, her notebook the same. As soon as the telephone was picked up the other end, she heard, not Clive Montfort's voice, as she had assumed that she would, but the beautiful rounded baritone of Guy Athlone himself. For the second before she announced herself she felt quite dizzy, but then she pulled herself together. She would be no use to him if she went all silly.

'Come round at once,' he said, crisp as ever.

'I have no transport.'

'I will send Clive for you . . .'

Freddie stared at the motor car coming up the drive.

'Golly, Aunt Jessica, look who's coming up the drive!'

Jessica took her glasses off the top of her head, and stared out at the drive beyond the window, while at the same time flapping her hand at the dachshunds, who were running around them both, barking excitedly.

'Not Clive again, is it?' she asked in a deliberately vague voice.

'Yes, it is, and look, Aurelia's getting in beside him . . .'

Freddie turned round and stared, but not at Aunt Jessica, at Daisy, who raised her eyebrows as far as they would go, which was really quite far since she had a good broad forehead. Neither of them needed reminding of the night before, of the fact that Aurelia had said that Guy Athlone had made a pass at her. They had joked that he was having her washed and brought to his tent, but the truth was that she really actually might be having to, as it were, go to his tent. Or she might even be about to go there willingly.

'I really think she might have come and told us where she was going,' Freddie said, in an effort to prompt her aunt to do something to save her friend from a fate worse than death.

'Oh, no, I hardly think so,' Jessica murmured, turning away. 'Clive is entirely to be trusted, as is Guy. No, no – it is perfectly in order for him to come and pick her up. I daresay he was passing by our gates, anyway. Besides, Relia told me that she had left her face compact behind, or was it her cigarette case? At any rate, now I come to think of it – so much on my mind, you know – they already told me they were coming to collect her. Longbridge Farm telephoned earlier. Yes, I seem to remember that is what happened.'

This at least was true. Jessica *had* been telephoned by Guy Athlone, not only that, but she had perfectly understood the need for Aurelia to return to the farm, that it was utterly necessary, and of course it was also unspoken that Jessica's discretion was guaranteed. It was not her business to question why Guy needed to have one of his 'little talks' with Aurelia, nor would she ever question anything that Guy asked of her. He and Jessica had been working away since the late twenties trying to prevent the war that was now all too inevitable. And as for fearing for Aurelia's virtue, everyone knew that Guy was currently having a raging affair – she paused, wondering to herself why affairs were always 'raging' – yes, it was the talk of London that he had started having an affair with his leading lady Gloria Martine, having ditched a society beauty by the name of Desirée Hamilton. And Gloria was a creature of such stunning looks that dear little Aurelia of the wispy Pre-Raphaelite locks would not stand a cat's chance of even attracting his momentary interest. Guy Athlone had exquisite taste, and when it came to women he had always taken care to love the best. He chose from the top drawer, or nothing.

Of course Aurelia knew none of this, she merely felt important, excited, and naturally quite passion-ate about what she now saw as The Cause. She had wanted to devote herself to Guy Athlone, and now she could. From this moment on, her life would be quite simple. She would do whatever he wanted, spy on whoever he wanted, pose as a waitress, or a hat-check girl, cloakroom attendant, anything. She was in love for the first time, and she knew it, but more than that she was needed. After a child-hood and youth spent alone in flats and houses, in an endless succession of rooms empty of everyone except herself while her parents socialised all over Europe, she was now a person in her own right, not just 'the Smith-Jones gel' left at school by her parents, always waiting for someone else to take her out for the day, befriended by the servants at home, but needed and loved by no one.

'You have done very well.'

Guy's expression was serious. From what she had been able to tell him of overheard remarks, this slip of a girl had done very well indeed, but something stirred in his mind – her name was ringing the wrong kind of bells.

'Miss Smith-Jones – I am going to have to cross-examine you now, not on behalf of the government, but on behalf of the private organisation to whom I supply information. You must understand that the name over the door is mine, and so if you let me down, it will be very, very serious indeed. The organisation has underground connections all over Europe and America, and so serious are these that if you let me down it might have pretty vile consequences for both of us, not to mention Clive out there.'

He nodded at Clive, who was busying himself in the office outside, one ear to the studio, one ear to the door in the eaves.

'The members of this private organisation do not take an oath, although the fact that I do know you socially is entirely natural, of course. But in future if we meet in London, we will acknowledge each other in a very flippant or cursory manner, you understand, making a joke of your helping me from time to time, that sort of thing.'

Aurelia nodded, thrilling to the whole idea that her life was becoming more and more like the movies.

'I understand, Mr Athlone. And I will do everything you ask, and more.'

Oh dear! Guy looked at her with sudden compassion. She was like every other actress that he met at cocktail parties. He just hoped that she would not start telling him how dedicated she was, for if there was one thing he dreaded more than sin itself, it was a dedicated actress. And then it came to him, in a really quite blinding flash. Of course! Smith-Jones! The name was now very clear to him, he could even see the relevant file at the office, see George going through all the society names, murmuring them, nodding, turning to the next file, both of them discussing the people concerned, and studying their photographs, which inevitably made them all look both mad and bad, and certainly not people that you would ever want to know.

'So.' Guy paused. 'Why don't you sit down, Miss Smith-Jones, and let's have a little talk, *"of shoes and ships and sealing wax, of cabbages—"'*

She finished the line for him and continued the verse, quite cheerfully, as they both sat down, and Guy smiled at her with sudden appreciation. He always did like people who knew their *Alice in Wonderland*. He looked dreamily past Aurelia, thinking of his happy childhood days, bicycling to get his comic and a banana chew from the village shop, lying in the long grass beside the stream immersed in the antics of his favourite cartoon heroes. After a short pause, he opened up again, on a completely different literary tack.

'The Mole had been working very hard all the morning . . .'

157

He paused, looking at Aurelia, eyebrows raised.

'*Spring-cleaning his little home,*' she continued, realising he was waiting. '*First with brooms, then with dusters; then on ladders and steps and chairs . . .*'

Guy appreciated people who knew their *Wind in the Willows* off by heart even more than those who knew their *Alice in Wonderland*.

'I think we are going to get on very well indeed, Miss Smith-Jones, truly I do.'

Aurelia smiled without realising that her smile was stunning, and that to his astonishment it made Guy's heart turn over several times, because it was so heartbreaking in its innocent delight. It was the sun coming up in the morning in his garden. It was the light bouncing off the windscreen of his sports car as he drove back to Longbridge Farm. It was the warmth of someone's arms, someone whom he had loved so completely as a young man, and who had loved him – and who had died.

'I will do anything to help you, Mr Athlone, and your organisation. Do you wish me to sign anything?'

Guy shook his head. No, that was not necessary, the Bros chose their people with great care. They would trust Guy's judgement.

After a pause Guy continued.

'I wonder if you *would* do anything for me and the organisation. I mean, when you say *anything*, what would you mean by that? Would you mean anything at all?'

'Of course!' Aurelia sat forward to better emphasise her dedication. 'Anything at all.'

Guy lit a cigarette.

'Very well.' He blew out some smoke, and removed a small piece of stray tobacco from his lip, because he had misplaced his holder. 'Will you therefore report to me everything that you know about your parents, their friends, and their activities?'

Aurelia's expression changed to shock. She loved her parents. They might be a bit too social, but she loved them, nevertheless. She loved them both as a dutiful daughter, and as an only child. She loved them in spite of the fact that they treated her as something to be taken care of by someone else, a bit like a favourite dog which, however lovable, will willy-nilly be thrown into kennels at the first opportunity.

'I don't think my parents are Hitler-lovers, Mr Athlone,' she said, at last. 'Truly, I don't. They just socialise so much that they probably know lots of pro-Hitler people, but . . .' her eyes widened as her resolve hardened, 'if that is what you want, of course I will do whatever is necessary.'

'Ah, there you are, Aurelia darling.'

Hotty Smith-Jones stood in the door of her daughter's bedroom, all ready to go out to a cocktail party. As always, she looked stunning. Jewelled cocktail hat wrapped around her face, girlish figure hiding behind a silk evening jacket, the edge of which was decorated by garlands of tiny roses. The effect was adorable, and Hotty knew it. But then that was what Hotty Smith-Jones

159

was all about. She was about presenting a picture that everyone, but everyone would want to see.

'You look stunning, Mummy, truly you do.'

Aurelia's mouth felt dry. For some reason, although they were not close, she was always sure that her mother could read her thoughts.

'I hardly think I look stunning, darling. I think you must be exaggerating, but I must say I am pleased with this jacket. It makes just the right statement for autumn, don't you think?'

Aurelia had never thought of autumn as needing a statement.

'We will not be very late, Aurelia. Possibly back about midnight, but don't wait up for us, will you? We have given the maids the night off. Help yourself to something from the larder, won't you, darling? But not the smoked salmon, please, that is for tomorrow's luncheon.' She paused. 'One other thing, sweetie. How long will you be with us, do you think, before you have to return to Twistleton?'

'I will probably be returning tomorrow,' Aurelia told her, but Hotty's eyes had already drifted to the clock on the mantelpiece.

For a second Aurelia wished that her mother was just a little more of an actress, a little better at pretending that she might miss Aurelia from her life, but after she left, drifting off in a cloud of expensive scent, Aurelia realised that it made it a great deal easier for her that Hotty wasn't good at pretending, that really it was only incumbent on Aurelia to do the acting. She waited, impatiently, until she heard her parents leave the house, heard the great heavy mahogany door swing shut, before opening it again, and listening to their chatter as they walked to their motor car. Then she shut the door once more, and turned back, with every intention of rifling through their belongings.

She had hardly started to go through the small bureau in her mother's dressing room when she heard a key in the front door again. Terrified, she turned round, expecting her mother was returning for something she had forgotten. She bolted out of the alien room, and into the corridor outside. But the person she confronted was someone so surprising that she found herself covering her own mouth so as not to yell out, even as he covered his lips with two fingers to indicate silence.

'Hush!' he whispered. 'Whisper who dares. Mummy and Daddy might still be downstairs.'

There was no doubt about it, Freddie was fast losing interest in the navy. Perhaps it was all the talk of gassing, and all the underlying fear that everyone was feeling, but all of a sudden it seemed wrong for her to go into either or any of the armed services.

'It's the fact that they are called the *armed* services,' she told Jessica, half-apologetically. 'I really think, much as I hate Hitler, I couldn't be responsible for killing someone else, at least not directly.'

Jessica looked unsurprised, which actually surprised Freddie.

'Well, dearest, I would say that is hardly a shock, coming as it does from you. So you want to nurse, I daresay.'

Jessica turned from counting the stores in the cupboard under the kitchen stairs.

'How do you know that's what I want?'

Jessica stuck her pencil in her ear, like old Budgie at Twistleton Meads Station when he was busy collecting tickets. She smiled, and sighed humorously.

'Who was it I seem to remember had an animal hospital in the stables round the back of here? Who was it who mended an owl's leg? And who was visited by that same owl for weeks afterwards, if not months, if not years? Who found a pair of old cricket gloves and nursed the old ram that bit everyone else? Not Blossom, and certainly not *me*. No, I think if my memory serves me right, that it was someone called Freddie Valentyne.' Jessica smiled, and walked up the back stairs to the main part of the house, Freddie following her. 'Come on, let's go to the library and have a sherry.'

Going to the library and having a sherry, despite its being only eleven o'clock in the morning, was Jessica's way of telling Freddie that as far as nursing was concerned, she had her blessing, and they both knew it.

'Are you quite sure, now?' Jessica handed Freddie a beautiful old engraved glass, the last of a set. It was a great compliment.

'Yes, quite sure. It came to me when I was trying to go to sleep last night that I actually am not the right material to be in a regiment, or in the navy, and I certainly wouldn't want to fly an aeroplane. I want to make people better, not worse, no matter what their nationality. Does that seem frightfully unpatriotic, and not at all Twistleton?'

'It seems frightfully Freddie Valentyne, and that is frightfully all right with me,' Jessica told her, smiling, and she raised her own sherry glass. 'Good luck, Freddie dearest. Now, where shall we start? You have plans, haven't you?'

Of course Freddie had plans. She had been up in the night looking up all sorts of things, making her way from the stable yard where they were all still housed, back to the library, where she had found what she wanted.

'I thought I might start by going to help out at the children's hospital at Bramsfield.'

'Good idea. VAD stuff needed there, I am sure, but of course you do know that the Hall will probably be turned back to its Great War duties, as soon as the balloon goes up? Nursing wounded officers is quite a skill.'

'I don't really want to go to the Hall, not after what has happened to Daisy.'

'Fair enough.'

Once more the unspoken silence between the Hall and the Court hovered in the air, and Freddie, not knowing what to say to add to what she had already said, was only too glad to escape in order to fetch Aurelia from Twistleton Meads Station.

*　　*　　*

The train was on time. Budgie blew his whistle, and the little station with its ladies' waiting room, and its flower-filled boxes, soon bustled with passengers.

'This place is getting more like Piccadilly Circus every day,' Budgie announced to no one in particular, as he took the sixth and last ticket of the evening.

'How was London, then?' Freddie asked, and then regretted asking such a banal question, for Aurelia was looking so pale and anxious. It was obvious that it could not have been much fun.

'London was full of people either trying to ignore the growing crisis in Europe, or people determined on leaving it as soon as perfectly possible,' Aurelia announced, after a considered pause.

'And which have you become?'

'I have become the second.' She sighed. 'Your aunt has been ever so kind, saying that I may stay at the Court for a few more days.'

Freddie frowned. It was all very strange. Jessica had less help than ever, everything was in quite a flux, and yet here she was happily asking Aurelia down to the Court, as if nothing else was going on and as if Blossom was still in the kitchen. Surely Aurelia, who quite evidently still had a crush on Guy Athlone, should be encouraged to stay as far away as possible from their neck of the woods? Whatever was the truth of the matter, it would have to wait until after they had finished trying to help Jessica and Branscombe cook supper, which in the absence of the redoubtable Blossom was an interesting experience if ever there was one – the result being even more curious.

'The thing is, Relia, I have decided to take up nursing, and I was wondering if you would like to, as well?'

It was late evening, and they were standing by the gate to the field at the back of the house, and staring up in awe at the night sky above them, as they always used to do when they first met. The light from their torches showed up the colours in the frost, a myriad of sparkling colours, and their breath as they spoke was making pretty little patterns in the air, and somehow the situation in Czechoslovakia, and the coming war, seemed, momentarily at least, as frozen as the ground.

'I am sure you will make a wonderful nurse, Freddie, you were always the first to rush to the first-aid box when any of us were hurt. Remember when Daisy pushed me in the stream, and I broke my wrist? You knew just what to do.'

Freddie threw her long plait of brown hair over her back, and frowned up at the sky. Everyone seemed to be remembering her healing ways a great deal better than she did herself.

'I just don't want to kill anybody, not even a German. Someone else's son, maybe someone who didn't want to fight a war any more than we did. I couldn't do it, I suddenly realised, just couldn't.'

'And I couldn't go in for nursing, I'm afraid,' Aurelia told her sadly. 'I faint at the sight of blood.

Besides, I always think if only people would try harder they could get better in a minute. I've no patience with sick people – as a matter of fact, I only ever want to shake them!'

They both laughed.

'So what will you do?'

'I already know what I will do, Freddie.'

Aurelia's tone was very serious.

'Oh well, then, that's all right.' Freddie dropped her gaze from the night sky and stared at Aurelia. 'Hang on, I've suddenly twigged. There's a war coming on, you're going to marry Guy Athlone, aren't you?'

Aurelia shook her head.

'No, I shall never marry Mr Athlone, Freddie. No, I am not his type. No, but I am going to work for him. I shall be going from here to Longbridge Farm, and I will be put up in a flat above the garage, where I will help him with his work, part-secretary, part-dogsbody.'

'But you can't even type.'

'There won't be much typing,' Aurelia told her with absolute truth. 'But quite a lot of other things. Of course I shan't always be at Longbridge, some of my time will be spent in London until the outbreak of war, after which I probably shall be there far more.' She, too, dropped her gaze from the sky. 'The thing is, I can't go back home to my parents. It's just not possible.'

Freddie understood from her tone that it was not possible for her to say another word on the subject and, what was more, she didn't *want* to.

166

'I see. So why did you come here first?'

Aurelia couldn't say. She couldn't explain that she had come down to the Court bringing information to Jessica, who had known Hotty very well before she married, so she could be the first to scrutinise and decode the information that Aurelia had brought to her.

Not that an actual code had been used. It was more a social code, its source being, of course, Hotty's diary, littered with the names of pro-Nazi friends, and notes of meetings that they had all attended in each other's country houses. It had been most unpleasant having to copy it all out – she had felt as if she was thieving from her mother – but it had also been a turning point. Never again would she be able to live at home, knowing what she did, realising just how many people known to her parents had helped the Nazi cause.

It was Guy, who had let himself into the house only minutes after her parents had left for the evening. Of course, his sudden appearance had given Aurelia the fright to end all frights. So much so, that after stopping herself from screaming when she found him in the corridor outside her mother's room, she had then had the most terrible attack of giggles.

'Nerves, Miss Smith-Jones, pure and not very simple. Now, do remind me to make sure that you are supplied with a skeleton key like this one—'

He had fetched her a glass of water and told her to pull herself together, after which he had shown

167

her the professional way to rifle through everything in the flat, and taught her how to copy out the most crucial details from her parents' diaries and address books. Finally, he had left the place as beautifully tidy as ever, slipping out of the flat again with not a hair out of place.

'Your aunt is so kind,' Aurelia told Freddie once more, out of the blue, which, following on Freddie's question, was meant to distract her. 'She puts us all up without a murmur, as if we were all still at finishing school here. Ah, here's Daisy, back from her ARP meeting and bristling with indignation as usual, I daresay.'

It was a great relief to find Daisy making her way towards them.

'Hardly a person in the village is willing to go on guard duty when the time comes. I truly think they are imagining that someone from the Hall or the Court can be left to do it, and there's no need for them, they have other fish to fry.'

'Perhaps if they had something to defend themselves on duty *with*, besides broom handles and frying pans, they would understand the necessity a little better?'

But Freddie's light sarcasm was lost on Daisy, who in her turn was staring up at the night sky, wondering if she would ever find herself flying through the dark, even above the stars, or past the moon? She was due to make her first solo flight the following morning, but when the day dawned there was such low cloud and heavy rain that she could do nothing but help Jessica and Freddie, for it had been decided that the front hall of the Court should become a first-aid post.

'So all that rolling of bandages will not have been for nothing,' Daisy commented as Jessica went out to see Aurelia off to Longbridge Farm.

'It certainly will not,' Freddie told her, giving the heap of bandages an approving look. 'However, let's hope that we still might not have cause to use them, shall we? Not that I'm an appeaser, you understand, I just can't look forward to seeing all these bandages being used. Oh, good, the rain's stopped: best if we go and help Branscombe with some double-digging.'

They both changed into overalls and wellington boots, and Daisy, in suddenly thoughtful mood, followed Freddie round to the walled kitchen garden. She was ashamed to admit that, unlike Freddie, she was actually looking forward to there being a war, not only so that she could fly as often as possible, but also so that all the dreadful waiting and worrying would be over.

As Freddie handed her a spade, all clean and shining from Branscombe's precious garden shed, the realisation came to her that Freddie was thinking only of the horrors of it all. Freddie was not like Daisy, who saw the coming war as a mighty and necessary battle to be fought against an evil empire, Freddie saw it only as a future bloodbath. Daisy refused to do this. She envisioned victory, not death. She began to dig, and as she did so she pushed away any doubts that she might have about the morality of fighting for

169

freedom, or fighting at all. Daisy was no pacifist: she would fight for Twistleton, for freedom, even for Aunt Maude – and fight to the death, too. She whacked the ground suddenly, imagining it to be a German.

In the drive Jessica was busy pulling at the dachshunds to stop them diving under Clive's wheels, while at the same time trying to discreetly hand him a folder which contained all the names she had culled from Hotty's diary.

'Tell Guy that there's very little in there that we don't know already, but a few new names *are* of some interest, some linking up in unexpected ways to the webs of relationships that we've already mapped, and some rather too royal to be comfortable. However, doubtless it will all change pretty soon.'

Aurelia climbed into the passenger seat, and Clive shot off down the drive in his usual hurried way. Jessica watched the car for a minute. Clive was tall, handsome, blond, blue-eyed and unmarried. With any luck Aurelia would notice him instead of having eyes only for Guy, although she somehow doubted it. Most unfortunately, Guy had that mysterious thing called star quality, whereas Clive did not. Guy was so startlingly talented that he gave you the feeling that at his birth the gods had showered him with almost too many gifts. Once or twice Jessica had teased him about not having a wicked fairy at his christening.

'Oh, but you are so wrong, Jessie. I am quite sure that Aston Proudfoot was there, lurking behind the pews,' he had joked back, referring to a famous drama critic who loathed Guy's plays, and had waged a long, and finally futile, war against the West End's favourite son.

'Anyway, life has a way of coming back at you, Jessie, believe you me, it does. The boomerang of success returns to hit you in the side of the head as sure as *oeufs* is *oeufs*.'

Jessica went indoors. Never mind all that now. She had to get going on the hall, which, she realised, looked surprisingly large now that she and Branscombe had taken most of the furniture and paintings out and stored them in the basement.

She looked round, frowning, imagining the place as it might well be soon. Here they could put the civilian wounded, until they could be taken on to the relevant hospital; there the shell-shocked; while over there any lost children, babies and so on.

A desk had been put in place, and soon there would be the relevant paperwork to set out. Everything in preparation for the sorrows to come. Suddenly it seemed too real. It was all starting again. The telegrams – *'regret to inform you that . . .'* Soon would come the sorrow, the grieving, the injuries, the trying to be cheerful, no matter what.

She stood still as she remembered hearing the news that Esmond was dead, killed so soon after returning to the trenches. Remembering the reality of all the boys over there in France, and how helpless everyone in Twistleton had been to do anything to help their loved ones. The boys, and they had only been boys, some as young as sixteen, all going off with a smile and a wave, thinking that it was all going to be a bit of a lark. And then, once they had recovered, having to send them back to the Front again, after all that nursing, after all the caring. It had been hardly bearable then, and now it was going to be hardly bearable again. She sat down suddenly, all alone, with only the dachshunds wandering about aimlessly sniffing the floor, and to her shame she started to cry. After only twenty years of peace it was happening all over again, and there was nothing she, or Operation Z, or the Bros, or George, or Guy, or any of them, could do about it. She was suddenly quite, quite sure that there was nothing to be done.

'Well, let's hope we can actually get on with the thing soon, that's all,' she finally murmured to the dogs. 'Preparation might be everything in this life, but endless waiting for something to happen has nothing to be said for it *whatsoever.*'

She stood up, feeling embarrassed and even a little ashamed at the way she had let go. She had been brought up never to cry, and certainly never to cry in public. Her parents would have refused to speak to her if they had seen her giving way emotionally in front of either the servants, or anyone else. It was just not done. What was done was to get on with your duty, and that was precisely what she was going to do, get on with all her duties in the village – and at home, just kick on

172

and hope for the best. Above all not look back, that was unbearable.

Laura was the only one to stay in London over the next few months. She had reversed her decision, and decided not to leave the Grosvenor Square flat until the bombs actually started dropping. For something better to do, besides monitoring her father's love life at a respectable distance, she joined the Women's Voluntary Services. She wrote to Daisy.

The WVS are the only organisation that will have anyone and everyone, and find even those who are thick as planks (namely me!) something they can do efficiently, even if it is only sweeping floors or sewing on buttons, or making pillows for hospitals, anything really. At the moment, besides monitoring Father's increasingly complicated love life, I am helping to plan the evacuation of thousands of poor little blighters from the East End and elsewhere. If and when the time comes there will be about a million and a quarter children on the hoof. What a fearful thought! Actually our branch is run by one of Father's exes, so it is very amusing to hear about all his antics . . . Well, quite amusing, not very, actually. Apparently he is now entangled with a Great Society Beauty. God help her indeed, she said piously.

In fact the planning of the evacuation seemed, finally, a little too dull, and since she had now become proficient at driving, she decided, on the recommendation of a friend, to do the decent thing and join the First Aid Nursing Yeomanry, always and ever known as the FANYs, if only so that she could send her father the bill for her uniform, a very crisp affair complete with lanyard, which the tailor explained was actually now forbidden, but which the FANYs still defiantly wore.

So pleased was she with the final look that Laura walked straight out of Mr Greaves's shop in it, carrying her civilian clothes in a large bag. It was heaven to feel so different, and to know that, so unused were the passers-by to seeing a girl in uniform, they literally stopped and gaped at her.

She was busy pretending not to notice the looks she was attracting, when a young man crossed the road, and stood in front of her, barring the way. He, too, was in uniform, but not army khaki: air force blue.

'Congratulations,' he said, removing his cap. 'I have to tell you that you are the first girl I've come across in uniform who has good legs.'

Laura stared at him, astonished.

'How do you mean?'

'Well, what do you think I mean?'

'I have no idea.'

'Well, I suppose I think I mean that you have stunning pins, Miss?'

'Laura Hambleton.'

Laura had been out with many young men, but not with any who had made the slightest impression on her, for reasons that up until now she had never really brought herself to consider. Perhaps it was the fact that she was always so bored at balls and society gatherings, either with her own conversational efforts, or with other people's. So it was only now that she was faced with a young man not in a society situation, and one who was instantly enthralled by her – and judging from the admiration reflected in his eyes, not just by her legs – that she felt something. She gave in to the moment. Why not? For God's sake, a war was just about to start, who cared where anyone met, or how?

'Laura *Hambleton*.'

He rolled her name around his mouth.

'Laura Hambleton,' he said again.

'Look, I do have to get back, truly I do. I have to pick up my car, and take it to a garage.' She indicated her uniform, the lanyard on her shoulder, her FANY look. 'I need to try to learn a bit more about the internal combustion engine, and where the oil goes and all that. I mean, I can make it go forward, oh, and backwards, too, but I think I had better find out a little more about how it works, or something terrible will happen and I won't know how to mend it . . .'

She started to walk past him, but he stopped her.

'Look, I know that this is a bit cheeky—'

'A bit cheeky! It is completely uncalled for!' she teased him.

'Yes, but even so – I can teach you about engines

and things, truly I can. I am, as they say, a born mechanic.'

Laura looked at him. He was tall, and dark, and, well, tall and dark, and the expression in his eyes was sweet and beguiling, and his very cheekiness was really very acceptable. She did the only thing she could do, she invited him back to her father's garage, where they opened up her car's bonnet, and after only a few minutes both of them found they had become completely enthralled with the engine, and each other, naturally.

His name was David Moreton, and he was from Sussex, only recently joined the Royal Air Force, and due back at RAF quarters all too soon.

'Let's go to dinner, before my pass runs out.'

'Oh, very well,' Laura said, having hardly allowed a decent interval to pass before agreeing. 'And after that we could drop into The Four Hundred.'

He immediately looked embarrassed, so she knew, equally quickly, that he did not know The Four Hundred, and that she might have made herself sound really quite blasé and beastly.

'I am afraid I only know London a little,' he said, coming clean immediately. 'Came up on the off chance of meeting a friend, but he failed to show up, and then I saw you.'

Laura smiled.

'You're staying . . . ?'

They were outside the garage now, and she found herself quickly looking up the street to make sure that her father wasn't about, or drawing up in a taxi, or driving off in his own motor car.

'I'm staying at Browns.' He seemed even more embarrassed, as Laura looked vaguely amazed. 'I know, I know, but a great aunt decided to give me a treat, and I think that's the only hotel in London that she knows.' He gave Laura a pleading glance. 'Please don't think less of me because of where I am staying. I shall be out of there pretty quick.'

'Look, I'll meet you at Browns, I love it, it's a lovely safe hotel. We can have a drink and then go on to the Berkeley for dinner, and after that The Four Hundred to dance, and don't worry, the Rossis know me there, so everything is taken care of. We even have a bottle of my mother's favourite champagne waiting there, for whenever we should want it. I don't go there to drink, though, I go there to dance. You do dance, don't you?'

David nodded. He danced all right. He loved to dance. He had sisters. They all danced back at home, rolling back the rug in the second half of the drawing room and putting on a gramophone record whenever they could.

Laura chose her dress for that evening as carefully as Mr Greaves had tailored her FANY uniform for her. It was pink, and had an embroidered top, which came off when you wanted to dance, revealing thin silk straps and a marvellous bodice with tiny appliquéd butterflies. She knew it was perfect for what she wanted, which was to make David fall even more wildly in love with her, which of course he did, and long before they began to dance.

'What is it about dancing that is so particular, so special, so perfect?' David asked once he had led her back to their table.

'The joy of it, I suppose?'

Laura looked at him through the low lights that made evenings in places such as The Four Hundred seem even more attractive. Although on the surface David was no different from any other young man in the room – black tie, perfectly cut evening jacket, crisp white collar – he was actually not like any other man that she had met so far. It was not just that he had joined the RAF instead of some smart cavalry regiment, and that he was not from a so-called top public school, it was his outlook. He was so aware, so bright, so determinedly himself.

'Let's go for a drive,' she said, suddenly getting up from their table, and snatching her evening bag.

David followed her, half-pleased, and half-puzzled at their sudden exit.

'You drive!' She threw her keys at him, and he caught them, and they drove off.

'Where to, Miss Hambleton?' he asked, still feeling puzzled, as they motored.

'Anywhere, anywhere you choose,' she told him.

'Anywhere being?'

'Out of town, Richmond Hill, perhaps, to watch the dawn come up? Just drive out of town.'

Laura stared ahead of her, trying not to think of what she had just witnessed in The Four Hundred, and yet knowing all too well that in a few hours she would be forced to do so.

'You might have told me, Father. I mean, I am your daughter.'

Arthur was drunk. He had actually arrived at luncheon well over the eight – he liked to call it 'well over the nine' – and had become progressively ever more drunk, to his own satisfaction, and his daughter's distress.

'I meant to, Laura darling, I did really, but you know how it is. Dora put it all together so quickly I hardly had time to think, let alone think about telling *you*, sweetie, truly. And anyway you had gone off and joined the army, so it seemed like a good idea just to get on with it, and then settle everything later.'

'I have not joined the army, Father, I have joined the First Aid Nursing Yeomanry.'

'That's what I mean. You were so busy climbing into uniform I had no idea where to find you, Laura. What with that and leaving so early for your work with the WVS, or whatever it calls itself. How could I find you? In fact I couldn't. And you know, Dora has been a widow for so long, she wanted to get everything over with as quickly as possible, so it was off to the registry office, and then on to dinner and The Four Hundred.'

'Yes, I saw you there, Father, the other night.' Laura stared at him. 'I saw you, but I didn't know who you were with. It could have been anyone, although she was very beautiful, so it

179

was obviously not just anyone, but someone, most particularly since you seemed to have gone and married her.'

'Oh, so you did see me with Dora?' Her father looked rather satisfied by that, a little bit of the peacock showing despite the amount he had drunk. 'She is very beautiful, I must admit, very beautiful – and rich, I am happy to say, very rich.'

'You do realise that now you are married once more, you will have to behave yourself, don't you, Father?'

Arthur stared at Laura.

'Oh, I doubt that, darling, after all, I never did before!'

He laughed heartily at his own joke, and as he did Laura found it was her turn to stare at him.

'How did Mama ever put up with you, Father?' she asked him slowly. 'Or perhaps *why* did she ever put up with you? You're really a rogue, aren't you, Father?'

'I suppose she must have loved me, sweetie. Women do find me irresistible, you know. Now, ducks, do please be good enough to wish me luck. I am off on honeymoon this afternoon, so let's at least you and I drink to Father's long and happy new marriage, shall we?' He turned to the waiter. 'More champagne, please.'

Laura stood up.

'I have to go, Father. I'm meeting someone. And if you're going on honeymoon, you had better go off and meet your new wife, hadn't you?'

'Dora's waiting for me at Claridges, where she

is living at the moment. We're going to pop off on honeymoon, have some fun.'

'I wish you every happiness, Father, and Dora, too, whoever she is. I wish you every happiness you can snatch before our world comes to an end, which it assuredly will, quite soon.'

Laura hurried out into the street, feeling wretched. Bad enough that he had married without telling her, that she had a stepmother she had never met, but the fact that he had had to get drunk to tell her, for some reason she could not name, seemed to make it all far, far worse.

And then she saw David, and hurried forward. He had managed to make it to London for a few hours. They would be together for a short time. Maybe they would even marry?

She stopped.

She was not yet twenty-one. She couldn't marry David without her father's consent, and she knew he would never give it, not in a million years. He would see David as being from a different class because he had not been to Eton like Arthur. David would not be good enough to be Arthur Hambleton's son-in-law. How ironic that Arthur could marry whoever he wanted, caring nothing about his daughter's feelings, and she couldn't move an inch without his say-so.

'Come back to the house,' she said suddenly to David. 'Father's going off on honeymoon, the house will be empty of everyone. Not even the maids will be about, only the caretaker in the basement, and we needn't worry about him.'

181

She caught his hand and they both started to run. It was a wonderful moment, and one that neither of them would ever forget. Somehow it seemed to Laura that they were running away from everything that had hurt her, and that she need not mind any more about Arthur or his new wife, or the whole of the world being about to enter into some new and terrible conflict. As for David, he felt he was running towards a temporary respite, a moment of hoped-for, longed-for union, of happiness held for a second and then released, his hands freed once more to go round the controls of his fighter plane.

Chapter Six

Daisy could hardly believe the sudden rush of relief she felt on hearing Chamberlain's broadcast, as in sombre tones he declared that Britain was at war with Germany. The euphoria she felt – that at last something, rather than nothing, was happening, that the dreadful suspense was over – was swiftly followed by guilt as she saw Jessica's ashen face turn away from the wireless. In that split second Daisy realised that despite everything that the older generation had said, despite the planning, and the plotting, despite the lists and the stores, they had all still clung to a tiny thread of hope; hoping, always hoping, that something would happen, that a solution could be found, that war would be put off in favour of a less terrible alternative, that a nation which had already devastated Europe could be stopped from doing it again.

'Of course nothing could be done once Germany made a pact with Russia,' Branscombe said, standing by the back door to the kitchens, puffing on a cheap cigar. 'Nothing at all. And so I said to Miss

Jessica – and Miss Blossom, when she was back on the weekend. Although she never thought there would be any other outcome, no more than Miss Jessica, not really. And when you think about it, Miss Blossom has been busy in the factory now for longer than we care to think about, poor soul.'

Daisy passed Branscombe, quickly making her way to the Daisy Club above the stables, a home from home indeed, still filled with jolly things begged and borrowed from the Hall.

The last weeks had been spent notching up her flying hours, and attending flying school – which was brief and to the point – while also helping Miss Valentyne. She had done all that she could to pretend that she was not feeling horribly frustrated, while at the same time knowing that until someone, somewhere, saw the sense of using girls like herself to do what they could do just as well as the men – flying aeroplanes – they might well lose the war before it had even begun . . .

At least now, though, they had the off.

Daisy paused, half-remembering Chamberlain's words.

'For it is evil things we shall be fighting against, brute force, bad faith, injustice, oppression . . .'

Yes, they would be fighting against all that, and Daisy would be in the forefront of the fighting. She was sure of it. She would never give up until she had become part of the fighting force, doing what she was now quite sure that she was good at: namely, flying aeroplanes.

At long last a letter came from Gervaise, written hastily, as his letters always were, but signed off with his usual caricature.

Now you are eighteen and you have a private pilot's licence and the statutory hours logged, all you have to do is to prove fitness, and pass a couple of tests. So go to it, my goddaughter. They need everyone they can get to fly the aircraft from the factories to the airstrips, so don't take 'no' for an answer. Turn up here and tell them I sent you, much good it will do you, I daresay – [He had scribbled the appropriate address.] *And good luck. My friend Gerard d'Erlanger has been banging on about the need for amateur pilots, women too, to be allowed to duty fly from factory to airstrip for these past God knows how many years. No call-up papers needed, you will be glad to hear.*

Daisy needed no further encouragement.

'Right, Miss Beresford,' the flying instructor called up to her. 'You can start. Remember,' he went on, raising his voice and speaking with over-clear enunciation, as if to a child, 'you have to climb to two thousand feet and—'

But the rest of his words were drowned as the aeroplane took off in a high wind, and Daisy resigned herself to her task, which was landing within a hundred or so feet of the object that the training officer had chosen. Up, up, up she went, and it was exhilarating, no doubt of that. The only trouble was, in his wisdom, and obviously all-too flustered by having to deal with a *girl*, the instructor had failed to tell her what the object might be, and she, arriving late and in a fluster to get on with the job, had forgotten to ask.

Up she climbed in the Tiger Moth, and off they went, circling with ease the airstrip attached to the motor-racing circuit, Daisy feeling exultant, free, liberated at last, as she did so. She was on her way, up into the sky, two thousand feet above the countryside, two thousand feet away from the chains that had bound her to the rest of the world. Now all she had to do was land somewhere vaguely near where she was meant to.

Jessica held open the door for Daisy, and Daisy strode past her, finally collapsing at the bottom of the hall stairs.

'You look a bit wind-blown, Daisy.'

'Phew!'

After a short pause Daisy looked up at a startled Jessica, and started to laugh, before reaching into her top pocket and lighting a cigarette.

'Do you mind if I swear?'

Jessica took her glasses off the top of her head, and stared at Daisy.

'Do you have to?'

'Well, yes.'

'Very well, but allow me to cover my ears, would you?'

'No, it's all right, no need. I'm beginning to see the funny side.'

'The funny side of . . . ?'

Daisy stood up, and leaning against the newel post she laughed and laughed. It was a full minute before she could speak, or Jessica could make much sense of what she was attempting to tell her.

'I went for my test, as you know, and I climbed to the required two thousand feet, and having climbed up there I was then required to land within a hundred and fifty feet – or was it yards? To tell you the truth I couldn't have cared less by then. At any rate, pretty close to an object on the ground, thus proving accuracy of plane and pilot. Good old Tiger Moth, she did as she was told, despite the wind, and up we were, at just the right height, everything as it should be, only trouble was that my instructor had somehow failed to say, or else I had forgotten to ask – either way I realised that I had no idea what the object might be next to which I was supposed to be landing.' She swallowed the laughter that welled up once again at the memory of the flying instructor's face. 'So I thought the object must be him, and nearly finished by landing in his lap!'

'And?'

'He wasn't very pleased, you may be sure.' Daisy wiped her eyes. 'But there was not much he could do, really. At any rate, despite all that, to my amazement, he passed me, if only to get me off his patch.' She paused, finally recovering. 'Now all I have to do are half a dozen figures of eight at six hundred feet. At least I think it's six hundred feet—'

'Sounds rather low, dear,' Jessica said, turning

187

away, glad only that Daisy was safe, at any rate for that evening.

'Oh it is low, and fairly dangerous, but great fun. I love doing figures of eight.'

'All well and good then, time for supper,' Jessica called back, trying not to seem at all interested.

Daisy followed her downstairs to the basement, where they now ate in what had been, long ago, the servants' hall.

'Do you want to come and see me do my figures of eight, Miss Valentyne?'

'No, Daisy dear, I would really rather not, if you don't mind.'

Daisy looked so disappointed that Jessica sighed, realising suddenly that the time had come to tell this wonderfully dizzy girl what someone should have told her years ago, but then, seeing her face – so eager, so full of life – she couldn't bring herself to do it. Besides, she had to ask herself, what good would it do? And more than that it might do harm, and also it might stop her ever flying again, and, after all, they were going to need good pilots now.

Along with just about everyone else Freddie had done a first-aid course, and then put in to become a Voluntary Aid Detachment nurse, which was only natural since both the Hall and the Court had long-time voluntary connections, reaching back to the Great War, with the VAD. So into that she went, only to decide after three months that if she was going to nurse, she must do it properly.

'Very sensible,' Jessica told her, not looking up from her list of evacuees, most of whom seemed, for some reason, to be destined to be put up at the Court. 'If you want to do something you have to do it properly, perfectly understandable. So where were you thinking of heading?'

'Nursing school.'

Jessica looked up at that.

'Might not take you, ducky, because of not having passed your matriculation. Being schooled here won't really count, I'm afraid, and being bright won't be enough. You must have a piece of paper to say that you *are* bright.'

Freddie looked resigned.

'I can't see myself passing exams at this time,' she said, busily running a pencil down a list of names of children to be picked up at the station. 'You know how I have always been, Aunt Jessica: all right on my feet talking the hind legs off the nearest donkey, but sit me at a desk and put a piece of paper in front of me, and I become as frozen as an Eskimo.'

Jessica stood up.

'In that case best to stay where you are, and do what you can in the VAD. After all, you have a motor car, which should be excellently useful for both your and their purposes, always providing we don't run out of petrol, for rationing is just about to hit us. Now, off you go to the station. I will follow in the old Vauxhall, and Branscombe in the pony cart. What a thing that so many are coming to us! I think the authorities must think we're the size of Texas, which we most certainly are not. Poor old Twistleton: no central marketplace, no town hall, and yet it looks as if we are being sent over fifty evacuees.'

Jessica knew she must have summed up the numbers about right, as the train drew into the station, and Budgie's eyes seemed to bulge to match his nicely rounded stomach.

'Well, I never did! Have you ever seen anything like it?'

Jessica had not seen anything like it, certainly never seen anything like *them*, and nor, it would seem, had Twistleton.

For some reason, among all those skinny children with their name labels attached to their coats, and their hats held down by tense little hands, their grey socks anchored somewhere around their knees with elastic garters, there were only a clutch of mothers. Jessica did not know whether to be pleased or appalled, although it certainly meant there would be fewer places to find with Twistleton families. She turned as Jean hurried up to her.

'I will be able to take two in my cottage, and Dan Short will take one, which is good of him, really. Oh, and I just passed Mrs Huggett of Holly House – she is waiting outside the station in a pony and trap. She says she will be taking three, but doesn't seem too enthusiastic, even though it still leaves her another five bedrooms for her own use . . .'

Jean's voice tailed off as her eyes searched for a couple of the smallest children, for given the size of her cottage she had to be careful not to choose anyone too tall, or they would be leaving their brains among the lathe and plaster before you could say Adolf Hitler.

She glanced sideways at Jessica, who she knew must know of her association with Joe, gossip in the village being what it was, but Jessica's expression was impassive. The truth was that those with the largest and most elegant houses had proved to be the least willing to take in any of the children.

'Afraid for their silk covers, I daresay,' Branscombe had opined, when Jessica discussed the matter with him.

'Well, it's very short-sighted, for in a few weeks' time we may none of us have anything to put covers on, Branscombe.'

Branscombe looked resolutely unimpressed.

'You can't blame them really, Miss Jessica, not really.'

'No, I can't blame them,' Jessica agreed. 'On the other hand, I can't sympathise with them either, I'm afraid. By taking in these children we are saving the future of our country, and that really is the truth.'

Jessica sympathised even less when she realised just what a miserly intake of evacuees was going into the bigger houses, and saw how generous was the welcome from The Cottages, with everyone there doing their best to welcome as many as possible of the dazed and forlorn little scraps standing about the station platform.

'I'll take three, Miss Valentyne,' Budgie

191

announced suddenly, as the crowd of those taking them up dwindled to nothing, and three small rejects were left on the platform huddled close to Jessica, while a wind blew the last remaining petals in the arrangements at the station window-boxes in a flurry around their feet.

'Does your wife know about this, Mr Budgeon?'

Budgie nodded, turning away, but Jessica stepped in front of him in an attempt to make him see reason.

'Your wife may prove to be a little shocked by your generosity, Mr Budgeon, if she hasn't been expecting to take anyone in.'

'Got to do it, Miss Valentyne, Lord bless us, most of them look half-starved. Got to get them into a hot bath and give them a nice plate of Mrs Budgeon's steak pie.'

Jessica mentally shrugged her shoulders, not wishing to tell the dear man that Mrs Budgeon's cooking might not be to East End kids' tastes.

'Off we go,' she said, realising with a sinking feeling that she was sounding all over-bright. 'One, two, three, four, climb in, won't you?'

Three children dutifully followed Budgie out of the station platform and from there down the road to The Cottages, while the four brothers destined for the Court followed Jessica. Once at the car, as the others climbed in, all thrown together hugger-mugger, the youngest started to cry.

'I ain't gettin' in that thing!'

Jessica picked him up, and despite realising that

he was not the sweetest-smelling of little person-ages, she hugged him to her.

'Come on, Johnny,' she cajoled. 'Your brothers are all sitting in the car, and they're not frightened. Tell him, Alec,' she called to the tallest of the Lindsay brothers, above the sound of the wailing. 'Tell Johnny that going in a motor car is going to be great fun, will you?'

'Shut yer cake hole, Johnny,' Alec, the eldest, called across to Johnny. 'Or I'll knock yer block off.'

This idea, rather than the idea of a motor car ride being fun, seemed to make great sense to little Johnny, because he immediately stopped crying, and climbed into the front passenger seat without fuss.

The Lindsays were all to be put into a big bedroom together on the second floor. Freddie and Jessica had gone to great trouble to make it look as bright and welcoming as possible, with patchwork quilts and colourful blankets and teddy bears on each pillow, but despite all this, the four Lindsay boys stood in the doorway, looking at the room with suspicion, refusing to move any further. Finally Alec turned to Branscombe who had shown them up.

'Yer going to lock us in 'ere?' he asked, a stubborn look in his eyes as the other three stared at the floor, feeling only too grateful that they had an elder brother who could act as spokesman for them.

Branscombe, whose childhood had been far from sumptuous, understanding immediately what the problem might be, turned to the bedroom door.

'See here,' he told Alec, swinging the door. 'No lock, no key, just a handle to turn.'

'Yeh, but s'posin' you take the handle off of it?'

'Then the door won't work, see, the door just won't work, and besides,' it was his turn to point, 'you have a rope ladder there, fire precautions, see? You can just throw it out of the window, and it will stretch down to the ground. And you can go where you like after that, always providing you can see your way around the grounds, of course.'

Alec stared around him, beginning to trust his surroundings a little more, but then not wanting to let go of his discontent, he finally pointed at the beds.

'I'm too old for toys,' he told Branscombe, accusingly. 'I dun have no teddy bears, and that.'

Branscombe walked up to the first of the beds, and picked up the teddy in question.

'Very well,' he said in a dignified voice. 'Since this is my personal teddy bear, Master Alec, and I was quite prepared to lend him to you, you will forgive me if I take him back to my room, where he will be more appreciated.'

Alec stared at Branscombe, realising that he was talking to someone with authority who was neither a policeman, nor a doctor, nor a teacher, nor a school bully.

'I'm fourteen, see?' he said, by way of a sudden

explanation. 'If it got back to Dad I was in bed with a teddy, he'd knock my block off.'

Branscombe sighed.

'There seem to be an awful lot of blocks being knocked off where you come from, Master Alec, but enough of that. Time to take off all our clothes and have a nice bath. If you follow me to the basement there is a tub all hot and soapy, ready and waiting for you lot there.'

Branscombe was so tired after all the scuttling about that the day had brought that he could have willingly climbed into the tub himself, and never mind the evacuees, but Johnny obviously didn't feel the same. He let out a sudden, vigorous, and fresh howl.

'I ain't havin' no bath, I don't have no baths, baths make you weak, my nan says!'

Branscombe turned away, half-closing his eyes, and his hand went out to the now really rather controversial handle on the door. He had tried to warn Miss Jessica just what they would be in for, taking in London children, but as always she had become instantly deaf when confronted with something she did not want to hear. Besides which, she was the area officer in charge of evacuees, which meant, she maintained, that it was imperative that she set a good example.

'Just stay here, until further notice, if you don't mind,' he said, raising his voice above yet more wailing, and yet more threats of blocks being knocked off. 'And I will be back with a change of plan.'

195

As he went slowly down to the ground floor, he came across Freddie in the act of descending to the basement with an armful of bath towels fresh from the linen cupboard.

'No point in bothering with those for the moment, Miss Freddie,' he announced. 'No point at all. Apparently the Lindsay brothers will not take a bath for fear of weakening themselves.'

'Oh, I expect we can overcome their prejudices, unless they are based on some kind of religious principles, in which case we will have to call in the vicar!' Freddie joked, continuing on to the base-ment, followed by Branscombe.

'Never mind their prejudices against bathing, Miss Freddie, it's my prejudices against nits that we're going to have to deal with just now.'

Freddie turned slowly.

'Nits?'

'Yes, Miss Freddie, nits. Never mind the bath-ing, we have an army of the little blighters to cope with up there, so it's out with the coal tar, and the paraffin, Miss Freddie, and believe me, that is just the beginning, because nits breed like Catholics, and some of them are up at Holly House, which won't make Mrs Huggett too happy, because, as I understand it, she hates Papists worse than nits!'

They both laughed, and Freddie followed Brans-combe dutifully to the storeroom, for despite their jokes, her heart was beginning to sink. The idea of taking in evacuees had seemed so romantic. She had imagined herself running about the park with them, gathering flowers, teaching them to ride a bicycle, that kind of thing, not having to cope with paraffin and coal-tar shampoos.

'All good training for the VAD, Freddie,' Jessica told her crisply, when Freddie moaned at the smell of the stuff they had to mix.

And that was before they attacked the poor boys' toenails, which were, as Branscombe put it, pithily, 'More like devils' toenails than anything human.'

Freddie agreed, little realising that coping with the Lindsays was actually going to be as nothing compared with what she would soon have to face.

Maude turned as one of the maids came in with a paint pot and brush.

'Surely we have finished dealing with the blackout by now, Pattern?'

The maid shook her head, more than a little hopelessly. Complying with the blackout was a slow job at the best of times, but when you were faced with as many windows as there were at the Hall, it was impossible.

'No more materials not anywhere, nowhere at all, not in Bramsfield, not Cudlington, nowhere. Can't get any more black paint for the pantry, neither. We have run out of material, only green velvet left at Mr Hartley's, and none left of black paper, and now no more paint, neither.'

Maude sighed. She had been warned by the wretched Chittlethorpe, before he went off to sign up, that she would be in for a hefty fine if she had so much as a small chink of light showing any-where.

'Just carry on, then, as you were, and if we run out we run out. I shall only be using a couple of rooms for these next few days, making do with daylight and candles, so I doubt if we will ever be in trouble with the authorities.'

The maid hurried off, and Maude stared out of the window. She had agreed to allow the place to be turned into a hospital for wounded officers, but then had been informed that the Hall should be made available for wounded soldiers, not necessarily just officers – soldiers of all ranks, which had not happened before. When she was in London for the Season, a friend of her mother's, who had nursed all ranks, had told them that the language of the ordinary soldier was appalling, but that if they were with you long enough, you could stop them using bad language just by creating the kind of conditions where it was simply not necessary any more. Maude could only hope and pray that this was right.

She had put away her photograph albums for good, now, and with Daisy's dismissal from the house, she no longer went for jolly drives wear-ing motoring scarves. She went to bed as the light faded, which, in the grip of a bitter winter, as they were now, was really not much later than teatime. Once in a bed smothered with blankets, she read by the light of a torch. She wanted to see no one, and she was quite sure that no one wanted to see her.

She had her faith, of course, not a very strong one any more, not since the horrors of the Great War, when the clergy blessed the guns, but it did give her a little comfort, as much as it gave her anything.

Sitting listening to the rector was very dull, but daresay the poor man did his best, he just had very little to say of consequence. She was still furious with that wretched Jean Shaw for planting out those ugly fields of potatoes and cabbages, although now they were coming in useful in her kitchen, her anger, like her despair at having to face another war, had abated a little.

Of course she knew she should be making herself of some use, other than waiting to see if the Hall would become a nursing home for the wounded, but she really did not know whether she had much to offer any more. She could sew still, and she supposed she could nurse – perhaps that skill never went away. But what was missing from her, what she did not want to admit had gone, was the *will* to do her duty for God and the King.

She was still standing in the landscape of her recurring dream. Wherever she went, there was no one. Somehow, losing Daisy to her obsession with flying had been the last straw. The outcome would doubtless be the same as it had been before, and knowing this had taken away her last half-inch of optimism for the future. Maude knew it was sad, and yet she could not even be moved by her own plight. She knew she should never have treated Daisy as she had, turning her away like that, but she simply could not stand by and witness any more tragedy, could not watch as yet another person she loved was sacrificed to some new and ever more hideous war.

She sighed, and picked up the candlestick from the same table where the footmen used to place them ready for the family to take them to bed when she was a child. And then she made her way up the shallow oak stairs to the landing above. It was a dark, silent walk from there to her bedroom, where the shadows cast by the light from the single candle seemed strangely oversized, as if they were figures from the past coming towards her, as if they were determined to dance about her room, mocking her with their lack of substance, with their sense of life being really just like them, badly in need of light.

'Stupid old woman,' Freddie said, shaking her head as she drove past the Hall. 'First throwing Daisy out, and then refusing to take in any evacuees, as if there wasn't a war on, as if she couldn't put a hundred children up in that place.'

She and Aurelia were going to help out at the VAD centre. Aurelia had taken her one day off a week to do it.

'What have we ahead of us, Freddie?' she asked, sounding nervous. 'I am really not much of a person for blood and guts, as you know.'

Whether or not she would prove to be of any use, Aurelia was only too glad to be away from Longbridge Farm. It took her mind off the fact that

200

her parents were, for reasons best known to them, still abroad enjoying themselves in some swanky skiing resort. Such idiots, going to Europe when they must know they were already at war. It made no sense.

A postcard from them had said it all: *'Phoney War still on, lots of friends out here, marvellous snow!'*

Certainly Guy and Clive themselves seemed to be spending a great deal of time flitting backwards and forwards to Paris on behalf of Operation Z, and had even managed to smuggle some delicious luxuries back for Aurelia – stockings, and scent, and a pair of beautiful gloves.

'We didn't know all your sizes, so we had to guess a bit – couldn't bring you back some under-pinnings until we knew better,' Guy told her in a detached voice, as if he was discussing something rather more ordinary, like tea towels, or dish cloths. 'Clive here will take your measurements from you, and we will remedy that next time round. You're not exactly large, so I should be able to conceal any little silk items about my person.'

By the time he reached the end of this speech Aurelia had turned the colour of a ripe plum, and seeing this they had both burst out laughing.

It had occasioned a verse from Clive which Guy found and read aloud in his light baritone.

Miss Aurelia Smith-Jones is waiting for mee
To bring delicate items from gay Paree,
Nothing too big for this English pearl,
Nothing too brash for a shy little girl.

Suffice it to say, when I am away,
It's to Miss Smith-Jones that my thoughts often
stray.

'Just as well it's me and not you that's the writer or
we would all be starving,' Guy told Clive, screwing
up the verse and throwing it into the waste-paper
basket. 'But please be good enough to take Miss
Smith-Jones's measurements, Clive. I fear she will
be badly in need of a great deal of undies before
the war is out, and no one does underwear for
women better than the French.'

'You should know better than most, Guy,' Clive
murmured, but seeing Clive's look of hurt, Aurelia
went to the waste-paper basket once Guy had left
the room, and retrieved the piece of paper.

'I think it's lovely,' she told Clive in a light voice,
and more to make him feel better than for any real
desire for French underwear she laughingly scribbled her measurements on a piece of paper and
gave it to him.

Once she had left the room, Clive kissed the
piece of paper and put it into his wallet with a look
of solemn reverence, before slipping the wallet
into his inside pocket, next to his heart.

'Well, here we are,' Freddie announced in a firm
voice as they arrived at the local hospital. 'Time to
roll up our sleeves and jump in.'

Aurelia felt herself paling. Despite the fact
that Freddie had persuaded her to do a very
rudimentary first-aid course, which so many

people from Twistleton had done, she still felt sick at the idea of even going near someone who was ailing in any way. It was something she knew she would have to overcome, but she had hoped that the challenge would not present itself so soon. She had actually put together a uniform of a kind, but as both Freddie and she had agreed, it made her look rather more like a nanny than a nurse. This might well have been the reason why, soon after they arrived, she was promptly dispatched to the children's ward, where she made the rounds with Sister, and then stayed behind to help with nappy changing and reading to a little boy who was about to have his eighth operation.

All in all, by the time she was dropped back at Longbridge Farm and her day off was over, Aurelia felt properly humbled, which was just as well because she had hardly bathed and changed when the telephone rang.

It was Laura, and she was in tears.

It seemed she had been in London for the day to attend a luncheon party in aid of Polish refugees, when, on coming out of the hotel, she had passed the billboards shouting out their hourly alarms and scandals. Normally she would have rushed by them without buying a newspaper, but today she found she was forced to actually get one.

'They've been arrested, Relia. Your mother and father were arrested as soon as they arrived home. It's all over the evening papers, screaming headlines, them and goodness knows how many others have been taken off to prison for the duration of the war. Your parents have been arrested as being a danger to this country. I can't believe it.'

Aurelia sat down. She had known that something was going to happen, and possibly something pretty awful, when Guy and Clive had suggested it might be better if she simply called herself 'Miss Jones', and dropped the 'Smith' bit. Of course she hadn't asked, wouldn't ask, but she had known it must be to do with the information about her parents given to Operation Z, information with which she and Jessica and Guy had been able to supply them after going through all their papers. She could still see Guy's intense expression in her parents' house – he had been unusually deft and quick at searching for hidden documents, and more importantly, replacing them exactly where they had been.

'Did you hear me, Relia? Did you hear what I said? It's your mother and father, your parents: the authorities have taken them off, for questioning or something. They are going to put them in gaol. Too awful for them, and for you.'

Aurelia knew she *should* be crying, and yet she couldn't even pretend to burst into tears, not even to Laura. She had long ago known that her parents would probably be punished for their stupid ideas, and that it could only be a matter of time before something happened to them. Now they were into what some people had started to call the 'Phoney War' the truth was that with everyone in security kicking their heels, waiting for something to happen, for Winston to take over – they were bound to turn their attention to sweeping up all the loose ends, and goodness knows people like her parents certainly were that – hanging around the outskirts of society, waiting, always waiting for their hero Hitler to tidy up Europe for them, turn their little island into a Fascist paradise . . .

'It was bound to happen, Laura,' Aurelia said, at last. 'You know my parents have always been politically so right wing, hating everyone who didn't think like they do. It's the eighth wonder of the world that they haven't yet fallen off the globe.'

'Yes, but what are you going to do, Relia? I mean, this is really serious. They could be shot, or something.'

'No, I don't think they will be shot or something, Laura, but I do think I will have to pack a few picnic baskets, fill them up with dainties, and visit them behind their prison bars.' Aurelia could hear Laura making a sound between a gasp and a laugh, and quickly realised that she was sounding just a little too flippant, too like Guy Athlone, or someone in one of his plays. 'It's all a bit too real, isn't it, sweetie? But war is real, very real, and heaven only knows what will happen next. The only thing of which I am sure is that in a few months' time we will think that my parents being taken away for questioning is really too trivial to talk about. We will look back and think: why did we imagine that was something serious?'

Laura put the telephone receiver back, and

stared at it. It was the first time she had realised just how hard Aurelia had become. She never used to be like that. Was it because she was so ashamed of her parents, or perhaps the shock of the news? Or was it something to do with her crush on Guy Athlone? For a moment, on the telephone, it seemed to Laura that she had even sounded like him.

Laura stood up. She was due to go and visit David. She was driving miles and miles just to be near him. Longing to be near him. She'd never thought she'd feel like this about anyone. She straightened her uniform jacket, but first she had to go on duty. Duty, stern duty, always waiting around, waiting for someone somewhere, waiting to assuage the guilt by helping others. Soon she knew she would be driving about London, being outwardly busy, while in reality only waiting for the bombs to start dropping, waiting for the smell of gas. She picked up her gas-mask case, but not before she had slipped her lipstick into it. After all, a girl had to be prepared.

The cold of that winter was so terrible, so biting, it froze so hard, that not only did Laura not get to see David, not even meet him half-way, but neither could Jean join up with Joe Huggett.

Guy Athlone and Clive became temporarily marooned in Paris, and it became impossible for Aurelia to visit Hotty or her father in their separate gaols.

At Twistleton Court Jessica and Freddie, not to

mention Branscombe, having burnt everything they could to keep themselves warm and the boiler going, each took to staring at the various staircases around the house and wondering, privately, when they might have to start burning them. The water in the taps was frozen, so each drop, when they could draw it, had to be quickly conserved, and boiled up – not just for drink, but for everything else.

The Lindsay brothers were miserable, which was only understandable, but at least they were clean. It had taken desperate measures to get them into any kind of hygienic state, but it was at last arrived at – not without cost. They might look scrubbed-up, and fit to be presented to the King, clean clothes, shoes shining bright. They might warm the cockles of Jessica and Freddie's, not to mention Branscombe's, hearts, but all they themselves wanted to do was to go home to the East End.

'If I could send you home, I would,' Jessica told them, but as she spoke she could not help feeling both hurt, and relieved. Hurt that they preferred the East End and its tough conditions to being at Twistleton, and yet relieved at the thought that they wanted to go back, and if they did she would be freed from worrying about them. 'At this moment in time it is taking, not hours for people to complete their journeys, but days, and I mean that, whole days.'

'I still want to go home, dun care how long it took,' Johnny murmured. 'I want to see my nan, and my mum. I don't want to see my dad, but I want to see my nan and my mum.'

'You can want away, I'm afraid, Johnny dear,' Jessica told him. 'And so can I, but there is no train, and no bus, not even a car that can get you home at this moment. There will be soon, don't you worry, when the thaw comes, and as soon as there is, you will be on it, or in it, or whatever is appropriate, and it will whoosh you home to your dear ones. Meanwhile, why not come and help crack some ice and bring it in to melt in the kitchen? Plenty to do. Or else you can walk the dogs around the grounds with me, if you prefer?'

As Johnny slipped his rough little hand into Jessica's and went downstairs to put on muffler and coat and go walking with her and the dogs, something which Jessica found always seemed to calm him when he was upset, it occurred to her that there was nothing more touching than a small homesick boy.

'You know we have to fight a war, Johnny, and that being so we all have to make what is called *sacrifices*. We have to do something, or be somewhere, or with someone we don't like. That is a way of defeating the enemy, being somewhere we don't like.'

'You're not,' came the succinct riposte.

Jessica looked ahead, a little ruefully.

'True enough, but I won't always be here at the Court, not always, Johnny. I have to go off one of these days, when the weather gets better. I shall have to go off and help out in the hospital here, or do some other work, and leave Branscombe to cope, but by that time you will be back home with your nan and your mum, and everything will be to rights. So just try to be cheerful, that's all, try to think of some nice things about being here at Twistleton, if you can, things like the dogs and Branscombe playing ping-pong with you. Just try to think of nice things.'

Johnny stared ahead of him, trotting by her side to keep up while holding tightly on to her hand. He was silent for a second or two.

'Can't think of any nice fings,' he murmured finally, before kicking a stone.

Jessica, too, stared ahead as they walked. The truth was that no one could take in someone else's offspring and hope to be of real comfort.

'It'll all come right soon, just you wait and see, Johnny, and you'll go back home to Mum and be as happy as a bird in a tree.'

Just then a frozen bird fell out of the tree they were passing, dead as a nail. Jessica looked away, and to distract Johnny she quickly pointed out an aeroplane passing overhead.

Hotty was looking as Aurelia had never seen her look before. Still beautiful – the bone structure had always been remarkable, and that of course was still in place – but her wonderful skin, always so carefully guarded, was now pale and sallow. Her nails, usually long and red, were now short, and there were white flecks in them – from lack of some vitamin, Aurelia supposed. And of course the worst thing of all was that she was still Hotty, absolutely determined to make a party out of her situation, to *kick on*, as the riding master used to shout at Aurelia, to do her best to make her situation a bit of a giggle.

'Of course, there are some very strange people in here,' she finally admitted. 'I mean, some of the women simply hate the way I talk, which is killingly funny, but I got round that one, darling, by asking them to teach me to talk like *they* do! They actually think I am coming on a treat, would you believe? I now know not just how to ask for the lavatory, not the aunt, but also a little bit of cockney rhyming slang, and even a little bit of Scottish; although Welsh is not my strongest point *en ce moment* . . .'

'Well done, Mummy.'

'You are a sweetie to come.' Hotty smiled. 'I don't know why they want to put me behind bars, Relia darling, but if it makes the powers-that-be happier, then this is where I have to stay, isn't it, sweetie? I will probably be able to give lectures on prison conditions when I get out of here, finally, to all those poor dear women who read the *Daily Telegraph* and pontificate at all times of the day and night, but don't know what it's like. But I must say, I would never be able to be like those suffragette people and allow myself to be force-fed, because that would be just too de trop.'

Hotty smiled the kind of smile, eyebrows slightly lifted, pretty mouth parted just a little, that she would have given an attractive young man at a cocktail party when she was in her salad days. 'I mean, I shall be able to tell all those ladies who might need to know such things just how to make use of the prison walls. For instance, you can rub your hand across whitewash and then quickly pass it over your shiny nose. Do you know, Relia darling, the other women have been absolute bricks about showing me how to wash my hair, and in return I have given them a cabaret.' In answer to Aurelia's surprised look she said, 'Yes, I know, I know you would never think I could, but I manage really quite well. I sing some of Guy Athlone's amusing songs to them, you know the sort of thing? I sing "A House Is Not A Home", and "Relax, Relax, Relax" which always gets a good laugh, and also "Some Way", and all those others. They like the gentle romantic ones . . . You would never think that they would enjoy Guy Athlone's songs, but they love them, and of course they tease me terribly because they know I love to be teased. So all in all, I'm really very lucky.' She leaned forward. 'Do you know some women are in here simply because they had a baby out of wedlock, and their husbands thought they had betrayed them, things like that; but even they consider themselves lucky not to be in a mental home, which is the lot of so many who slip up, poor little things.'

And so it went on, Hotty being even more Hotty, despite her prison clothing and her white, white face, which made her eyes look even larger and more beautiful. And of course her voice, so cultured, so well-articulated, so musical, seemed even more so in that place where she had been condemned to be, Aurelia knew, by none other than her only child.

Aurelia walked back to the car park, and seated herself in her car. It would take her hours and hours and hours to get back to Longbridge Farm, hours when the tears would be allowed to flow freely, and the guilt would start; perhaps, like the war, never to end.

When the thaw did come, it was an anticlimax, everything dripping and bursting, and the well in the yard, from which they still drew their water, too full for comfort. Only Daisy was exultant, beginning her training proper, feeling really chipper about the fact that she had been chosen to be what was already being called an Air Transport Auxiliary, or ATA girl. Exultant, and not a little proud, until she saw who else had been rounded up to fly aircraft from factory to aerodrome.

'Talk about a motley lot!' she moaned to Jessica. 'You should see them. There are only about three other girls like myself. The others all look like chuck-outs!'

Jessica laughed as Daisy went on to describe the odd bodies, 'including myself, of course', who had logged up enough hours to be trusted to fly planes from the factories to their take-off points. Middle-aged men, too old to be taken up by the RAF, bottle-nosed, hearty, and all too often hellish. Bitter young men whose eyesight was just not good enough for flying fighter aircraft in combat. Ladies like Twistleton's Miss Manningham, who would go anywhere, do anything daring, to prove that they were really the boys for which their benighted mothers had so longed. All these and more began their training with Daisy, and all of them would, one way or another, become her friends. Because, being thrown together as they were, rejects from the other services, or just madcaps like Daisy, they had begun to realise that they were complete misfits. Worse than that, they knew they were considered to be what Aunt Maude called 'people of no consequence' – in other words, expendable.

'And what is harder,' Daisy joked, 'is that the girls are not even allowed to wear trousers. You try wearing a safety harness, with a strap fastening up the middle of your skirt! You can't imagine how uncomfortable that is. And – and what happens if you bail out? But our head of everything, the brilliant Gerard d'Erlanger, will not hear of anything else. We wear skirts, and that's it, no argument, and since he's been in our corner, and has been for years . . .'

Jessica stared at Daisy.

'But that's terrible,' she said, placing a bowl of home-made vegetable soup in front of Daisy, while the dogs yapped around her feet, and Branscombe quaffed a pint of cider he had found as treasure trove in the cellar.

'No, it's not terrible, it's beastly!' Daisy attacked the soup and the side helping of home-made bread at the same time. 'Can you imagine what

213

will happen if I decide to bail out and have to land with my suspenders and stockings on show, and my skirt around my ears? I will opt to fly to Berlin rather than that, I promise you!'

They both laughed, but Jessica turned away even as she did. Knowing what she knew, she could hardly bear to hear Daisy joking, see that bright look in her eyes, remember other laughter, other bright looks, shining from what suddenly seemed to be the very same eyes. So much to forget, so much that now must be forgotten.

PART TWO

Chapter Seven

Guy Athlone put his cigarette in the end of his holder and lit it, before walking over to the window and staring out. He had just handed Clive a cutting from the *New York Times* – May 1940. If he had allowed himself to be affected by it, Guy knew he would have given way, but as it was he simply refused to let the side down.

So long as the English tongue survives, the word Dunkirk will be spoken with reverence. In that harbour – such a hell as never blazed on earth before – at the end of a lost battle, the rags and blemishes that had hidden the soul of democracy fell away. There, beaten but unconquered, she faced the enemy . . .

Clive finished reading it, and then slipped it into a folder on his desk.

'I daresay you could do with a snifter?' he asked after a few seconds, because they had both stopped counting just how many of their friends were still in France.

*   *   *

The happily vast hall of the Hall, now devoid of its inlaid marble table, was crowded with people on crutches, with nurses and stretchers, not to mention men from the village who had been roped in to act as orderlies. Trains that were bringing the wounded back from Dunkirk stopped at Twistleton Meads Station, and Jessica, who was in charge of so much in their area, had telephoned to Maude to tell her what to expect. At first just the lighter cases came off the trains bearing the wounded – those that did not need operations, those that were not badly burned, or had already had amputations – but the fact was that some of the worst-affected had to come to the Hall, because no one could face leaving them to continue on without relieving their pain in some way.

Jessica and Maude hadn't spoken since the Great War, since the telegram had arrived telling his family that Esmond had been killed at the Battle of the Somme, and now that they were speaking again neither of them felt any warmer towards each other. In fact they both realised, with a kind of dull surprise, that neither of them felt anything at all after all these years, except a strange acceptance. There was nothing left to feel, they just had to get on with the job in hand, do their duty, and use their organisational and nursing skills to keep up morale and to mend the boys back from France. But what they both did know, what was unspoken, was that whatever happened, whatever the outcome, even if the German Army were outside the doors of the Hall, their boots ringing out on the stone steps, both Maude and Jessica would stand shoulder to shoulder, they would be there armed with croquet mallets, broom-handles, medieval pikes taken from the walls of the Hall, anything rather than surrender.

'Whoever thought it was a good idea to go to France in the first place – army half-wits, I suppose?' Guy demanded before climbing out of his car, followed by Clive, both of them hurrying into Twistleton Meads Station and up to the train carriages from which many of the wounded were being handed.

'Careful, Guy, you know it's against the law to lower morale by seditious talk.'

'While the people at the top make decisions that would make you weep,' Guy carried on, regardless as always. 'Oh well, we will win the war despite the politicians and the mad generals. Despite everyone and everything, we, the people, will win this war.'

The first casualty to be brought off the train that morning had been in a quite appalling state, but for some reason that Clive could never understand, Guy was able to cope with the poor fellow as well as any trained nurse. More than that, his hail-fellow-well-met manner meant that he could joke with the men, offering them cigarettes, taking their minds off the ghastly pain that so many of them were experiencing.

But all that was as nothing compared to the way he coped with Maude Beresford.

'My dear Miss Beresford, what a privilege!' he called out as he helped yet another stretcher-case into the Hall. 'You're looking even younger than when I last saw you!'

Maude, starched and white in her Great War nursing uniform, tried to pretend that she had not heard Guy. She had never seen any of Guy Athlone's amusing comedies, but she had met him once or twice when they were younger, on the few occasions when he had been brought to the Hall to play and sing before an invited audience in aid of the village memorial, and other such causes.

She had formed the impression then that, theatrical though he might be, Guy Athlone was very much on the gold standard, and so he proved over the next days. In between such work as took him to London, he was always in and out of the Hall, not just anxious to help, but better than that, easy to have around.

The Hall was a strange place to be, with men of all ranks placed in beds that had been moved out of everything from maids' bedrooms to nurseries, so that at any one moment a tousled bandaged head could be seen propped up against a carefully painted picture of a pink fairy, or a mahogany four-poster could be found housing two Frenchmen busily smoking and playing cards.

'We've brought as many Frogs back from Dunkirk as ourselves, I sometimes think,' Corporal Bastable commented to Maude, when he was up and about, albeit supported on his good arm by a crutch.

Maude, who to her relief had found that her nursing skills from the Great War had not deserted her, smiled. She had been personally responsible for setting young Bastable's leg, not in plaster, which when she nursed at the Front had not been the practice, but in splints and bandages. This meant that the bones could be checked at reasonable intervals, and there was no possible risk of malformation, as had happened so often since the practice of using hard plaster had come in, with the result that people were often left with limps and bad backs, with arms that were useless – all sorts of unnecessary handicaps arising simply from careless setting that could not be checked before the bones knitted.

Maude had hoped that the sister in charge of the intake along the line from Twistleton Meads Station would be an old friend of hers, but to her disappointment she was replaced at the last minute by a new woman. A tremendous organiser, the new sister had brought with her from various local points a clutch of nurses, all of whom had immediately been reorganised into groups. There were experienced, trained nurses who attended the operations, nurses who were good at organisation, and those that waited on the patients, doing what the sister called 'personal nursing'.

'No point in operating successfully on someone if you then leave him to die of thirst,' was her motto.

Much to her relief, Freddie was co-opted into

the last category, personal nursing, and so found herself doing anything and everything for men of all ranks, including writing letters home.

'*Dear Clare.*'

There was a long pause while Corporal Bastable, who had not only had his leg badly injured, but his right hand blown off, thought through what he could say to Clare.

'*Dear Clare,*' he began again. 'I hope you are well.'

Freddie dutifully wrote this.

'*I hope you are well . . .*'

There was another long pause as he stared past Freddie.

'Can I see that?'

Freddie held up the writing pad so that he could read what he had dictated, which Bastable did, nodding with solemn approval, and then he looked at Freddie, and looked away, and then back at her again.

'I don't know how to tell her about my hand,' he confessed. 'That's what I'm trying to work out, how to tell her. I think she'll want to chuck me if she knows. On the other hand, I can't wait till I get home, can I? I mean to say, give her a worse shock, I should have thought.'

Freddie could see his point, and it was a sticky one.

'How about if you put it just like that?' she asked. 'Say what you have just said to me, but perhaps like this. "*The thing is, I don't want you to chuck me, but I understand if you do. I have sustained serious injury to my right arm and leg, as a result of which I now only have a left hand."'*

'I think you're right, Nurse. I think that would be all right, to put it like that.'

Freddie dutifully wrote as she had suggested, and showed it to Corporal Bastable.

'That's good,' he said approvingly. 'And then I could make a joke of it after that. Say *"As you know I never did like my right hand much, the left always being my favourite."'*

Freddie wrote that, too.

'How is Murphy? I hope he is not missing me too much?'

Freddie paused, guessing at once who Murphy was.

'He's my mongrel sheepdog,' Corporal Bastable told her proudly. 'Very good dog, happily for me, considering everything that's happened. He responds to the whistle, don't need a lead!'

Freddie smiled, suddenly, for no reason she could think of, wondering about Blossom and how she was getting on. And then wondering about the Hall and how long it would be used for mending young soldiers like Corporal Bastable. Somehow the Court, despite all its colourful characters, seemed to be fading from her, and she couldn't have said why. It was as if they were all in a painting that was about to be bought by someone else – which was ridiculous because everyone knew that the Valentynes had been at the Court since for ever, and no one could move them on, but no one.

*   *   *

At The Cottages, now that summer was on its way, Jean might have been forgiven for feeling smug, since her new potatoes and cabbages, and other vegetables, were all doing so well. But what might have been a cause for celebration was cancelled out by the misery of the Muggleton children put into her care, their homesickness, and their inability to adjust to country life. On top of that the Hall, serving as a temporary hospital for the wounded British Army returning from Dunkirk, was a vivid reminder that the lull that had fallen after the outbreak of war was now formally over, and the gloves were well and truly off.

'I don't know what to say or do to cheer my lot up,' Jean confided to Freddie, when she dropped in for a late-night cup of tea.

'Oh, don't worry, the Lindsay brothers are the same, they hate everything, but everything. The food, the village, all of it. They constantly complain that there is nothing to do, and we have to pretend that our carrots have come out of a tin. They thought eggs came out of a shop, and when I showed them that hens laid them, and where they came from, they were so disgusted they refused to touch one ever again. Not that you can blame them, when you come to think of it!'

They both laughed.

'I haven't heard from Joe at all, not since he went back,' Jean suddenly confided.

Freddie, who had found out about Joe from the usual village gossip, looked sympathetic, although she couldn't imagine taking the time to fall in love just as a war broke out, or anything else, really – she just couldn't. She wanted to mend people, not marry them.

'I expect he's training so hard he doesn't have time to pick up a pen.'

'Oh, I know, and I have nothing at all to do, and yet I find time to write, in between throwing myself into the fields at five in the morning, and looking after that lot upstairs.' She jerked her head up towards the ceiling, indicating her clutch of evacuees. 'Mind you, I have had a bit of a vee for victory with Miss Maude Beresford. I did not ask, but she has offered to put up some land girls to help with the farm work. Really very decent of her considering how much she has disapproved of my growing potatoes and cabbages in her fields.'

'What kind of land girls are they going to be?'

Jean shrugged her shoulders. Who knew?

Freddie left Jean at The Cottages, walking back to the Court, her torchlight catching the newly planted vegetables of all kinds that had taken the place of flowers in all the Twistleton cottage gardens. Making compost to feed these vegetables was the new hobby of everyone in the village – they used everything from manure and old bits of horsehair mattress to sodden newspapers.

The Dig for Victory campaign had started the previous September, and had caught fire. There was not a park, an allotment, a council flower bed or a station yard that did not now sprout everything from leeks to shallots, from potatoes to cabbages.

Even by torchlight it was all too evident that it had changed the look of the village, but on the other hand, no one could say that the sight of the vegetables did not give cause for optimism. The rows of fronded tops and rounded shapes, interspersed with marigolds to protect them from disease, were defiantly pretty – perhaps as pretty as any flower border, once everyone grew used to not expecting flowers.

The following morning Freddie dressed as usual and, after breakfasting the Lindsay brothers, drove up to the Hall, the back of her car filled with all the usual necessities, only to find Maude standing on the steps outside.

Maude, as always nowadays, in her Great War nurse's uniform, was as neat as a pin, but today she was wearing not just her starched apron and headdress, but an expression on her face as shut as the car door that Freddie was now closing.

'Everyone is to be moved on,' she told Freddie in a flat voice. 'No one is to stay. Orders have come this morning, via Sister on the telephone. She does not agree with them, but apparently every case is to be assessed and then appropriate measures taken to place each patient in a specialist unit. Some of them will even have to go to London for repair work. London!'

Maude raised her eyebrows at Freddie, her look giving Freddie to understand that she thought this the maddest idea of all, since everyone knew that once the bombing and the gassing started, London would be sure to be the worst hit.

'Do they not think we are coping?'

'Nothing to do with how we are doing, Freddie dear, all to do with the top brass wanting everything in neat little packages, and please tell me when do they not? Everything done on a map, everyone a number, no thought to what it does to the patients' morale to be moved on just as they are feeling better. No thought to the harm it could do our patients physically, to be bumped about in the back of a converted lorry, or some decrepit ambulance. Oh yes, and it seems that a great deal of our work is too old-fashioned, and we are using too many VADs by dividing up work into sections as we have – that, too, is old-fashioned, it seems. Well, I mean to say, Freddie dear, it seems to me to be the Great War all over again! Nincompoops everywhere!'

Freddie stared at Maude. She had never ever called Freddie 'dear' before, but not only that, she had never talked to her at any length, least of all voiced an opinion.

'It has always been my experience that people in authority are put there because nothing else can be found for them to do. When we nursed at the Front, we who were good at the nursing did the work without complaint, but there was always someone who was hopelessly incompetent who had to be found a job. So they put them in a position of authority. Someone would be brought in who would make life more unpleasant, both for the patients, and for the nurses. Of course class came into it, too. The worst jobs for the aristocracy was the rule of the day, probably still is. Corpses to be laid out, bed-pan duties – gracious, and who is this coming up the drive?'

They both turned and stared as a dilapidated car slowly made its way to the front steps of the Hall.

The young girl who climbed out was carefully, if poorly, dressed. The glove on the hand she extended to Maude and Freddie was much mended, but meticulously clean. She wore a felt hat, and she had a light tweed coat, which was a little too short for her dress, so that it showed an inch or two beneath. Her shoes were sturdy, and her stockings carefully darned.

'I have come for Corporal Bastable,' she stated, looking from Maude to Freddie, and back again.

'Corporal Bastable? Yes, of course. You must be Clare?'

'How did you know?'

Freddie couldn't say because she had written to her on his behalf, so she only smiled.

'Corporal Bastable is not ready to come home yet, Miss.'

'Oh, I think he is. See, he wrote to me that he wants to come home, and that he misses me so much.'

Freddie's mouth went a little dry. Oh, dear heavens! The truth was that she had written a few more things at the bottom of Corporal Bastable's letter, more than the good man had perhaps meant

228

her to put. She had said that he was missing Clare, and because he had touched on their woodland walks together, Freddie had put that he missed those walks with her so much. Oh, and she had put a little something about moonlight, and about love, and about how often he thought of her when he saw the stars, and how happy they could be together once the war was over, or perhaps even before? Crikey!

'I'll take you to see him,' Freddie said, ignoring the warning look that Maude had given her. 'They'll all be breakfasted now, and up and about, shaved, too. I shaved him yesterday, but someone else will have done early duty today.'

The reunion between the good corporal and his girlfriend was muted. To say that the young man looked amazed was, Freddie thought afterwards, like saying that Hitler was *rather* horrid. The poor one-handed young man's face almost fell apart, emotions tearing through him – joy that Clare was there mixed with fear that she would hate seeing his lack of a hand and all the rest of his injuries, and then incredulity that she had made the journey from so far away, and that she had driven herself.

'You're coming home, Benjamin Bastable,' she told him. 'Coming back to Murphy and me.'

Only trouble was Maude was far from pleased by the notion.

'Can't just let him go AWOL, Freddie dear,' Maude told her. 'It won't do.'

'Surely we can manage something?'

Freddie looked at her pleadingly.

'I daresay you have a plan?' Maude was now looking, for Maude, almost amused.

'I have to admit to feeling a plan coming on,' Freddie admitted. 'Well, Miss Beresford, since they are all going to be turfed out, surely, one way or another, Corporal Bastable can just be found to have been turfed out a little earlier than the others? See, here we have the lists of patients. My point being that we have them, and we can hold them, distract Sister, and then, whoosh, suddenly Corporal Bastable will be gone with all the others, a big tick by his name, but somehow he gets lost the other end, but with a war on, albeit so far only the Phoney War, one wonders who will bother about him.'

Maude surveyed Freddie's guileless if freckled face with equanimity, while Freddie looked up at her, wide-eyed.

Maude sighed, lightly.

'With you on our side, Freddie dear, victory will surely be ours within months. I certainly can't see the little corporal from Germany defeating you.'

So Corporal Bastable and Clare drove off together, and that night Freddie finally left the Hall to bicycle home without lights, hoping that she would arrive back to some sort of supper left out for her by Branscombe or Jessica, which happily she did.

'Still up, Aunt Jessica?'

Freddie looked from the delicious tray of food laid out by, she guessed, Branscombe, to Jessica who was sitting knitting at the kitchen table.

'Yes, Freddie dearest.' Jessica nodded briskly at the tray. 'Tuck in, duckie, you must be starved, on your feet all day as you are. Eat and then sleep, sleep and then eat, it's the only way to keep going.'

Freddie took off her cap, and undid the pin that had secured her hair, quickly re-braiding her hair and throwing the plait back over her shoulder in her characteristic way.

'Everyone is to be sent on. The Hall is finished as a nursing home. Don't know why, and nor does Miss Beresford. I shall have to go back to Bramsfield and take orders from there.'

Jessica paused, momentarily, in her work, the sock she was knitting swaying a little between the three needles.

'I heard from Aurelia that Longbridge has been cleared of everything, that it is to be requisitioned by the army. Perhaps it is only a matter of time before the Hall is, too?'

She shook her head and resumed her work, the sock seeming to quickly lengthen to a man's size foot even as Freddie ate.

'Longbridge Farm with the army installed is not a pretty thought,' she murmured.

'No,' Jessica agreed. 'Life is about to change immeasurably, yet again, thanks to Dunkirk.' She stopped knitting and thrust all three needles through the ball of wool in a short savage gesture. 'Hitler thinks we've had it, Freddie, and perhaps we may have, but we just must not go down

231

without a fight. Doesn't matter what happens, we must fight to the last. What we need above all . . .' She stood up. 'What we need is aeroplanes. I heard from Blossom yesterday, they're short-handed. So. I'm going to join *her* lot. Aeroplanes, aeroplanes, aeroplanes, that is what we need, Freddie, and I want to be part of building those fighters. And do you know what? I shall kiss each piece I contribute, and murmur to it: "Go to it, and kill". What a thing for a God-fearing person to say they hope to be doing, but I shall, believe me – I shall be leaving at crack of dawn tomorrow. If we don't cross paths, God bless you, darling.'

She leaned forward and kissed Freddie briefly.

Freddie watched Jessica leave the kitchen, and stared down at her empty plate. With Aunt Jessica gone, and all her friends, that just left Branscombe and the dogs.

'I'll manage,' she murmured, and then felt ashamed that she felt desolate, that the house was too large, and she for some reason too small for it.

She stood up. Time to get going again. She had to drive through the dark to the hospital. They were desperately short-handed, everyone needed, patients coming in from all directions, the flow from Dunkirk still being constant, not to mention the pregnant mothers that had been evacuated from Wychford to make room for the wounded.

For the first time in her life Daisy was beginning to find out what it was to be really tired, and it was a salutary experience. She had known that ferrying aeroplanes from factory to airstrip, again and again, and yet again, would be quite a task, but had sadly underestimated the battle fatigue. No time to ask questions, just get in and get on with it. They had to get the planes to the men – young men, most of whom had barely finished their training, some of whom had not even finished it – waiting, playing cricket, smoking, wondering whether their number would be up, or whether they would return. France had seen the loss of three hundred fighter pilots. To make up the numbers the Fleet Air Arm had to be called in, the Royal Canadian Air Force, too, and squadrons now desperate for men were manned by escaped Czechoslovakian and Polish pilots.

The rumour was that over a hundred squadrons were needed, and yet even with all the additions, they still only had sixty.

'There are no ground forces at all, unless you count the Home Guard, who are armed with everything from old muskets to broomsticks and frying pans, and no anti-aircraft guns to speak of, so how we will defend ourselves on the ground I don't know . . .'

Guy shook his head. He lunched and dined at the top tables, heard everything, and could do nothing; peeling away every few hours from some new stiff-upper-lip gathering, only to have to attend another, experiences which were far from uplifting.

He and Clive were now based in London. It was

rumoured that the theatres would soon reopen, although when, exactly, no one quite knew. However, Guy had other plans besides presenting his clever little comedies.

'I hope to be fielding a troupe of players, taking them out to the provinces, going to sing to the workers in the factories, because that, after all, is what I am famous for, is it not, dear Miss Jones?'

Now that Aurelia was in London all the time, her role of looking after Guy had both increased and decreased. He did not need her in connection with his particular work, but he did, it seemed, need her for other duties.

'It will be your task, Miss Jones, to go around and about, to be seen everywhere, the Savoy, the Dorchester, all the while, of course, keeping your pretty little ears open in order to bring me back relevant information.' He paused, pulling on his cigarette holder. 'We want to know everything that is being said, and even everything that is not being said. There are still British-born Nazi spies and agents all over town, and we want to know about them. Not everyone has a file on them, you know, not everyone in society is open about their political affiliations. We need to know more about these society Fascists, a great deal more, and you after all have the entrée to society. You know these people because you have grown up with them, Miss Jones.'

Aurelia flinched at that. Her last visit to her mother had revealed that Hotty had a quite serious chest infection, and her father had already lost over a stone in weight, which succeeded in making him look both younger and more lined. However, thanks to Clive Montfort's behind-the-scenes influence they had both been moved to less harsh surroundings, sharing their quarters so that they could look after each other, which was a great relief to Aurelia, although a source of open disgust to Guy.

'Why the special treatment?' he asked Clive, disapproval written all over his face as he lit a cigarette.

'Not special, old boy, just different.'

'Appeasers! Fellow-travellers! Fascists! Why?'

Clive looked across at Guy. He did not share either his confidence, or his black-and-white vision of the world, which was probably why Guy was a successful playwright, and he no more than his secretary.

'Thoroughbreds and carthorses, old boy. Different treatment. Some live out, some live in, some have thinner skin, some have thicker. Can't treat even the naughty ones all the same. Mercy in war is as much a victory over the enemy as defeat, as some great man once observed.'

But Guy had walked away. Nothing that should have been done to prevent the war had been done, and everything that was happening now was just a confounded waste of beautiful lives. If he had had a heart he was sure that by now it would have broken, and yet the proper war had hardly begun. Everyone was going around calling *now* the Phoney War.

235

The Bros at Operation Z had told him that someone truly bright had suggested bombing the Krupps arms factory, which would after all have put paid to a lot of, if not all, their present difficulties; but needless to say the idea had been firmly vetoed in cabinet, because, it seemed, it would offend the French! Well, with the Nazis crawling all over France at that very moment, the French were well and truly offended now, and if that was not the truth, nothing was.

Jessica knew that both Branscombe and Freddie would look after the dogs and the house. She also knew she was expendable at the Court now that the Lindsay brothers were being put to work in the fields and garden, not to mention the house, for even little Johnny had stopped crying, and had learned to trot after Branscombe chattering his head off, while Branscombe contented himself with the idea that had he ever been able to attract a wife, which with his wounds from the Great War would never have been possible, little Johnny could have been his grandson.

The girls who had been occupying the cottage in the stables were now dispersed, while Alec, the eldest of the Lindsay brothers, had gone to work for Jean alongside her army of land girls. She sometimes heard him getting up in the morning at the same time as she had just done, tiptoeing downstairs as the light came up, that perfect light that was pale pink and grey, and blue, and somehow purer than at any other time of day.

She had to walk to Twistleton Meads Station, leaving the car behind for Branscombe's use. Even at a brisk pace the walk between the Court and the station took some time, and when she did arrive she knew she would be forced to sit in the ladies' waiting room with her knitting, waiting for hours to get on a train that might take as much as a day to travel to the factory where Blossom was working.

As she sat knitting, the silence around her seemed ominous, as if even the countryside was waiting, even the awakening birds, the wild rabbits, the squirrels, the foxes, the badgers, the sheep and the cows. As if they were all waiting for the sound of that siren that would signal, not the arrival of the train, but the arrival of the enemy. She wished that she could knit faster, and faster, just to stop thinking, because thinking brought back memories of that other war, of that time of such despair, that time which was upon them again, except the war was to be here, above them. Not in France, not in some foreign field, but here in their own fields.

Her fingers ached, her arms ached, and yet the blasted sock did not seem to be getting any bigger. She pushed her needles out in front of her, examining the neat work in which she was pretending to be engrossed, remembering now that she had been told that all those socks they had knitted for the troops in the last war had been used to clean guns! What a futile occupation, to be knitting something which would probably end up cleaning a gun! But it was something to do, better than nothing. Nowadays she couldn't read, couldn't write, had no one to whom she wanted to write, just had to do something repetitive.

At last the train arrived, at last the peace was thankfully shattered by that reassuring sound of brakes applied, steam and noise welding into one effect, people staggering with their luggage, doors opening and closing – thank God for noise, for people.

Except, perhaps not!

As she walked into the factory where Blossom had been working for some time now, it was Jessica's turn to be shattered. She had never imagined in all her wildest nightmares that such noise could exist, never imagined that a place could be in such ferment, the air filled with such a fog of cigarette smoke that it would be difficult to see anything beyond your own work. She had hardly been there a minute before the effect on her eyes and her breathing was noticeable. In a matter of seconds, when she saw the hideous conditions under which everyone was expected to work, Jessica found herself envying anyone who was not in the factory that day; and then she remembered exactly why she was there, and felt ashamed.

She glanced briefly up above her. The roof had been blacked in to prevent the factory being seen from the air, and targeted. For obvious reasons therefore, the work had to be done by artificial light, which made it even more tiring, because you had to peer through a fog at what was in front of you.

The head of her group beckoned to her, and then to another young woman, who immediately joined them. The leader mouthed to Jessica that she would be shown what to do, but before starting to take note, Jessica could not help glancing down at her watch. In eleven hours' time they would go home, perhaps to their own homes, or perhaps, like Jessica, to temporary lodgings. Blossom had written to her that the work was long and hard – but not just necessary – vital. Without it they would lose the war. The hours just had to be put in.

Jessica braced herself, and then tapped the pocket of her boiler suit, the one where she had carefully placed the photograph of Esmond. She didn't care how long the day would prove to be, she knew for whom she was doing it. It was for all those other Esmonds, all those other young men waiting 'at readiness' – some playing cricket, some smoking, some sitting in cockpits, all of them waiting for the order to scramble, to climb into the skies and defend their country, perhaps for the last time.

Daisy knocked back her drink.

'I'd like to be in the RAF if they would have women,' she confided to one of her newer, older, flying friends. 'But I don't know that I could stand the waiting. I mean, at least we fly in and get on with it, whereas the others have to hang about

239

waiting for the starting bell. It would get on my nerves, truly it would.'

Her companion looked at her, shaking his head, and then he laughed.

'But you don't have any nerves, do you, Daisy?'

Daisy thought for a minute, and then frowned.

'Oh, I think I do.' She stubbed out her cigarette. 'In fact, I'm sure I do.'

They were in a pub much frequented by airmen, and one which had become quite used to the sight of uniformed women customers.

'Although—' Daisy stopped suddenly. 'Actually – maybe not. I always think I will be nervous before take-off, but I never am.'

'Some people just don't suffer from 'em. Let me buy you another snifter. Same again?'

'Oh, very well, hung for a sheep as a lamb.' Daisy turned back to the bar once more, thinking that if Aunt Maude could see her now, drinking and smoking in a pub, she would have fifty fits, and then her eyes widened. 'Good Lord, Joe Huggett!'

They shook hands, and as they did so, Daisy turned back to her drinking companion. 'This is Brian Ashford, Joe.' Then to Brian. 'Joe and I are from the same village, Twistleton . . .'

It was obvious Joe was not going to stay for more than the minute or two it took him to knock back a drink. He just wanted to get back to Twistleton. He was on twenty-four-hour compassionate leave from his training – how he had swung it was anybody's business – but he had to see Jean, had to get back to her lovely arms, just for a moment, and feel her body against his, perhaps for the last time. Who cared, who knew? It was all he could think about now he was on the ground.

'Can't stop. See you around.' He smiled suddenly. 'But look who's here, too!' He thrust out a hand in greeting to a tall, immensely handsome airman who had just swung into the bar. 'David Moreton.' He turned back to Daisy. 'Daisy, this is a shocking man. He and I were at school together. How are you, old boy? Top form, as far as I can see. Sorry, I can't stop – my girl awaits me!'

They all laughed, and shook hands.

'I was just teasing Daisy here that she has no nerves,' Brian joked, while at the same time wishing that he was not a middle-aged man with receding hair, but as young and handsome as David Moreton. 'Daisy flies with flair, better than the rest of us by miles. The way she lands and takes off would make a bird jealous.'

Daisy looked embarrassed.

'You must forgive Brian. He likes to blow a trumpet for our poor old skills, because he thinks you lot look down your noses at Air Transport Auxiliary, and I daresay he is right.'

Taking in Daisy's long elegant legs, her beautiful face, blonde hair, and startlingly blue eyes – but most of all the faintly mocking manner that told him she was quite a girl – David felt odd, dizzy and strange, as if he had been flung out of his cockpit and his parachute refused to open.

'You should be in the RAF proper,' he heard

241

himself say, after a short pause. 'Cheer us all up no end—'

'No, no, old boy,' Brian interrupted. 'If the RAF took Daisy, she would be running the whole show by the end of the year, and you would be taking orders from her.' Brian joked on, determinedly, while knowing all the time that he might as well talk to himself, for it was quite clear that there were now only two people in the room as far as David was concerned, and not even a bomb dropping would get him to take his eyes off Daisy.

As for Daisy, she didn't seem to notice him noticing her, concentrating on her, but turned to introduce him to other friends who had arrived. She carried on as normal, but then that was Daisy – she always scythed her way through admirers, leaving them gasping for more.

All leave for the FANYs had long been cancelled, which meant that as soon as the bombs did start dropping on London and the south-east, Laura found herself driving a much-needed canteen nightly to the increasingly beleaguered East End. Driving in the dark with the sirens wailing and fires blazing became so much a way of life for her, that it was not until the end of the first month that she realised she had enjoyed so little sleep that she did not know whether she would ever again be able to doze off for more than two hours at a time. In fact, sleeplessness had become such a habit that she had actually managed to convince herself she only needed those two or three hours.

And the East End was not the only place in need of refreshment.

Since the people of London had taken it upon themselves to remove the locked gates to the Underground, the FANYs had been ordered to help with subterranean canteen duties, tending to the crowds through the night. Once down the steps into those dark regions where trains still ran even now, Laura had discovered an unlooked-for resilience that was humbling, for here was a set of people determined not just on surviving the night, but on doing so with as much strength and courage as they did above ground. Until at last dawn came up, and they re-emerged into daylight, pale-faced, tired, but alive, summoning up the energy to resume the daily struggle, standing behind boards that read: *'STILL OPEN FOR BUSINESS'.*

Once again, as night fell, down they went below ground with their families, everyone carrying food and drink, and anything else they imagined they might need.

Over the days a fairground atmosphere had gradually come into being, everyone hoping against hope that the increased bombardment would soon be over, while knowing all the time that there was worse to come.

And there *was* worse to come, for everyone – including Laura, who, with the other FANYs, was only too willing to drive her canteen across a London which at times seemed to be exploding, to bring what little she could to the heartbreakingly cheerful crowds in their dark hiding places – had started to wonder if indeed they *would* be able to take it . . .

'Carry on, carry on singing, all of you. I'll join in "Roll Out the Barrel".' It was the Prime Minister, Winston himself, fresh from dinner, a cigar clamped in his jaw, his eyes taking in every detail of the faces in the shelter.

There was something about him – not just his voice, or his manner, certainly not his height or his looks, but the whole of him – that made everyone straighten their backs and want to smile and cheer. He radiated an almost childlike energy, as if he knew just how badly they all needed to feed off his belief in them. And although he was only with them for a few minutes, and was all too soon escorted off to some new place – leaving behind the inevitable smell of cigar smoke – after he had gone Laura noticed that it was as if he had left behind a brazier, as if in their imaginations they felt they could all put out their hands to the spot where he had stood, and feel themselves warmed.

'Good old Winston,' someone near to Laura said in a cheerful voice. 'Imagine him having time for us, with all that he must have on. He sang "Roll Out the Barrel" like a Cockney good 'un, didn't he, now?'

A few minutes later the ground shook so hard that everyone fell to the ground, and Laura found herself starting to pray – and she was not in the least religious.

*   *   *

Aurelia stared at Jean.

'I thought I was, too, a bit ago, but I wasn't, I just couldn't remember what had happened after an evening out. The thing is, the chap I was with drank gin, and it didn't take much for him to persuade me to try some.' She shuddered. 'Never touched the stuff again, never will. Nothing worse than thinking you are *you know what*, and waiting and waiting, and then finding out that all along you have been wasting your time, and you simply passed out from too much tiddly and nothing happened. Most especially if it's a married man, as, in my case – he *was*, or is still, for all I know!'

Jean smiled wanly. She knew that Aurelia was trying to cheer her up, but she didn't dare tell her that it was quite useless. She was quite sure that she *was* what Aurelia called '*you know what*'; and there was another thing: she and Joe had dashed into a registry office and dashed out again. In other words, they were married, but she didn't want to tell Aurelia, or indeed anyone else that, either, because Joe hadn't told his mother and father, and judging from the expression on his angelic face, probably never would. It had been a joke between them, but now Jean suspected that their one-night honeymoon had resulted in pregnancy, she imagined that someone might have to tell the Huggetts, although perhaps not until the next time Joe had twenty-four-hour compassionate leave. She looked at the date on the wall of the farmhouse kitchen. It had an unreality about it that she couldn't quite understand.

Aurelia, too, was looking around the kitchen, but for a different reason. She and Clive had been made responsible for shutting up the farmhouse – or rather, emptying it, putting everything in store, preparatory to its being taken over by the army.

When the news came through, Clive had found Guy groaning in the kitchen.

'Longbridge will be like a bomb shelter by the time we get back to it, if we ever do get back to it.'

He stared round at the facade of the old house, its mellow exterior catching at that part of him which he liked to pretend didn't exist, namely his heart.

'We've had some wonderful times here,' he murmured. 'Some marvellous parties, and some unforgettable evenings. Let's just shut it all up, and be thankful.'

But as always when Guy said 'we', he really meant everyone else except him. He fled back to London, to Operation Z activities, and rehearsals for his latest comedy, everyone being much in need of laughter.

'I had better get on.' Aurelia pulled a little face at Jean, at the same time feeling that since there was very little she could do to help her, hanging about and talking was not going to add much to the situation.

'Sorry I can't help. Have to get to cracking the whip behind my lot.'

Jean leaned forward and kissed Aurelia on the cheek. It was not something she had ever done to anyone before, so she found herself reddening.

'Look, take care, won't you?' Aurelia smiled.

Jean nodded, and then hurried out to where she had left the tractor. Happily she had parked Old Faithful well out of sight of the farmhouse, so she was able to be sick without anyone seeing her – or so she hoped.

Laura was waiting outside a cinema for Daisy. They had arranged to go to a film that had been made from one of Guy's comedies. Watching a comedy seemed a pretty strange thing to do when a war was raging, but everyone knew that it was all part of the general plan to stick two fingers in the air at Hitler, all part of the 'we can take it' attitude. No matter how many bombs dropped, they had to keep going as if nothing was happening.

Daisy eventually appeared, looking stunning. Laura stared at her. Daisy had always been beautiful, but now, in her ATA uniform, its very boyishness seemed to show up her femininity all the more. They smiled, touched each other briefly on the arm, and hurried into the cinema.

The film was frequently interrupted by the manager coming on to the stage to ask the audience to leave for the shelters, and would then be re-started once the all-clear sounded. This happened so often that the audience started to laugh every time the poor manager came on to the stage. Of course, this was just the thing to keep everyone's mind off the bombs dropping. Finally the audience refused to move, just carried on staring at the screen and laughing wherever possible, seemingly impervious to what was happening outside, perhaps reckoning that what would be would be, and that if their number was up, not much could save them anyway. There was little Laura could do but sit still, pretending to be more nonchalant than she felt, while knowing that she was fighting a losing battle, not just with fear; she was fighting a losing battle not to fall in love with David Moreton.

Afterwards, when they had retired to the basement flat beneath Gervaise's London house that Daisy was now intermittently occupying, Laura confided to Daisy that she thought she had fallen in love with this RAF chap she had met called David Moreton.

'But that's so exciting, isn't it?'

Laura looked shy. It was exciting, but much as she loved Daisy, she did not dare tell her just *how* exciting. Nice girls like herself and Daisy were not meant to have love affairs, they were meant to wait for marriage. She knew she would now be considered damaged goods, at any rate in the eyes of society, but the worst of it was that she did not care.

'I hope to see him again soon,' she said, but before she could elaborate further, the wail of the sirens started up, and they both disappeared under the kitchen table.

'A fat lot of good this is!' Daisy moaned. 'But do go on about this chap, whatever he's called. Who knows? I might bump into him. He picked you up, did he? How quite marvellous. And you both took it on from there. I love that kind of cheek.'

The building shook, and they flattened themselves, not even Daisy being able to go on pretending to be interested in Laura's romance as the world about them rocked – and then, for some reason, the world seemed to steady itself. At any rate, quite enough for them to be able to share a much-needed cigarette and have a laugh. It was only when they were both scrambling up the area steps, tumbling over dustbins, cursing themselves and everyone else, that Daisy realised exactly what Laura had just told her.

The bar was crowded with RAF and a few ATA girls, the air so thick with smoke that even the barman was leaning forward and frowning in an effort to see what drink he was pouring into which glass, while the chat, like the smoke, rose up to the dark, yellowed ceiling, accompanied by that particular laughter that comes out of relief at still being alive. David made his way through it all, across the crowded bar to the girl he couldn't get out of his head, who was standing with a crowd of others. He pushed himself to her side.

'Miss Daisy Beresford,' he announced, quite unnecessarily.

Daisy turned, seeing him suddenly, and wishing that she hadn't, wishing that he would go away.

'Here you are again—' Daisy heard herself saying.

'Yes,' David agreed. 'Here I am indeed – again.'

'It doesn't seem possible . . .'

'You mean you were hoping it wasn't possible?' he asked, raising his head a little to move away from the smoke of his own cigarette, but also so that he could get a better look at those fabulous legs.

'Guess who I saw last week in London.'

'Vivien Leigh?'

'Laura Hambleton.'

'You know Laura?'

He looked surprised, and at the same time embarrassed, as if Laura was already a name from the past.

'I believe you picked her up!' Daisy went on purposefully.

'Yes, I did,' David agreed. 'And what is more I showed her how the internal combustion engine works. Very important when you're in the FANYs.'

'Yes, I suppose it is.' Daisy found that she had dropped her eyes, because it was obvious from David's expression that he was not very interested in talking about either Laura or the internal combustion engine. 'Laura and I were at Twistleton Court together.' As David looked understandably puzzled, she went on. 'Twistleton Court was a sort of finishing school where we learned how to do a court curtsy, and climb out of a car in an elegant fashion, swinging the legs out first, *comme ça!*'

To demonstrate, Daisy put her long, elegant legs together and swung them neatly, in an exaggerated fashion, off her chair, which made David laugh.

'Any good for climbing in and out of Spitfires and Hurricanes?'

'No, hopeless, I'm afraid. Particularly since they will not let us wear trousers, which makes life both tedious and embarrassing at the same time.'

Daisy quickly lit a cigarette. All that finishing school side of life seemed not just silly now, but ridiculous – and yet at the same time, very dear, too. She now thought of those months at the Court, when she had managed, at long, long last, to escape Aunt Maude and life at the Hall, as something that must have happened, not before this war, but before the Great War.

'I expect Laura rebelled a great deal, didn't she? I seem to remember that she told me she hated parties, hated having to socialise, that her father and her godmother had insisted on her being a debutante. She found it all a stupid waste of time, just wanted to run out. I expect she made a bit of a hash of finishing school, didn't she?'

Daisy stared at David, realising that whether *he* realised it or not he was still talking about Laura as if she was in the past, which at once made her heart sink.

All of a sudden she found herself thinking that she hoped to God he would not lean forward and murmur, *'Let's forget about Laura, shall we, and think only of us?'*

She determined at once to talk about Laura before he could further embarrass himself or her.

'Laura?' she stated with perfect diction, and very obvious loyalty. 'Laura did everything perfectly at Twistleton Court, as she always does. She is a very beautiful young woman, and she and I, and the others that did the course together, are all the greatest friends.'

David seemed to accept this, although she noticed that he did throw back his drink rather too quickly.

'This is all rather awkward,' he said, lighting a cigarette.

'What is?'

'This, everything, all this, you and I, both of us here. The war. It is all a little difficult, at least so it seems to me.'

'You're not really making a great deal of sense, which is only understandable.'

David looked at Daisy, who tried to give him her best casual look in return, while actually looking resolutely vague.

'No, I know, well, I wouldn't make sense, would I?'

'Being at war—' Daisy began again.

'Nothing to do with being at war, I only wish it was.'

Daisy looked away this time, trying like mad to avoid his disturbing intensity.

'Look – we have to sort this out.'

Daisy stood up.

'No,' she said firmly. 'No, we don't have to sort anything out. I must go – so much to do before tomorrow.'

David stood up as she left their table, but she knew that his eyes were following her, and that they both knew that she was lying.

As for Daisy, she was only too happy to drive to the relevant factory the next morning and fling herself into a plane, and fly off into the skies. She would not and could not have anything more to do with David. It would be a betrayal of everything that she believed in, most particularly friendship and loyalty. They were more important than some passing attraction, and always would be.

Chapter Eight

Freddie was aware that she should be busy hating the enemy, but though she tried hard she could not do it. For her, war was not about hatred, it was all about trying to put innocent people together again, people of all kinds, and of all nationalities. It was no good hating someone you were trying to mend.

Jean knew no hate, either, being a part of the land, being guided by the weather, living by the seasons – hay hastily brought in before the weather changed, wheat ripening, cows grazing, hoping, always hoping, for good things to come had been part of her young life since her grandmother had first taught her how to milk a cow, which was why when she saw what she recognised as pure hate in Mrs Huggett's eyes, she was stunned.

'You are what?' she asked Jean.

'I am having a baby.'

'Not here, you're not, my gel. Not here. You can take yourself, and your so-called baby, somewhere else.'

'But, Mrs Huggett, but – Mrs Huggett—' Jean

suddenly discovered what swallowing hard and having a dry mouth, both at the same time, was like. 'This is Joe's baby. And we are married.'

Mrs Huggett's eyes seemed to grow smaller and smaller until they almost disappeared into her face, so narrow did they become.

'You married Joe? You married Joe? *You?*'

Jean had never heard anyone say 'you' like that before. It made her feel as if she was something on the back of the dung cart that still called regularly at The Cottages – and not a very nice something, either – but she was determined not to show her fear, or how awful she felt.

'Well, actually, Mrs Huggett, Joe married me. On a twenty-four-hour pass from training college.'

Mrs Huggett breathed in and out again, and for a few seconds it seemed to Jean that the older woman's chest was a pair of bellows, very well-covered bellows, of course, but bellows none the same.

'Joe,' she finally said, 'is no longer at training college. He has been pulled in to fly ops, despite not finishing the course. They need everyone they can get, even unfinished boys.'

There was a small silence as Jean frowned, and wondered whether this made any difference to their being married, and then, realising it couldn't, remained silent, if mystified.

Mrs Huggett stood up.

'Look, I am very sorry you have got yourself in the family way,' she said, altering her tone of voice to that of a rector's wife visiting the unfortunate.

'But the truth is that I can have nothing more to do with you, and when Joe gets back I shall have to tell him so. We do not cross the tracks in our family, we simply do not, and it is just as well for you to know that from now on. Whether you like it or not, you are on your own, Miss Shaw.'

'Mrs Huggett, actually.'

Susan Huggett rang the bell to the side of the fireplace and waited, and then, remembering that the maid had left that morning to go to work in a factory, she sighed.

'I will show you out, Miss Shaw—'

'Mrs Huggett—'

'But please do understand, you will never be welcome here at Holly House, never, ever.'

Jean walked down the hill back to The Cottages and let herself in. Her new evacuees were all busy in the back garden planting out heaven only knew what, and only heaven *would* know. Her first evacuees having been taken smartly back to the East End by their mother – because they couldn't cope with no chip shop, no cinema and no indoor lavatory – the dear Ropley boys, newly orphaned by the war, had arrived to take their place, and settled into Twistleton and The Cottages as if they were born to life in a small village.

Not only that, but what with being outside all day long, and helping about the farm from dawn to dusk, they were both now proud possessors of healthy appetites, and having swiftly grown used to appreciating Jean's home cooking, would not now care to eat anything from a tin. Which was another source of pride to her, or would have been had she not become pregnant, since when cooking had become an agony of discomfort, most particularly in the early morning.

She could tell almost no one about her changed state, for the good reason that Mrs Huggett would not acknowledge that she was Joe's legal wife. And since Joe and she had tied the knot many miles away – for obvious reasons – their marriage and her pregnancy had remained a secret, although as time passed that would, of course, stop. She did, however, tell Freddie, because she knew that Freddie could help her when the time came for her to go to a hospital or find a doctor – or nowadays, more likely, a midwife.

'I am so happy for you,' Freddie said, and then she walked back to the hospital, where, she knew, she would soon be busy helping to deliver even more babies. Yet, even as the warning wail of the siren started she could not stop worrying about Jean. How would she manage to farm the acres she had valiantly taken on, and look after her cows and sheep, if she was pregnant, and then, later, saddled with a baby?

A few minutes later there was little time to think about Jean, and even less to help get patients out of their beds, and safely underneath them. If they couldn't do this in an air raid the nurses had been told to cover the poor creatures with whatever was at hand.

A few minutes later she heard herself saying to

an elderly patient, 'Don't try to get out of bed, Mr Taplow, you're going to be quite safe. We're going to protect you by putting this door over you.'

Really, what a thing – poor man! As Mr Taplow shrieked with terror at the idea of being covered by a door, Freddie turned to Sister, who was always at such pains to try to do without help from the VAD nurses and murmured, 'I'm not sure that this won't make matters worse . . .'

'An order is an order, Miss Valentyne, no matter what,' Sister said, raising her voice to a commanding level. 'Mr Taplow must be covered, and we have been advised that for those patients unable to get under their beds, being covered by a door will be most effective.'

Her mouth tightened, and she walked on, leaving Freddie and a fellow-VAD nurse to pick the door up from under Mr Taplow's bed, and cover the hapless fellow, an action which, Freddie imagined, was likely to kill him quicker than any bomb.

The news vendors in London were daily recording victory over the enemy, their boards suggesting more that a cricket match was being fought overhead, than a fight to the death for the survival of a nation: 'MESSERSCHMITTS SEVEN – HURRICANES THREE'. And even this score would soon be changed to give a more hopeful result, a little moment of forgivable fiction on behalf of the vendors, knowing as they did that even as the buildings behind their stands crumbled, everyone needed to think that the battle overhead was being won.

Daisy, herself, was fighting a losing battle. In the ghastly chaos of those weeks when German victory seemed imminent, she had tried to avoid even thinking of David, and yet the more the losses overhead mounted, the more she realised that fighting her desire to bring loving comfort to at least one young pilot was ludicrous. They were both in the same fight. Maybe Laura would not mind? Maybe Daisy should, after all, answer the little notes David kept sending her, begging her to meet him.

She struggled to find a reason not to see him again. She wrote to him that she was too busy, and yet all the time she knew that he might be dead tomorrow, so what did it matter what happened between the sheets? The last straw was when one of her new ATA friends was killed by, of all things, friendly fire! All of a sudden 'what did it matter?' became a cruel reality, and more than that, she realised that it was not just David who might not be alive tomorrow, it was her, too. And she knew that she needed love, quite desperately.

When they met up again, in the pub of course, they both knew it was hopeless, and having chucked back their drinks they ran off into the night.

They did not speak, they looked, and unexpressed thoughts became action as they tore each other's clothes off and climbed into bed together, refuge having been found in a local hotel.

'Passion and war have always gone hand in hand,' David murmured afterwards, perhaps to assuage his own guilt, even as Daisy realised with gratitude that he knew about women: what they liked, how they felt. Then she allowed her guilt, and the realisation of what she had undoubtedly done to Laura, to hit her.

'We must never speak of this to anyone,' she said, having managed to run a bath of two inches of rusty water. With a few expert movements, she brushed out her long blonde hair, put it up, and stepped into the water.

But before she could begin to wash herself with a precious piece of soap, David took her in his arms. Why would they speak of it to anyone else? he wondered silently. To whom would he speak? A matter of moments passed. They washed each other tenderly, and then they re-dressed in their uniforms, Daisy doing up her long suspenders to hold up her knee-length stockings, David watching her with a strange feeling of possessive pride. Daisy kissed him goodbye, upstairs, and then they both left by separate entrances, knowing that they might never see each other again. It was only as David drove away that he started to wonder: would Daisy give the same comfort to all the pilots? He drove faster, telling himself that he did not care if she did, knowing all the while that he cared far too much.

Daisy returned to her ferrying duties as always – thankfully, welcoming doing anything and everything to take her mind off what was happening to David – and then, returning on leave to Twistleton Court, was met by a white-faced Freddie.

'Who?' she managed to ask.

Freddie shook her head, unable to speak for a little while.

Daisy wanted to shake Freddie, and scream at her, *Is it David Moreton?'* It was ridiculous, because Freddie wouldn't know David Moreton from Hermann Goering. Instead she stood stock still as Freddie collapsed on a hall chair, and the message that had been brought from the village fell to the ground. Daisy picked it up. It was from Jean. Joe Huggett had been killed twelve hours earlier. His plane had been shot down.

Daisy was staggered, quite unable to believe that Joe, who had always been such a mischievous cherub, Joe the baby of the village, always being cuffed by someone, and hugged by someone else, was gone, that they would never see him again. She couldn't cry, wouldn't cry, because crying was such a blasted waste of badly needed energy. That was a lesson that the war had already taught her – you had to conserve what little reserves you had, from minute to minute, not even hour to hour. Don't waste energy, hang on to every ounce. Besides which, there was usually no time to cry, which was another lesson quickly learned.

'They've only just been married, and now—'

Freddie had to hurry down to The Cottages to comfort Jean, who had sent the message up to the

Court, but before she went she and Daisy kissed each other quickly on the cheeks, which everyone had lately become quite accustomed to doing, even if they were only going shopping, knowing, as they all did, that it might be the last time they saw each other. But then, before Freddie could leave, Daisy stopped her.

'Wait a minute, when did Joe and Jean marry?'

Freddie turned impatiently.

'I don't know, I'm sure. Besides, what *does* it matter when they married? What does it *matter*? I just hope the shock doesn't cause her to lose the baby.'

'Baby? Baby? She's having a baby?'

'Yes, you know, one of those small things that people push about in prams, that have to be given bottles, and aren't nearly as pretty as foals.'

Freddie fled out of the door as Daisy put the message on the table, and went to sit down on the chair that Freddie had vacated. But she couldn't settle. For some reason there was no one else about at the Court – they were out, or busying themselves somewhere – and only Daisy was left alone with her thoughts, restless, unable to even switch on the wireless for fear of hearing of some new disaster, new bad news, brought to her by courtesy of the BBC.

Oh dear God, little Joe Huggett, dead. Loved by all, would be missed by all, never known to have done a bad or an ungenerous thing. Lovely, funny Joe no longer coming back. Lovely funny Joe, one of those rare people whose warmth came into a room with him, leaving it colder when he left.

Over the next few hours she became obsessed that it had been one of *her* planes that Joe had been piloting. Maybe that Hurricane that she had delivered so proudly, and in record time, to the airstrip after she and David had made love? It was not long before making love to David, Laura's love, turned into an indigestible lump of guilt. Maybe it was her wickedness at making love with her friend's boyfriend, whom she *knew* to be her friend's boyfriend, that had brought bad luck to Joe? Maybe it had.

For want of anything else to do, Daisy went outside and started to walk round the grounds with the dachshunds happily following her. Walking, and walking, and walking, trying to get Joe's cherub-like mischievous young face out of her mind. His too-long hair, his engaging grin, everything about him, but everything, a tribute to youth and gaiety.

'I can't stay here,' she told the trees they were passing. 'I just can't. I can't stay and be amidst all this silent sorrow. I have to get back.' And as she passed the trees she thought she could hear Aunt Maude's voice murmuring of the silent cities that were the war graves in France, of Maude's beloved Beresford brothers all but one lost in the Great War, and she remembered with shame how she had turned away from her aunt's silent sorrow, impatient with the grief of the previous generation, eager only to get on with her own life.

Unable to face any more guilt, Daisy fled back to the house, packed her overnight bag, shut the dogs in the boot room, and headed out to her car. Branscombe, having hoarded petrol in everything from what looked like jam jars to feed buckets, quickly filled up her tank for her, and Daisy drove off, leaving Twistleton without regret.

As she drove back to the factory, she realised it was not just her guilt over David, it was also the fear that she might suddenly bump into Laura, that had driven her back to her duties in less than a day. She also knew that she was too cowardly to face the sight of Jean's grief. It was despicable, and it meant that she was even less of a good person, but on the other hand, at least when she was on duty she knew what she was doing. She had to fly every and any make of aircraft sometimes two and three times a day, from their factories to the airfields waiting for them, and do it all without the guidance of a radio, following the rivers and towns, often in appalling conditions – because there was no alternative. But even so, it was easier than coping with the reality of sorrow. Battling on, fighting, was easier than facing the awful solemnity of grief.

And they did all have to battle on, stunned with horror at what was happening to their friends and their homes, trying to forget the news of losses, making plans to shoot themselves rather than be captured.

Over the next few weeks the overhead battles between the might of Hitler's air force and the slender resources of the British increased to an unbearable extent. Yet the British quickly learned to use their Spitfires to pass beneath the German bombers, while the Hurricanes attacked the 'Flying Pencils' and the Spitfires provided top cover. It was to prove a winning tactic.

The losses were nevertheless terrific. Day after bloodied day, the realisation of who would never return was set aside by the brave young pilots, until, at last, they came to realise that, amazingly, somehow – and nobody really knew how – the Nazis had been temporarily rebuffed.

It was not that the war had stopped, for even as Churchill warned that it was only the 'end of the beginning' people everywhere had grown all too used to seeing dog-fights overhead, trails of smoke streaking the late summer sky, so that even schoolboys only paused momentarily in their work to watch parachutists gliding down to earth. The aerial battle had become such a common sight. And now, the first of these battles had been won, but at what cost they could not contemplate. They only knew that somehow, and no one really knew how, the worst had not quite happened. They had won a victory in the air. The Nazi invasion was temporarily halted.

Branscombe had watched Miss Daisy driving away with mixed feelings. He liked Miss Daisy, more than that, he had grown really quite fond of her over the years. Well, he would have, wouldn't he? After all he'd watched her growing up, albeit from afar, given the continuing silence between the Court and the Hall. She had turned out a good 'un though, that Miss Daisy. Quite a sight, nowadays, in her air uniform, an ATA girl indeed, from the tip of her blonde head to her shining heels; not to mention being a chip off the old block, if ever there was one.

Not that anyone ever spoke about the coldness that had always existed between the two houses, as they wouldn't, Miss Jessica being Miss Jessica, and Miss Maude being Miss Maude. All a long time ago, that business of Miss Jessica falling for Miss Maude's middle brother Mr Esmond, and he going off to war, hardly past his eighteenth birthday, because Miss Jessica's family had forbidden her to marry a younger son with no prospects. And so he had gone off to prove himself a man, and never returned, leaving Miss Maude, so rumour had it, blaming Miss Jessica for his death, because Mr Roderick, her favourite and youngest brother, had followed Mr Esmond out there, the two of them being such pals. And of course he, too, had not come back, and that had been the last of them, once Daisy's father had gone down in the drink, being flown to Deauville for lunch, of all things . . .

Branscombe sighed, and then frowned. Someone was coming up the drive. He narrowed his eyes, staring, as he realised that it was a uniformed dispatch rider on a motorbike, and felt a familiar feeling of relief that it was not the postman astride a pony, carrying a telegram.

Branscombe, quickly assuming his peacetime role of butler, stepped forward on to the front steps to greet the new arrival.

'Miss Valentyne is on war-work duties, and not expected back for some time—' he told the man, who presented him with an order sheet. *'Twistleton Court is commandeered by the army'* – Branscombe stared from the dispatch rider to the order sheet, and back again.

'There must be some mistake, sir – these houses are all privately owned. This is our village.'

The dead-eyed look Branscombe was given said all too clearly what the older man did not want to know, namely that there was a war on, and that the authorities could do as they pleased.

'I think you will find that the army owns Twistleton Court now, *sir*.'

'The army can't take over private property without so much as a say-so or a say-not.'

'The army can do what they like when they like, *sir*. Brigadier MacNaughton will be arriving at 0800 hours tomorrow. Meanwhile, orders are to start evacuating the village now – *sir*.'

Maude was thinking quickly, as she had to do.

'The Hall is not part of Twistleton proper. They can't commandeer the Hall, or its grounds, or its demesnes. I would very much doubt that they could do that, for it is most certainly not part of Twistleton proper, and never has been.'

Branscombe looked relieved at this. If the Hall

could be saved from imminent military invasion, that at least would be something.

'I shall have to send someone to fetch Huggett, at once. Do you know where he is, Branscombe?'

'As I remember it, he is busy organising the Look Duck and Vanish Brigade, is he not?'

'Mr Huggett is head of the LDV, yes, of course, I remember now, he did mention it.'

'The LDV may be able to cope with a Nazi or two, but they will be helpless against our army, Miss Maude . . .'

On hearing the news of the military takeover of the village, Maude, for reasons even she did not understand, had promptly disappeared upstairs and changed into her nurse's uniform, so she now straightened her starched apron, and consulted her fob watch.

'I see they have given us only twenty-four hours to get out of our houses. Surely even the Germans would give us a little more time, would they not, Branscombe?'

'The Spread Eagle could have taken five people upstairs, but The Spread Eagle, too, is requisitioned. The whole village must be emptied.'

Maude's lips tightened, and she stared past Branscombe, and into what seemed to her to be an all-too-graphic picture of the future. It was not a very pretty sight. She knew what the army could do to villages, she had heard and seen all too much of what armies did, in the Great War.

'I heard that with the threat of invasion many towns and villages near the sea have been evacuated, and we are too near the sea; but this is not what they are doing here, is it, Branscombe? They are requisitioning the village for training purposes, which means, in effect, the end of Twistleton. Twistleton will become a desert.'

Maude felt her throat tighten. She felt older than she was, older than she should – and worse than feeling old, she felt hopeless.

'I was only an ambulance driver in the Great War, Miss Maude,' Branscombe confessed, looking uncomfortable, as if he half-expected Maude to pin three white feathers to his old, faded black jacket.

'Jolly brave too, Branscombe, jolly brave, and it cost you one of your eyes, as we all know. Absolutely first class, men like you, couldn't have done without you.' She paused, and to Branscombe's surprise she went to a silver cigarette box, took out a holder, and a small Turkish cigarette, and lit it with a slim gold lighter. 'No, this is not what this wretched order is all about, Branscombe. Of course Huggett may say different, but with official papers you must always try and read what they are not saying. And what they are not saying here is very unpleasant indeed, very unpleasant.'

Branscombe frowned. Surely there could not be anything more unpleasant than the army taking over your village, the village where you had lived all your life?

'What they are not saying here, Branscombe, is that they are taking over the village with the aim of making it a playground for tank and target practice, a training ground. Of course they will promise compensation, the army always do, but the truth is there will hardly be a building left standing after this Brigadier MacNaughton, or whatever his name is, has taken us over.'

There was a small silence during which Branscombe, too, felt suddenly helpless. How would he tell Miss Jessica? What would he tell her? He would hardly know what words to use to her, or Miss Blossom. What could he say? He felt as if he had let them down in some way, let in the army when their backs were turned, while they were working all day and all night building planes.

Finally Maude consulted her fob watch as if she was once more on duty on the ward.

'We will have to call out the LDV to help us, Branscombe.'

Branscombe looked startled. Would there be a new war, then? Would it be the Local Defence Volunteers of Twistleton versus the Territorial Army? Broomstick and musket versus guns and tanks? He had seen the volunteers marching through the village street – the lame, the old, and four schoolboys just about summed up Twistleton's LDV.

'Meanwhile I will ask you to go to the rector and tell him to ring the church bells. Everyone must start packing up at once. Just as well all the evacuees have gone home.'

'Not ours at the Court. The Ropleys have gone, but the Lindsays, they haven't returned home, Miss Maude.' Branscombe managed to look rueful, while feeling vaguely proud. He had finally won over not just Alec, but all the Lindsay brothers, to country life, not one of them now wanting to go home, not even little Johnny. Which was just as well, since it seemed that their mother wanted them back about as much as she wanted tooth-ache. 'We still have all four Lindsay brothers with us at the Court.'

'Oh, you do, do you?'

Maude looked vaguely astonished, before writing a note to advise the rector of their new and thoroughly unwelcome situation.

'Yes, they are all well and happy at the Court, and not likely to be wanted at home again, at least not for the duration.'

'I *perfectly* understand what you are saying, Branscombe. You will therefore, please, after giving the rector this note, return to the Court and pack up your evacuees, and yourselves, and all necessary effects.'

'The dachshunds—'

'Of course, the dachshunds, poor creatures. You will pack them all up, and bring them here. Let us hope they can cope with the pugs—'

'Petrol and car?'

'Everything. You will pack them all up—'

'Pony and trap—'

'Of course. And you must please tell the rector to cut along to the Hall as soon as he is able, as also Huggett. I have put here: "*Emergency. Invasion. No, not Nazis, the army requisitioning the village.*" Yes, you will tell them all to bring everything they

271

can, here to the Hall, Branscombe. Yourself and all your et ceteras must all be put up in the stables, I'm afraid. We will have our work cut out to make them habitable, but habitable we must make them, for the duration.'

'And what about the rest of the village, Miss Maude?'

'The rest of the village? The rest of the village must be put up in the house, Branscombe.'

'In the house, Miss Maude?'

Maude nodded.

'Yes, in the house, Branscombe. With Bowles and Pattern and the rest gone we have at least, I don't know – twenty bedrooms now, not including the basement and attics. What there is, when all is added up, is perfectly enough room to accommodate everyone. Hugger-mugger it will be, of course, but hugger-mugger is what war is all about. And let us face it, with the young going off, and soon women being called up, the numbers will doubtless thin out, and we will probably only be left with the remnants of the LDV, and all the rest will be thrown into the melee. Off to the factories, or the army, they will all soon be gone, and only you and I left to marshal them, but marshal them all we must, so you had better get to, Branscombe, and start ferrying the folk from The Cottages up here.'

As Branscombe turned to do as directed – feeling, and doubtless, he was sure, *looking* flustered – he tried to imagine old Dan Short from Number Five The Cottages sitting down to break bread with Miss Maude. He turned back. 'Miss Maude?'

'Yes, Branscombe?'

'You do mean *everyone* from The Cottages, do you?'

Maude nodded briskly.

'I certainly do, Branscombe, I certainly do.'

'Up to and including Dan Short, and the Tumps?'

'Oh, yes, everyone.' Maude turned back to put out her cigarette. 'Although,' she paused, 'although, maybe the Tumps should be in the basement – better for bicycling.'

'They don't have any bicycles, Miss Maude, I wouldn't have thought they own bicycles.'

'Maybe they have no bicycles, but we do. My brothers all had bicycles, and they are in the basement. When all is said and done, that is one thing that a house as big as the Hall is good for, bicycling down long corridors . . .'

Branscombe thought for a minute. He didn't like to think of the Tumps, a rowdy, scruffy lot at the best of times, having first pick of the Beresford bicycle shed.

'May I, with the greatest respect, suggest that we put Dan and the Tumps up in the grooms' quarters above the stables, and we put my lot from the Court, the Lindsay brothers, in the basement here?'

Maude thought for a minute.

'I tell you what, Branscombe, why do I not appoint you billeting officer for the Hall? You make all the arrangements that you think appropriate once you have alerted the rector and Huggett. You can be billeting officer, while I myself will become head of nursing and so on, allocating beds and such matters that looking after a small community will doubtless bring.'

Branscombe turned. He could not help remembering that Miss Maude and Miss Jessica had always been known to differ in their attitudes to the idea of another war, Miss Jessica often being called a warmonger by so many, while Miss Maude, seeing no one, never reading a newspaper, going nowhere, had been more than happy to sit in her vast house living off her memories. Now it would seem that she had sprung to life. Perhaps she, like so many, had needed a war to feel wanted again? Although why she had chosen to cut Miss Daisy out of her life was quite another matter.

The brigadier stared at Maude. He was not used to dealing with women that he could not bully, and he was certainly not used to a woman with the look of a latter-day Britannia about her addressing him as if he was some kind of a nincompoop.

'I am sure, from the army-issue map that I have here, ma'am, that this house, the Hall, is included in the village of Twistleton, and it is the village of Twistleton that we have been ordered to requisition, preparatory to army training and exercises, as you know. Most villages near to the sea have been evacuated, in case of invasion, as you are doubtless aware. I can only suppose that the smallness of Twistleton, its size, has meant that your village has escaped notice to evacuate so far. Perhaps the authorities thought it too negligible, but from 0800 hours tomorrow Twistleton village will be requisitioned. I have been given my orders.'

Maude gave the brigadier her coldest look.

'Perhaps you have the authority to requisition Twistleton, the village, Brigadier, but with the greatest respect, the Hall is not part of the ancient village of Twistleton, and never has been.' She paused. 'If I may explain. In 1086, my ancestor Sir John Beresford was given the lands and grants to what is now known as Twistleton Hall and Twistleton Farm. If you look at these ancient maps, you will see that the people of Twistleton were ceded grazing rights then to the common land of their village under ancient law, and indeed it was the same in each village south of here. The Hall and the Farm, while bearing from the middle of the nineteenth century onwards – and purely for the sake of convenience for the new postal service – the name of Twistleton, have never, ever been part of the village. In fact, as you will see here, as Mr Huggett can point out to you . . .'

Maude looked across at poor Huggett, his face edged with grief above a black tie. She was only too thankful that she had written a condolence letter to him and his wife, for now that it seemed they were all in the soup, she needed to lean on him in a way in which she would never have done had times been different. Grief needed time and tranquillity, but there was a war on.

Whether by intent or design poor Huggett had brought with him a map of such age that it was immensely difficult to make out county, village or any other demarcation lines. He now pointed at a faded line with an authoritative finger, and assumed an expression of legal gravity, before beginning.

'Here you will see, from these lines, lands granted to Gwillem of Twussel in 1103 by King William. This land, in time, passed not to his son – I think he was killed on a crusade. At any rate, the land passed not to him, the only son of Gwillem, but to his cousin, one Bardolph. The land thereafter passed in 1184 to Thomas, and from Thomas to William, always known as the Saint, because he was said to have healing powers. At any rate, where was I? Yes, it was then that the family name changed to Berrenger, following titles and deeds passing on the marriage of William, son of William the Saint, to the heiress, one Mathilda, only daughter of Thomas Berrenger, and—'

But what happened after Mathilda, only daughter of Thomas, was lost to those present as the increasingly familiar sound of a siren rang out, and they all retreated to the basement.

Perhaps the brigadier had been cowed by the ancient map, or perhaps he had no taste for history, for he left the Hall an hour later, entirely dissatisfied with the stance that its owner had taken, but somehow realising that he could not prove that Maude's family home was indeed part of the village, and the Hall open to be requisitioned by the army.

'Well done, Huggett,' Maude said quietly. 'We have repulsed the enemy. At least we at the Hall have a temporary respite from his horrid invasion. I must do all I can to help the village, although for how long, we cannot know.'

For a few seconds Roger Huggett looked, if it was possible, even more sombre. Only he knew what few other people knew: that in her quiet way Maude Beresford had always been financially active in every area of the day-to-day life of Twistleton – helping out with anonymous donations whenever possible. The fact that she was now opening her home to the whole village in their hour of need was not surprising. Miss Beresford might be cold in manner and detached in voice, because she was very much of the old school, but he knew, if only from her letter of condolence about Joe, that she had a golden heart.

'If we have to pour boiling oil from the first-floor windows that man and his troops are not going to invade the Hall, Huggett. He has no right, he *shall* have no right here. War or no war, an Englishman's home is still his castle. Now, would you like a gin? You certainly deserve one.'

Roger accepted the gin and downed it really rather too quickly, while Maude sipped hers, quickly making sure to refill his glass.

'It's very difficult for you, at Holly House, I know, but we must all just bite on this particular bullet. The army will offer compensation, it will only be a question of time.'

Roger thought of his poor wife, already distraught at the loss of their youngest son. It would be only a matter of hours before poor Susan would have to come up to the Hall, the owner of a few suitcases and not much more.

'Some places, I hear, have been given so little time to evacuate their homes that the army have even requisitioned their pets. My wife was talking of having to put the dogs down, but—'

'Tell her she must do no such thing, Huggett,' Maude interrupted, appalled. 'She must bring them here. Whatever happens we must save what we can before the ghastly dawn of tomorrow. But we must hurry, Huggett, we must indeed. The Cottages alone will need our help in such matters as livestock. There will be Dan Short's hens, and Jean Shaw—'

Roger turned away abruptly at the mention of Jean's name. Maude had heard the rumour about young Joe Huggett's marriage to Jean Shaw, from Bowles of all people. The maid had come to take her leave of Miss Maude, in order to go into the armaments factory near Bramsfield, but of course Maude hadn't believed her story about Jean. It was not Maude's way to listen to hen-house gossip; yet seeing Huggett's face, she now believed that Bowles might have been entirely correct, and that Jean Shaw was indeed both pregnant, and a widow.

Maude felt a momentary sadness, but it was only

momentary as there was too much to do to allow feelings to get in the way. What she could do, and what she would do, was to ask Branscombe to put aside the best bedroom on the first floor for the poor girl. In the circumstances, that was the least they could offer her.

Freddie was travelling to London to see a patient in a newly set-up burns unit. Daisy had just flown a plane to Scotland and was facing a very long return trip indeed; while Laura had been sent to Norfolk to take charge at a recruiting centre, so none of them knew what was taking place at Twistleton.

Neither did anyone care to try to get hold of Jessica and Blossom, since they seemed to change their lodgings every few days – bomb dodging. All anyone knew was that they were still slaving away at the aircraft factory.

Despite the mind-bending, back-breaking, agonising days spent painting aircraft, or slotting metal, the pause in the German assault that had come from the skies had given renewed energy to the girls and women in the factories. It was as if someone from above was patting them on their heads and saying, 'Without all that you are doing, and have done, we would be Hitler's lackeys.'

In fact Jessica had taken up lodging in an old inn some miles from the factory. It was said to be haunted, but no spirit had, as she now often joked, 'a ghost of a chance of waking me up after my shift'.

If she was on dawn shift, which she often was, she was able to throw herself into the pub bar, and enjoy a drink, always providing there were any to order.

Too often there would be a sign saying, 'NO BEER. WAITING DELIVERY', or another saying, 'SORRY FOR THE INCONVENIENCE. UNEXPLODED BOMB IN THE ROAD'.

The quiet while a bomb was being dealt with outside in the road was, indeed, the silence of the grave. Happily, the second time it happened, there was beer to be had, and she and the other regulars were able to toast Phil and his friends from bomb disposal, who had brought about a happy outcome.

Phil was older than the rest of his team, but nevertheless he had that same bright-eyed look that a friend had told Jessica the young officers of the Great War had possessed, before they went over the top. This particular night, after a successful lift of an unexploded bomb in the neighbouring town, the little bar was filled with young men, eager to drink away the reality of what might have happened.

'Your hands had a bad time of it, in that place?'

Phil nodded at Jessica's hands, which were now so marked that she had to wear gloves.

'I am afraid so. Still able to hold a glass though—'

Phil watched Jessica put the glass down, and handed her a cigarette.

'And a cigarette?'

Jessica nodded.

'That, too,' she agreed, laughing suddenly.

They started to talk, and as they did so, Jessica realised that although Phil might be ten or perhaps even as much as twelve years younger than she was, and not from the same background, nevertheless they might as well have been born in the same year. They talked, as everyone did nowadays, about everything *except* the war. They talked about the films they had seen and the books they had read, about travelling abroad – carefully leaving out the words 'before the war' – and by the end of two rounds of drinks, and even more cigarettes, Jessica was quite sure that whatever else happened, she had to make love to him.

As with Esmond, there would probably only be time for it to happen once – and as with Esmond, it would be something that would remain with her always. As also with Esmond, she did not care what people thought, or that the publican winked at her as she passed him to go upstairs, Phil following her, after a statutory few minutes.

What did it matter? There was a war on, and she knew what war did: it took people for ever. So when they were with you, you made sure that you made them happy, and when they were not with you, you knew that you had at least brought them some last-minute love.

Afterwards – when break of day had dawned and nudged them both into leaving each other's arms, and going back to the war – instead of Jessica's thoughts reaching out to Twistleton Court and darling old Branscombe, to Freddie and the dogs, instead of drawing comfort, as she usually did, from her memory of the old place with its soft stone, its benevolent aspect, and its delicate air of having always been there, she found that she was only remembering the last few hours of the night. The factory work might be cruel in every way, but as her badly gashed and bruised hands reached out to push open the dark door that led to the factory floor, as she faced the start of yet another smoke-filled twelve hours, of yet another truly back-breaking day, another day of community singing to the sound of *Workers' Playtime*, she found she was remembering only the passion and tenderness of the night.

Chapter Nine

While the sun showed still weakly on the horizon, the first rumble of army tanks was heard in the village below the Hall, the ominous noise rising above the sound of the distant sea and the gathering wind and rain, above the sound of people pushing anything from hand carts to wheelbarrows up to the Hall, their only place of refuge against the coming invaders.

Maude had been up for some few hours, busily making up beds with poor grieving Susan Huggett. Bedroom after bedroom, and in an awkward silence punctuated only by small instructions from Maude, they carefully observed the usual routine, moving from room to room, making hospital corners at the side of each top sheet, and equally carefully straightening all the blackout blinds at the windows, not to mention dusting all the mahogany furniture.

'That is the last bed we need to make up in the house, I think, Mrs Huggett. Branscombe has been busy in the basement, so that area will not need us. He has found any amount of furniture from the outhouses in the stables, and is dragging them in for the Lindsay boys, while Dan Short and Mr and Mrs Budgeon and the rest are taking up the stable flats.'

Susan Huggett nodded dully, and then made a sighing sound.

'Why those Lindsay brothers have not been sent packing back to the East End, I simply do not know. You could use that basement flat for other, better purposes, Miss Beresford, better purposes than for the benefit of those slummy boys.' Susan turned away, her face a picture of misery above her black blouse, and her black suit . . . 'There is all too little *thought* being given to us, the village proper. All too little, really there is. Our homes have been taken from us by this wretched army. And what a thing for us to know that we have been occupied not by the Nazis, but by our own army!'

'You are having a very bad time of it, Mrs Huggett,' Maude said quietly. 'But we will all help you as much as we can. In my experience—' She paused before repeating, 'As much as we can help, we will.' Just for a second she felt more than unusually helpless.

How could she help a woman who had just lost her son?

But Susan turned away. What experience could a woman like Maude Beresford have had of loss? She had never had a child! She could not know what it was to truly grieve.

'In my experience . . .' Maude carried on with

dignity. 'In my experience,' she said again, still to Susan's back, 'work and more work is the only answer to grief, as Doctor Johnson once said.'

'Doctor Johnson.'

Susan repeated the name in such a contemptuous manner, as if the famous literary figure was a family doctor with a bad reputation, that this time it was Maude who turned away. She left Susan listening to the news *'read by Alvar Lidell'* – thinking, as she did so, how very strange it was to hear announcers giving out their names.

She went in search of Branscombe and found him arguing with Dan Short . . .

'They will be perfectly happy in the stables, Mr Dan—'

'They will be no such thing.'

Maude took Branscombe aside.

'Look here, Branscombe, if Dan wants the Tumps with him in the house or whatever, let's see to it. Anything for peace when in the midst of war . . .'

'No, no, nothing to do with the Tumps, *they've* gone to their nan in Isleworth only this morning, no, this is his *hens*. He wants the *hens* in with him, in the flat, don't trust them not to be rustled by the troops.'

'Well, he does have a point, Branscombe. The troops will take one look at his hens and think only of bread sauce and sausagemeat.'

'It's not hygienic, Miss Maude,' Branscombe said, lowering his voice. 'You know how much hens do, and then it's not as if they don't walk it about, and that's before Dan starts doing the same.'

Despite the steady downpour the atmosphere in the large, square stable yard, with its old stone sets and its arched entrance, was thick with resentment. Maude could see at once that the housing of the hens had become a matter of The Cottages versus the Hall, and that would never do.

Dan continued putting up a steady defence of his hens.

'I'm not putting my girls in there, Mr Branscombe,' he stated, nodding at the stables. 'Not no how, Mr Branscombe, not no how, not never . . . They'll be targets for every wassailing soldier, not to mention every fox in the county, what with no huntin' and no nothin'. I might as well wring their necks and eat 'em myself. Foxes can jump stable doors, as Miss Beresford here's old hunter used to do, I'm a mind to remembering, as I am sure she does.'

Branscombe shrugged his shoulders, his one good eye shooting a desperate look at the mistress of the Hall as he did so.

'Mr Short can't seem to understand that living with hens is not going to be what is wanted here, Miss Maude. What about the others? That is what I think we should be thinking of, the others what are going to be living here too, in the other flats and cottages. They'll be kept awake by the cock crowing at dawn, any old how, I am thinking.'

Maude knew Dan of old. He had always been immovable, entrenched in the old ways.

'I don't see why Dan can't have chickens in with

him if he so wishes. The hall of the flat is quite large enough, isn't it, Branscombe? After all, if he puts a coop in there, he can at least go to bed at night knowing they can come to no harm, and then he can let them out into the yard during the day. No harm done, I shouldn't have thought.'

Branscombe shrugged his shoulders, yet again, and sighed, and then found he really did not care if Dan put the hens in his bed with him, he just hoped that he wouldn't have to clear up the feathers and the rest of the mess when, at the end of the war, Dan went back to The Cottages.

'With Christmas all too soon, by 1941 there'll be half the countryside coming after my girls, mark my words,' Dan went on, glowering at both Branscombe and Maude as if he suspected they might be about to put a chicken in the Hall oven.

'We may well not even be here at Christmas, Dan,' Maude murmured, turning away. 'Let us go to church and pray that we will be, but we cannot and should not take that particular idea for granted, as I am sure you will agree?'

Still as busy as ever on ops, Daisy had found that as far as the second Christmas of the war was concerned she had drawn a pink ticket, and was able to snatch a bit of precious leave before returning to her duties.

As she drove into London to try to do some shopping, and to meet up with Freddie, Aurelia and Laura at the basement flat Gervaise had lent her, it occurred to her that wartime London did not look very different from the countryside now – what with sheep grazing in Green Park and vegetables flourishing not only in the parks, but in every front garden. So when she galloped down the basement steps Daisy was unsurprised to find Laura proudly showing off a cabbage plucked from her own front garden. She was also busy in the tiny cupboard that passed as a kitchen, already wielding a saucepan and starting to make what seemed to Daisy to be a particularly sad-looking soup.

'I am not touching that, Laura ducky,' Daisy told her, putting her arm round her. 'Not with a bargepole, let alone a spoon.'

Laura looked at Daisy calmly.

'It does look filthy. Even so, I think you will find that it will fill a corner tonight.' She glanced down at her watch. 'The other two are bound to be late, they're queueing for presents. Freddie's mad keen on getting the Lindsay boys things like Meccano that they very likely won't even know what to do with – bless her.'

A scrabbling at the door announced the late-comers, Freddie with arms full of Meccano that she had indeed been queueing for since dawn, and Aurelia with some soap and talcum powder for Hotty, now under house arrest and being deprived of all the little luxuries that she had always taken for granted.

'So now everyone's going to have luncheon on me,' Daisy announced. 'I have enough coupons saved to feed the entire population of Twistleton, let alone the members of that oh-so-exclusive club, ye Daisy Club, so fall in behind, it's off to scoff we go!'

'Don't you mean everyone at Twistleton *Hall*, Daisy?'

Daisy took the stub out of her cigarette holder and carefully put the tiny bit that remained of it in the ashtray.

'I certainly do not mean everyone at the Hall, since I am *persona absolutely non grata* at the Hall. Why would I mean everyone at the Hall?'

The other three looked at each other, and then at Daisy.

'Didn't you get my letter, Daisy?' Freddie asked. 'I wrote to everyone care of their lodgings, about Twistleton. I sent yours here.'

Daisy finished powdering her small delicately made retroussé nose, before snapping the compact shut.

'No, I did not hear from anyone until Laura rang my lodgings last night. Why? Is there something that I should know? Has Aunt Maude run off with Branscombe, or taken to driving tanks?' She said this flippantly, looking from one face to the other – but not at Laura's.

It was almost impossible for Daisy to look at Laura. She did not know whether David had even told Laura of their meeting, let alone anything else; because of this she glanced with determined nonchalance from Aurelia to Freddie, and back again, only realising as she did so that the expressions on *their* two faces were fluctuating between gravity and embarrassment, before changing to uncharacteristic bitterness and fury.

'You mean you don't *know* what's happened to Twistleton?'

'Well, I know that most of the evacuees have returned back to their mums because like Johnny Town Mouse they found the country too quiet. Mmm. Now what else? Well, I know that Freddie here has been a Trojan helping in the hospital – not to mention acting as an ambulance service when that bomb dropped on the Wychford canning factory after the East End raid, and—'

'Shut *up*, Daisy, you're being de trop, truly you are,' Laura snapped suddenly, which immediately gave Daisy the feeling that Laura *did* know about her and David Moreton.

'Twistleton,' Freddie said, her expression serious, 'has been requisitioned by the army, and Miss Beresford and everyone else think that it will not be long – what with regular mortar practice and tanks on exercise, and having to practise urban fighting, oh, you know, all those things that it seems the army have to practise – before the whole place has been razed to the ground.'

Daisy stared at the three faces that were now staring back at her.

'I'm afraid I don't believe you, you must have got it wrong,' she said slowly. 'I flew over Twisters only a few days ago, on my way to "somewhere secret", and it was very much still there, I know it was.'

'It may have been, but not for long, it won't be, if any of the other requisitioned villages are anything to go by. As a matter of fact, none of us know why Twistleton wasn't cordoned off years before, but it seems it was too small and tucked away to matter, with too little access from the sea. The beach is so narrow. Somehow it got overlooked – until now, that is . . .'

Daisy shut the front door again, took out a cigarette, placed it in her holder, and lit it.

'Tell me all, fellow members of the Daisy Club, concealing absolutely nothing,' she said, looking embarrassed as she realised how flippant she must sound. 'Come on, let me have it,' she said slowly through the holder firmly wedged between her teeth, a recent habit, because, somehow, when her teeth were clenched on the holder, she felt, for no good reason, a little more able to cope.

'It happened overnight,' Freddie said quietly, while they were all still standing in a strange little queue by the front door, as if they half-expected it to be opened and a parcel to be handed out to them by a beaming butcher or fishmonger.

'Oh well, let's go and have luncheon anyway, before we all proceed to Twistleton,' Daisy commanded. 'After all, when all is said and done, it is Christmas.'

This time it was the turn of the other three to look embarrassed, waiting for the penny to drop that the Hall was open to all of them, but not to Daisy.

'I suppose you might be able to spend Christmas

in the country with your godfather?' Freddie offered, as they walked round to the restaurant.

At last Freddie could see that the penny had indeed dropped and Daisy had realised that *they* were all going to be hugger-mugger at the Hall, but without her, because she had been banished.

Daisy, teeth still clenched on her cigarette holder, walked a little faster.

'Oh yes,' she agreed. 'Of course there is Gervaise, but I heard on the grapevine that there's a new girl in town, his driver, and they are having a bit of a time of it, between whatever else is happening, or not happening – and I daresay she might not want a goddaughter hanging around the Christmas tree. But I can always ask him. He's such a brick, I'm sure he'll extend the godfatherly hand to me.'

She smiled gaily at Freddie.

'Come on, let's scoff!'

Freddie and Branscombe had been put in charge of the lower regions of the Hall, and so it was up to them to invite everyone downstairs for Christmas luncheon, which they did, all, that is, except for Maude, who they imagined would still eat her festive luncheon upstairs amidst the portraits of her ancestors, the old glass, the silver wine-coolers, and the mahogany furniture.

'As you know, Miss Maude is one of the old school,' Branscombe explained tactfully to Freddie, but Freddie was not impressed.

'She is hardly older than Aunt Jessica, Branscombe, and you know it.'

'Miss Jessica is expected back for Christmas?'

'No, Branscombe, neither she nor Blossom think that they should come back. I wrote to her again about the army taking over Twistleton and the Court being used as headquarters for one thing and another; and this time she did get the letter, and she wrote back.'

Freddie pulled out a letter from her apron pocket, and passed it to Branscombe, who shook his head, arms covered in flour, up to his elbows trying to make wartime dumplings.

'I'd rather not, Miss Freddie. You know how it is; bad enough trying to read this Marguerite Patten recipe, let alone Miss Jessica's handwriting. Barbed-wire entanglements was how her brothers used to describe Miss Jessica's handwriting, barbed-wire entanglements!'

Freddie put aside the turnips she was trying to peel, and started to read the letter out aloud to Branscombe as he ploughed away at what looked like a really rather odd mix.

Dearest Freddie,

Well, Blossom and I were really sorry to hear about the village, but war is war, and I daresay there'll be something to come back to, when it's all over. The poor old Court will probably survive because the officers will be kind to it, and we'll just have to piece it together after this is all over. Miss Maude sent Blossom a very nice letter from Algy

293

and Bertie, and Blossom was glad to hear that they were getting on so well with the pugs, especially dear old Trump, who is not famous for liking newcomers!

Freddie looked up at that, and she and Branscombe both smiled. 'Dogs first, as usual with those two! Now where was I? Oh yes . . .'

Freddie cleared her throat, and went on reading.

The work is very hard on the hands so I have to remember to wear my gloves when not in the factory, for anyone seeing my hands as they are now would call out the Red Cross! I often think of everyone hugger-mugger at the Hall now, and how you must all be pulling together as we are here. Don't forget to give darling old Boy his bran mash on Sunday nights, or he will not thrive and pull the pony trap up Kingstarte Hill as he should do. I daresay Jean will be able to spare him something, or Chittlethorpe?

I have to say Blossom and I could do with a bran mash, too! Now, Freddie darling, take care, and remember not to look beyond each day as it comes, that is what we do here. Blossom sends everyone her love, as I do,
Your loving Aunt Jessie

There was a small silence as Branscombe frowned at his hand-written recipe, taken off the wireless the previous day. Then he said, in a considered voice, 'Well, I daresay, with so many mouths to feed over Christmas, it is just as well that Miss Jessica and Miss Blossom are staying put, staying where they are, and I daresay, too, they'll get the day off at Christmas, although knowing Miss Jessica she won't take it . . .'

Freddie nodded at the turnips, which somehow seemed further away, a little more blurred, since she had first started to read the letter aloud to Branscombe.

Christmas would not be Christmas without Aunt Jessica and Blossom, but they were doing the right thing, saving petrol, saving themselves the long journey, working to save Britain, if not – as far as they all knew – the civilised world.

'What are we going to do for the smaller boys' presents, Branscombe?' Freddie asked, anxious to change the subject.

'Miss Maude asked me just the same thing, only an hour or two ago. I told her that you had queued for the Meccano for Alec and Dick, but that we were a bit flat for ideas for Tom. Johnnie, as you know, won't be here for Christmas. I thought it might be a plan to go up to the attics, there'll surely be something for Tom's age group up there, I daresay. Although I don't think Miss Maude has paid it a visit since before the Great War.'

Freddie thought back to the rainy days spent in the attics at the Court, and how the Huggett boys, when they came to tea with her, used to love to play sardines, just so they could go up there, fighting their way past the three-legged chairs, and the old magic lanterns, stumbling over dusty trunks, and large wooden cases that held, well – who knew what?

'Oh my goodness, what was that noise?' Freddie started, and Branscombe looked up, an expression first of fear then of embarrassment on his face.

'What a thing to be so scared of your own troops! Miss Freddie, you look as white as a freshly laundered sheet!'

'I don't trust that lot. Come on, Branscombe, under the kitchen table with us!'

'That's mortars, I expect, Miss Freddie. They're doing an exercise through the village – there's a visiting general, or some such, coming. I heard it on the grapevine.'

Freddie straightened up, and her mouth tightened.

'On exercise through the village is a very tactful way of saying that they are busy blowing the place up, Branscombe, and we both know it.' She wiped her hands on her apron. 'I went past The Spread Eagle yesterday evening. It was crammed, but *crammed*, with drunken soldiers. I wanted to fetch a new wheel for the trap, and I remembered that there was a spare in the tack room at the back of the place, but could I get through? What a fuss! I had to show my identity card, I had to ask to speak to old Mr Justin, if only so he could vouch for me, and then, at the end of it all, I had to sign for the wheel, which was mine, anyway! I mean, really. I cannot tell you how rude those men were, and that was before I was confronted by the sergeant who, well, never mind, just let's say you wouldn't want him to be eating Christmas luncheon with you. By the time they'd finished with me I felt like saying what the Duke of Wellington did about his troops—'

'He didn't know what they did to the French, but they scared him all right, didn't they?' Branscombe smiled in such an affectionate way it sounded to Freddie as if he was talking about an old friend. 'The good old Iron Duke, we need him now, don't we? If it wasn't for Winston . . .' He sighed, and started to roll his mixture into dumplings. How he had got his hands on so much suet from the butcher was nobody's business, and nobody's business was how it was going to stay. Just thank God that he had.

Later, Maude was waiting for him. She had just got in from the hospital, where she was now helping out as often as she could, not minding what she did: cleaning floors, cleaning bathrooms, anything and everything that she could put her hands to. Reading to patients, checking on the young nurses who were so unprofessional that if there was an air-raid warning they were hard put to remember to wash their hands before they came back on the wards. Of course, since Dunkirk, everything was running short, all of what was necessary going, as was only proper, to mend the rescued soldiers.

'I thought we ought to do a roll call.' As Branscombe looked appalled, she went on. 'No, no, not call everyone together here. No, they are all far too busy. No, just you and I do a *list* of who is here now, or expected for Christmas, or else we will lose count of who and what we are meant to be doing, and how they are, and so on. Now, I am at the hospital for most of the week. I don't know about you, but I am losing count of who is here and who is not.'

She picked up a list she had previously started to make, and which Branscombe could see announced at the top *'Wychford Hospital Do Not Remove'*, a command that obviously did not apply to Miss Maude of Twistleton Hall.

'Very well,' she said, sitting down at her antique desk, and taking up her old ink pen from its silver holder. 'Very well, here we are. We'll leave aside the villagers for the moment, and start at the top with ourselves, and so on. We have obviously, yourself, myself, and Miss Freddie. Miss Aurelia Smith-Jones and Miss Laura Hambleton, who are both expected, although not until Christmas Eve. Miss Valentyne and Miss Blossom are not expected on account of the length of the journey, and being needed for the work at the factory. Miss Jean, or rather *Mrs* Jean Huggett, and Mr and Mrs Roger Huggett—'

'No, Mr and Mrs Roger Huggett went back, this morning, to her people in Yorkshire. Provided they can get through the snow, they will be there for the duration, if not longer, by the time the army has finished with Holly House. It has come to our notice that Brigadier MacNaughton has a woman who passes as his housekeeper in there with him, and if it is true that an army marches on its stomach, he won't be marching very far – he definitely hasn't chosen her for her cooking.'

Maude looked up at that.

'Huggett never said anything to me about going. They have left the Hall, and with a grandchild on the way?' Maude thought for a moment. 'How did they get the petrol?'

'No one knows, but there was talk downstairs in the kitchen of Mr Huggett having swapped all the foodstuffs from the larder at Holly House for enough petrol to get them up to Yorkshire. As to the grandchild, it appears that they are not going to recognise it, if and when it arrives, not now, not ever.'

'If and when it arrives, Branscombe?'

Branscombe looked matter-of-fact.

'You can't be too sure with babies, the little that I know about such things . . . At any rate, as I understand it, whatever happens they cannot accept Miss Jean as being one of them, most particularly since Mr Joe will not be coming back. She has never been, nor will she ever be, accepted, it seems . . .'

'I see.' Maude looked down the list. 'So, where are we? Ah, yes. We have Mr and Mrs Budgeon, and their evacuees—'

'They've gone from the stables, Miss Maude. Mrs Budgeon found being at the Hall too countrified for her tastes, she is just not used to the sound of birds and that, only really likes what she's used to – the sound of trains. So she is making do with them and living in the ladies' waiting room at the station, and using the station facilities, and the evacuees that she took in, well, they only wanted to be with their mother for Christmas, so off they went. Before the army came here, yes, off they went back to East Ham.' He paused, starting to count on his fingers the rest of the people currently housed in the stables. 'Then there is Mr Dan, and the two land girls, and Miss Jean. Miss Freddie and myself, and of course—'

'I have already noted that, Branscombe.'

Maude looked down the list.

'Not as many as I thought there would be, considering, Branscombe, not nearly as many as we started with, at any rate.' She frowned. 'Oh, but then there are the four Lindsay brothers, of course.'

Branscombe cleared his throat yet again.

'Only three Lindsay brothers, I think you'll find, as of the next few days, Miss Maude. Their mother wants young Johnny back with her. Doesn't mind leaving the others, but young Johnny must go back to be with her, to be with his mum in Peckham.'

Maude frowned.

'Does little Johnny want to go back and be with his mother in Peckham?'

'As a matter of fact, no, he doesn't. As a matter of fact, I think it is the last thing that little Johnny wants.'

There was an even longer pause, and then Maude said, 'I'm going up to the attic in a minute, Branscombe, where I hope to find some suitable gifts for those children who are left to us. I am sure there must still be some toys, toys that belonged to my brothers, that will bring a little joy to those poor boys.'

Branscombe had never heard Miss Maude mention her brothers before. Like Miss Jessica, the subject of those lost in the Great War was never touched upon, except on the appropriate day of the year when everyone lost was remembered by the whole nation.

'I can come up—'

'There's no need—'

'I can hold the torch for you while you look, if you would like?'

'That is much appreciated, Branscombe.'

They climbed up to the third floor, which had once housed as many as six or seven young maids, all working in the house for the Beresfords. They made their way through the dark, empty rooms, devoid of anything except floorboards and blackout blinds, to an end door, which opened on to the place where all Miss Maude's family heirlooms and mementoes were housed.

'I haven't been up here since – since, well, for many years, you know, Branscombe,' Maude murmured, making her way past the usual medley of lamps and trunks, to where there was an old cobweb-festooned rocking horse.

Maude stared at her old friend. She and Roderick had loved Paintbox, as they had christened him. She went up to the horse, and by the light of Branscombe's torch she took out a handkerchief

301

from her uniform pocket and dusted his face with it. She wiped his nostrils and his mouth, not to mention the insides of his ears, so expertly, as if her handkerchief were a stable sponge, that for a few seconds Branscombe was quite sure that Paintbox was a real pony.

'There, Paintbox, there you are.' Maude stood back. 'There now, I think we can get you down the stairs for the children to ride on you.'

Branscombe looked at Paintbox. The only boy that he would suit, even vaguely, would be his Johnny, and Johnny was going back to Peckham.

'I think they're a little old for Paintbox, Miss Maude. I think maybe we should be looking for something to amuse older boys.'

Maude nodded, her expression serious.

'I daresay you are right, Branscombe. Besides, boys are never quite as keen on the horses and the ponies as girls, are they? Although Mr Roderick did love Paintbox so.' She moved on to a line of old trunks, only stopping when she reached one with the initials R.B.B. – Roderick's old school trunk. She remembered how she had helped her mother pack up all the boys' trunks: each one with their initials stamped on the lid held their old school uniforms, their toys, their school reports, every-thing as neat as pie.

'Ah, now here are some things that boys will like all right, wouldn't you say, Branscombe?'

'I would say,' Branscombe agreed. 'I would, in-deed.'

'There is much to do to get some of these

ready and repainted, Branscombe, much to do indeed.'

Daisy had been as bright as a button throughout luncheon with Freddie and the rest, but Aurelia had noticed that she looked suddenly, and uncharacteristically, sad as she kissed them all goodbye.

'Stupid old woman, Miss Beresford,' Aurelia muttered to Laura a few days later, as they met up briefly for an evening drink. 'I mean to say, locking poor Daisy out of her own home, and at Christmas, and all that. I mean to say, with a war on you would think there would be some sort of reconciliation. Honestly, families can be such a pill.' She stopped grumbling as she realised that this time it was Laura's face that was crumpling. 'Oh, sorry, Laura, I forgot your lot are still on the away list, still AWOL. I am sorry, it quite slipped my mind.'

'Why wouldn't it? Besides, it is of no matter. Knowing my father, he's probably holed up in some swanky hotel, eating and drinking and leading the life of Riley.' Laura tried to smile, and failed. 'Thank heavens, there has been too much to think about to worry about them. Either they've both got through to neutral Portugal, or they haven't. I know Dora has relatives all over the Continent, so they *should* be all right. It just might be nice to hear from someone. Except I have quite given up worrying, because with all this happening—' The wail of the sirens started and they began to pelt down the area steps of the Hambletons' flat in Grosvenor Square. 'What possible good does it do?'

'I'm quite sure I should be fire-watching to-night, not sitting under a table with you having a brandy,' Aurelia confessed, some time later, as the all-clear sounded. 'Only trouble is the place I was meant to be watching from is, as of yesterday night, only a ton of rubble. Cheers.'

They clinked glasses, and drank.

'So we'll meet again at the Hall for Christmas, my dear?'

'If we're allowed in. Apparently it's all cordoned off.'

'I can get us in.' Aurelia nodded importantly. 'With my new pass I can get us in anywhere you want. That's one of the good things about the new job that Guy has shoehorned me into accepting: you get a pass that makes even the military police wave you through!'

Guy himself, while still working secretly for the Bros at Operation Z, had, with what he called 'my other hat on', grown fed up with trying to infiltrate society and send on information of which no one ever seemed to make any good use, so he had taken himself off to entertain workers of every kind, factory workers in particular, everyone, all round the country, singing and playing sketches to the entertainment-starved population.

'They far prefer to listen to the wireless, but I try to

pretend I am not noticing,' he had written to Aurelia, after making sure that she was posted on, with a recommendation from him, to take up a position at Special Operations Europe in Baker Street.

Since Aurelia had lived abroad, on and off, all her young life, travelling through Europe in the company of a young nanny, who then became her governess *en titre*, as it were, she was pretty nearly bilingual in both French and Spanish. No surprise, then, that she was placed in the French section in SOE.

It was a bit of a change, to say the least, to go from working for a theatrical personality such as Guy Athlone, to sitting with a drawer full of cyanide tablets, one of which was always handed out to all agents before they were dropped into France. But of course she could say nothing of this to Laura, who was still whizzing around London in the FANY tradition, doing everything and anything that was needed.

'Listen, let's go to the Hall together, that way we can share my car, you can get us through with your pass – don't forget to wangle one for me, too, if you can – and everything will be tickety-boo.'

They parted, kissing each other fondly, then Laura made her way to her car, Aurelia back to Baker Street, both of them passing such depressing sights of devastation on the way that Laura found herself staring at the pavement, at her feet making their way through rubble and glass, passing everyone else doing the same as firemen played hoses on burning buildings. They all pretended that they didn't know that there were dead people inside crushed houses, or living ones still trapped, and that they were useless to help, that they just had to get on, because not to get on would be no help to the war effort.

'So, Johnny,' Maude said gravely. 'You are to go back to be with your mum for Christmas?'

Johnny looked up at what seemed to him to be a very old lady – despite the fact that Maude was hardly past her fiftieth birthday.

'Yes, miss.'

'And your mum is to meet you at the station?'

'Yes, miss.'

'You like trains, don't you, Johnny?'

'Yes, miss.'

'I thought so.' Maude turned back to the Christmas tree that had been placed, as always, by tradition, in the hall. 'Father Christmas, knowing that you were going back to Peckham to be with your dear mum, left you an early present. Would you like it, Johnny?'

Johnny looked up at Branscombe, who nodded encouragingly, so Johnny deemed it safe to look back up again at Maude and nod.

'Yes, please, miss.'

Maude bent down and retrieved a present wrapped in old wallpaper found, along with so much else, at the back of the laundry cupboards. She presented the parcel to Johnny, who scrabbled at it eagerly, eventually exposing a box, faded by the years, but inside of which was a beautiful train and carriage.

Johnny looked at it in silence. Maude, knowing something of what he must be feeling, was also silent. Branscombe frowned, wishing that Miss Jessica, who had taken such an interest in young Johnny, was there to see the little chap's face.

Johnny looked up at Maude.

'Father Christmas is a good un, int' he, miss?'

'I think he knew you liked trains, didn't he, Johnny?'

Johnny was silent once more, clutching the box against his thin little chest.

'I fink so, miss.'

'Did you put that you would like a train on your letter to Father Christmas, the one that you posted up the kitchen chimney?'

Johnny nodded, leaning closer to Branscombe.

'I dun want to go back from 'ere,' he announced, in a low voice.

'You want to see your mum, I expect, and you will be going in a motor car with a kind lady. And remember your mum, she wants to see you.'

Silence greeted this statement, such a long silence that it gave Maude time to think.

'I know why you wanted that train, Johnny,' she told him, eventually. 'It was because you knew it would bring you back to us, wasn't it?'

Johnny looked up at this, and after a second he nodded.

'You knew that a train may take you to Peckham, but it will bring you back to the Hall, to us here, too, won't it? That's why you wanted a train, wasn't it?'

Johnny nodded, and for a second the sad look in his eyes changed.

'Yes, miss,' he agreed.

'Come on then, young man, the lady from the WVS is out there waiting for you, just arrived, I see. She's going to take charge of you, and she's probably got some sweeties set aside for the journey. I heard someone say those volunteer ladies have always got a sweetie or two in their handbags. And there's another little boy with her, he's probably like you, going back to see his mum at Christmas, so that'll be good, won't it?'

The sad little duo turned away, and walked down the hall, and out into the bitter winter day, Johnny on his way back to who knew what.

Maude turned away. War was a blasted thing, a really awful, blasted thing, but then she said silently to God *'sorry for swearing'* but really, it was true, war was a blasted, blasted thing.

Of course Gervaise would have been too diplomatic to turn Daisy away. Knowing this only too well, Daisy was far too proud to admit to anyone that she was going to be on her own at Christmas, so as the cold, cold weather set in, bringing with it yet more misery, Daisy crouched in her basement flat, the air so damp and miserable that once or twice she thought it might have been cosier, and certainly more cheerful, to spend Christmas down the Underground singing and making tea, helping babies being born, anything rather than being on her own at Christmas.

Before they went down to the Hall for their Christmas, Laura and Aurelia were due to drop by for a shot of gin, and a giggle.

There was much that was new about the little basement flat, not least the sign above the door.

It read: 'THE DAISY CLUB. MEMBERS ONLY! NO NAZIS!'

Where Daisy had found the paint to do what she had done, or managed to borrow or steal the bright rugs, or the cushions, they none of them thought it quite right to ask, but from the moment they walked down into the basement, duly signing the new visitors' book, it felt just a little like being back at Twistleton Court in their shared flat in the stables.

'How have you done this? Have you found an Indian gentleman with a monkey across the way to send you all these lovely things?'

Daisy laughed.

'That is exactly what I have done, Laura ducks, and no mistake.'

'You've made this place look like a home from home, Daisy. Despite the fact that two doors down has gone, and opposite is no more, it is so cheerful here you wouldn't even know it,' Aurelia stated, as Laura crouched by the one bar of the electric fire, practically burning her still-gloved fingers on it, in her urgency to get warm.

Daisy, who had been too busy taking coats

309

and making stiff drinks to notice the change in Aurelia, looked up quickly.

'Apparently it *was* a bit noisy last night, and we were lucky the gas mains didn't blow up,' she admitted. 'So much so that when Gervaise rang and told me, I thought I might stay on ops rather than pelt down here, but then I thought I'd cock a snook at Hitler, and I strong-armed Gervaise's people upstairs to lend me things that he will never notice have gone AWOL, make it as much like Twisters Court as perfectly possible. Cheers!'

'Bottoms up, whatever that means! I say, don't let's ask!'

They all clinked glasses, and it was only as they did so that Daisy really took in Aurelia's wan face.

'Why the look of the drowning maiden, Relia? Nothing happened to Guy, has it?' she asked as Laura downed her gin and left them to go to the telephone in the upstairs hall, in an attempt to call headquarters about something that was concerning her.

'Guy.' Aurelia said his name so flatly that Daisy knew at once that her passion for the famous man must have abated considerably. 'No, nothing to do with Guy Athlone, Daisy, no.' She looked away, struggling to speak, not knowing what to say, but having knocked back her gin too quickly she burst out: 'It's being in SOE. I shouldn't say this, not a word, because I mean they are all great people, of course, great people, and a great mix. And one thing and another. But. But. Well.

310

You *see* everything. Maps! People there, and not there.'

Daisy looked at her, her expression sombre.

'It's bad, isn't it?'

They both knew how bad.

'It's not as if they – you know. I mean, every time I hand them—' She stopped. 'I shouldn't be saying this . . .'

'Don't worry, I haven't heard,' Daisy assured her. 'I'll just telephone the War Office and have you arrested once Laura's through with the phone.'

Aurelia leaned forward, glass in hand, which Daisy instantly filled.

'Every time I have to give them their Goodnight Vienna pill, as I call it, I keep hoping that they'll take the damn thing, whatever happens. I even find myself praying for that, praying for that for *them*, that they will have time to take their Goodnight Vienna, not be captured. So where is the sin of Judas, then, Daisy? I mean to say, and I really hate to say it, but I don't believe in much any more, and I don't think I ever will, not after this. It's turned everything upside down for me, truly it has.'

'Well, it would,' Daisy said, and she put out a hand and touched her arm.

Aurelia had always been a bit of an hysteric, the least likely of all people to cope with so much that happened in a war.

'That is what I keep hoping, that they have time to take their pill, have time,' Aurelia repeated.

'Well, you would,' Daisy agreed, again. 'After

311

all, that really is a better fate, to die by your own hand rather than – well, anything else . . .'

'I have been trying not to think about any of them, trying not to remember anything. Once I leave the place for a few hours' kip, I put it out of my mind, what they looked like before they went off, that kind of thing. And I was doing quite well, until, well, until the awful news came through!'

Daisy turned away. Whatever it was, she didn't want to know.

'You had better stop there, Relia, or we really will both end up with our heads on a spike above Tower Bridge.'

Aurelia looked shattered. It was true. It was treason to speak of what she knew, but she couldn't help it.

'I have to tell someone.'

Daisy wanted to say, '*Yes, but not me, please, please, please, not me.*'

Aurelia leaned forward.

'If I whisper it, it will be easier.'

She whispered.

Daisy leaned back, appalled.

'Dear God. Not true?'

Aurelia nodded.

'I am afraid so,' she went on, still whispering. 'I don't think Laura ever knew that – that, well, that her father and stepmother, were, well – not ever. At least I knew about mine, so it was less of a shock when they were thrown into jug. A little less of a shock,' she went on, thinking back. 'Still a shock,

312

of course, but at least I knew what they were, or are, at least I knew.'

'You can't tell her, of course.'

'No, of course not.'

'Agony.'

Aurelia nodded quickly as Laura came back into the room.

'Agony?' Laura asked, over-brightly. 'What is agony?'

'Childbirth,' Daisy said raising her eyebrows and shaking her head. 'Catch me having a baby. We were just talking about poor Jean. Any minute now. Big baby on the way.'

'She tried to get the Huggetts to acknowledge it, but they won't. Just won't. Can't stand the thought that a grandchild of theirs is being brought into the world whose mother is from The Cottages. Just won't acknowledge her at all.'

'Poor Jean.'

Jean was enjoying life at the Hall. Somehow, within the courtyard atmosphere of the stables, there had grown up a camaraderie not unlike that she had known when she was growing up cheek by jowl with Dan Short and the rest. The two, now three, land girls who had been sent to help were a bit of a mixed bunch, inclined to flop out at a moment's notice if you didn't watch them, so unused were they to hard work; but they, too, seemed determined to make the best of their situation, despite the fact that they wouldn't be going home for Christmas.

313

'It's only one day of the year, Jean,' they all kept saying, repeating it so often that by the time Christmas week did finally come about, Jean, more than anyone, was convinced that they almost believed it. 'Nature doesn't stop for Christmas. There'll be lambing and calving all too soon after that, and Boy has to be groomed and put to the plough, the pigs fed, the milking done every day and the vegetables dug, *if* we can dig them, that is. It is non-stop down on the farm, isn't it, Jean?'

The basic problem of hunger was being solved at the Hall, thank God, Branscombe thought, busy as ever in the kitchen, by the countryside itself. They were not in for as lean a time as the towns and cities, for while it was almost impossible to dig up root vegetables from a ground that was frozen enough to break precious spades, nevertheless unlike the cities there was much meat to be had, from wild rabbit to pork and mutton, and this, accompanied by milk and precious stored vegetables, did at least give them enough energy to get them through the long hard days when, gas masks at the ready still, Jean and her land girls toiled to keep the farm going. Happily, the harvest having been good before the onset of such a harsh winter, they had flour back from the local mill, and much else for which, with so many mouths to feed, they had to be truly thankful.

'Very thick jam this, boys . . .' Branscombe said, speaking to the motley collection of dogs collected in the old kitchen.

He stared at some plum jam sent from the local

314

Women's Institute, and shook his head. He knew it had to be sturdy to stop it from spilling when it was being carted about, but this lot looked like cement. 'But thick or runny, into the tarts it will have to go, and when all is said and done, thank God for it.'

Once autumn had come Branscombe and Jean had set the Lindsay brothers to pick blackberries by the ton from the hedgerows, and every apple that had ever fallen into the orchard grass. All this Jean had duly delivered by pony trap to the Women's Institute centre at Wychford. She had turned a blind eye to the Lindsay brothers, under darkness, secretly picking apples and pears – and plums, of course – from the abandoned gardens in the village. These also had been taken up by pony trap to the centre, Boy pulling the trap across the uneven fields, well away from the prying eyes of army guards, whose boredom at being landed in such a quiet country place was all too evident.

'Now, Algy, Bertie, Trump, George and Dixie, mustn't forget to make a very small apple pie for Johnny's teddy, must we—'

Branscombe stopped. What a thing! So ingrained was he in always making a little pie for Johnny's toy, he had, momentarily, forgotten that Johnny wasn't at the Hall any more, no longer playing at the back of the kitchen, or trotting after Branscombe with a large feather duster as they attempted the usual household chores.

Branscombe sighed. It seemed that even quite new habits died hard. His thoughts ran to where he imagined Johnny must now be, on his long, long tiring journey home. With a bit of luck, quite a lot of luck, by now Johnny should be making his way across London. Branscombe imagined the little fellow, clutching his small cardboard suitcase which contained hardly more than a change of clothes, a toothbrush, and inevitably his precious new toy train. At least the WVS ladies were used to those journeys, even if they did take for ever to do them once they arrived in a city or a town, what with the sirens and the all-clears sounding, and re-sounding. Doubtless Johnny would have forgotten London, but doubtless, too, he would be looking forward to seeing his mum, and the rest of them, spending Christmas with them in the old way.

Branscombe turned away. Christmas. Sometimes he wished it didn't happen, somehow it always seemed to highlight everything all too much, especially in war: loneliness, dashed hopes, other happier days – before the war.

Despite her transformation of the basement, despite the gaiety of her hand-painted notice over the door announcing her club, Daisy tried not to think of how lonely she felt, how much she would have liked to have been with Freddie and all the rest at the Hall, how good the old tree that they dug up every year would be looking, how Aunt Maude would insist on climbing a ladder at the start, to put the angel at the top. She tried not to remember how she and Aunt Maude, and all the maids, poor souls, would all sing hymns on Christmas Eve very badly indeed, their reedy voices trying to follow Aunt Maude, who would seat herself at the piano and lead the well-known carols in a very pretty singing voice.

Daisy smiled. At least that was something that the maids would not be missing, having to sing no matter what, although they would miss the lovely presents Aunt Maude had always chosen for them.

Her one cheerful thought was that David had promised to try and visit her, if he could, which was another reason why Daisy had not asked to spend Christmas Day with Gervaise. She was hoping against hope to see David just this one more time. She had promised it to herself, and after that – well, it would have to stop. Just have to.

She recognised with a dull guilt that she should have told Laura about knowing David, and left her to guess the rest, but after what Relia had told her (which of course she never, ever should have) it had simply not been possible. Once Laura had found out about her father and stepmother for herself, well, things would be different, but just at that moment Daisy simply did not have the courage to face her. Besides, she had convinced herself that when Laura had left Daisy and Aurelia, and gone up to make a telephone call in the hall, that that call had been meant for none other than David Moreton. And, of course, the fact that Laura herself now never mentioned his name was in itself an indication that she was still in love with him. Freddie had always said that. She had always insisted that when a girl was in love with a man she never talked about him, that the only men a girl really talked about were the ones that were of no interest whatsoever, the hangers-on, and that they used them as distractions, as feints.

Daisy lit a cigarette. Guilt was piling very nicely on guilt now, and piling on thick, too. But what could you do? When you fell in love, you fell in love – particularly in war.

That was one thing which she had discovered. Love was not like anything else. It was irrational, inconvenient, and dangerous. Only a few days ago, she had been so busy thinking about David's latest thrilling note to her, saying that he was going to try to meet her in the basement of her godfather's house on Christmas Day, that she had just missed slicing the Hurricane she was taking to Scotland in half on an overhead cable.

'Daisy?'

'Yes?'

Daisy stared hazily out at the face she could see beyond the half-glassed door.

'It's me, David.'

'David?'

'Yes, you know, David Moreton? Remember we met – I wrote to you that I would try to come, re-member?'

Daisy swayed a little. She had been dreaming of someone, but she couldn't quite remember who, or what had happened in the dream – it had all been tumbling buildings, faces, strangers, people that she had never met before. Where had they all come from, those very real people? Disembodied faces, voices and clothes that were so lifelike that they were more vivid to her than the voice coming from the darkness beyond the door.

'It's two o'clock in the morning—'

'I know, Daisy. I should do. I don't know how I got here. Do you think you could open the door, and let me in? I have driven through the night to get here, and I am dying for a great many things, most of all a drink. Please, old girl. Let me in.'

'Old girl' was so very RAF. Daisy was suddenly completely awake. Good God! It was David. David! She wrenched the door open, and they stumbled against each other in the dark.

'Come in, come in! I fell asleep waiting for you. Actually I never thought you would come, that you could come, that you would get compassionate leave.'

'I had to come: twelve hours with you was such a spiffing thought, worth everything.'

He kissed her so hard that Daisy – which was not at all her – started to feel faint.

'Just a minute, just a minute.' She stepped back, knocking into the sitting-room door. 'I have to make sure you really are who you say you are—'

'As a matter of fact, I'm not. No. Listen, old thing, who I am is – I didn't like to say, didn't want to put the foot down too hard, but I'm really Air Chief Marshal Sir Hugh Dowding . . .'

'Yes, of course, I would have recognised you

anywhere. Come this way, Sir Hugh. I have laid out the best glasses, the best whisky, and the best meat pie you will ever have tasted in your life, but first I must light a candle or two.'

They stared at each other through the candle-light, and somehow, even though the journey had been as long as hell, even though he had to get back on ops sooner than he cared to think, Daisy looked so beautiful that David knew at once that every minute with her was going to be golden. He knew that whatever happened to him, in his last moments – if they came sooner rather than later – he would always think of her as she was at that minute, slightly sleepy-eyed, slightly tousled, wearing a now rather crumpled Christmas party dress with sequins around the top. He had never seen her in a dress before, only in her ATA uniform. The cut of the silk followed the contours of her body, showed the outline of her small rounded breasts.

'God, you are so beautiful, Daisy, you make me feel as if this war had never started. Stay as you are, don't move. Let me always remember you like this!'

He raised his glass to her, and as he did so there was the sound of a siren, and they knew they should get under the table, or go to the coal cellar, but they didn't, they went to her bedroom, and David undressed her, and they made love so beautifully that even the picnic in the sitting room was forgotten in favour of lying together until the dawn of Christmas, when they were woken by the telephone ringing. Daisy was wanted back by the ATA, as soon as possible. She shrugged her shoulders as David moaned, 'But it's Christmas! Surely we can have a few more hours?'

But apparently not. Christmas during the Great War might have meant a ceasefire, but now it meant only a few hours before the bombing and the destruction began again, and Spitfires were wanted, Hurricanes were wanted, everything was wanted, and sooner rather than later, when it might be far too late.

'One of the aircraft factories has been hit, so it's all hands to the pump, old thing!' Daisy said, determined to be light-hearted.

David looked mournful.

'A few more hours?'

She shook her head.

'We've gone through our emotional coupons for the moment, and you know it.'

He turned away from her. They both knew, had always known, they were only sitting in an oasis for a few hours, and then it was back to the harsh reality, of death lurking behind every burnt-out building, behind every telegram regretting to inform the recipient that someone was 'missing'. Such was the sorrow of the times that only love relieved the pain, and youthful energy fuelled the duties ahead. That and the will to win, or rather, not to be defeated.

Daisy pinned up her blonde hair and pulled down her uniform jacket. Time to go.

'I won't look back, and don't you wave,' she

called to David as she sprang up the area steps into the dawn light. 'Whatever happens, don't wave.'

David turned, and it was only when he reached the front door of the basement flat that he noticed the sign reading: '*THE DAISY CLUB – MEMBERS ONLY! NO NAZIS!*'

Once inside he saw the visitors' book, with all the girls' names signed in. Taking up the pen that lay beside it, he cheekily wrote his own name under theirs, and then went back to bed for a few hours.

Christmas luncheon at the Hall, in the basement kitchens, prepared by Branscombe, was as sumptuous as he could make it, helped and sometimes abetted as he had been by his many helpers. There was not just one turkey, but two to carve, and many side-dishes of extravagant pre-war delight, three sets of Miss Jean's potatoes, once so despised by Miss Maude, and plenty of cabbage, also once the cause of Miss Maude's disdain.

No one asked where most of the food had come from, although Dan did bolt back to his flat to make sure that, 'No one's gone and stealed my girls', in exchange for the turkeys, or done some other piece of nifty barter at their expense.

Of course they all knew that it would have spoilt everything to have known the exact origins of the turkeys, let alone which of the pigs had gone to make the sausages – which were out of this world. Since there were so many of them, Branscombe and Freddie had designed the meal so they all

322

started by eating a piece of Yorkshire pudding. Branscombe had suggested this to Freddie, knowing that by starting with a piece of pudding, as in the old way, the guests' appetites would be kept at bay, just a little.

Of course Freddie had always been aware, since she was quite little, that Branscombe had a pretty special hold on the rest of the countryside around Twistleton. His contacts were second to none. Also, since his father and grandfather, on his mother's side, had been in the Connaught Rangers, 'foraging' was second nature to him. Or as Aunt Jessie had always said, 'it was in the blood'. So nothing was said about the enormity of the spread at Christmas luncheon, food that they had spent several days preparing, although, inevitably, eyes came out on stalks at how crowded their plates were allowed to be.

'Won't always be like this,' Branscombe murmured, as he heaped up yet another plate, and another contented guest reeled off towards the kitchen table staring down at their helping with disbelieving eyes.

For the first time ever, Miss Maude had changed her mind about where she would spend her Christmas luncheon, and now that she had, she was very glad about it, although it had taken some effort on her behalf to break with her time-old tradition of Christmas in the dining room. But when the time came, after they had all been to church, she was quite relieved to find herself *not* upstairs, pretending that everything was still the same as it had always been. The truth was that she and Daisy, all alone with only one of the luckless and understandably resentful maids serving them, had been really playing a game of pretend. They had been pretending, or rather Maude had, that everything had not changed since the Great War. All quite absurd, now that she came to think of it.

'Pull the wishbone with me, Miss Maude?' Branscombe asked.

Maude nodded. She had always hoped to be the one chosen to pull the wishbone by their father, if only so she could offer it to young Roderick, who always closed his eyes and said his wish out aloud, inevitably spoiling the whole effect.

'Look at that, you've only gone and won it!' Branscombe nodded approvingly at the wishbone that Miss Maude was holding. 'Now, I wonder what you will wish for, Miss Maude?'

Maude closed her eyes. She knew just what she would wish.

She wished, how she wished, for her darling Daisy to come home to the Hall.

She had known now for some time that she should never have behaved the way she had towards Daisy. Her only excuse was that she had found it unbearable seeing her going off like that, seeing the look in her eyes, the replica of that in her poor dead mother's, Maude's sister-in-law, who had been piloting a plane to Deauville just after the war, when it had crashed, leaving Maude to bring up Daisy. Maude just hadn't been able to face even the idea of losing Daisy, so had disinherited her, cut her off rather than have to wait around in that unbearable way, waiting, always waiting, to hear that she had been lost.

She knew now she had reacted in a way she should never have done. She must make it right after Christmas, make everything right again.

Mentally she raised her eyes to heaven. Sorry, God! Awful war, awful war, it did it for one finally, one reacted in a foolish fashion, and then regretted it.

Branscombe stared at her as she opened her eyes.

Maude stared back at him, waving the wishbone.

'I was just wishing that Miss Daisy would come home!'

Branscombe smiled, but at the same time he shook his head.

'Never reveal your wish, Miss Maude, didn't your nanny tell you that?'

They both laughed, and then Maude turned away. Well, never mind that, she had told her wish, and nothing could be done about it now. The truth was that just the sight of Daisy would be the best Christmas present she could have had. Just the sight of her swinging through the double doors into the Hall, eyes sparkling, bubbling over with excitement, bursting to tell her old Aunt Maude a story.

The worst of it was just how much she despised herself for being so scared of loss that she had banished the one person she truly loved from her life. The truth was that the burden of her grief, untold for so many years after the Great War, had somehow swelled up inside her, and she had been unable to contain her dread of losing Daisy. She had banished her instead, when she should have known that nothing could protect a loved one, nothing but prayer, and hope.

Chapter Ten

The calendar said February 1941, but as far as Jean was concerned it was really saying 'only three weeks to go'.

'You should be careful about that baby of yours,' Freddie had spent the last few months warning her. 'It will be born running, and much sooner than it should, if you go on as you do.'

Jean shrugged her shoulders.

'If it was going to be born sooner, Freddie, it would have happened in the trap by now. Bounce, bounce, bounce!'

Freddie, half-asleep after her night-work, gently pushed Jean back down into the old kitchen chair, and for a few seconds she sank gratefully back against the old Liberty flower-printed cushions that lined it.

'Sit you down, Mrs Huggett duckie, and let me make you a nice cup of warming tea.'

Jean struggled to get up.

'I can't stay for a cup of tea, Freddie. I have to get on, truly I do.'

'Those girls of yours, what are they for, Jean?

Leave it to them, for goodness' sake.'

'Those girls of mine, as you call them, are all down with influenza. High temperatures, the lot. Doctor Blackie called last evening when you had gone off to the hospital. Came across on his horse, and he says that half the troops in the village have got the same bug. I could see he was hoping that it wasn't Spanish flu.'

Both young women looked at each other. They had grown up with people talking in low tones about the Spanish flu epidemic of 1917, which had taken off millions of people. When it did not kill, it had often left people unconscious to the world, graven images locked into hospital beds, unaware of their condition, their loved ones left grieving for people who were dead, and yet not dead.

'What a winter! Enough to get us down, it is, really,' Freddie murmured, putting a kettle on the old kitchen range. It would take so long to heat up, she knew that they would be lucky to have a cup of tea before dinner was on the table.

'Trust the troops to bring a bug into Twistleton. Doctor Blackie said that we haven't had anything like this for years and years.'

'The trouble is most of the men, well, they're not from these parts, so they have no respect for anything or anybody. If they were the North Wessex or the South or North Wiltshires it might be different, but no, they're from all over, and care nothing about Twistleton and us.'

'I gather most of the village street has been

shelled since General what's-his-name graced Twistleton with his presence.'

Jean stared at Freddie, realising at once from what she had just said that she could hardly have left the Hall for weeks.

'Are you no longer going to the hospital, Freddie?'

'Of course I am,' Freddie asserted stoutly, throwing back her plait of brown hair. 'I'm on nights at the moment, and in between I take charge here, trying to help out as much as possible. I go across the fields on my bicycle, with no lights at this time of year – it is certainly very interesting, my deah!' she joked.

Jean seemed satisfied by this, but she still refused the cup of precious black tea on offer, and after struggling to her feet she finally walked off into the bitter weather to try and do something useful about the place. Cows had to be brought in for milking.

The cows were out today, and they might be hard to get in, but they were good girls all of them, no trouble to milk, no trouble to feed, not a kicker amongst them, and, despite the land girls being down with the influenza, with the Lindsay boys to help her she could cope.

Freddie yawned as she watched Jean waddling off, bursting out of her woollies and clumping along in her farm boots. Then she gave a small exhausted sigh. She could hardly put one foot in front of the other. She closed her eyes, and sat back down in the chair. Jean was still a very pretty girl with her wild black curls and her beautiful complexion, but nowadays, despite the pregnancy bloom, she was looking tired and anxious. Frankly, now that she was so far gone, she was nothing but a worry, and to Branscombe too. Both he and Freddie complained almost hourly that Jean was doing far too much, most especially in her condition. And now, of course, with the girls all abed with fevers, the nagging feeling that she should have her feet up, and not be chasing cows over all but frozen fields, persisted.

Freddie never thought she would think it, let alone say it, but only the previous evening she and Branscombe had raised their poor old glasses, and thanked heaven for the Lindsay boys. Without them there would be cows with full udders all over the place, not to mention vegetables not dug, pigs not swilled, and eggs not collected.

In the end a decision had had to be made, and Freddie had made it the week before. She was so worried about Jean that she had swapped her duties at the hospital for being on nights, the better to keep a sleepy eye on the poor girl during the day. Branscombe could keep an eye and an ear out for her at night, since they were both housed in the stables.

'The moment that baby starts, Branscombe, if it starts at night, you must send Jean to the hospital. If you can't go with her, send Alec, send Dick, send anyone, not Miss Beresford, obviously, especially not now that she has the influenza.' She stopped.

'Have we checked on Miss Beresford, by the way, Branscombe?'

Branscombe nodded.

'Doctor Blackie visited this morning, after he was called out to the stables to the land girls. Don't you worry, Miss Freddie, I made sure of that. But you know Miss Beresford, it is all I can do to make her stay in bed, even though Doctor Blackie told me her temperature is worryingly high. Of course one of her troubles is that her room is such a freezing great barn at the best of times, and now – well, frankly, you would be warmer standing outside.'

Freddie felt impatient. She couldn't help it. Everything at the Hall, unlike the poor old Court, was half-done, nothing really completed, tiles off the roof, pipes still stuffed with last year's leaves, chimneys with rooks' nests. Had the army not been occupying the Court, she would have suggested that they all move into Aunt Jessica's house, but that was not possible, or even permissible, now. She paused, remembering how hard Jessica had worked to keep the Court going, to keep it in model-farm condition, and now even to pass it on foot or bicycle was too painful for words. She was only thankful that her aunt was away, and could only hope that by the time she came back, something would have happened to right it. Although she somehow doubted that.

Branscombe kept saying, in a sombre voice, 'Once the army have been in, Miss Freddie, a house never recovers.' Needless to say, it was a statement that did nothing to cheer the listener. Now he was saying, 'We could try and light a fire for Miss Maude in that little grate in her bedroom, but I'm afraid that it will catch the chimney on fire. There are so many birds' nests stuck down all the chimneys they start to smoke within a minute. It's a wonder the whole place hasn't caught fire years ago, really it is, Miss Freddie.'

It was true. The rooks had long made their homes in the myriad chimneys above the Hall roof. With their nests preventing any fires, it was no wonder that Miss Maude's room was such a freezing great barn, and all the chimney-brushes Branscombe had managed to find had been too decrepit to use, or too short for the flues. Cleaning these chimneys would be a job for a professional, whenever they could find one.

Freddie dreaded going up to Miss Maude's room. It was not just that it was freezing, and that the jugs of water in the pretty flowered basin and carafes were literally iced over. It was that, despite its lovely Edwardian furnishings, its many covered tables of floral chintz, its plethora of silver-framed photographs, its mahogany bed with velvet trimmings and graceful curtains of such intricately pleated silk that they caught the eye even more than the paintings of ancestors on the walls, it was the saddest place in the world. The room of a spinster daughter who had been left alone to struggle on, to cope as best she could, winter after winter, with burst pipes and freezing weather – and, worst of all, with impossible standards, keeping up the facade all alone, when everyone else had gone.

There was a painting over the chimneypiece of a young boy with dark curly hair, who was staring out at the onlooker as he must have stared out at Gainsborough. He had a slight frown, as if he was hoping that this dull business of sitting for a painter for his portrait would be over soon, as if he was longing to be allowed to scramble out of his red velvet suit with its large lace collar and its large lace cuffs, and run off into the grounds of the Hall with the gardener, or the gamekeeper, or his tutor – anyone who would allow him to pick up his fishing rod, or chase after his dog, or shoot a rabbit, anyone who would allow him to enjoy himself as he wanted. Freddie knew from something that Miss Maude had said that the boy in the painting was the spit of her brother Roderick, and it made her sad, so that when she went into the room she dropped her eyes rather than catch sight of the portrait, however beautiful.

'I will check on Miss Maude later, Branscombe, before I leave for night duty, but for the moment I think she should be allowed to rest. So, don't you worry about it.'

'Miss Maude is a tough old bird,' Branscombe muttered to the dogs, once Freddie had gone back to bed. 'Take more than a bout of influenza to carry off Miss Maude, take more than a regiment of Nazi soldiers, take more than I like to think. Come on, off up the kitchen stairs, time we all went for our constitutional.'

Branscombe looked round at the gaggle of assorted dogs, and then once again, out of habit and before he could check himself, he looked round for young Johnny.

Dear, dear, he really must be getting old to keep on looking for what was definitely not there. He climbed up into the hall followed closely by the dogs, his old army coat wrapped tightly round him, his mittened hands holding on to various leads. He hadn't heard from anyone about Johnny. Hope he got delivered to Peckham all right. Hope the train was all right. Hope that he wasn't missing Twistleton Hall too much, and his brothers of course, hope he wasn't missing them. The Lindsay boys were all turning out to be the mainstay of the place. Alec and Dick helping with the cows and the rest, and Tom always on hand to run errands. They were a tribute to Peckham, and to themselves, really and truly they were. And more than that, the fact that they had changed physically so much for the better was a source of some pride to Branscombe. Where once their faces had been pallid, and their ribcages like toast-racks, now they were well-covered, and their eyes bright as the pony's when he saw his feed bucket coming towards him on a frosty morning.

Branscombe pushed open one of the pair of old half-glassed doors and gasped. *Brrrh!* The marble-floored hall behind him was hardly what anyone would call warm, but once the door was open, and the dogs squeezing past him, the full force of winter cold seemed to hit him not just in the face, but, even as he gasped, in the back of his mouth. The truth was that the air was so cold it hurt.

Branscombe pulled his knitted hat further down his ears, and his old coat tighter round him, thankful for once that he had only one eye uncovered, one eye exposed to the cold. The dogs pulled him along their usual route. The lake ahead was frozen over, and the trees so stilled and frost-covered that they might have been sculptures. The studs on his old army boots rang out on the hard ground as he walked briskly along, the pugs on their leads, the dachshunds at his heels. He liked to cover a good distance after luncheon – it gave him much-needed energy when he needed it – thankful always that the park was so hidden that neither the army in the village nor those at the Hall could see each other. So there was no grim sight of tanks on manoeuvres, although the sounds that rang out of poor old Twistleton these days made his heart sink, and he an army man since he was a boy.

He stopped suddenly, the dachshunds crashing into his legs, the pugs reeling back against their taut leads.

There was someone at the large old gates, guarded as they were by two lead dogs on plinths. Someone in a dulled black uniform, pushing a bicycle. Someone with a black cap on his head, someone with bicycle clips, and he was carrying the unmistakable, the unwanted, the much-dreaded dull little envelope. A telegram.

*   *   *

335

Aurelia stared at herself in the mirror. Why was she doing this?

Her face, looking, if the truth be known, a great deal more bleached than usual, was a mask of suppressed terror.

'I am doing this,' she replied to her mirror image, 'to prove to myself, and everyone else, that I am not an hysterical little nobody, and if I come through – *IF* I do – I will be able to respect myself. That is why I am doing this, and for no other good reason.' She stopped. 'Well, there is one other good reason, and that is that I am trying to prove to Guy, and to Clive, and to Laura and Freddie, and Daisy, that I am a worthwhile person. And not just someone content to be desk-bound, hearing about other people being brave, while being rather less so myself.'

It was a good lecture, and one that seemed to satisfy her mirror image.

'Very well, now I am fully equipped,' she went on, speaking silently to herself. 'Nothing to do now, except put myself in my motor car, and drive to the destination which has been designated, and get on with the job in hand.'

The aeroplane that had just been delivered was not of the usual type. It was something quite special, and faster than normal. Aurelia, as she climbed into it to sit alongside others on the same mission, wondered fleetingly if it was one that Daisy might have delivered. If it was, then she hoped to goodness that it now had been checked-over by a competent mechanic, because, as she well

336

knew, the planes flown from factory to airstrip often had modifications made to their instruments at the last possible minute, which meant that the girls flying them – girls like Daisy, who delighted in flying but did not court danger – had to have a great deal more guts than they were actually ever given credit for. Especially since, together with the worry about whether the controls were going to work properly, they never knew exactly what they were going to have to fly. And also, they had no fighting training, their aircraft never contained ammunition, and there was a distinct possibility that they might meet an enemy aircraft while in flight.

'Girls of no consequence, that's us, old thing!' Daisy had often joked, on the few occasions when they saw each other, either fire-watching, or queueing for some futile necessity.

Aurelia had the feeling that the same could be said of her. She was a girl of no consequence, hardly trained in parachuting, hardly able to think of the danger she was putting herself through without feeling so faint that she had to cling on to the nearest piece of furniture, but – and this was the important thing – she was determined.

She was so determined, to do her bit. She would come through if only for Guy – and Clive – most particularly now that Guy had been imprisoned.

'What for? I mean what do they think putting Guy in prison is going to do? What is it for? Why have they put him there?' she had kept asking Clive when he met her for a much-needed drink.

It had been difficult for Clive to explain it to Aurelia, not just because they were both so devoted to Guy, but because he could not tell her all that he knew. And of course, after a little while, Aurelia had realised this, and stopped throwing questions at him, and they had both repaired to a dark corner of the pub.

'Guy has enemies, Aurelia, many enemies.'

'Why should he have enemies? Who could dislike Guy, for goodness' sake? This talented man with so many gifts who always works so hard to make everyone happy with his plays and his songs, who could possibly dislike him?'

'You would be surprised how many people dislike Guy,' Clive had said, lighting a cigarette, and passing it to Aurelia. She had immediately started to smoke it too fast, while he lit one for himself.

'But why should anyone dislike him?'

Clive had looked suddenly affectionate, paternal, protective, and loving, all at the same time.

'Guy is disliked by many, many people for a very, very good reason, Aurelia.'

'Because?'

'Because he is talented. As he himself said, shouting over his shoulder to me even as they led him away – bless him – *"Don't put your head above the parapet, Clive. See what happens if you do?"'* Clive blew a smoke ring which he watched for a second, waiting for the memory to pass. 'It's only for a month, he has only been incarcerated for a month. And knowing Guy, he will soon make friends with everyone in the prison, have the gaolers eating

338

out of his hand, everyone singing his best-known songs, and be out before anyone can say West End. Then, you may be sure, he will be writing a play about it in two minutes flat, and shortly after that he will be found moaning that they want to put Mavis Arledge in it, and it will be over his dead body, because she hasn't been able to remember a line since 1921.'

'Of course, the charges are trumped-up, aren't they?' Aurelia had asked in an urgent voice.

'Of course,' Clive had agreed, without giving the question much thought, because just at that moment, after night after night of fire-watching, he had found acceptance a great deal less fatiguing. 'The authorities, or someone in authority, wanted to make an example of someone famous, wanted to crack down on people flouting petrol restrictions. They hoped the rest of us would go about saying, "Well, if that can happen to Guy Athlone, it can happen to me, so I had better behave." And believe me, it will work. It will work, and the authorities will congratulate the person responsible, in fact he will probably be given a knighthood after the war, and no one will remember why. His friends and acquaintances will only assume that he has done something quite terrific, which, of course, in the eyes of our dear government he has: he has effectively terrified everyone into taking account of petrol-rationing and abiding by the rules, car-sharing, and so on and so forth. Time was when people were knighted for brave deeds. Think of that.'

'Exceeding the petrol-allowance!' It had been Aurelia's turn to sound bitter.

'Of course the irony is that he was on government business, but because he has to look after his own paperwork just at this moment, because he is always dashing about doing work for you know what—'

He had nodded in such a significant way that Aurelia had known that he meant Operation Z, and the mysterious brothers, who were still running networks of rescue teams all over Europe.

'He has been working day and night for the people who do so much to help the cause, and because of that he has not paid much attention to rules and regulations. It is only understandable. And really it took – what? – just a few gallons over, or something like that, and they got him.' He snapped his fingers. 'Just like that, they got him. A ghastly woman, may all her hair fall out and her toenails curl over, a woman scorned targeted him, just for revenge. Anyone can bring anyone else down, innocent or guilty, it doesn't matter at all – and that goes on even more when a country is at war.' Clive sipped his drink, before reflecting on the good times he and Guy had enjoyed, and looking, without his realising it, suddenly sad. 'Never have anything to do with being famous, Aurelia. There's always someone waiting to cut you down to size if you are famous and, worse, talented. They were waiting for Guy, and they got him. So they must be very pleased with their work.'

'And he can never now be vindicated, I suppose?'

'Because of Z,' Clive had lowered his voice, 'because of the Bros, no. What an irony, when you think what he has done, and how hard he has worked, and yet he will go down in history, not just as a wonderful writer of comedies and songs, but as a cheat! Guy, of all people, one of the most generous men you could ever meet, as open-handed as he is open-hearted.'

'It could turn you cynical, truly it could, could it not?'

'Yes, it could. Of course, despite his age barring him from being called-up, the publicity was still angled in such a way as to make him look as if he sidestepped the army in favour of the bright lights of the West End. Ha, ha, ha.'

Aurelia closed her eyes, shutting out the engine noise, as she remembered the sad look in Clive's eyes as he had pretended to laugh, and it strengthened what was left of her resolve, which was very little. She had to remember – every minute of the next few days – just why she was doing this. It was for Guy and Clive, and everyone like them; and because she hated her parents, who loved Hitler and Fascism in equal measure. After even the little bit of the war that she had been through she didn't care too much for them at all, any more. She was also doing it so that places like Twistleton would always be Twistleton, and Britons would never, ever be slaves, and all that kind of thing.

Besides which, as she kept joking to her teacher on the short course they were all dragged through – 'It will make a man of me!'

And what a hilarious course it had turned out to be, with the poor man in charge of all the girls due to be parachuted into enemy territory not knowing whether to laugh or cry at their antics, and the girls not knowing whether to or not, either, when they saw what the powers-that-be expected them to wear. And as for the handbags that were meant to conceal heaven only knew what! Once across the Channel carrying one of those ghastly creations, they would be arrested at once, if only for offences against fashion.

'Jones!'

Aurelia jumped.

Or rather she was pushed, and as she was, miracle of miracles she managed to make her parachute open, thank *God*! Might have been a bit of a squish if she had made a bish of it.

Suddenly it was all real, the wind rushing up to her as if in greeting, the sound of the sea a long way behind her. Normandy! The place where she had so often holidayed as a child, alone with her French nanny. The place where she had first started to speak French. Not polite French, either: country French, with a country accent, which she could still do, despite having been taught what was called 'drawing-room French' or 'salon French' as Miss Valentyne called it.

That was how she had realised just how useful she could be to the war effort. It was when she saw all those pegs being removed from the board, and realised what bad French all those blown agents had spoken; all the crass mistakes they had made, like not crossing their sevens, and not knowing their slang properly, and forgetting to eat with a piece of bread, rather than a knife. Stupid, stupid things that had cost them their lives, because they were not in the *way* of being French, didn't wave their hands about enough, all that. It was when one of the prettiest and cheekiest of the agents was blown that Aurelia had known, without any doubt, that she had to volunteer to be dropped into France. The truth being that she was perfect for the job with her ability, not to mimic, but to reproduce really good country French, not to mention her knowledge of Normandy – not the well-known places, but all the little lanes and by-ways, places where she had walked, and walked, and walked some more, when she was a child. She was perfect agent material.

'Ouch! Double ouch! Triple ouch! Not to say *merde alors!*'

She pulled herself free of sudden pain, with some considerable difficulty.

Dear God in heaven, she had just landed in a stunted tree, which had disobligingly attempted to slice her in half. She rolled free, cursing silently, and then quickly untangled herself. There were torches ahead. She was sure of it, torchlight. She had to hide somewhere. Happily she was dressed as a simple French girl, papers all tickety-boo, everything as it should be, even her hat with a provincial label from a French shop sewn in the back. She was Yolande Marie Charbonne. Just please, please, God, help her get out of her boiler suit, and hide her parachute in time! Please, God! But God, it seemed, was not listening, because the torches were getting nearer and nearer, and she was certain now that she would never be able to hide her parachute in time.

Jean was bringing in the cows with Alec, the eldest of the Lindsay brothers, when the telegram had arrived. She liked Alec as much as she liked anyone, now that Joe had been taken from her. He was quiet, and he was strong, and he liked cows. He respected cows. He knew that a cow-kick could come quicker than any horse-kick, and that they could kick from the front, and just when you least expected it. He knew the names of all the cows, and had thought up some of them himself. Alec knew about cows because Jean had taught him, and also because he had taken the trouble to learn about them.

At night, when the other two were asleep, Alec had told Jean, he studied farming books by the light of his precious torch, old leather-covered books that he had found in the library at the Hall. They were old-fashioned all right, but they taught him about land, and the way of it, and he and Jean talked about land, and cows and sheep, and how animals all had different personalities, and how you had to know them, same as humans, or you would slip up. It was as important as how you fed them.

Nowadays most of the cows came when they were called. Alec had learned to make a 'yip-yip-yipping' sound. He had learned it from Jean, of course; but more than that he had learned to do it with difficulty, because he was shy.

Jean respected his shyness, just as she respected the way he had learned to make a cow-calling sound, because he was anxious to fill in for her when the time came, when the baby arrived. Of course they never talked about the baby, or its imminent arrival. Why should they? It wouldn't be right, and it wouldn't be decent – no one talked about the baby – but they all knew it was there, and that it would be coming soon, no matter how much Jean tried to hide it with long pullovers, and farming clothes of every kind pulled down over her land girl uniform.

Alec had heard enough babies arriving in his time not to be impressed by the idea. As the eldest of four boys, all born at home, he knew all about kettles being boiled (although he still had no idea what they did with the hot water), and the local midwife arriving, and when he was old enough he had rounded up the others and taken them out, to the park if it was daytime, or to play outside The Duck and Horse if it was evening. Playing in the road, in the dirt, was better for them, he had always reckoned, than watching their father boil kettles, and listening to their mother yelling her head off.

'Ow, ow, ow! Oh my God, why did no one tell me? Why did no one warn me what would happen, ow!'

Alec was way up the hill, but because of the cold still air he could hear the sound, and it reminded him of when Tom and Johnny – oh God – it was Mrs Huggett! She was two fields away, but he could hear her sharp as anything, hear her cries. Maybe old Goldie had kicked her in the baby? In the front!

He started to run, but he was too fast, and he fell, he fell flat, and he cut his face and hands because the ground was so hard it might as well have been made of concrete, or granite. It really was that hard. Might as well have been a Peckham pavement that he had fallen on, really it might. He picked himself up, and stumbled on again, groaning a little as he tried to wipe the blood from his eyes, where he had cut his forehead. The blood dripped down over his hands, which made him suddenly realise what a good idea it might have been to take Branscombe's advice, and pack a handkerchief into his back pocket.

If his father hadn't always leathered them for swearing, Alec would have said every swear word he had ever heard, but he respected himself too much nowadays to swear.

That was what Miss Maude always said to him: 'You respect yourself too much to use bad words, don't you, Alec?' And she was right. He did. He told himself this as he staggered up through the fields to where he could see the black of Miss Jean's farm coat, and hear her cries.

'You been kicked by Goldie, then, Miss Jean?'

Jean looked up at him.

'Oh, Alec, you're here. Good boy! No, no, I haven't been kicked. I fell and I think it's brought the – I think I have started. Can you go for help?'

'Shouldn't I go and bring the cows in first, Miss Jean? They're that full of milk they'll burst.'

'No, no, Alec. No, I tell you what, pull me up.' She sat up. 'I don't think I have broken my ankle, just twisted it, but the suddenness of the fall, it has—'

Alec nodded. He knew a bit about childbirth, knew what to expect. He looked away discreetly as he pulled Miss Jean to her feet.

'You got nuffin to fear, Miss Jean,' he told her quietly. 'Nuffin at all. Truly.' He remembered old Nana Stanton saying that to his mother when Tommy was being born, so now he repeated it. 'You just lean on me, now.' He bent down a little because he was considerably taller than Jean, and carefully placed one of her arms across his shoulders. 'There now, we can go along like this, and we'll be back at the Hall before we can say knife, or butter, for that matter.'

Poor Alec could not help casting a glance at the immense udders on the cows that they were passing, wondering if he would ever be able to get back to them before it was dark. Wondering if any of them could be got in before night-time came and the blackout came into force.

'We should never have let them out, not in this weather, but with everything as it is, and the top fields clearing under the sun this morning, I thought it would continue fine. It was only at midday that the weather turned, didn't it, Alec?'

Jean stopped to gasp as another pain hit her.

'Yup. It was only at midday. This morning, it were cold, but it were sunny, and you could see the grass all right,' Alec agreed. 'It's that kind of winter, though, in't it, Miss Jean? Difficult to tell whevver it will be anything but hard ground and no fodder, or we keep them in and find ourselves running out of winter feed. That's the kind of winter it's gonna be, I reckon.'

'Ouch!'

'Lambing will be late, I should have thought, very late this spring,' he went on conversationally. 'And then there'll be the crops to sow. There was a good harvest this year despite everything, though, weren't there, now?'

Jean stopped suddenly, and started to laugh instead, which was a great relief to both of them.

'To hear you talk, Alec, you would honestly think that you had lived in the country all your young life. You sound so country it makes me think that you've been here since you were born!'

Alec smiled his shy smile. He was only really repeating what he heard Branscombe and the rest saying so often when they were in the kitchen and he came in for his tea. And Miss Maude, of course, she always did like to hear what was happening on the farm, so he always did have a mind to go and tell her whatever was happening.

'Thought you might like to hear me going on, take your mind off of it,' he told Jean in a calm and gentle voice. 'I know our mum used to like to hear talk when she was as you are now.'

Jean stared at him, suddenly realising what he meant. Of course! Alec had brothers, he came from the East End, he would know all about babies and such like, it was natural to him. No going off to hospital for the likes of his mother, it would be a bed in the front room and kettles boiling every ten minutes, and, just like in Twistleton, doubtless a bevy of women hovering on the doorstep waiting to know the size of the baby, and what 'make' – as her father used to say, never tiring of his joke.

'Thank the Lord, it's not a girl,' Alec remembered the women on the doorstep always murmuring as each of the boys arrived in turn. 'Can't bring trouble home. A boy brings money in, a girl will bring another mouth to feed long before she's old enough to read.'

All this came back to Alec as they, eventually, far too eventually, he thought, reached the Hall. Jean limping, both of them stopping when Jean gasped as another pain hit her, Alec praying all the time that the baby would not arrive before they reached the comforting sight of the old grey stone house.

'Nearly there, Miss Jean, nearly there,' he kept saying, and finally they *were* there, and his hand was reaching out to the back door that led to the kitchen, and the door was opening, and he could feel a little warmth from the mix of kitchen fires and old ranges, not much mind, but enough to boil kettles, he was sure. He was about to call out, quickly and urgently, when he realised it was useless, because from the inside was coming an unfamiliar sound of a girl sobbing.

'You lean against that wall, Miss Jean, and I'll just spy out the land, and then go for a doctor, or a nurse, or a—' He didn't complete his words, but walked hurriedly ahead of Jean into the boot room, and from there through the drying room, until he eventually reached the kitchens.

He pushed the kitchen door gently open and stared in. Branscombe was standing by the large old kettle, which he had placed on the range, as if he had known all along that Alec was going to come in with Miss Jean, and that she would already be in labour. His face was very grave. At the kitchen table, which looked vast, since there was only one person seated at it, was Miss Freddie. She had her head in her hands and was sobbing her heart out.

Alec stood and stared at her. He had never seen a woman crying before. He had *heard* them crying, all right. When his father came home drunk and took his belt off to his mother, and of course when the cat was run over by the brewery van. Mum hadn't been too good about that, but he had never ever seen a member of the opposite sex crying, not in real life. With no sisters, he wouldn't, would he?

'Best if you make yourself scarce, young Alec,' Branscombe told him in a low voice. 'Bad news, very bad news, I'm afraid.'

Alec went to say something, but since he didn't move, Branscombe pushed him a little.

'You heard what I said! Best if you make yourself scarce. We have bad news, indeed.'

Alec still held back, so Branscombe continued to push the young man's seemingly immovable body out of the kitchen, and closed the door behind them both.

'Miss Freddie, she's in a bad way. Not surprising.' He paused, clearing his throat a little. 'Factory where Miss Jessica and Miss Blossom worked, it took a direct hit. Nothing left. Bombed to extinction. They're targeting the factories all the time now. No. There's nothing left of anything or anyone,' Branscombe repeated. 'Nothing.'

Alec didn't know what to say. Why would he? Shy at the best of times, he found he was wordless now.

'I, er – I, er—' He pointed helplessly at the scullery door. 'I got Miss Jean in there, Mr Branscombe, and she's in a bad way.'

Branscombe stared at him.

'Have you been in a fight?' he asked, as the light caught Alec's blood-streaked face.

'No, Mr Branscombe, I fell. Nothing to it. No, it's Miss Jean, she's hurt herself. Fell in the field – ground so hard, all of a sudden. Cows shouldn't have gone out. They're still out. And I heard her, and ran, and I fell. No fight, no fight, but the baby – it's coming out, I think.'

Branscombe brushed past him impatiently.

'The baby is coming out?'

351

Alec nodded.

'We'll need hot water, and—'

Branscombe took one look at Jean and saw that she was clutching at the lower part of her body. They were going to need more than hot water. Beyond them, beneath the outside archway, through the half-glassed door, the older man could see something. Alec carefully draped Jean's arm around his shoulders and they started to walk very, very slowly towards the kitchen and the still-insistent sound of Freddie sobbing. Branscombe, walking ahead, inevitably was the first to see just what none of them wanted to see at that moment – snow.

As the torchlight hit Aurelia's face, she was sure that every inch of colour that might have been there had now fled, which was hardly surprising since she was well aware that she must now have had it. Someone must have blown her cover, someone must have known that there was to be a drop at that very place that night, or else why the welcoming party?

She put her hand up to her eyes, and said in French, and in as calm a voice as possible, 'Good evening, sirs, may I be of any help? Or will you be of help to me?'

A hand descended on her shoulder, a heavy hand. It smelt slightly of oil and petrol. Aurelia frowned up into the face that held the torch.

'Welcome to France, Mademoiselle Charbonne,' the voice said, and as Aurelia stared up into that round, friendly, reddened face, she knew that somehow, or other, heaven only knew how, considering the awful landing she had made, she had managed to fall into a friendly field. 'Come to the farm. We must switch off our torches now we have found you. There are others, too, but you are the first!'

The hand turned her round, and the stout, short farmer walked ahead of her, while two others, their torches also extinguished, walked behind.

The farmhouse was unlit, until you went inside, and then there were discreetly placed candles. There was only one other woman there, and she was silent, placing some wine on the table for Aurelia, and nodding to her to drink it, while carving her a piece of baguette, which she pushed towards Aurelia together with some cheese.

The men sat down, and they too drank some red wine, but, perhaps because they had eaten earlier, they did not share the bread and cheese, or perhaps they were holding back out of good manners? Aurelia indicated the food, silently offering to share it with them, but they smiled and shook their heads, watching her all the time.

Eventually the man whose house, Aurelia imagined, they were sitting in spoke to her in a measured way.

'You are better than the others, Mademoiselle,' he told her. 'Truly much better. The others they sent to us—' He shrugged. 'They did not even know how to eat, how to drink. They were soon—' He drew a finger across his throat, and then shrugged his shoulders. 'I have better hope for you.'

Aurelia nodded, her expression serious. She had papers she had to pass on. She had to get them into the right hands. She knew she could trust these people. She looked from one goodly farmer's face to another. She knew she could trust them, she said aloud, slowly, looking from one face to another. She did not add that she knew she *had* to trust them, because there was nothing else she could do. As far as she was aware, it had not been the plan for her to be picked up only minutes after she landed, so her insides were still trembling from fear that her cover might be blown before she had accomplished her mission. Perhaps her feelings showed in her eyes, because her host leaned forward and started to talk.

There had been reprisals the night before, many dead. All plans cancelled, a double agent. They knew who he was. They would wait for him. They had been told to wait for him. He was done for, as far as they were concerned. An Englishman, they said, with some relish, but by the time they had finished with him he wouldn't know what he was. His wife had been shot, some time ago, but he had escaped, alas! Never mind. They knew where he was. He thought they didn't know where he was, but they did. He was good, though, you had to give him credit: spoke perfect French, perfect German. Strange to think that an Englishman should be betraying his own like that. In Normandy such a man would not be tolerated. In Paris perhaps he would, in Paris they had heard that many had turned out to welcome the invaders, but not in Normandy.

This was not getting Aurelia very far, but she was too well-versed in French country ways to try to hurry things along, and she continued to listen, while all the while wondering, over and over again, if she would ever make contact with the relevant agent, and whether he would recognise her, given the chaos that was obviously rife beyond the farmhouse building. All of a sudden England did not seem far away, it seemed a world away, and she a very small figure in a lonely place. Until she heard Miss Valentyne's voice, from what seemed like another century, but was actually only a few years before, saying, 'If you're ever in a tight spot, always remember two things. Charm is not just an aid, but a tool to helping you. And you can never thank enough. Those two assets will help you out of any tight corner. That, and appreciating the flowers. *"Aren't the flowers lovely?"* always goes down well.'

Of course that advice had been given to help all of them out of a tight social spot. And looking around the simple farmhouse kitchen, the round, red faces, the serious expression of Madame, now seated at the top of her table, Aurelia was quite sure that appreciating the non-existent flowers would not get her very far, on the other hand, charm might be just what was wanted.

'It is such a beautiful thing to be back in

Normandy,' she began. 'The place where I have my happiest memories.'

At that moment there was a thundering on the stout oak front door. Aurelia half-rose from her seat. The three men and Madame remained still and seated, and then their host leaned forward.

'Take off your shoes, Mademoiselle, and follow me.'

Aurelia did as she was told, and he led her through a door to an anteroom, quickly followed by the other two men. The three of them then shifted what appeared to be a flagstone of immense proportions, and pointed to Aurelia to climb down the steps to the hay store below.

'Hide well behind the hay,' one of them whispered, as she clambered down into the darkness, even as they quickly stripped off to their underwear, and Madame likewise, and hoofed up the stairs to the rooms above, where they lay down, Madame having whisked the glasses off the table, and tidied away every suggestion of a repast.

There was more hammering on the door, and eventually one of the top windows in the farm-house opened and a voice called down.

'What is it, at this time of night? I have a gun, if you are a robber, I have a gun.'

Aurelia had always suffered from claustro-phobia, but never more than at the moment when they pulled the stone into place above her, and she had to fight her way through what seemed like a sea of hay to the back of the cellar. She lay underneath it, frightened to death, her heart beating so fast that she felt that it must very soon explode.

She must have slept long hours, for she finally woke to the sound of an unusually educated voice speaking French. Either that, or the thin streak of light coming from the tiny window half-buried in the ground must have penetrated her covering of hay, because she found herself moving towards the tiny inset glass and staring up at the dawning scene above her.

The men were in the farmyard, and they were laughing and smoking with a tall man, well-dressed, too well-dressed for the countryside. His outfit stood out strangely against the coarse clothes of the farmers. The educated voice belonged to the man, but it wasn't that which froze Aurelia's blood, it was the fact that she knew his face, but where she knew it from, she could not at first say. And then it came to her exactly where she had last seen that slightly florid, self-satisfied, handsome – but finally unattractive – face. It had been at Twistleton Court.

The owner of the face had come down to visit Laura. Aurelia remembered him now, only too well, because he had felt her bottom in a beastly way, and had he not been Laura's father, she would have kicked him in the whatsits, or slapped him across his horridly handsome face.

Aurelia leaned back. She knew now that she had had it. She was sure of this because she had already known that the Hambletons were traitors, known

357

it from being in Special Operations Executive, but never thought to come across them in Normandy, of all places. They were meant to be in the South of France. Meant to be – what did meant to be mean when there was a war on? What was *meant to be* when it was at home?

And the worst of it was, she rapidly realised, the worst of it was that her farmer friends were his friends, so quite briefly, and not to put too fine a point on it – she had actually *had* it, and little grey matter though she might have, even she could recognise that she was done for.

She started to slip her hand down to the place where she had hidden her pill, when something stopped her.

One of the farmers had taken out a gun, and was pointing it at Arthur Hambleton, and not in a nice way. (Come to think of it, *could* you point a gun at someone in a nice way?) And the others were still smiling at him, but they were leading him towards an old van, and stuffing him into it.

Aurelia stared. The van started, and as it was the oldest-looking van you had ever seen, that was something of a miracle. One of the farmers climbed in the back after Hambleton, leaving another to drive off, while her host, the one she had imagined to be her friend – and who still could be – walked slowly back towards the house, smiling.

Freddie stopped sobbing, and looked up briefly at Branscombe.

'Stiff upper lip, Miss Freddie, stiff upper lip,' the face above her with its eyepatch and sad expression said. 'It's the only way we'll get through this – stiff upper lip.'

Freddie mopped her eyes with a tea towel.

'My upper lip has gone soggy, Branscombe. Nothing to be done, I know there isn't, just nothing to be done—'

A long forceful, silent shudder ran through her young body, and her normally buoyant expression seemed to have fled, so much so that her grief seemed forever set to stay.

'Something has to be done, Miss Freddie. Miss Jean's having her – *ahem* – I think the *ahem* is on its way into this world, and it's snowing, hard. We'll never get through to the hospital at this rate, really we won't, unless we act fast, and pretty fast at that.'

Freddie frowned up at Branscombe. What was he saying? Aunt Jessie and Blossom had been wiped out, and he was muttering about Jean. What was it he was saying? At that moment Jean gave an involuntary gasp, and Freddie looked round to see Alec leading the poor girl to the old kitchen armchair with its squashy faded Liberty-print cushions, and its air of always waiting to receive someone.

She stood up. She had to pull herself together, get into uniform, go back into the fray. No time to cry, no time to do anything except get on with whatever her life dictated she should get on with. She moved over to the chair where Jean was now

359

seated. Freddie's eyes were sore, and her lips were still trembling with the effort not to go on crying. She felt ashamed at breaking down, and at the same time ashamed that she was ashamed. Why shouldn't she cry for Aunt Jessie and darling old Blossom? What was it about war that meant you were not allowed to cry? And yet. And yet she knew it was just not done. Crying took up too much time, took up too much energy. If she saw her, Aunt Jessie would turn away, embarrassed, and if Blossom saw her, she would look appalled. She would say something like, *'Not snivelling, are you, Freddie dear? Mustn't snivel. Bad for the troops.'*

Jean gasped. The sound seemed to ring through the kitchen, and Branscombe and Alec found themselves standing in a little ring around the old kitchen chair as Freddie, now changed, bolted back down to the kitchen.

'Oh God, Jean, you've only started!' Freddie stated, rather too obviously for everyone else present. She threw back her long plait of brown hair, and stared down at Jean, trying to suppress an overwhelming urge to shout at her, *'You can't have it now! Not when I have just heard about Aunt Jessie and Blossom. You can't start it now, it's just not – fair.'*

But when was life fair, and why should it be fair to her?

She leaned forward, and taking the tea towel, she carefully wiped Jean's forehead with it, then went to the kitchen tap and wrung it through with fresh cold water.

360

'Don't worry, kid,' she said, suddenly putting on a perfectly terrible American accent. 'We'll get through this together, see if we don't.'

Jean looked up at her and tried to smile.

'No need to take me to hospital just yet, eh?'

Freddie shook her head, placing careful hands on Jean's stomach.

'Well, love,' she said, now giving a passable imitation of one of the ward sisters. 'If it was me, I think I'd get my skates on! Come on, chuck! No harm done to get you to the hospital, and then if things are not too busy, they can give you the once-over, and if things are just how they should be, send you right home with us!'

The truth was that Freddie was using different voices simply to hide the fact that she was petrified. She had stood by, helping to deliver a number of evacuee mothers, poor souls who had been sent from one hospital to another, until they finally ended up at Wychford, for want of anywhere else to go. Alone and terrified, the poor young women had always been so far from home that there was never anyone to visit them, or indeed take any interest in them, or their babies. Each time the babies she had attended had arrived normally, so normally that she could now feel, from placing tender hands on Jean's stomach, that her baby was by no means the right way up. Little that she knew of childbirth, she did at least know that feet first was not a way to arrive in this world.

Freddie knew she could deliver a baby normally, she also knew she was not capable of coping with a breech birth. She had heard that obstetricians, even very capable nurses, had managed to turn babies, but that once the mother's water was broken, it was impossible.

'Come on, kid!' Freddie smiled. 'Time for us to get into the car and make for Wychford and the hospital.'

'Just put me in a cow byre, I can have it in the straw,' Jean said, protesting as Freddie and Branscombe pulled her to her feet.

Branscombe turned to Alec and muttered, 'Fetch a spade, a blanket, a bottle of water, and a bottle of brandy, and bring them to the car.'

The car. That was all they had now. One car, one set of tyres, one set of brakes, one can of petrol left, until Monday. One can was enough until Monday, enough to get them to the hospital. Branscombe's mouth tightened as he thought of all the ruddy receptacles, all the Kilner jars, and God alone knew what, that he had filled with wretched petrol, and how it had all come in so useful, and yet, now, when he really needed it, he had only one can left.

If one thing happened to stop them on their journey, would the car start up again? What if the brakes gave? Oh, shut up, he told himself sharply, as he helped to wrap Miss Jean in a large pink woollen blanket. Shut up and don't trouble trouble until trouble troubles you, see? He had got through the Great War, he was going to get through to the hospital, and if the baby insisted on arriving – well, Miss Freddie was a nurse, wasn't she? Except. He glanced over at Miss Freddie. Except Miss Freddie had just had the most dreadful shock, well, they all had – but there was something else about that pretty face with its tiny rounded chin, and its bright, albeit at that moment reddened, eyes that gave him cause to worry. Miss Freddie and he, well, they had developed a kind of telepathy, which happened with troops in the trenches, with cooks in a kitchen, and with two people trying to cope with a large house, and a great many and very varied sets of personalities, all with their own different demands. This meant that he and Miss Freddie could look at each other and know, without speaking, what the other was thinking. It was just a fact. Now the fact was that Miss Freddie was not looking at him, so he knew that she did not want him to know something, that she was hiding something. Branscombe's heart sank. Heaven only knew what it was, but he had the feeling that all was not well with Miss Jean.

The car made its careful way, Branscombe driving, Alec sitting up beside him through the narrow country roads. Leaving Twistleton was not as easy as it used to be. Now they were stopped by guards, and had to show their identity cards.

'Jean's left hers behind!'

'Can't let you through, I'm afraid.'

'I can vouch for her. I've lived here all my life,' Freddie protested from the back of the car.

'No, sorry, miss, rules is rules.' The snow was

piling on top of the guard's cap as he peered through the window at Branscombe.

Branscombe stared up at him, infuriated, and then he pushed the car door open, careful to keep the engine running, and stood up outside. Pointing at the back seat he said, trying to control his temper, 'That girl in the back is about to have a baby. Now, do you want to deliver it, or do you want the hospital to deliver it?'

'Sorry, sir, so sorry. Of course.'

The soldier waved them through, looking appalled.

'Identity cards! They'll be asking for them for unborn babies soon, they will. They'll be asking for them for unborn babies.'

Jean gasped again, this time clinging to Freddie, her hands digging into Freddie's clothes, holding them tightly.

'Oh God, oh God!'

'Don't worry, kid, we'll be there soon.'

Alec glanced at Branscombe, who was driving as fast as he dared.

They both knew that 'soon' was a little bit optimistic. Alec also knew from Branscombe's expression that he would probably rather be back in the trenches than driving a young woman in childbirth through a snowstorm to a hospital that suddenly seemed to all of them to be a thousand miles away.

Jean gave another gasp, and then another, and then the gasp seemed to be turning more to a scream, and Alec wished to God he could get out of the car and run off, as he had done when his mother was having his brothers. But he couldn't.

'I don't think we're going to get through, not without you walking in front and digging a path for us, Alec,' Branscombe muttered.

In the back, Jean looked up through pain-filled eyes at Freddie.

'Will you look after my baby for me, Freddie?' she asked in a pitiful voice. 'Will you look after him?'

Freddie shook her head.

'No, I will not,' she said in firm tones, as Branscombe stopped the car to let Alec get out and fetch the spade from the boot to clear the deepening snow. 'No, I will not: you're its mother, his mother, or her mother. You will look after him or her, not me.' Freddie wiped Jean's sweat-filled forehead tenderly.

Jean shook her head.

'No, Freddie, I shan't be here. I know it. I dreamed last night I saw him christened, and you were holding him, not me. I wasn't there! I wasn't there!'

Now Freddie found herself wiping Jean's eyes.

'Hush, hush, it was only a dream,' she said, seeking to reassure her, but even as she did her blood was running colder than the snow outside the windows, and the sound of Alec's spade scraping at the snow on the road in front of the car seemed not optimistic, but sinister.

*   *   *

The sight of German uniforms was somehow so shocking that Aurelia, dressed as Mademoiselle Yolande Marie Charbonne, and smilingly surrendering her papers to be examined, thought for one moment she was going to disgrace herself and faint. Happily she had, even though she said so herself, very pretty legs, and the guards were so busy appreciating her very pretty legs that she was able to control her desire to run off, and continue on her way, slowly and gracefully – Miss Valentyne would be proud of her – to the inn where she would be staying until such time as her contact decided to fetch up there.

The second sight that nearly caused her to faint again was the food at the inn – oh, and the smells! Coming from wartime Britain, those chips, that steak, that sauce! But again, to seize on the food and scoff it would be appalling. It would mean that she was unnecessarily hungry, and as she was meant to be staying with her uncle, a Normandy farmer who kept a good table, and was known to be married to a splendid cook, someone might notice her unhealthily large appetite and report it as being sinister. So, with her tummy rumbling to beat the band, she sat up at the bar, and ordered a Cassis, and read the paper that her 'uncle' had provided her with, and waited for her contact.

It was actually quite a simple job, she told herself for the thousandth time. She simply had to take the relevant information provided in yet another newspaper, exchange it for the newspaper she had been given – she hoped to God that her contact would have the same newspaper, with, more importantly, the same date on it, or else she would be well and truly scuppered, and that comforting little pill in her inside pocket would be in her mouth before she could say – she turned as someone arrived at her shoulder.

'Bonjour,' the voice said in perfect, educated French. 'Is this seat taken?'

Aurelia had not been told who to expect, not the name, nor the sex of her contact – in case of being captured and tortured. All she knew was how to answer the relevant questions.

'No, this seat is not taken,' Aurelia answered in her sturdy country accent. 'But I daresay it will be soon, given that the food and wine in this auberge is so good!'

She smiled, and her contact smiled back at her, and, careful not to look at each other, she – because it was a she – slipped on to the seat beside Aurelia.

The barman smiled at the two pretty girls seated opposite him.

'It is my lucky day, huh?' he asked, as the room started to fill up with hungry German soldiers, accompanied by some of their French girlfriends, local lasses – shame on them – determined on fraternising, doubtless for the sake of the men's wallets. 'Not one, but two pretty girls.'

Aurelia smiled, and sipped her drink, which was, all of a sudden, all too necessary, for she found that her mouth had gone so dry her tongue might have been made of sandpaper.

'There is almost too much choice on the menu, do you not find?'

This was the second phrase arrived at, less than originally, by their people.

Aurelia nodded, folding her newspaper, so that it sat neatly beside the other newspaper. The two were identical, she was quick to note.

'I do find there is too much choice, but as it happens, I must be careful. I have a condition that limits my choice to fish, which happily is well represented.'

Aurelia had actually protested at this line because, as she kept saying to the chaps instructing her, 'Supposing there's *no* fish?'

But the chaps had just laughed and said that the sea would have to dry up for there to be no fish on the menu in an auberge near the French coast.

'I am luckier, I can eat steak, and some of Monsieur's wonderful chips.'

Aurelia nodded.

'That is good.'

They had got through the ridiculous dialogue all right, but happily neither young woman had looked at each other, because if they had, Aurelia was quite sure that she and Laura would have had to have been carried out, they would have laughed so much. Their cover would have been blown, and everything would have been finished, especially them.

Happily, their orders were taken, and the newspapers were exchanged with a deftness that, in less dangerous circumstances, would have made them feel proud, and they were able to start talking in the kind of code that only girls who know each other very well can employ.

'How come you are here, too?' Aurelia asked.

'Oh, I live just up the coast, now. Besides, my family are round here and I would like to see them. It is some time since I saw my father.'

'Of course. Do you know where he is?'

'No, I do not know his whereabouts at present. My father and his wife are holidaying, so they would not tell me. They have been holidaying for some time.'

Aurelia lowered her fork into the fish that had just arrived. So difficult not to eat it too quickly. Oh, and the smell of the chips! But even her overpowering, if stifled, greed was losing out to the memory of Laura's father being taken off to be – as her Normandy host had told her in an understandably gleeful tone – shot. His body had been fed to the pigs – apparently a very efficient way of disposing of double agents who had had a hand in some nasty reprisals.

'I think many of the people holidaying here have now gone back to Paris.'

Laura looked at Aurelia, her own fork poised.

'Yes, perhaps they have,' she agreed. 'But since I am here to enjoy my own holiday in the Normandy countryside, it does not really matter if I do not see my father for a little while.'

Aurelia sighed inwardly, with relief, and at the same time her thoughts raced back to SOE or whoever had sent Laura to France. Why in God's name did they think it was all right to start using FANYs? Laura was a FANY, she did not work for what was euphemistically always known as the 'War Office' or the 'Foreign Office'. Then she remembered how many of those little pegs had been taken off the map of France, and she realised that, like the aeroplanes, like the food, like the petrol, the clothing, everything – they must be running short of agents, too. They must just be grabbing who they could, or whoever was mad enough to volunteer, and knowing Laura, with her father and stepmother still missing somewhere in France, she would not have stepped forward, but jumped forward, because that was Laura.

Freddie sat slumped on a bench outside the delivery room. All she could hear was Jean's voice, and her own voice, insisting that Jean would live.

But Jean had been right, and her dream had been correct, she had died, and doubtless Freddie *would* be holding the little boy at the christening. As the corridors filled up with people covered in dust and blood, luckless people fleeing from the latest bombing raid, Freddie sat on, wondering dully about the reality of dreams.

Could someone dream of something that then took place? She shook herself mentally, and then shook herself physically.

'Can you take the baby on, Nurse Valentyne?' It was the friendly northern sister. 'The gentlemen over there have both indicated that it was the wish of his poor mother.'

Freddie shook her head, and then, seeing the look of astonishment in Sister's eyes, she realised she was shaking her head instead of nodding, which was what she was really meant to do.

'Yes, yes, whatever you wish. Yes, his mother did wish it,' she agreed. 'We can take him back to the Hall.'

'He's a good weight, love, a good big bouncing boy.'

Freddie stood up, and then as she suddenly swayed, Sister caught her, and put her own arm around Freddie's shoulders.

'Come on, love, I'll make you a cup of tea, and after that we can get on with everything. It's been a bad night, and likely to get worse, but we both deserve a few minutes out before going back to the fray. No point in getting in a worse condition than your patients, I always say.'

The black tea was indeed comforting, so comforting that it gave Freddie the strength to say, 'Could we have saved her, Sister Andrews?'

Sister shook her head.

'No, love, not the most experienced obstetrician could have saved the poor girl. She haemorrhaged. It sometimes happens in childbirth, and once it does, there is nothing to be done. Had she been here when she first went into labour, maybe we could have prevented it happening, but as it was, by the time she arrived, as you know, it was all we could do to save the little fella, let alone his mum.'

Sister walked towards Freddie, who had turned away, her lip far from stiff.

'Here, give you a quick hug, and then back to our duties, eh?'

Freddie found herself clutching this suddenly maternal figure. She had never been hugged before, let alone by anyone older. It had just not been what had happened when she was growing up.

She pulled away from her.

'Don't be too nice to me, Sister, or I'll be useless to you!' Freddie protested, wiping her eyes.

They both laughed a little hysterically, and then, straightening their aprons and their caps, they went back into the fray.

Chapter Eleven

Gervaise stared at his goddaughter.

'I have no idea, Daisy, none at all, and no – I can't pull strings for you, truly I can't.'

Daisy looked, and felt, miserable.

'It's just that, you know – we were all at Twistleton Court together, absolute friends; and nothing has been heard about her, or from her, for such a long time. Not for nine months, as a matter of fact.'

Gervaise wanted to say 'I have rather more important things to do than help you find out about one of your finishing-school friends' but he didn't. Instead he plumped for looking sympathetic, which he didn't feel.

'All I can do is, if, or when, I hear something of interest from France, I will contact you at once.'

Daisy nodded. She knew Gervaise could not wait for her to skidaddle out of there, and so, rather than hang about, she did just that, bolting back down to her basement flat, and shutting the door behind her. She had to get back to the war, must get back to the war, but she had promised Aurelia at least to ask Gervaise – who knew everyone, but everyone in government – to see if it was known what had happened to Laura Hambleton. For, despite being very much at the centre of certain things, Aurelia could find out nothing, or perhaps because of being at the centre of things, she was not telling?

Daisy stopped, and then realised, for the first time, what an idiot she was being. Of course! Laura's disappearance was not something that Aurelia could speak about, even if she wanted to. Her officers would not want her to know if Laura had been blown, would keep Aurelia thinking that Laura had merely gone into hiding, for fear it might affect Aurelia's own work.

Numbers everywhere were shrinking, pilots' numbers, workers' numbers – there were just not enough people to go round.

Women were now to be conscripted, and the rumour was that older women would be next, and men, grannies and grandpas – anyone would do. Just as had happened in the Great War, boys hardly old enough to have begun shaving were now being called up, quickly trained, and flung into fighter planes, or seated at the back of them with guns, and sent off to do their bit to defend their beloved island.

ATA girl numbers were down, too, accidents had been too frequent lately, and the people who had reported being shot at by friendly fire while trying to bring in planes to land had grown far too numerous for comfort.

Very well, it was nobody's fault, it was just one of the thousand other hazards of war, but flying through mist was bad enough without being shot at by your own guns!

Daisy lit a cigarette. It was so hard, so bloody hard. God, her language had deteriorated. She had damn well better pull up her socks and start dropping the bad words. Yes, she had. She stared at herself in the mirror as she smoked. She looked quite pretty smoking her elegant holder. She had to admit that she did. David had given her the holder to replace one she had lost. They had not seen each other for aeons. There were reasons for this. The main reason being that Daisy, now that Laura was known to have gone missing, out of guilt, out of despair, out of – well, you name it, out of so many emotions – had written and told him that they must not meet again.

She had not heard back from him, as she knew she would not. And although it was now nearly Christmas again, she did not expect that she *would* ever hear from him again.

Smoke curled around her head as she continued to stare at herself accusingly in the mirror.

It was the 'supposing' that she had not been able to conquer. That was the truth.

The 'supposing' that Laura had volunteered to be dropped into France because she had not heard from David?

Supposing Laura had been dropped into France because she knew that Daisy had fallen for – and indeed made love with – her David?

Supposing David had told Laura, but not told Daisy?

Oh God!

Daisy turned away from her image. She had never thought she would become this sort of tortured person. Was this what war did to you? Did it completely change your character? Did it send you from being a positive creature, not much to go on, but optimistic and cheerful, to this? That's what she had been, and now look at her! Talk about yesterday's rice pudding, she was last week's custard, if anyone could get any.

She picked up her shoulder bag, and swung it on to her shoulder.

Time to go back to the war. As she went out she passed the closed visitors' book, not wanting to see inside it, not wanting to see Laura's dear hand-writing and the words she had written: *Back soon, don't you worry!*

True to Jean's dream, her baby boy was christened in the little chapel next to the Hall. It was a family chapel, very small, very much of the Beresford clan, filled with plaques commemorating former Beresfords killed in battle, killed fighting for King and Country, for their homelands, for the honour of their families. And goodness, Freddie thought, looking round for the rector to arrive, the Beresfords were an honourable lot. Their intractable nature, their love of their country, it all seemed to be in the air of that small church. So full of the history of a family was that church, that the chapel's very existence seemed as much a symbol of the history of England as any far greater edifice.

'Who stands as godparent to this child?'

Freddie nodded. She did. She looked sideways at Miss Maude. Miss Maude did, too. They both raised their hands, as did Branscombe and Alec.

It had actually been at Miss Maude's insistence that Edward Joseph Frederick John Shaw Huggett had been christened in the Beresford family chapel.

By the time Miss Maude had recovered enough from her bad bout of influenza and was out and about, many weeks later, helping outside with the harvest, or bringing the cows in, or any other thing that her now restored health was able to allow, Ted, as the little chap was now known, was practically a toddler.

But christened he must be, whether his true grandparents the Huggetts were there or not. It mattered not at all, Miss Maude had insisted, to Freddie and Branscombe, and Alec and Dick and Tom, who had all looked and felt astonished, if only because they all knew just how much at odds Miss Maude had been with Jean, but that had been before the war. Now everything was different.

The christening cake, as was now the custom, was made for the most part of decorated cardboard, covering a make-and-do recipe of sponge; but the tea was as bumper as could be managed, with sandwiches, and biscuits made of grated carrot, and all sorts of other treats that the land girls, the

Lindsay brothers – not to mention old Dan, and Budgie and his wife – could find.

'No wine to wet the baby's head, though,' Branscombe had muttered. 'Only gin . . . Well, I daresay that will have to do.'

Maude overheard him, and went up to her vast cold bedroom, and without more ado produced an enormous bottle of vintage champagne which she had hidden behind her old ball gowns.

'No baby christened in our chapel goes without his health being toasted in champagne,' she murmured to the portrait of the little boy, before staggering downstairs with the jeroboam.

Of course, thanks to the baby having come through both winter and summer, and now winter again, proving to everyone's relief that he was a bonny bouncing little chap, the christening party was a wonderfully joyous occasion, as it should be when vintage champagne from long ago is flowing.

That night Ted was put to bed by Freddie, one of his two new godmothers, in an old cot that, in its turn, had been found and painted up by old Dan. Freddie could not leave him alone in her flat, and so she sat knitting and listening to the wireless, which was now her habit. She was back on day-duties at the hospital, leaving Ted with Maude, Alec, Tom, Dick and Branscombe, and sometimes Mrs Budgie, who now came up to the Hall from the station to help on the farm. They all took it in turns to look after him until Freddie was back from her duties, and perhaps because he had become used to so many different faces, Ted seemed to be the least nervous and fractious of babies.

Freddie stopped knitting, looking about her dimly lit room, with its old whitewashed walls, suddenly having the feeling that she was being watched.

She did not feel frightened, but she had the definite feeling that she was not alone. It was as if someone was above her, and smiling. She could also smell flowers. It was as if she had been presented with a bouquet and she was now leaning forward, and smelling them. The light scent was beguiling and reassuring, as if promising something good to come.

She picked up her knitting again. Before the war would she ever have thought to see herself as she was now? Knitting for half the night, looking after someone else's baby. She had never really liked babies when she was growing up, just not a very maternal girl, loved animals, but neither dolls nor babies had been attractive to her. Now she had Ted, it was all different. She loved him with all her heart, and although rushed off her feet at the hospital, she looked forward to coming back to the Hall, longing only to see his cheerful face – so like his father Joe's – loving to pick him up out of his cot and play with him before bedtime.

Freddie sighed suddenly. She could not now remember what she had wanted to be and do, before the war. And yet, after thinking that she smelt flowers, and feeling someone who loved her was watching her, she felt reassured. It was as if she knew that they would now win through. God knows how she knew, and only God did know, but that scent of flowers, the feeling of warmth in the cold room, had meant something. Tomorrow was Sunday, 7 December 1941. This year there would be no turkey. Branscombe, despite his well-earned reputation for foraging, despite what Freddie jokingly referred to as his not black market activities, but 'back-door market activities', had not been able to come up with much. He was always at pains to conduct his nefarious goings-on discreetly, and even more importantly, well behind Miss Maude's back, for he knew that Miss Maude would have had sixteen fits if she had known what he was up to.

But this year it seemed Branscombe had not been able to fix anything at all, not for Christmas lunch, nor indeed for any other lunch. They had to make do with what they had, whatever that happened to be.

Despite all this, Freddie felt something good was going to happen. She could not have said why, until she heard on the kitchen wireless that Japan had attacked Pearl Harbor.

The celebration at America at last coming into the war was muted, as it should be; but after that, as another wartime Christmas came upon them, yet again, everyone in England kept going about saying 'we are no longer alone in the war'.

No one said such a thing in front of Maude, because they knew that if they had done they would have had the worst of her tongue. Brigadier MacNaughton, up at the Hall for reasons he did not at first feel inclined to explain, did have the misfortune to say exactly that to her, and was given the full treatment.

'We have *never* been alone in the war, Brigadier! To begin with, we English have had the Welsh and the Scots with us. We have had Canada with us, we have had Australia and Tasmania with us, we have had New Zealand with us, we have had Malta with us, we have had India with us, we have had the Irish – yes, the Irish – eighty per cent of the male population of Southern Ireland have crossed the Irish Channel to come here and fight with us. We have had the Gurkhas, we have had the Tongans, we have had the Maoris, we have had the Norwegians, the Danes, not to mention the Polynesians, the Maltese, the Poles, the Czechs, the Hungarians, and the Free French. It is sheer nonsense to say that we have been alone! We have not been alone, we have had everyone with us, and now we have more people with us, now we have America. Well – that will be a help, but never, ever say, never let anyone say, that we have been alone. It is ridiculous, and what is more, it is mistaken, and it is utterly and stupidly wrong.'

Brigadier MacNaughton was so astonished by this speech that for a second or two he quite forgot what he had come up to the Hall to say. He frowned at the splendidly upright figure of Maude Beresford.

'Quite so,' he finally said. And then again, 'Yes,

quite so. However, it is my duty to inform you that there is some disagreement about the entitlement of Twistleton Hall to be exempt from being requisitioned by the army. I have papers here that indicate that the Hall is as much part of the village as the Court and so on and so forth, and always has been from earliest times.'

There was a short silence which Maude was disinclined to fill.

Perhaps for want of something better to do, the brigadier produced a sheaf of papers. Maude took them and, after giving them a cursory glance, put them on the table in front of her with a look of such disdain it seemed to the brigadier they might have been contaminated with Spanish flu.

Since he had sent an outrider up to the Hall announcing his intention of coming up to see her, Maude had elected to interview the brigadier *in* the hall, the inference being that that was precisely as far as she would allow him into her house, to be greeted by its owner. She remained seated behind her table, he was not invited to sit, and no chair was provided for him, either.

'Well, that is interesting, Brigadier,' Maude said finally, adopting her sweetest and most charming tone, which if Branscombe had been present would have immediately made him feel a little bit sorry for the brigadier.

Never was Miss Maude more dangerous than when she used a sweet or charming tone.

'Very interesting,' Maude continued. 'And I

suppose you came by this information via some sort of county officer, or some such?'

The brigadier nodded. He had. He smiled, looking round. He could not wait to set up shop at the Hall. Not that Holly House was not a nice and comfortable bivouac, but it was not grand like the Hall. Here, in the hall of the Hall, he would be able to stride about, his boots ringing against the marble stone floor, pretending that the portraits were of his ancestors, not this fearful old woman's.

'I know the character who would have provided you with this, Brigadier MacNaughton. I used to know him quite well, because he *used* to work here, years ago, after the Great War. He was not the most reliable of characters, not even capable of being a boot boy. I am afraid to say, he can hardly have changed, for this information is what is known by you and me as *mis*information, and I am afraid he has led you sadly astray.'

Maude opened a leather folder embossed with the Beresford coat of arms.

'Here,' she said, and she could not help sounding both sweet, charming, and thoroughly self-satisfied, since she had always known that this day would come. 'Here are papers from the Minister of Labour himself, from the Minister of Agriculture – even from that good man Mr Bevan – from many and varied ministers, guaranteeing the safety of the Hall from being requisitioned, simply on the grounds alone, quite apart from anything else, that we are a working farm here. You cannot at this time requisition what is not part of the village

383

proper, nor can you requisition my working farm. Good day, Brigadier.'

She stood up, and nodded to him, and when Aunt Maude nodded, as Daisy had often said – *'you take flight'*. A nod from Aunt Maude was as good as a kick in the pants.

She watched him go to his car, which was parked, sheer impertinence she thought, right at the bottom of her steps, and, anxious to make sure that he was going to be seen to go, and not hang about, she followed him out on to the steps, and watched his driver open the door to him.

It was then that she noticed the driver. A woman, in her thirties, slim, pretty in a vaguely vulgar way, but wearing the kind of expression that Maude particularly disliked. It was the good-as-you expression of a jumped-up piece of tat. The see-if-I-can't-get-back-at-you expression of someone who has a score to settle.

This young woman, so smartly uniformed, was none other than the dreadful nursemaid who had, it seemed, made young Daisy's life such a misery, and who had been dismissed and replaced by the delightful Nippy. Maude watched as Patty Bywater carefully closed the door on the brigadier's portly figure, and then made a well-known Churchillian gesture of victory at her former employer.

Maude stood on, expressionless. Victory Miss Bywater might think it, but not when it came to a Beresford.

Maude watched the car drive away. Of all the people she would not want to see shipped up on her doorstep that young woman was one. She turned to go back into the house. Women drivers were being used everywhere, and not just for driving, either. How in all that was unholy had that young woman managed to pull herself up by her bootstraps? Maude did not like to think. She closed the hall door behind her. Hadn't Branscombe told her the brigadier's housekeeper was of dubious virtue? Patty certainly had not got where she was by saying her prayers, of that Maude was *quite* certain.

Maude leant for a few seconds against the half-glassed door and thought about the implications of the brigadier's visit. She knew, she was quite certain, that the wretched man would not leave it at that. He would stop at nothing until he got his foot in the door once more. It was only a question of time. But by then perhaps, please, please, dear God, perhaps the war would be over by then?

With the army occupying Longbridge Farm, Guy had found a cottage in the Buckinghamshire countryside in which to spend Christmas. His experience in prison had been unpleasant, to say the least. He had only been there a couple of weeks when he contracted double pneumonia, an event which made Clive moan, 'Must you do everything to excess, old boy, even pneumonia?'

In the event the infection had nearly carried Guy off, but now he was out and about in the West End again – or at least out and about in what was left of it – he was beginning to feel better. An actor and a playwright once more, seeing the people he understood, being with the people he cared for, and who cared for him. He might be thinner, older, and not at all wiser, but he was still alive, and while his heart would never be the same again – since he knew very well the lady behind the trumped-up charges brought against him – on the other hand, his heart being free, he was now at liberty to fight even harder for victory, without giving a thought to anything else.

He summoned Miss Jones, of whom he had heard nothing but good, to his office.

Aurelia, freshly back from France, came to see him, marvelling at how strange London had become, not just because she had been in France, but because, with no familiar landmarks, it was so difficult to find anything that you remembered. Happily it was not difficult to find Guy, as he was at work in one of his favourite theatres, ensconced once more among the old theatre posters, in his dear old cabin, with its red velvet curtains, above the upper circle.

'How are you, Miss Jones?'

He laughed lightly. As a child actor Guy had been taught how to laugh lightly, and it had always stood him in very good stead, not least when he was in prison, where he had found that his 'light' laugh seemed to cheer up the other lags no end.

'How am I? How are *you*?'

Aurelia stared up into Guy's thin, taut face, a face much changed from the last time she had seen it. Inevitably the expression in her eyes was one of undisguised maternal anxiety, which made Guy smile. She was far too young to look so worried.

'How am I? You may well ask, indeed, how I am. Well, I am as well as can be expected after prison, and double pneumonia,' he told her, indicating that she should sit down.

They both lit cigarettes and stared at each other through the smoke.

Miss Jones had now, Guy noted, a great deal to be said for her. She had matured into a charming-looking young woman. All the schoolgirlish awkwardness had been knocked off her, and she was now slimmer, her whole demeanour calmer, stronger. In fact she was really rather beautiful. He found he could appreciate her in a way that he could not have done before, and had he not known that Clive was smitten, and had he not had enough of love, for ever and ever amen, he might have been tempted to fall in love with her himself . . .

For her part, Aurelia found Guy much changed. It was not just that he still had that strange pallor that even a few weeks locked up in jug was traditionally meant to give you, it was not just that his face was thinner, his figure much depleted, so that his immaculately cut suit seemed to have been cut for someone else, it was the expression in his eyes. It was as if he was struggling all the time not to give way to bitterness, to keep believing in human nature, and yet she had the feeling that despite the brave fight that he was putting up, he was losing, minute by minute, and of course the war could not have helped.

'Miss Jones, might I call you Aurelia?'

'Yes, of course, Mr Athlone.'

'Good.'

He had not indicated in return that she might call him 'Guy' which she appreciated. He, after all, was still, no matter what, *Guy Athlone*, and Aurelia was well aware, indeed appreciated, that they could never, ever be considered to be on the same level.

'As you know, Miss – as you know, Aurelia – I have been in prison, and am to a great degree, outside of the theatrical world, of course, disgraced. It was entirely my fault, and I know it; not, I hasten to add, that I overstepped the mark by making a mistake with my petrol rationing, but because I trusted a woman with whom I was once in love, and who once loved me – but a woman scorned is a very dangerous creature.' He paused, tapping his cigarette on the side of the ashtray in front of him. 'Love is a dangerous game, as you will doubtless discover, although it need not be. But in my case, love, fame and success have almost led to my downfall. I say almost, because I am not one to accept defeat, and my public have remained with me, as the receipts at the box office will show – and so have those few friends whom I love, and who love me.'

Aurelia was aware that Guy's speech was making it clear to her that he was not just a changed man, but a very changed man, which his frail

388

appearance underlined, and that just as his long-time love affair with Gloria Martine was over, so, too, was his ability to love, except in friendship.

'I hope I may be considered to be a friend and admirer,' Aurelia ventured.

Guy smiled.

'You may, Aurelia. Young as you are, you may. For you have not only proved yourself a friend, sending me such an amusing letter while I was in prison, but you have proved yourself a loyal supporter of a certain organisation, for which, as you know, I have worked for a long time, many years, even before the war.'

'Yes, yes, of course—'

'Now they are looking around for someone to take my place, because obviously, since I went to jug, I am now a marked man. I suggested Clive, but he too is a marked man, having stayed loyal to me, silly fellow, so he has taken on a desk job at the Foreign Office, and is keeping his eyes and ears open, as we all must. But I wondered if you knew of anyone who might be interested in becoming part of this particular set-up?'

Aurelia frowned. She could think of no one.

'No name occurs to me, I am sorry to say.'

'Never mind. You yourself are, of course, very busy?'

'Yes.' Aurelia stubbed out her cigarette. 'Yes, pretty much so, too. And likely to be busier.' She had again volunteered to be dropped into France.

Guy stared across the desk at her.

'You were determined to be brave, weren't you,

Aurelia?' he stated, quietly. 'I find so many people of a nervous disposition so often are.' He smiled. 'Your parents continue well?' he asked, after a slight pause.

Aurelia coloured. She knew just how much Guy loathed people such as her parents.

'Yes, they are well, which they perhaps do not deserve to be.'

Guy stood up.

'Yes, quite. It doesn't seem fair, does it?' he demanded, all of a sudden. 'People like that, the architects of our present hell, sitting in comfortable circumstances, while people like you jump into battle on their behalf!' He stopped, because his voice had become too emotional. 'Now, look,' he went on, in a calmer tone. 'It's Christmas in a few days, you won't want to spend it with them, I am sure, and you won't be busy-*busy*, until after the festivities, I don't suppose.'

His way of saying 'busy-busy' at once conveyed to Aurelia that he knew that she had volunteered to be dropped into France. She wasn't surprised. Guy knew everyone, he might even know too many people, which was perhaps why he had been thrown into prison on trumped-up charges. 'You'll come and spend Christmas with me. I know you will. Clive is coming, and one or two others. It will be fun. A touch theatrical, of course, but you won't mind that, will you?'

Aurelia smiled. She would love to spend Christmas being a touch theatrical.

Guy looked at Aurelia. He knew that Clive would

be thrilled. He also knew, absolutely, that Aurelia's crush on him, Guy, had passed, and about time, too. He could not tell poor Clive, in case it raised his hopes. Poor Clive did not hold just a single torch for Miss Jones, but a whole set of them.

Daisy received Aunt Maude's letter a few days before Christmas.

'*I hope you have forgiven me, dear child?*' she had written. '*Forgiven a stupid old woman.*'

Daisy smiled. Aunt Maude wasn't *that* old.

'*Do come and join us for the festivities if you can. Can't promise much of a Christmas luncheon, but there will be enough to go round, be sure of that. Your loving Aunt Maude.*'

Daisy folded the letter and slipped it into her shoulder bag. She would be flying two and three times a day right up until Christmas Eve, and then, whatever happened, she would get back to the Hall. She might be so tired she could hardly put one foot in front of the other, let alone hop into a car and drive down to Twistleton, but drive down she would.

As she eased through the country roads back to her old home for the first time for – for how long was it? Daisy frowned. Must be a clutch of years at least. She wondered at the fact that it was easier and faster to deliver a plane than it was to get around English roads. It was bad enough driving in the blackout, or coming back on trains that took as much, or sometimes more than, a day, standing

391

all the way – but driving in thick fog, even in daylight with no lights, was hell on wheels.

To take her mind off the beastly conditions, she imagined the welcome she would get once she drew near to the Hall, imagined that once she was through the security checks surrounding the village, had shown her identity card, and was on up the drive to the great old wooden doors, she would find the fire burning in the old hall grate – using wood from the fields. She imagined Aunt Maude standing on the steps to welcome her. So many images came to her, and of course her imaginings made her drive faster.

After many, many hours she arrived outside Twistleton, and all was as she had thought it would be. The security checks, the grim sight of the village already half-tumbled-down from army manoeuvres, the Court looking like it surely could not have done since the Black Death – windows broken, iron gates missing, the long drive a mess of mud and weeds, flattened by army use. And yet the excitement of coming home at last would not leave her.

Soon she would be bumping across the old broken road that led up to the gates of the Hall. Soon, very soon, she would be looking at the old facade, so beautifully set amongst its own gardens, its little park. She duly passed slowly through the wrought-iron gates, guarded on each side by stone pillars, atop of which sat the lead hunting dogs of which Aunt Maude was so fond. It was strange and marvellous that they had not been torn off their plinths and taken by the army by now, but no, they were still standing, seeming from their proud looks to be silently rejoicing in the knowledge that somehow they *were* still there.

But as Daisy drew near the house, as the bend in the now grassed-over drive gave way to a new vista, she instinctively knew that the place was quite deserted, that something was terribly wrong. She stepped out of the car, stiff as a piece of ice after so many hours of driving, and only too thankful for her already quite aged flying jacket. Whatever happened, at least she was home. She stretched back into the car for her shoulder bag, before walking slowly up the front steps to the double doors.

She pushed open the right-hand hall door, and walked in. There was no fire burning in the grate, as she had hoped, and no Aunt Maude waiting smilingly to greet her. She walked to the foot of the great old wooden staircase with its carved newels of ancient wood, and its polished shallow steps. She called up the stairs, and hearing no answer she started to walk up to the first floor, calling, and calling.

There was no answer. She stopped half-way up, knowing suddenly that she was calling to no one, and walked slowly down again, this time descending to the kitchens, still calling. But the kitchen was empty, even of the dogs.

She went out into the stable yard, calling, still calling. No one answered. She stood still, looking around. Freddie had written to her that they were

393

all now housed in the stables, but it couldn't be true, because calling into all the flats, pushing open their doors and calling 'cooee!' – such a stupid sound when all was said and done – she received no answer.

She didn't know what to say, or do. To say that she felt lost was to say the least. Her heart was beating hard, and she knew now, without any doubt, that something must be terribly wrong.

Then she heard it. The single sharp bark of a dog, and it was coming from the house. She ran back to the house, glad that she had a small revolver at the bottom of her handbag, although it was, unhappily, not loaded.

Still no one in the kitchens, and yet above her in the library she thought she heard the sound of feet moving. She took out her stupid little pearl-handled revolver and crept up the stairs. Whoever it was, whoever they were, the sight of a woman with a gun always struck fear into the hearts of the opposite sex.

She flung open the library door and stepped boldly in, her expression at its most defiant.

What she saw inside was something she would never forget.

Aurelia was trying not to laugh, but it was very difficult. The game they were all playing was that they had to mime a phrase or saying. She had just been handed a slip of paper with her phrase or saying on it, and it was distinctly naughty.

'Very well.' She held up one hand and showed

five fingers to indicate how many words there were, and then she paused, and finally, after some serious thought, made another gesture, which evoked a chorus from her small audience.

'Sounds like!'

She nodded, and started to mime watched by Guy, Clive and the other guests.

She was, of course, particularly watched by Clive, who was then watched by Guy, whose heart went out to his old friend, for if ever a chap was in love – it was Clive.

Mind you, watching Aurelia miming away so prettily, and with such touching enthusiasm, would have made most men in the room love her, if not fall in love with her.

'Very prettily done,' Guy said, applauding hard, not least because Aurelia was on his side. 'Very prettily done.'

Aurelia sank down beside Clive, her face flushed. If she had not been to France, if she had not worked in SOE – oh, a thousand *ifs* of one kind or another – she would never, ever in a million years have dared to play charades, and word-games, and heaven only knew what, in such illustrious theatrical company. She would have gone and hidden in her bedroom, and stayed there until it was time to go home.

Clive looked at her, trying his best to keep his expression affectionate, rather than loving.

'I expect now that you have won your turn, you feel you could climb Mount Everest?' he murmured.

Aurelia nodded, still staring ahead, not really paying much attention to the continuing game. She did feel she could conquer anything now. She thought of her parents, under guard in their barren lodgings, she thought of Laura, somewhere in France – she hoped – and then she thought of Daisy, and she hoped that she was safe back at the Hall, all forgiven. She hoped that so much. Daisy was not just her friend, she was her heroine. Daisy flying planes, who knew how, who knew what – apparently there was never any time to be told how to manage some new design that had been rushed out of the factory – flying not just by the seat of her skirt, as she so often joked, but with a heart of oak, a courage made of steel. It was people like Daisy, young *women* like Daisy—

'Your turn!' Clive said, in a gently teasing voice.

'What, again?'

'Aurelia – you were asleep!'

Aurelia stared up at Clive, and then around her. The room was empty, and she could hear laughter and talk from the cottage dining room, and the piano being played by Guy.

'Oh good gracious, how terrible!'

Clive pulled her to her feet.

'Not terrible at all. But we none of us felt inclined to wake you.' He smiled. Seeing her fall into a well-deserved slumber, the other guests had crept out, leaving Clive to watch over her. 'Come and dance. There's dancing next door!'

Aurelia looked up at him. Perhaps because she

was still sleepy Clive seemed to have changed. He looked not just very 'Clive' but startlingly handsome.

'What are you staring at?'

Aurelia shook out her hair.

'I never realised before that you were so handsome, that's all,' she said, laughingly, as she smoothed her evening skirt down. 'Guy gave me this, you know,' she went on. 'It was left over from a production of *The Marriage Mart*. Gloria Martine, playing Lola Margritte, refused to wear it. He said it's usually hats with actresses, so it was in that sense an unusual refusal, but I daresay you know all that?'

Clive took her hand.

'No,' he said, in a firm tone. 'The only thing I know at this minute is that I want to dance with you before Christmas Day is over.'

'Are we about to melt into each other's arms, do you think?' Aurelia asked, as he pulled her out of the sitting room and into the dining room, where the rest of the party had pushed the furniture against the wall, and were waltzing happily, blackout curtains drawn, candles lit.

'Not only shall we melt into each other's arms, we have a very good chance of staying there,' Clive told her.

'Surprise!'

Daisy stared around her at all the familiar and unfamiliar faces. She stood stock still, not moving, and as she did so she imagined running up to each

397

person in the room and hugging every single one of them – Mr and Mrs Budgeon, the Lindsay boys, Freddie and Branscombe, Dan Short – flinging her arms around all of them. But of course she couldn't, but only because she knew it would have embarrassed Aunt Maude. Instead she went up to her only living relative and kissed her briefly on the cheek, and that was before turning back to the others. As she did so, a wave of almost overwhelming grief washed over her, leaving her speechless, as she realised in one single awful moment just how many Twistleton friends were missing.

Jessica and Blossom, Jean, Laura – not Aurelia of course, she was spending Christmas with Guy Athlone – Joe Huggett, he was gone, and two from The Cottages who had been in bomb disposal. She thought of Jessica at the Court, and what the Court looked like now, and then she shook her head – now was not the time to remember – and smiled and laughed instead, and, bending down, greeted the mad assortment of dogs that had accumulated in her long absence.

'Bless you! You have given me the shock of my life!'

'We wanted to surprise you,' Maude said, with quiet satisfaction.

'And you certainly succeeded!'

It had been Maude's idea to give her a party. She knew she would have to do something to help them both get over the embarrassment of their reunion, but didn't know quite how to do it.

Then Freddie, perhaps guessing that there would surely be an awkwardness, suggested putting on a surprise party, which, as it turned out, had been ideal.

'I'll have to run and change!' Daisy looked down at her uniform.

'No, don't, you look wonderful—' Freddie exclaimed, putting a hand on Daisy's arm.

'I must change,' she insisted.

'Very well, shake a leg, but be back in five seconds,' Freddie commanded.

Back once again, Daisy looked as beautiful as ever, but a great deal more the thing, her long blonde hair caught up into a topknot of velvet ribbon. Her slender figure was admirably suited to the pre-war long silk dress that Maude had donated to her, long ago.

Freddie, too, looked admirable, despite having to carry Ted around on her hip, because he couldn't be left in his playpen very long without putting up a fuss.

'I'll take him,' Daisy said, hands reaching out.

'I thought you didn't like babies?'

'As a matter of fact, this is the first one I've tried!'

Daisy took Ted, gleaming with health and Christmas clothes made by Freddie and Maude from heaven only knew what – and heaven only did know – all found, as always, in the attic. His bottom half was made out of an old dressing gown, his top half out of an old nightdress, but he looked as smart as new paint.

Daisy, tired from driving and, well, the war, put Ted down after a few minutes, and as Maude started to play the piano, instead of carrying him she began to dance up and down with the toddler, as they all sang 'Away in a Manger' to Aunt Maude's playing.

'This little baby has a crib for his bed,' Daisy told him. 'This little baby is a very lucky Ted, isn't he?'

She looked round at the variety of people singing, and thought how much jollier it was that they were all there under one roof, all singing hymns to Aunt Maude's playing, no one feeling awkward, all the coldness of the old house quite gone.

Freddie, too, looked round, and with justifiable pride. The three Lindsay boys were grouped around Aunt Maude's piano, all singing lustily, and nearly in tune. Their once-wan faces had changed so much in the passing months, and that despite all the shortages. The fresh country air had given them the colour of autumn apples, and their dark heads of hair neatly cut by Freddie into nice shapes – no pudding-basin cuts for them – showed up their newly handsome looks. White shirts, and home-made bow ties, old-fashioned Edwardian jackets – once belonging to Aunt Maude's brothers, but now altered to fit the Lindsays – showed off their strengthening physiques. Looking at them, Freddie thought with sudden pride that if the Lindsays had been three young horses that they had all brought on, she could not have been more proud.

'Time to put on the hay bags!' Branscombe announced, following which they all poured, chattering and laughing, down to the kitchens below, where there were so many cooking pots bubbling, and there was so much going on in the old ovens, that the fact that most of the food was not what it once would have been, even a year before, was quite forgotten in the warmth of the moment.

'Will you have to go back quite soon?'

It was almost like the old days, with Freddie and Daisy sitting up in a flat above the stables, only, this flat was at the Hall, not the Court, and they were each nursing a gin, which they would never have done before the war, and there was no notice declaring that only members of the Daisy Club were admitted.

'Yes, tomorrow, I am afraid. I must go back and carry on. The war may be being won on the factory floor, but it is also being won *from* the factory floor!' Daisy joked.

Freddie looked crestfallen.

'Oh, I had hoped that you would be able to be with us a little longer.'

This statement amused Daisy, because it now seemed to her that their roles were reversed, and that where once Daisy had been the daughter of the Hall, now Freddie seemed to have taken her place, in every way.

'You are coping so well here, it seems that really, in essence, the village has become the Hall,' she said, changing the subject in an attempt to cheer Freddie up.

Freddie gave a weak smile. Coping! She would hardly call what she did 'coping' – struggling, perhaps, but not coping.

'Everyone is pulling together,' she conceded, after a second. 'But we all miss you terribly, Daisy. We pray for your safety every night. Specially Aunt Maude, she misses you so much. She is so different now you are back, smiling unexpectedly, and laughing, which she hardly ever does, or has done. And I miss you, and the Daisy Club, so much, really I do. It would be so nice if you could come back more often, but you can't: what you are doing is vital.'

Daisy sipped her gin, realising from what Freddie had just said that Freddie must be very lonely. More than lonely, if she was missing Daisy so very much. Freddie's war was very different from Daisy's war. Freddie had to cope with all the various people now clustered, one way or another, under the roof at the Hall, and yet, at close of play, she had no one with whom she could go to the pub and have some fun.

Daisy might be flying planes, she might be delivering them to airfields which on one day would seem to be seething with young pilots, and the next completely deserted – if there had been a lash-up – but at least she was with people her own age.

Freddie, when not rushed off her feet, nursing under very trying conditions, or looking after Ted, was really quite friendless, particularly now Jean was gone.

But it was Freddie's turn to change the subject.

'The Huggetts won't acknowledge Ted, you know.'

Daisy stared.

'Why ever not?'

'Because, you know – Jean. Well, Jean was from The Cottages.'

'Snooty?'

'"Snooty is as snooty does" is what Branscombe says.'

'I hate snobbery, do you know that?' Daisy stated with sudden passion. 'Preference is fine, we all have our likes and dislikes, but snobbery is so cruel, and has nothing to do with good manners. Snobbery makes me feel quite sick. I was thinking the other day that if there was one thing about the war, it does seem to have brought everyone together, and done away with petty attitudes.'

'I think it has. I see that on the wards, everyone helping everyone else. Yes, war has brought us together, everyone not caring who or where someone is from, not minding in the least, only wanting what is best – except for people like the Huggetts!'

'Perhaps they don't know about Ted? Perhaps no one has told them about Jean and Ted?'

'Oh, they know, all right. Your aunt wrote to them several times. Wrote to them about the christening. Wrote to them about how many teeth he had, what he was getting for Christmas, all that kind of thing, but not a word back. She is furious, you know, as well she should be. Abandoning a grandchild like that is inconceivable, most especially since he is Joe's only child, his son.'

Daisy knocked back her gin, and then lit her cigarette.

'Anyone heard anything from Laura, do you know?'

Freddie shook her head sadly.

'Nothing. And we're not allowed to know either, although Aurelia wrote to me in heavy-handed code that "a friend of our mutual acquaintance is at this time missing, believed to be abroad".'

'Laura was a FANY. FANYs don't go abroad, they stay at home ferrying officers about in military motor cars and getting taken out to The Four Hundred.'

'Not all of them, Daisy.'

'Damn, damn, damn. I suppose – oh God, I suppose she has only gone and volunteered for something madly dangerous?'

Freddie looked away.

'She'll be back soon, I expect. We all hope – back soon, don't let's trouble trouble, eh? I know the last time I saw her at the Daisy Club, at your flat, she was looking pretty determined, pretty whiz-bang, a bit of a Catherine wheel look about her.'

Daisy looked away, guilt now pouring over her like molten lead, like boiling oil, blistering her very soul.

*   *   *

The following morning, making sure this time to kiss everyone firmly on the cheek, she set off after a breakfast composed mostly, it seemed to her, of fried eggy bread, and chicory coffee.

'Don't wave, don't wave!'

Waving goodbye was now said to be bad luck, just as kissing people, if only before they went to the shops, had become routine.

Maude and Branscombe, with baby Ted on his leading reins, did not wave her off, but watched Daisy, manoeuvring the car as fast as possible down the grassy, bumpy path that had once been the drive, until the moment that she disappeared from sight.

'I only hope that she doesn't drive the whole way at that speed. If she does she'll have run out of petrol before she reaches Wychford,' Branscombe remarked, as they all three, baby Ted leading the way, turned to go back into the house.

Maude nodded. Branscombe was right. She pushed the hall door open. She sighed, and sighed again. Suddenly feeling tired, because she was all too aware now that every time she said goodbye to Daisy she did, as the song said, die a little. It was her age. Or it was memories. Something. But the truth was with each 'goodbye' a little of her went away, never to come back.

Sensing Miss Maude's mood, the dark cloud hovering above her – at which he was now getting quite adept – Branscombe turned to the mistress of the Hall.

'Can I leave Ted with you, Miss Maude? Got to

get on with my carrots and turnips, and all that. His playpen's in the library, and I lit the fire.' As Maude looked at him, shocked at this, he nodded in agreement. 'I know, I know, shocking stuff. But I found an old door at the back of the shed that leads to Fallow Field, you know the one? And I chopped it up. A bit of cheer before New Year.' He stopped. 'A bit of cheer before New Year? I am a poet, though I didn't know it . . .'

Maude smiled, and followed him into the library. Dear thing, he always thought he was being so subtle, but really he was about as subtle as a dog with his head under the table that had forgotten that his tail was sticking out!

Branscombe went down to the kitchen and started to cook, and as he did so he listened to the wireless. His old wireless from the old days, from Twistleton Court. Somehow that wireless meant the world to him, taking him back to the days before the war.

He missed Miss Jessica and Miss Blossom, every day. They were always at the back of his mind, but just now he really had to get to grips with pushing carrots through the mincer, a job and a half at the best of times.

Chapter Twelve

All Johnny could hear were the voices above him, and sounds as if water was running, and all he could see was an arm sticking out. He stared at the arm. It looked familiar, but since he could hardly see for the dust and the dirt clogging his eyes, he could not be sure. He tried to remember what had happened. His mother pushing him under the stairs, was it? Everything so quick, so sudden. Him playing, and then suddenly, before he could do much more than snatch up his toy, a feeling that the whole world was falling on top of him, and his mother was screaming and pushing him under what was now on top of him. He tried to stand up, but his head hit something. The kitchen table, that was what he had been pushed under, by his mum, or was it his nan?

'Anyone in there?' a voice called out, a little more clearly. 'Anyone in there?'

Johnny tried to call back, but his mouth was so full of dust he could hardly make a sound. Eventually he managed 'Help!', and then 'Help!'

again, and although he was lying down, he knew he had made a sound that had been heard by someone, because a voice said, 'I think I heard a voice, I think I heard something.'

'Help! Help!' Johnny called again. 'I'm here! Johnny Lindsay! It's me!'

After saying that, he lay back against the rubble, exhausted, while above him – or was it around him? – he could hear the sound of bricks being moved and voices coming nearer.

'It's me!' he called again, eventually. He wondered in a dazed way why he kept calling '*It's me!*' Until he remembered Mr Branscombe reading to him at night from that funny book, and the bit about Kanga and Roo, when Roo was covered in dust, and Kanga pretended not to know who he was, and how Roo had kept saying, 'It's me, Kanga!' Or something like that. That was what he was like now, that was what Johnny was like now: he was like Roo, he was covered in dust, and his mum would never know him. He lay still, toy in hand. Someone would get him out and wash off the dirt, just like in the story. He believed that, he really did.

Aurelia stared into Clive's eyes.

'I have to go, Clive, you know I have to go. Christmas is over, the war is not.'

'But you're probably doing something frightfully dangerous, and I won't see you again, just when we have fallen in love, and everything about us is golden.'

Aurelia reached up and touched Clive on the cheek.

'Love,' she said, a little hopelessly.

'Is what it's all about!'

'No, just at this moment it's war that it is all about, and we must win. We must defeat the Nazi devils, put them to the sword.'

'But, but, you might be pregnant!'

It was his last shot at delaying Aurelia, but he could see from her stubborn expression that it was futile. Aurelia shook her head.

'No, Clive, I am not pregnant.'

'How can you be sure?'

'Because, my dearest, dearest Clive, I am!'

Aurelia remembered the dreadful time when she had thought she was, and felt ashamed. It had been foolish of her – but also terrible. What a thing to happen! And then for all your friends to know, and make preparations in case you were. It didn't seem possible now that she could either have been so naive, or so open about herself in that way.

She paused, looking back with something approaching repulsion at the person she had once been. An hysteric, at the beck and call of her beautiful mother, darling old Hotty, and her father. Always on the verge of tears, always embarrassing everyone, especially girls like Daisy and Freddie who had backbone. Well, now she had backbone too, and she was going to show it. She would be dropped into France as many times as it took. She was determined on it.

She would take messages, and she would come

back with messages, and during all that time she would look and look for Laura, until she found her. She would not leave her friend on the other side of the *English* Channel, she would bring her back. Whatever happened she would find her, or find out about her. She had to.

'Clive, I know now that I am in love with you,' she said, with her usual straightforward candour.

'And I with you, but then I have been in love with you ever since I first saw you.'

Aurelia was dressing with her back to Clive, but at this she turned to look at him, astonished.

'I never knew that,' she said, looking around for one of her stockings. 'That can't be true.'

'It is true. Ask Guy!'

'Guy knew that you were in love with me?'

Clive nodded.

'Of course. We have been friends since time began.'

'Oh, I see. So he knew, and that is why he asked me down, is it?'

'Good gracious, no. He asked you down because he trusts you and he likes you. He is not someone who will ever ask anyone anywhere if he does not trust or like them. The only trouble now is that since he was thrown into jug, since the press turned on him, along with everyone else, except people in the theatre – and some of them, too – he trusts and likes so few people that, as he says, he would be hard put to fill the broom-cupboard at Longbridge with his friends, let alone the drawing room!'

Clive laughed shortly, and then swung his legs down to the floor. He had been hoping to make love to Aurelia once again, but he could see now that this was not going to happen. He could see, not just because she was dressing, but from the *way* she was dressing, that Aurelia's thoughts were with the war, that love had been put away on a top shelf. Her expression was very set – not grim, but set – and she slipped her slim feet into her shoes, and pulled on her suit jacket, in such a determined fashion that she might already have been on her way, not just going to her suitcase to pack.

'You can't tell me what you are doing, but you can promise me to keep away from all those sexy Free Frenchmen at Baker Street, and those passionate Poles and cheeky Czechs, can't you?'

Aurelia turned and smiled, the expression in her eyes one of amusement. Just how many Free French and passionate Poles she would be seeing in Normandy or Brittany was open to question, but nevertheless, given that she would probably only meet Communists – those who made up the now very active underground – Nazi soldiers, and Normandy farmers, it was easy enough to promise that she would keep away from the men that Clive imagined were a danger to him.

'I promise that whatever happens I will be faithful to you,' she said, putting up a hand to touch his cheek.

Clive took it and kissed it passionately, but even as he did, he knew in his heart of hearts that there was something that Aurelia was not telling him.

411

Something that said that she was not just returning to SOE in Baker Street.

Daisy had returned to ops with a heavy heart, for the truth was that being back at the Hall had weakened her dreadfully, in that way that people being kind to you so often did. If she did not know just how desperately people like her were needed, if she did not hate Hitler so much, she might have been inclined to throw in the towel, and take Jean's place on the farm.

Laura, on the other hand, had not returned from France for a very good reason. She was having an affair, and not only was she having an affair – her second, she realised just a little ruefully – but she was having an affair with a Communist, for goodness' sake, although, really, goodness had very little to do with it.

The fact was that the lines being run by the British through France would not have been possible if it had not been for the Communists. Without their single-minded hatred of the Nazi invader, without their grudge against the bourgeois middle classes, most of whom had thrown in their lot, all too willingly, with the Nazis – running agents would have been quite impossible.

The next, and undeniable, fact was that the Communists were as brave as anything. They were just what you wanted, the kind of fighters that most generals would give not just their eye teeth for, but most of their stripes. They were the *sans-pareils* of the underground movement.

They gleefully blew up bridges even as the Boche crossed them, and set booby traps with hair's-breadth timing for motorcades. They were also adept at running messages through the lines so carefully laid by people like Laura. Ice-cold in their daring, intent on thinking that in winning this battle, they were not just winning France back, they were winning back a *new* France.

Laura had been picked up by John François – always known as Friquet, for reasons she had never bothered to ask him – hardly a moment after Aurelia had left her in the restaurant.

Of course Laura had been told to expect some-one, but not someone like Friquet! Tall, handsome, insouciant, with a look in his eyes which told everyone that not only did he like women, but he knew that women liked him.

He was posing as a newspaper reporter working for a pro-Vichy rag, our man on the spot, as it were, which he seemed to find hilarious. Laura had been told that this was the type who would be her contact, but not exactly what he would be like. Even as he sat down on the bar stool so recently vacated by Aurelia, Laura knew that whatever happened now, whatever battle was ahead, being instantly attracted to Friquet was one fight she would willingly lose.

As it turned out, after they had made love several times, Laura found out that Friquet was not just a Communist, but an aristocrat, too. He came of an ancient French line, steeped in history, and his ancestors had somehow escaped the guillotine thanks to being rescued by English cousins.

'Although it is always possible that, as the last of the line, I may not have the same happy fate!' he joked. 'My family went to England, where they lived until it was safe to return, by which time our chateau was a little the worse for wear, but we managed to restore it, over the next hundred and fifty years – these things take time in France, as you know – and thereafter we have lived in it, deep in the heart of Normandy, unlike some, eschewing Paris, which was very sensible of us. But now, alas, the chateau is shut up once more, a desolate house, deserted by everyone except the mice. So, I the Communist son must once again fight for what is right, and, indeed, what is mine, or should be mine.' He shook his head, and as he did so, and turned to light a cigarette, Laura realised that his profile, with its head of dark curly hair, was reminiscent of the Michelangelo sculpture of David. And not just his profile either, like the statue of David there was no doubt that Friquet was very well made in every way.

'We must go back to the fight.'

He stood up, and they both quickly dressed.

'You must not be seen too much with me, because of retaliation,' he told her, taking both her hands and kissing them in a particularly Gallic manner.

'Hang on, no need to kiss my hand, I'm not a married woman!' Laura joked.

'It is time to be serious, *mon ange*.' As much as they both disliked being serious, Friquet most particularly, it was very important that Laura knew the dangers into which she could run. 'Listen, please. If you are seen about with me too much, it is not the Boche that will get you, it is the Maquis. They are very badly organised, or else, ask yourself, why would they be using me? No, you must not be seen with me too often. Now I think of it, we must not be seen together in the towns at all. We can meet here in this little seaside inn, because the landlord downstairs is a cousin of my married uncle, and he would rather take his own life than give us away, but nowhere else. You understand? As I am posing as a pro-Vichy newspaperman I, too, am in danger of what you English call 'friendly fire', but it is easier for me, because I speak the same language, whereas you, my dearest little Englishwoman, while speaking impeccable French, nevertheless do not speak the language of the Communists, or the Maquis.'

'I could learn, you could teach me.'

Friquet laughed heartily at this.

'No, Laura, you could not even begin to learn it.'

'Why is that?'

'Because, prettiest of creatures, because there are too many bad words!'

He left her, and Laura watched him go down the path that led to the coast with feelings of both delight and regret. Delight that they had made love so beautifully, more beautifully than she thought could have been possible, and regret that he had to go.

She lay back on the bed in the little white-washed bedroom, and thought of what lay ahead. She knew she must stay in France for the moment, that she was more useful here than she had been driving about London with a canteen, or down the Underground. Very well, she had come to France not just to set up lines of communication across the vast French countryside, but also to find her father and Dora. Where were they?

She had wondered that so often that it had become painful. Wondered it over and over again. Where were they? Why had they not come back? Why had they not fled to Portugal as so many caught in France had done? Why had they not taken a boat from the South of France as, again, so many of the English had done, packing their few jewels into a small suitcase, leaving the Nazis to take over their villas, their paintings, their silver and gold?

And yet, if she knew that she could find out what had happened to them. If she had already found them, too, would she really have volunteered when she had heard that a few French-speaking FANYs were needed to go to France? She doubted it. No, she knew she would not. She had come to France to find her father in order to prove to him that, little though he might love her, she loved him, and was willing to risk her life to find him. That was how deeply she felt about him, and her country, too.

She looked at her watch. She was due to meet a Madame Bonnet at a certain point in a village some few miles away.

She rolled the name around her tongue, saying it out aloud, as she did so, '*Madame Bonnet?*'

She imagined her, a goodly woman, a rollicking good sort, all black bombazine and woollen head-scarves. She yawned nervously. In half an hour she would go downstairs, and, slipping out of the back door, take a bicycle and a torch and start out on her journey. It would take her some time, but Madame Bonnet could not be met until midnight. Laura's contact had told her this.

Even as the village clock was striking the midnight hour Laura, pushing her bike – which happily did not squeak – found the street where she was to meet Madame Bonnet. She had a watertight story, thank God. Madame Bonnet was an aunt. She wanted to see Laura to put in order certain family matters, a little business of a will, something that the rest of the family must not find out, something that only Laura and she could settle, hence the lateness of the hour, because with so many Bonnets in that particular village, they did not want tongues to start wagging.

It was a good story, and Laura was happy with it until, after some time waiting, and *waiting*, clinging to her bicycle as to a lifeboat, she realised that the woman who had to be waiting for her, the woman going under the name of 'Madame Bonnet', was the tart saying goodnight to a German officer, who then drove off in a staff car, with a perhaps understandably happy smile on his face.

'Madame Bonnet? I think you are expecting me

– Marie Bonnet?'

The woman smiled, which Laura thought, fleetingly, was not a good idea. Her teeth were more than a little alarming.

'Come in, my dear.'

Laura walked up into a room lit only by red light. As she sat down she realised that this must be why places of vice were always called 'red-light districts'. How stupid! How stupid that she had never realised it before! She also realised that the lighting must make things easier, after all, not every man could, or did, look like Friquet.

'Where is your message, Mademoiselle?'

Laura produced it.

Madame Bonnet, if it was indeed she, read it briefly, and then with a look of unveiled contempt gave it back to Laura.

'My dear, this is of no use. It tells me nothing. Who gave you this?'

Laura was in no state to feel calm. She was in the upstairs room of a tiny village, which, if she did but know it, might well be stuffed with the Boche. Now was therefore not the time to look as scared as she felt.

'My apologies, Madame,' she said, at pains to at least seem polite. 'But I was given this message in good faith.'

As she spoke Laura's eyes were trying to take in, not the undoubted outlines and curves of her hostess, but the rest of the room. There was something about it that was not right. She had always understood that tarts' rooms were stuffed with dolls, and that kind of thing, but there was nothing like that here. With the single exception of the red light bulb in the rather provincial standard lamp, it was more the room of a respectable woman, right down to a reproduction painting of Monet's garden.

It was then that she heard the sound of boots coming up the stairs, and if she had not known that she had her little pill in her pocket, she might have screamed or fainted. As it was she said to Madame Bonnet, 'Are you expecting a guest, Madame, because if so I must surely leave?'

Before the tart had time to reply, Friquet came into the room. He recoiled dramatically the moment he saw Laura.

'Oh! *Nom d'un nom!*' he said, and then looked at Madame.

'I thought you said we would be alone!' He turned to Laura, and something in his eyes told her to react to his words. 'My darling! I am so sorry, but it has been so long – and you know, because you are so religious and deny me everything until our wedding, I have needs, masculine needs!'

Laura picked up how the scene should play immediately, and without more ado, she slapped Friquet hard across his face, and as she did so his expression was marvellously amazed. He put up a hand with undisguised shock to where she had hit him.

'I knew I would catch you out! One day I knew I would catch you. Thought you were being so clever, didn't you?'

She caught up her handbag, and marched past them both, and down the stairs to her bicycle. She hopped aboard it, and without looking back, she cycled her hardest out of the village.

Inside the room Friquet tried to look remorseful, and failed. He shrugged his shoulders instead.

'You know how it is with young girls,' he said. 'They don't understand men, they don't understand our needs.'

The tart, for such she was, also shrugged her shoulders.

'If you want to go ahead, it is double at this time of night.'

Friquet shook his head, but handed her a wad of money.

'I am sorry if you have been embarrassed, Madame,' he said, with great courtesy. 'It is just that – the mood is not quite right.'

She laughed a short, vulgar, ear-splitting laugh, and as Friquet ran down the stairs and out into the street, and wrenched his car door open before speeding away, he nevertheless had time to think that hell was surely filled with such sounds, thousands of such sounds. Nowhere else could produce something so hideous, falsely frantic, and at the same time, full of evil intent.

Laura arrived back at the inn first, and having hidden her bicycle in the usual wood pile, she bolted up the stairs, and poured herself a brandy. What was up? Where was Friquet? He would know what was happening.

Half an hour later, having carefully taken a very

different route, Friquet, too, arrived back, and followed Laura's route up the stairs and straight to the brandy bottle.

'What a lash-up!' Laura exclaimed. 'What happened?'

Friquet couldn't speak for a moment, nor could he tell her exactly how close she had been to being arrested by the Gestapo.

'There's been a clean-up, as well as what you call a lash-up,' he said, starting to laugh. 'The whole neighbourhood is crawling with the Boche. I got wind of it, from someone on the paper.' Friquet was improvising. 'What happened was that the real Madame Bonnet was arrested, thanks to the tart saying she was helping the Maquis. The tart was given orders to take your message, and to say it was false, so that she could detain you for a while. And then. Well, never mind. The truth is that it was, as you would say, "a narrow squeak".' He looked serious. 'That must not happen again.' He sat down quite suddenly, and stared ahead. The truth was that having Laura in tow was really quite a liability. He ought to send her on her way. He looked across at her. But he couldn't. He was like someone in a Greek fable, he had been trapped, enchained by love, and he a free spirit, *enfin*!

'I am a liability, aren't I?' Laura stated, reading his unspoken thoughts most precisely. 'I should go back to England, but I can't. The truth is, I want to stay and help, but not if it is going to endanger you.'

'My family's chateau is the perfect place to hide, you know that. It is more perfect than you can imagine.'

'I don't want to hide alone in a chateau. It would be cowardly. I can do that in England, if I want.'

'What do you want to do, therefore?'

'I can stay here, surely? If your uncle downstairs, or whatever he is, is trustworthy, and no one that he does not know comes here, this place is safe. Not many people pass by, and there is the sea. I can pretend to myself that I can see England.'

Laura was playing for time. She did not yet know how much she could trust Friquet. She must trust him, of course (what else could she do?), but she was still English, she was still alone, and she knew, instinctively, that if there was water, she could escape more easily. Once trapped in a lonely country house, there would be no way out. By the sea, on the other hand, there was always – well, there was always a boat, water, rocks, some feeling that you could get away.

'Very well, my dearest Laura. You may remain here, but you must only venture out for a walk to the shore when it is dark, never during the day. You are too pretty not to be remarked upon, even in your delightfully provincial clothes. Now, I must go. We will not see each other for a few days.'

Laura listened to him retreating back down the stairs, and as she did so she wondered whether her so-called feminine instinct was right. Was Friquet what he seemed to be, or was he, in reality, yet another double agent with a brilliant cover?

She was left alone in the inn, eating alone, sleeping alone, and wondering what to do next, for a few days. Once or twice she saw a lone fisherman coming in with a catch, and once, at night, she thought she saw torches flashing, but other than that, not wanting to make use of her radio, for obvious reasons, there was nothing she could do, but wait, and wait, hoping that something would occur to move her on, that someone whom she could trust would suddenly appear.

'Friquet!'

She fairly danced off the bed as he came into the room.

He pushed her away from him.

'You must go, my darling. No time to say more. There's a boat waiting, it will slip you round the rocks out there, and then take you as far as the opposite coast. You will be all right. They are very good, these people, they do it all the time. How, I don't know.' Friquet was packing up her things, and stuffing them into her shoulder bag. *Va! Va vite!* No time to waste, they are after you.'

Laura could not stop to question him, how could she? She snatched at the bag he handed her, and fairly fell down the stairs after him.

'Va! Va vite!'

As she ran after him, and down to the beach, and he flung her into a boat, and then helped a couple of very small but obviously very strong fishermen push it, Friquet wondered at the bad luck of it all. Poor Laura, she must never find out, must never know, that the people who would be after her, sooner rather than later, were not the Nazis, not the Gestapo, but the Maquis.

It was the surname that had done it. Hambleton. Arthur Hambleton. Laura had asked Friquet if he knew of this man, her father, if he knew of his whereabouts, and that of his wife. Well, his wife was long gone, but the father, it seemed, had been a double agent, and was also gone, but this Laura was not to know, ever.

'Good luck, my darling,' he murmured, as the boat finally left the shore, and Laura sat shivering at the back of it. '*Au revoir* – and let us pray to the good Lord that you return to me, when all this foolishness is over.'

He turned to go up the beach, but seeing torches above him, he thought better of it, and hid among the rocks until daylight, by which time whoever it was had gone. He walked up to the old inn, breakfast in mind – coffee, croissants – only to find the woman of the place weeping. Her husband had been arrested.

'Don't worry,' Friquet told her with his usual assumed nonchalance, 'I will get him out.'

'How? How can you?'

'Simple. I will tell the officer in charge that I will write about him in my newspaper. It always works!'

She stopped crying and served him breakfast, just as Laura arrived back in England after a journey which had seemed so fantastic as to be unreal. The brilliance of the men who had finally taken her on board, their ability to dodge not just shipping lanes, but landmines, was so inspiring that Laura felt ashamed that she had ever felt afraid. What had she ever achieved trying to lay down lines in France, that compared to that kind of brilliance?

'God bless England, and you!' she told them.

They smiled. It was nothing. They did it all the time.

'First time was Dunkirk, that was a bit of a baptism, but now . . .' They shrugged. 'It's the boat, you know, such a good old girl, really she is.'

Laura patted her keel. A converted pleasure boat, she had, it seemed, since Dunkirk, made the journey across the Channel under cover of darkness more times than they could tell her.

'It's her shape, see,' one of the boatmen said. 'Even if they see her, they have no idea what she's doing, or why, so they leave her alone. Simple, really. Go about in the unusual and people steer clear of you, that's what my old father used to say!'

It took longer to get to London by train than it had to cross the Channel, but at last she found herself outside the Daisy Club flat, putting her key in the latch. She had made soup for Daisy here, the last time – was it the last time? She could hardly remember. At any rate she remembered very well making that soup, and how Daisy had pulled a face at it. Now she would give anything for some of it, for any soup. She almost fell into the flat, and then shut the door.

She flicked her lighter just to see something,

and then, the blackout curtains being drawn, she lit a candle, and automatically turned to the visitors' book that Daisy still insisted, just like the old days at Twistleton Court, everyone must sign. She opened the book, and then looked round for a pen. No pen. She closed it again. No ink, no pen, no loo paper, no nothing. Suddenly France seemed to be the land of luxury, and she sighed for it, while at the same time feeling indignant. She would give anything for some food such as Friquet would now be eating at the inn. But this was England, and she must fight on.

Before she went to sleep she found herself praying for the boatmen, for the innkeeper, but most of all for her darling Friquet. He had got her out in time, before the Gestapo came for her. How could she ever repay him?

The men who finally unearthed young Johnny from the rubble and put him on a stretcher spoke to him in cheerful cockney tones, and they were careful not to move him until they were quite sure that it was safe. Then they carried him to the Red Cross centre and he was put on two chairs pushed together, while a kind lady washed his face and hands, and tried to brush his clothes.

As she washed him and brushed him the lady talked to him about what his name was, and what his mother's name was, and Johnny, still clutching his toy, tried to tell her, and he did but it was difficult for him to talk because he hurt so much.

'I were under the table,' he told the lady after a

426

while. 'Where's me mum? She was by me, she was making tea.'

'Is there someone who can come and collect you? Who we tell that you are all right?'

Johnny thought for a few minutes, and the lady waited. Eventually it came to him.

He had a brother called Alec, and he had two others, two other older brothers, too. They were away, in a place called . . . He stopped, frowning. He could not remember what the place was called. It was called something like a whistle. He stared up at the lady, trying hard to explain, but she kept repeating everything that he had said, which made him forget what he was trying to say next. Yes, he had brothers, and his brothers were all in a big house, and it had a hall, and they all worked on a farm, and there was a gent called Branscombe, and he was very kind, and looked after Johnny.

The Red Cross helper nodded, and then turned away. Yet another lost child, yet another evacuee to be placed.

She consulted her superior as to what to do.

'He'll have to be sent to another centre, we're full up here. And then, well – once they've identified the other bodies, he'll have to go to an orphanage, if all his family were in there.'

The Red Cross helper looked sadly across at the poor little chap lying between two chairs clutching his toy train. What a thing for a little boy. Bad enough to have lost both his parents, maybe all his family. Who knew if his brothers and the big house were not some sort of made-up story? But for the poor mite to end up in an orphanage would be terrible.

Freddie had not had a day off from anything since she had last seen Daisy, at least she didn't think she had. Not that she *should* have a day off, nor even a night off, nor even an afternoon off, why *should* she? No one else had 'days off', it was just that she liked to think that one day she would have time to take a walk, or go to the cinema – something that would let her off having to *think* any more, and also relieve her of the pressure of running away from what she thought everyone *else* was thinking.

It was the third year of the proper war, and everything was getting harder and harder. However much they all joked about being hungry, being hungry hurt. Sometimes Freddie, after a long, long day, would clutch her stomach and bang it with her fists because she felt as if she had an animal inside her, and it was eating her, and of course she did have an animal in there, and the name of that animal was hunger. And the worst of it was that they all knew they were very lucky, because they were in the country, and they could grow food, but it was trying to grow enough to spare that was so hard, and battling with the elements to get what they grew to the right places, and to the right people.

Each day now seemed more difficult than the last. It was not just trying to find enough food for Branscombe and herself to put in front of the rest of the household, but also having to feed the animals, help muck out, wash up, clean out, wring out, and any other things that happened to be needed. Hot water had never been in great abundance at the Hall, as she had discovered when she first arrived, but now it was even scarcer – what with the fuel shortage, the need to save electricity, and the need to do everything they could to save, and save, and save. It made everything so difficult, so tiring.

'You need an afternoon off, Miss Freddie,' Branscombe told her. 'Really, you do. You need to go to the cinema, or do something that will take your mind off the war. I'll look after young Ted here. You take yourself off, you look worn to a thread paper.'

Freddie frowned. Branscombe was obviously a mind-reader.

'I don't really think that I should, really I don't. Besides, the petrol, you know.'

'Tart yourself up, go on. Take yourself off. Put on your nurse's uniform, and hitch a lift, you'll be quite safe. Go and see something at the cinema at Wychford. Someone will take you.'

Freddie shook her head. Someone might give her a lift, someone might take her for a cup of tea, but to what purpose? She knew no one her own age. The army, grimly going about their training in the village, the land girls, who had their own club, their own language, Dan and Miss Beresford, little Ted, the Lindsay boys, there was no close friend with whom she could talk. She missed the Daisy Club, she missed having a gin with one or the other of them, or just a laugh. She missed friendship.

'What about tea?' she said in a dulled voice to Branscombe. 'I really should stay and help with tea.'

'Tea is as tea does. Off with you. I'll take care of everything.'

Freddie suddenly saw the sense in this. She dried her hands on a tea towel. She was back on nights at the hospital, going back to the Hall during the day to do what she could. She hadn't seen Daisy, didn't know where Aurelia and Laura might be, and hardly knew what a pair of stockings looked like, so scarce had they become. Some of the nurses at the hospital were now painting seams up their legs to make it look as if they were wearing them. Others had made friends with American soldiers stationed in the next town, although making 'friends' was perhaps a bit of a euphemistic way of putting it. Freddie was not up to making 'friends' with anyone, not even for a pair of nylons.

She opened her underwear drawer, and that was also a misnomer. She had managed to make new underwear for herself, out of some parachute silk, and very pretty it looked, but she turned away. She couldn't wear it, even on an afternoon off. She had to save it. She might need it one day, more than she did today.

Nowadays everyone hitched a lift, and no one thought anything of it. She straightened herself up, refreshed by just the thought of not having to do anything for the rest of the day, until she clocked into the hospital for night duty. She was just about to swing out through the hall doors, thinking that to see someone new, drink a beer, hear laughter in a pub, would do her no end of good, when she saw a car pushing itself slowly, very slowly up the drive.

'Who now?'

She spoke the words out aloud, and although they were innocent enough, the way Freddie said them they could have been swear words.

A young man climbed out of the much battered car, alone. Freddie frowned. Most unusual for anyone in this day and age to arrive alone. He stood staring around him. He was in civvies, and wore black leather gloves.

'Corporal Bastable!' Freddie saw at once who it was, and she went out to greet him, knowing as she did that this would mean an end to her beloved afternoon off. 'What are you doing here?'

'I'm driving for a few of our boys. They were wanted over at Bramsfield. I had an hour to spare, so came on,' he told her. 'Had to come back here to see, you know.' He stopped. 'Not much of the village left, now, after all. The army have certainly done a good job. But, had to see—' He stopped again, looking embarrassed.

'You came to see if we were all still here? Well, we are. A few of us. Come in and have a cup of tea?' she said, not really wanting him to do any such thing, because it would mean her outing to the cinema would go bang.

Benjamin Bastable seemed to understand this. He smiled.

'No, I won't impose on you, Miss Freddie. I just wanted to see you, see if you were all still all right, and you are.'

'And you? You married?'

He coloured slightly, and shook his head.

'No, I'm afraid nothing came of it, you know. She met someone else. I think she was put off by the war.' They both knew that he really meant by the loss of his hand. 'Still, I got left with the dog!' he joked, suddenly.

'Oh, I am sorry.' Freddie said this a little automatically, because she had suddenly found that she was not sorry at all.

'I mustn't keep you, Miss Freddie, I'll be on my way. The boys, you know, they'll be back from their doings before you can say knife – well, we hope so, anyway.' He noticed her coat. 'But you were going out when I arrived?'

'Yes, yes, I was just going for a walk – well, on an outing,' Freddie lied, because she didn't want to embarrass him by asking for a lift.

'Can I give you a lift to Bramsfield, or some such?'

It was Freddie's turn to colour.

'Well, if it's not an imposition?'

'Not at all. Do anything for you and Miss Beresford, you know that, Miss Freddie.'

'Freddie, please—'

'Ben.'

They shook hands as if they had never met

432

before, and Freddie realised that Ben's black leather gloves were a way of disguising his false hand, because he shook her right hand with his left one.

Once in the car, they never stopped talking, and perhaps because Freddie was the same age as Ben, and the war had changed them all so much, it seemed to her to be perfectly wonderful to be talking and laughing with a boy her own age.

'And where can I drop you?'

'At the cinema. I am having an afternoon off, before going back to the hospital. Pretty indulgent, I'm afraid, but there we are. Branscombe gave me a pink ticket.'

Benjamin nodded, understanding.

'If you want to find us, we're all meeting later for a beer at The Cock and Pheasant, at about six.'

Freddie paused. A beer with boys her own age! No patients, no one needing to be bandaged, or fed, or given an anaesthetic – if you could find any.

'It sounds like heaven, I'll see you there.'

She walked into the cinema, feeling that she had agreed to something pretty daring, but caring less than a farthing that she had.

While Freddie was out, a letter came for Maude in a very small, flimsy square white envelope. She stared at it. She did not know the handwriting, and as she opened it she suspected that it might be something untoward, which it was.

Madam,

I am a neighbour of Mr and Mrs Lindsay, whose boys I think are with you. Madam, I am sorry to tell you that those good people are no more. Their house and mine had a direct hit, but I was away in Penge with my sick mother, and so did not get killed, but they were not so fortunate. I promised their mother if anything happened I would let you know on account of them being, as I understand it, with you, and so that is what I am so doing, madam. I am so sorry for the boys. Myself, am childless and a spinster, so much better had it have been me. No more ink, the last!

Yours truly and obliged, Enid Broadstairs

Maude found her way downstairs with some difficulty, because Branscombe was so mad keen to save electricity at any cost. He only worked by one light in the kitchen, and there were no overhead bulbs on the landings. She really should have taken her torch, but the news was so grave she clung to the stair rail instead, and eventually, and gratefully, arrived in the kitchen.

'Branscombe?'

Branscombe turned as Maude stumbled into the room, waving a small piece of lined paper obviously torn from a school exercise book.

'This letter, it's from someone in the Lindsay family's street. They've been bombed out, the street has all gone. Bombed out. The family have all been bombed out. She thinks no one was left.'

Maude sank down into the old kitchen chair

and put her head back, closing her eyes. She had become so close to Alec, and his brothers, to Tom and Dick, but Alec particularly. He was growing into such a fine young man, and now this had happened. It would devastate them.

Branscombe took the letter from Maude.

'Is little Johnny gone?' he asked, and it seemed to him as he did that he could hear his own voice, and it was strangely steady, strangely matter-of-fact, as if he had been waiting to be told, all these months, that Johnny would not be coming back to them.

Maude opened her eyes.

'I am afraid that we must think that he is, Branscombe,' she said, and Maude's own voice seemed to her to be matter-of-fact, because she was so shocked.

And yet why should she be so shocked, for heaven's sake? Sending a little chap like that back to his mother to live in one of the most dangerous parts of England, what did they expect? What *did* they expect?

'I'd better go up and tell the boys. They'll be in the milking-sheds, poor lads.' Branscombe turned away. His gravy was about to burn. Gravy! No one could call that gravy, it was more like dish-water. He threw it with sudden force into the sink, where it drained slowly away.

'Alec, Tom – where's Dick?' He called them, and they came up to him, knowing at once from his sad walrus face with its black eyepatch that something

435

was terribly wrong. 'I am sorry to tell you, but your house, your home, has had a direct hit. They don't think that anyone has survived.'

Alec stood quite still, staring at him, and then he turned slowly away, and went back to his milking, Tom rushed off howling, and Dick sank against the wall, his face working with the struggle not to cry.

'I'm sorry I had to be the one to tell you, boys.'

Alec turned round, briefly.

'I'm not, Mr Branscombe.'

Branscombe turned away.

'Must get back to making tea. Make sure that Tom gets in, won't you, Alec? There's a good lad. He'll need something. It's a long day for all of you.'

'And for you, too, Mr Branscombe.' Alec turned once more, nodding. 'I'll be in to help you soon as I've got through Mrs Rommel, here. Can't leave her to anyone else. Kicks like a mule, as Miss Jean used to say.'

Branscombe nodded, and he went back to his kitchen. He sometimes wondered at how anything, or anyone, went on. Two wars, and they weren't even finished with this one. Two wars, and all those dead, and for what? For nothing that he could see. Oh, he could see that they had to get on with it now that they were in it, but how had they arrived in it in the first place? He shook his head. The devil, and only the devil, really knew.

*   *   *

Freddie could not wait for six o'clock to arrive. The film was terrible, but possibly it seemed all the more so because she was so looking forward to going to The Cock and Pheasant?

She had packed her precious pieces of loo paper in her handbag, and so was able to arrive early at the pub, and 'pop to the aunt', where she put on some lipstick, and combed her hair.

She stared at herself. She had grown so thin that Sister kept joking that if Freddie stood sideways they would never be able to find her.

She pinched her cheeks, and put her long plait into a twist at the back. Despite the shortage of shampoo, and having to melt down soap – if you could get it – she could not bring herself to cut off her hair, particularly since Jessica and Blossom had gone. Aunt Jessie had always been so proud of Freddie's long hair, ever since she was small. She had promised Jessica never to cut it, and she never would.

She climbed slowly up the stairs, hoping that no one would come rushing up to her and ask her what to do about their boils or their VD, or their asthma, or anything else that happened to be wrong with them, because one glance at her uniform, and a queue could form. Happily, Benjamin Bastable was waiting for her in the bar with a particularly eager expression.

'Beer?'

'Lovely, thank you. Can I?'

She opened her purse to help out with the round.

'No, you can't,' Ben said, looking shocked. 'You're my date, not my war chest!'

Freddie smiled, and they started talking, only to be interrupted a few minutes later by the rest of what Ben called 'our gang'.

'Of course you know he lost his hand helping us out, so that's why we have to let him drive us?'

Freddie smiled, knowing better, but also knowing that driving with one hand could not be easy. But then, flying a plane with no legs wasn't, either, and they'd all been told about a certain pilot who did that.

'There's dancing in the upstairs room. Want to come and jitterbug?'

'Don't know how to,' she had to admit.

'It's easy. I'll show you, as long as you don't mind catching my left hand. I can spin you, and you can follow my feet, just do the same as I do.'

Freddie looked down at her nurse's uniform. Would it matter?

'I was going to hitch a lift, and then go on to the hospital, that's why I'm like this,' she confessed, feeling suddenly awkward, as they were passed by girls who were really got up to the nines, if not the tens.

'You look cute,' Ben told her. 'No one to hold a candle to you. Come on.' He held out his left hand and pulled her after him. 'You don't know what fun is until you've jitterbugged.'

Branscombe nodded at Alec. He had given him a top-to-toe inspection, and fully approved of what he could see. It had not been easy to kit Alec out from the few clothes that they had, but kit him out they had. The only hitch had been finding shoes. Alec had, quite rightly, refused to wear a pair of dancing pumps that Miss Freddie had found in the attic, instead they had all agreed that the riding boots were the only solution.

Alec cycled to the station, one thing, and one thing alone, on his mind. He had to find out what had happened. Very well, the house had taken a direct hit, but he had to see for himself. He could not possibly bring the others, as it would leave the farm too short-handed, but Miss Maude and Mr Branscombe understood, he had to go back to London to see everything for himself.

The train, when it arrived, was so crowded that it was not just a question of standing, it was a question of fitting in at all. Mr Budgeon gave Alec's backside one last great shove, and thanks to him, and his skill at shutting the door, Alec found himself aboard, and on his way back to London.

He also found himself face to face, only inches away, from a dozen unfamiliar faces, who all stared at him.

'We were just discussing the movies we have seen,' a Canadian soldier said. They were standing so close to each other, that, as the soldier joked, a little later, 'Any closer and we'd have to marry.'

At that particular moment, though, the soldier smiled encouragingly, but to no avail. Alec had to admit that he had never seen a film, nor even been to the cinema.

439

'I live in the country,' he said, by way of explanation, and as he spoke he could see that his fellow passengers were staring at him, so closely that it was not difficult to see they were thinking he was like someone from Mars, if he had never seen a film.

'What's that like, living in the country, then?'

'You don't sound like a countryman—'

'No, I'm a cockney, but I live in the country now.'

'Well, tell us about it, why don't you?' The Canadian nodded encouragingly, once more, as the train slowly made its way towards the capital.

So Alec told his fellow passengers what it was like to be in the country, and how hard it could be, but also how rewarding. He told them about getting up at first light, and going to bed as it faded, about the kind of animals you saw, and the birds. How you could, if you were lucky, see a kingfisher, which was of such a startling colour that it made you wonder how it could survive. He told them about the army taking over Twistleton, and how all the birds and the wildlife had somehow seemed to have taken refuge at the Hall, away from the armoured cars and the guns and the mortars. He told them how Miss Maude went to nurse at the hospital, because she had nursed during the Great War, and how Mr Branscombe made soups for them all out of everything and anything, and how they set about the hedgerows in autumn, plucking what they could, from hazelnuts to blackberries; and how he had learned to shoot rabbits, and skin

440

them, too, and how he and his brothers milked the cows, and knew every one of them by name. He told them so much that by the time the train, very, very slowly, arrived in the middle of the night at the station, and they all had to take refuge in the Underground because the sirens were screaming, the Canadian soldier said in parting, 'Thank you, young man. Now I know exactly what we are all fighting for. And good luck!'

There was no point in Alec trying to make his way across London immediately. Instead he stayed down in the Underground, trying to enjoy the people, trying not to realise that he was no longer used to crowds, trying not to see what some of them were doing, trying to endure the smell, which was a hundred times more intrusive than the smell from a cow's stall or pigsty.

Once the all-clear sounded, he walked to Miss Daisy's basement flat, to which Branscombe had given him a key. He found the house eventually, by dint of asking anyone and everyone, and was at last able to turn the key in the latch, all the while not quite knowing what to expect. He had never been in this part of London before, and although the buildings were bombed, and the streets filled with troops and police, it seemed to him, as he asked for directions, that the whole of a very sophisticated world was being offered up to him. The people were so different from those with whom he had grown up, not just their voices, but their faces. He pushed the basement door open. Inside the flat the blackout was in place all right, and it was as dark as he had expected – which made it all the more startling when he realised that there was someone else inside, someone there ahead of him. He caught his breath as a voice spoke out of the darkness.

'Sign in!'

Daisy flashed a torch at him, before quickly shutting the door, and putting on a very small low-watt bulb.

'Miss Daisy!'

Daisy grinned. There was no other word for it.

'Yup, this is Miss Daisy, Alec, and this is my club, and you ain't going no further, young man, without signing yourself in.'

Daisy opened the visitors' book and pointed one elegant finger at the last name there.

'Sign there, Alec Lindsay!' She stopped suddenly, staring at the last signature. 'Laura – Miss Laura – signed in before you. Oh, and she has left me a nice little note, too.'

Darlingest Daisybags,
So sweet of you to say we could all return to the Daisy Club whenever we wanted. I have spent a wonderful night under the table, until the all-clear, and then a blisskins sleep on your ducky little sofa, and now I am off down to Twisters to see the other members of the Club, but meanwhile I send you love and thanks from your now really rather Froggy little friend – safely returned!

442

Daisy finished reading the note, put Alec into her bed, shared some chocolate with him – he had never had it before, bless him – and then settled herself down on the sofa to try to sleep. That sleep would not come was nothing to do with the comfort, or not, of the sofa, but everything to do with the realisation that David had signed his name in the book when he was last at the flat with her, Daisy.

She went to stand up, and then realised that the flat was so small she wouldn't be able to take more than five strides, and anyway she didn't want to wake Alec. She sat down again. If Laura had come here, Laura must have seen David's signature in the visitors' book. She just must have. Daisy lay back in the chair. She would have to tell her. Most of all she would have to tell her because she had heard from David for the first time in ages, only a few hours earlier. He was still alive, and wanted to see her again. Had to see her again, but fretted that she might not want to see *him*. Daisy did want to see him, but not before she had spoken to Laura.

The following morning Daisy insisted on taking Alec back to his home. It was a devastating sight, but the clearing-up of the street had obviously been going on for some time. She left Alec silently staring at the remains of his parents' house, and went to talk to some of the neighbours, the lucky ones who had escaped a direct hit, and who were now helping to clear the street of the remains of the unlucky ones. All the living told Daisy that they were determined to cling on to their homes, despite the lack of water, the lack of anything, really. They were still defiant, and unable to leave all that they loved, all that they had worked for.

Alec remained standing in front of the rubble that had once been his home, struggling not to show his feelings, his throat working as he realised just what had happened. He was biting on his fist, really biting, when he heard footsteps behind him, and looked round. It was one of his parents' oldest friends.

''Ere, Alec Lindsay, isn't it?' Alec shook the hand held out to him. 'I wouldn't have known you from Fred Astaire, you changed that much, young man.'

He stood back, taking in Alec's grown-up height, his whole demeanour, which gave Alec much-needed time to pull himself together.

'You've changed into a proper toff, you have! Look at you! Riding boots and all! Come with me, I've got something for you, my lad, something that will please you, too. A proper treat I have in store for you. My, but my missus won't half be glad to see you. She won't half. Come on, put your best foot forward, lad.'

It was Daisy's turn to look round. Alec? Alec? Where was he?

She walked rapidly down the street, calling out, stopping people, asking. They pointed to a house further up, the end-of-terrace house always so prized by those who lived in a row.

'In there!'

Daisy stopped by the gate, or rather by the half-gate, and then, seeing Alec by the door, she made a pretence of shutting it, despite it not being anything more than a few pieces of wood swinging off a hinge. She did it so smartly that Alec burst out laughing, but when Daisy saw who was standing beside him, she started to cry.

'You're not to tell Aunt Maude I blubbed. If she finds out she'll kick me out again, truly, she will.'

Daisy said this as the car turned into what had once been the long drive up to the Hall. They had driven back to Twistleton through a rainstorm, two security checks and a hail of bullets – it was the new Nazi pastime to fly low and shoot at civilians.

They had given two VAD ladies a lift, not to mention a very old member of the ARP, a kindly gesture which Daisy had soon regretted.

'Everything's initials now, isn't it?' he had said, grumbling. His whole personality had been infused with a sort of strange, suppressed boredom. 'People too lazy to pronounce anything any more.' He then proceeded to pronounce on everything from the conduct of the war to the black marketeers, and always in such a tired voice, as if he had quite given up on everyone else, for the good reason that they were not like him.

But that was before Daisy, all too used to identifying the sound of enemy aircraft, had driven off the road, and shouted at them to get out of the car.

And hadn't she been right? Bullets had indeed rained down from the returning German bombers, but happily, not on them.

After that, the elderly gentleman had not been at quite such pains to appear bored. In fact he had shut up, which was just as well, for if he had not, Daisy thought she might have chucked him out of the car.

Anyway, come hell or high water, and they had enjoyed a little of both, here they were at last, creeping up the drive to the steps of the Hall.

Before Daisy even had time to pull on the handbrake, Freddie and Branscombe and Aunt Maude were out on the top step to greet them, little Ted beside them. In fact everyone and anyone who could was standing behind them. Tom and Dick, on hearing the motor car arriving, ran from the side of the house.

'Johnny, Johnny, Johnny is back!' they all shouted, and laughed, and then shouted some more – and laughed some more, too.

Later Daisy explained that the Lindsays' neighbours, knowing that Johnny had been scooped up by the Red Cross, had taken him in, while all the time hoping that the rest of the family would contact them.

In spite of all the jubilations going on around him, Johnny was silent, while allowing any number of people to embrace him, allowing them to even kiss him. He himself even kissed little Ted, and patted the dogs, of course, but it wasn't until he was with Branscombe in the kitchen that he finally spoke, holding up a small brown paper package that he had clutched all the way from London.

Branscombe watched him.

'What's in that when it's at home, then, Johnny?' he finally asked, as he handed him a piece of pastry he had baked for his return.

Johnny gave Branscombe a sage look, and as he did so Branscombe noted that he now looked older than his years, as he would do after all he had been through, but he seemed strangely satisfied, too, as if something in which he had believed had come true.

'The train Miss Maude gave me, see, Mr Branscombe, she were right, see?'

'Miss Maude is often right, young Johnny.'

Johnny held up the toy train given to him by Maude.

'She said it would bring me back, and, see – it did.'

Chapter Thirteen

Branscombe's expression was immovable, stubborn, and intransigent, all at the same time.

'You will have to go and tell Miss Maude, Miss Freddie. You will have to go and tell her that this chap wants to marry you, and after only seeing you twice. It is not for me to say, but it does seem a bit precipitous, even for wartime.'

Freddie's expression was not unlike Branscombe's.

'I don't see why. I just don't see why it is precipitous. Why, only the other day I read of a couple who met on a train, fell in love instantly, got off at the next stop, and went straight to the registry office and got married.'

'The train must have taken a long time between stations, and doubtless had a stop or two in tunnels, too.'

Freddie stared round at Daisy, who pulled a face, not quite knowing where she might fit into the conversation, if at all.

'It is just the way it is done at the Hall, Miss Freddie.'

'But I'm not a Beresford. If I was, well, I would have to go and tell Miss Maude, or ask her for permission to marry, but as I am to all intents and purposes an orphan, and over twenty-one, I don't see why it is necessary, really I don't.'

Branscombe's expression remained unchanged.

'Do as you like, Miss Freddie, as you always do, but the truth of the matter is that you are at the Hall, and here things are done differently. It is only good manners, after all, Miss Maude acted *in loco parentis* when you were an orphan and a minor.'

Daisy and Freddie retreated to the flat. It was still bitterly cold, even though it was meant to be spring.

'I don't see why you have to tell Aunt Maude you want to marry Ben what's-his-face,' Daisy said, pouring them both a gin. 'I mean to say, she's not your mother, and you're only here for the duration. Once the war's won, you'll be off like a shot. Branscombe's being a bit stuffy, surely?'

'Both Branscombe and Miss Maude, they've both been a bit preoccupied lately,' Freddie went on. 'There've been a great deal of coming and goings, ever since young Johnny came back. Something's up, although what, I wouldn't know.'

'Now I'm based so much nearer, I can help you out here, you know, with everyone. All hands to the pump, and all that. And God knows you need all hands with that pump out there.'

Freddie shook her head.

'No, you stick to your planes, you'll only be an

449

extra mouth to feed,' she said, straight-faced. 'And really, we could do without that, and you. We can manage, we have done, and we will go on, until this bloody war is over! Excuse my English . . .'

Daisy laughed, and then decided to bite on the bullet, probably the effects of the gin.

'Freddie, I have to tell you something. I have done something pretty dreadful.'

Freddie put her hand up, after gulping her gin too quickly.

'Don't tell me any secrets, don't tell me anything. I am hopeless, I will only come out with it, and ruin everything.'

'I slept with David Moreton,' Daisy burst out.

Freddie wanted to say 'Is that all?' But she knew that it would not be the right thing to say, so she just stared at Daisy, not really understanding, and then the penny dropped.

'You mean David Moreton. David Moreton? The David Moreton that Laura was in love with?'

'Yes. That David Moreton.'

Daisy nodded, while at the same time finding she was unable to look Freddie in the eyes. And when she could, eventually, she saw that Freddie was not as shocked as she should be.

'I have to tell Laura, don't I?'

Freddie shook her head, appalled.

'No, you do not have to tell Laura anything. Do not even attempt to tell Laura anything.'

'But she must know, anyway, because David signed his name, silly fellow, in the visitors' book in London. He signed his name.'

'So?'

'So Laura must have seen it, because she has been staying at the flat, off and on.'

'And?'

'And, well, it is pretty obvious.'

Freddie leaned forward, and smacked Daisy lightly on the hand.

'That is for being so stupid. Why do you want to tell Laura something that she doesn't want to know, wouldn't want to know? Is it because you are thinking of her? No, I suggest, ladies and gentlemen of the jury, that you want to tell Laura because it will make *you* feel better, and for no other reason.'

'But what if she finds out? She is bound to find out.'

Freddie gave Daisy a vaguely maternal look. Daisy was very beautiful, and very brave, and very, very silly.

'If you are intent on getting married to David—'

'Or he to me—'

'Then there is no need to tell Laura when you and he met. It is of no matter. Frankly, when all is said and done, not only doesn't it matter, but it is none of her business. Besides, Laura forgot about David aeons and aeons ago, she is on to fresh fields, and certainly pastures new.'

'How do you mean?'

'How I mean is, silly, Laura wrote to me – I'll find the letter for you – she has met the love of her life, but she is going to have to wait for him, because he is not in England, and not an Englishman. (It somehow got through the censor, which was a miracle, don't you think?) So, where was I? Oh yes, so why would she now care a threepenny damn if you're going out with David what's-his-face, or anyone else, for that matter? She has a new love in her life, and it is the only one that now matters.'

Daisy could have burst into tears with relief. Instead she lit a cigarette.

'Are you sure of this?'

'Of course I am sure of it. Why would I not be sure of it, if it means that much to you, which it does. I should be boiled in a cauldron, if I was not sure of it. At this moment in time Laura has gone to stay with her aunt, who, it seems, is busy giving everyone perfectly delicious food and carrying on as if there were no war on, which is disgraceful, but Laura is revelling in it, just for a bit, and you can't blame her, really.'

Aurelia, on a flying visit to the Hall, had actually told Freddie what Laura had been doing. Well, what she had actually said was, 'She's been assing about in France.' This was no way to refer to someone putting her life on the line for her country, but Freddie had so far managed not to tell Daisy.

Daisy, in her turn, was still too stunned to care what Laura had been doing, or where, or to be able to even feign interest in it, so she asked nothing more.

'You are an absolute angel, do you know that, Freddie?' she said, eventually.

'Yes, I do. Now, staying on me, what am I going

to do about Ben Bastable and Miss Maude? Do you think that Branscombe is right, that I will have to ask your aunt's permission to marry him, because of being a minor and *in loco whatsit*? It does seem a bit Victorian.'

'She might be a bit stiff if you don't,' Daisy admitted, but although she was doing her best to be interested in what Aunt Maude would say, Daisy actually found that she was not very interested in Freddie's romance, so relieved was she that she could see David without feeling guilty. She had lost interest in anything else.

'Oh, very well, I'll ask her.' As Daisy stood up to leave to go back on ops, Freddie sighed. 'I'll ask her tomorrow, if only to make Branscombe feel happy.'

There was a long silence, and then Maude spoke.

'This Corporal Benjamin Bastable, you have been out with him twice, and now he wants to marry you?'

'Yes. He says he knew it the moment he saw me again, that I was the girl he should marry.'

That was very bold of Freddie, and she knew it, but she was dashed if she was going to be put through the hoops without being completely honest.

'Nice young man, Corporal Bastable,' Maude announced, after a much smaller silence. 'Lost his hand, as I remember it, and suffered one or two breakages, but altogether in not too bad a shape. What's he up to now?'

'He's studying for a degree in something or other – oh, economics – he thinks that after the war everything will be about just that, economics.'

'He's probably perfectly correct.'

'And then he's very keen to invent a new kind of bicycle. He draws beautifully, you know.'

Maude looked at Freddie, and smiled.

'My dear Freddie,' she said. 'I don't know why you thought it a good idea to ask my permission to marry this young man. Of course you must marry your clever young man, of course you must. As it happens it will serve my purpose very well if you marry him as soon as is perfectly possible.'

She took out some papers from her leather folder, and laid them on the library table.

'When you have read through these, you will know what I mean.'

There was no time to put together a wedding dress, and anyway, it was not considered quite right to do more than wed in your best suit with perhaps a corsage of flowers on your lapel. But Freddie did have a flowered hat, to go with her spring suit, and loveliest of loveliest of things, a fine pair of nylon stockings.

The honeymoon was spent in a cosy room above a country pub. Freddie thought that making love was wonderful, but did not have time to appreciate it quite as much as she wished, because she had to get back to her duties, and they both had to get back to the war.

'All that matters is that we love each other, not

how long our honeymoon is,' Ben said, by way of comfort.

'No time to bore each other, either, think of that!' Freddie joked, quickly plaiting her long brown hair and tossing it as usual behind her back. 'I've really enjoyed my twenty-four hours in civvies,' she added, dressing once more in her nurse's uniform. 'And what is more, since this is the first day of our marriage, I think I can say I have never been happier.'

Ben turned away. He hated leaving her, had loved loving her, but it was indeed time to get back to the war.

'We've been very lucky, haven't we? The Hall did us proud, what with the cake and the tinned salmon – don't know where Branscombe got that from – and the gin toasts.' He shook his head. 'When you think of some, it's into the registry office and out again, and not even time for anything more than a quick kiss.'

They kissed, and Ben dropped Freddie back at the hospital, just as Miss Maude was coming out, having done her bit for the day.

'Good evening, Miss Maude. Want to hop in, and let me drop you back before I go on?'

Maude settled down in the seat beside him, leaving her bicycle behind for Freddie to bring on in the morning.

'It was very good of you to say you would sign those papers for me, Benjamin,' she said. 'And you hardly married!'

They both laughed.

'Least I could do for you, Miss Maude, the very least. I must thank you for the wonderful wedding you gave us. You spoiled us, really you did.'

Maude glanced sideways at him, although she could not really make out his face in the dark.

'You're going to be very happy, both of you,' she said with some satisfaction. 'I know that you are, because you both work hard, and if you work hard, you make things happen, that is how it is. It means a great deal to see you all settled. I only hope my Daisy gets on with it, truly I do. She's so busy being a boy I think she has put love on the back burner, and that will never do.'

Ben knew otherwise, of course. He knew that Daisy had shot off to see David Moreton, about two seconds after he and Freddie were spliced, only just giving herself time to catch the bride's bouquet, which, after all, as they all knew, brought luck in marriage.

'I think she will find herself someone, Miss Maude, truly I do.'

'Don't want her ending up like me,' Maude said, getting out and shining her torch as she did so. 'Don't want her ending up a lonely spinster. I'll walk in front of the car, until we get into the drive, Benjamin. You just follow me.'

Ben did as instructed, and as he did so it seemed to him that Maude Beresford going ahead with the torch, and he following on, was some kind of metaphor – a new word for him – some kind of symbol of the past and the present, he, the younger man in the dark, she the older generation leading the way with a torch.

One of these days Branscombe was sure that one of them was going to fall down the stairs to the kitchen. Clatter, clatter, clatter, perhaps someone already had? He turned. Oh dear, it was Miss Maude, and she was white in the face, and pointing upstairs.

'Brigadier MacNaughton?' he asked.

She shook her head.

'No, worse than that, MacNaughton and his ghastly new wife, with the Huggetts, Roger and Susan.'

It had been a day they had all been dreading, knowing that one way or another it would come eventually.

'They've come for Ted, Branscombe, they've come for Ted!'

Branscombe slowly wiped his hands on a cloth.

'They have, have they? Well, they're going to be disappointed, aren't they?'

Maude stared. She had never been less composed, and yet Branscombe, it seemed, had never been more composed.

'How do you mean, disappointed?'

Branscombe gave Maude his long, one-eyed stare.

'I had a feeling it was going to happen, Miss Maude, as I am sure you did, too, and I got wind yesterday that it was going to come to this, but it won't. They can't have him, see, because he is not here.'

'He isn't?'

Maude looked round, only now realising that the kitchen was empty of everyone except the dogs and Johnny.

'No, young Ted has gone for a holiday, and will only be back once the adoption papers are through. And that might take some weeks.'

Maude sat down suddenly.

'What can we say, then?'

'Nothing. We say nothing. Only that his mother left him to Miss Freddie in her will, which she did, and that Miss Freddie and her husband have officially adopted him, and that they will be in touch, once Ted has enjoyed his holiday.'

Maude put a hand up to her head, always a forbidden gesture when she was young, no matter how ferocious the headache.

'I'm not sure that I can cope any more, Branscombe. Do you think you could take this message up to them? Say to them what you have said to me.'

'With pleasure.'

Branscombe took off his apron, pulled on his formal black coat, brushed his trousers, and said to Johnny, 'You stay here and guard Miss Maude until I get back.'

As soon as he saw MacNaughton again, and his new wife, Branscombe remembered how much he hated men like him, and wives like her, jumped-up tarts. He had been in the Great War with the MacNaughtons of this world, overbearing monsters, all of them. Couldn't wait to call their men cowards and shoot them, while themselves cowering behind the lines.

His one eye now took in the Huggetts. Most respectable, two or three generations into respectability, but so cold, so hard, so snobbish. They had hurt poor Jean Shaw's feelings to such a degree it didn't bear thinking of, it really did not. The poor girl, working her fingers to the bone on the farm, losing her husband, all she had wanted was for them to acknowledge her child.

'But they never will, Branscombe,' she had said. 'Not ever. So in the event I don't survive, I have left my baby to Freddie and you and Miss Maude to bring up.'

Of course Branscombe had insisted that she would live, which of course the poor girl did not, but she did make a will leaving Ted to Freddie, and, for her own reasons, Branscombe and Miss Maude.

It was Miss Maude, grown so fond of Ted – not to mention Alec and his brothers, not to mention Johnny – who had got it into her head that Freddie and Ben should adopt Ted officially. It was quick and easy enough to do, once the knot was tied, and in wartime, even quicker and easier than at any other time, when the authorities rubber-stamped any adoption, if only to get the babies into homes, and out of care.

'Ted is not here,' Branscombe began, rather enjoying himself.

'Ted? Who is Ted?' Susan Huggett asked her husband in tones of suppressed fury.

'Ted is Miss Jean's, Mrs Joe Huggett's, only surviving child. Her son. He is not here, if he is what you have come for.'

'Soon change that name . . .'

'He is away on his holidays, and will be back when they are over.'

'He will be found, and at once,' the brigadier rapped out, while banging one finger on the table to the side of him.

'Mind that table, sir, it has been here two hundred years, and it might not be feeling too well. Yes. Now, where was I? Yes, Ted Huggett is away, and will be back when, and not before, his holidays are over, after which he will be staying with his new parents, Mr and Mrs Benjamin Bastable. They have adopted him—'

'But they can't!'

'They have adopted him, in line with the wishes of his poor mother's will. He will keep his surname as Huggett, but he will be brought up by Mr and Mrs Bastable, in line with his mother's wishes.' He turned to the Huggetts. 'Since you now wish to take an interest in him, I am sure the Bastables will be only too happy to ask you round to tea, or let you visit him on previously arranged occasions. When he is older you will want to see him play in matches at his school, and that, too, will be perfectly in order, I am sure. But now, for now, I must ask you all to leave, if only because there is nothing more to stay for.'

'You haven't heard the last of this,' Roger Huggett shouted from the bottom of the Hall steps.

Branscombe shook his head at him. Huggett had always seemed such a nice man, before the war, but war changed everything, mostly people. He himself climbed carefully down the dark stairs to the kitchen, only too relieved that the whole unpleasant business was over.

'All done and dusted,' he told Maude in a matter-of-fact voice.

'How did you know that something was in the offing, Branscombe?'

'I have my spies, as you know, Miss Maude. The brigadier's wife, as you know, once worked here—'

'She did indeed.'

'She's a bit of a goer, as they say. One of the guards, well, what can I say? To put it another way, I came by information that she had been in contact with Ted's grandparents, about the boy. It happened because she and the brigadier are living in Holly House, where the Huggetts were. The rumour was that she wrote to them, the brigadier's wife, saying how much like Joe the boy was becoming, all that kind of thing. Mischief-maker, as so many women like that are. So down they came, eventually, and up to the Hall, as we saw this morning; but we got him out of here before any more mischief could be done, didn't we, Miss Maude?'

'It seems we did. Who's he with, Branscombe? Who is Ted holidaying with?'

'Why, Miss Daisy, of course.'

461

Maude stood up.

'That will never do. Daisy knows nothing about children!'

Branscombe threw her a suddenly affectionate look.

'It is more than Miss Daisy's life's worth for her to let anything happen to the little chap. Besides, it will do her good, Miss Maude, take her mind off her beau!'

'Daisy has a beau?'

'I believe so, Miss Maude. I believe so.'

'Well, you do surprise me. She's become so masculine, always in that uniform, smoking and doubtless swearing, in and out of planes. I'm surprised that any man has taken an interest in her!'

They both laughed, knowing that Daisy would never have any trouble in attracting men, only in settling down with one.

Daisy was lodging in the country, so it was easy for her to take on Ted – indeed she delighted in doing so – and even easier to find someone local to look after him while she went on ferrying planes. Mary Fry was a nice local girl with a fresh-faced complexion and an easy way with children, which was evident from the start.

'I'm the eldest of eight, miss, so there's nothing I can't tell you about children.'

'Gracious, no trouble for you when it comes to motherhood, then.'

Mary Fry looked across at Daisy. It was a look of such good-humoured cynicism that it actually made Daisy, who was half-way out of the door making for the factory, laugh.

'After bringing up my brothers and sisters, you're not going to catch me having babies, and a husband, Miss! I know too much about it.'

Daisy shook her head, seeing her point, and then shut the door behind her, dropping the latch back. Sauntering down the front path to the country road, it occurred to her that she had found the perfect nanny.

'What are you looking so complacent about?' David asked her as he drove her to the airfield, later.

'Nothing, and everything.'

He stopped the car.

'I'll pick you up tonight, and we can go back to the cottage and map out the rest of our lives – once the war is over.'

'Twenty-four-hour leave is usually arranged by clever people to coincide so that they can be together during that twenty-four hours, but not, it seems, the future Mr and Mrs David Moreton. Oh, expletive! My watch is slow – oh, double expletive! Look what I can see on the tarmac waiting for me! Only a something, something Walrus—'

David left her. Happily for both of them, the distance that the planes from this particular factory had to go was very short indeed. They were only short hops, and that meant David would be seeing her this afternoon, before he, too, went back to his duties.

Just before he drove off, he saw her turn and

wave back to him, and the sight caught at his heart. He loved his darling Daisy more than he would have thought possible. Now they just had to win the war, and then they could be married, not before. Both of them were determined about that.

As Daisy said, joking, 'We don't want to do anything in a hurry, do we?'

But it took so long to win the war. So long, and the end – well, it seemed that it would never, ever come. First it was going to be now, then it was going to be quite soon, then in a few weeks. First the Allies had to re-invade France, and just the thought of climbing up those Normandy beaches under fire made Daisy shudder, and then Paris had to be taken, and then, and then . . .

It sometimes seemed to them all that the war, the real war, not just their war – fighting their local difficulties – but the battles, and the news from around the world, was being won, or lost, by the wireless around which they all liked to cluster for the news.

Finally VE Day came, and finally, too, all the celebrations could happen, but not in Twistleton, only at the Hall.

At the Hall they had a bonfire, and the children all danced around it, and they had hot drinks, and Freddie and everyone gave out little whistles and paper hats they had made and painted themselves. It was good, and it was fun, but in so many ways, the adults knew that they were too tired to really feel anything any more. Too tired to really take stock, until finally there was Churchill, good old Churchill, on the balcony, and the King and Queen, God bless them, and the crowds were cheering really hard – and at this point most people had gone home. But, in the case of everyone at the Hall, they couldn't, because the army still occupied their homes, or what was left of them.

They had been told that they would be paid compensation, but none was forthcoming.

They had been told that the army would make good the damage, but they did nothing of the sort.

'It's disgraceful,' Guy exclaimed when he drove over with Clive and Aurelia, and they surveyed the ruins that had once been Twistleton. 'Bad enough winning a war without having to fight your own army, as well.'

Longbridge Farm was a sad sight, too, but not nearly as sad as Twistleton.

The new building restrictions meant that both the farm and the village would stay as they were until such time that the former owners could gain the necessary permissions, which Guy, because he was Guy, was able to do, but the people of Twistleton could not.

'They even shot the faces off some of the tombs in the graveyard, did you know that, Miss Maude? And off the gargoyles over the church door, sir. They even shot bits off our church.' The one-time owner of the pub shook his head, and tears filled his eyes. 'And now look at the Court, Miss Jessica's

465

old place: nothing left of it, except the ground floor. What will happen to that, I wonder?'

Guy shook his head, and Clive tugged at Aurelia's hand, and they all walked quickly on.

'What will happen now, Clive?' Aurelia wanted to know.

Clive shook his head.

'Probably blasted nothing,' he said, as politely as he could. 'Blasted nothing, but we must see, that is all we can do.'

They all went back to Longbridge Farm, knowing that it would take months and months, possibly years, before Guy could even begin work on it, but at least it was not a shell, at least it was recognisable.

But even there their spirits sank as they realised that the white sofas so favoured before the war looked a little silly now, more than silly, as objects of luxury always do when the bad times come. Guy found himself staring at them, wondering why he had prized them so much, thought them so smart.

'There will be parties here again,' he declared. 'We will laugh again,' he told the walls blackened by damp. 'We will overcome this next silent war, as we have overcome the last. We will live to be happy on another day, because not to be is finally to be defeated.'

Clive and Aurelia, married now, and living in what had once been old Bob's cottage, looked after the farm during the week, when Guy was in London or abroad overseeing the production of much-wanted comedies. They had no luck producing children, for no reason that they could ascertain, but after a while they settled for a great many animals, which seemed to make up for their lack of fecundity. Particularly, as Clive often remarked, the cats.

Everyone who had been at the Hall during the war was told that they could stay on, and for as long as they liked; but most wanted to go back to their civilian lives, where they could attempt to find some kind of peace and privacy, and start living properly again, which was only natural.

Freddie and Ben were renting a cottage near Oxford, where she could nurse and he could continue to study and work on the designs of his new bicycle. Naturally they took Ted with them, which was a wrench for Maude and Branscombe.

Daisy and David, and the redoubtable Mary Fry, went to live at the lodge of David's parents' country house, which had been turned into a school for the duration, and was now a wreck.

'It'll take about fifty years to put it all back to rights, won't it?' Daisy joked when they had finished walking round it. 'As a matter of fact, I'm not sure that schoolboys don't do more harm than the army.'

Of course this wasn't true, but putting the house back together would take many, many years of hard work, years during which Daisy produced four children, all boys, which seemed to satisfy her Aunt Maude in a way that Daisy understood, but never remarked on.

Laura went back to France and, to her great delight, married Friquet, who was also delighted. They, too, repaired to a country house much damaged, not by a school, or the regular army, but by German officers.

Again it would take years before they could put it back to rights, years in which Laura and Friquet lived in a wing, very happily, and put themselves to work on the estate, producing anything and everything so that they could save up to buy the necessary building materials to restore the old place.

Only Maude, Branscombe and Alec and his brothers lived on at the Hall.

Alec married a local girl, and produced children, as did the others, except for Johnny, who became a jazz trumpeter, which, as Branscombe noted with some surprise, gave Maude a great excuse to go to jazz clubs and smoke cigarettes.

The two older inhabitants of the Hall often thought back to the bad times of the war, finally agreeing, over a nice glass of whisky, that what had come out of it was not victory so much as the fact that they had all pulled together, and that many barriers had been broken, and lives changed, in a good way.

But the truth was that, optimistic as they felt, knowing that people of all kinds had become kinder and more tolerant for knowing each other, for being put hugger-mugger in an untidy way together – the village, their Twistleton, was still wrecked.

Letters were written. Why would they not be? All kinds of remonstrations were made, but no one paid the slightest attention to the fact that Twistleton lay in ruins, roofs off The Cottages, doors swinging free, gardens overgrown, no part of it habitable except the pub, and the church – and even they were no longer as they had been, prey to so much theft and destruction . . .

'Something must be done, something has to be done to help Twistleton,' the redoubtable old pair would say, and Alec, to whom Maude had finally willed the Hall – along with his brothers, and their descendants – would overhear this, and silently vow that he would do what he could when he could.

Epilogue

Guy stopped beckoning to the rest of the Daisy Club, and dropped his hands, indicating that they could all now sit down and enjoy their picnics.

It was their annual meeting, and no one, but no one, missed it, on pain of being dropped from the club. In the case of an absent member even sick notes from doctors had to be produced, which Daisy thought was a bit much, but which Guy nevertheless insisted upon, as he also insisted that all children and dogs were left at the Hall in the charge of Branscombe and Mary Fry.

They all shared their picnics and their drinks, and there was plenty of everything to go round, despite the fact that there was still rationing. Soon would come the speech, which, if it was raining, and the picnics had to be held in the old bomb-shelter to the side of the woods, was usually drowned out by the sound of the water pounding on the tin roof.

Today, however, was different, and they all

knew it. Today, they had made up their minds, was the day when they were all going to decide once and for all on a plan of action.

'We have had enough of talk,' Guy told them to the sound of murmurs of assent. 'Now we have to plot a plan of action, and make sure that we carry it through – and we can carry it through. We have enough strength and purpose.'

'But when can we do it?'

'On a day when no one is looking, when everyone will be out celebrating, when the whole of this island will be celebrating the crowning of our dear Queen. That is the day we will reoccupy our dear Twistleton and fly the flag above the pub, and ring the church bells.'

'How can we? What about the army? There are unexploded bombs everywhere.'

'Not any more, there aren't,' Guy told the speaker, with his usual assurance. 'Not any more. They have had it, as from next week they will be no more. I made sure that Gloria Martine—' There was a pause for laughter. He went on, 'I mean the few people who still owe me for having me thrown into jug. I made sure through them that the powers-that-be arranged for them to be defused.' They all looked at each other in amazement, unable to quite believe what was being said. 'And once that has happened we can start in on your beloved village, and let no man or woman step between it and us! So let us drink to being in this place this time next year, and our own beloved victory.'

Clive looked across an assortment of heads to where Guy was raising his glass to victory. He loved doing this sort of thing, and what was more he was very good at it. And of course the fact that he was back, all cosy at Longbridge Farm, made him feel for the villagers of Twistleton, who longed, constantly longed, to get back to their beloved homes.

The rest of the day was spent laughing and talking, and finally they all packed their picnics up, and headed back to the Hall for more drinks and a buffet, all part of their annual reunion.

As they left their seaside view and trailed back up the field again, their faces a little burned by the sun, their baskets feeling oddly light, their rugs not as smartly packed as they had been, Daisy thought about all the people they were missing.

Of course they had been replaced by the next generation currently being given tea by Branscombe and Mary up at the Hall, but they would never be quite the same as those who had gone – those bright-eyed spirits who had so willingly given their all to defend their homeland. She wondered for a thousandth time where they *were*, everyone whom they had known and loved, and who were now gone. Where *were* they?

And then it came to her. That they were the wind moving through the grass, the heads of the flowers swaying, they were the sea coming up to the edge of the beach, they were the rocks against which it tested its strength. They were the mystery of everything they had done, and the beauty of everything they had been. They were the length and breadth of love and kindness, and because of that, they would never be forgotten.

THE END

Charlotte Bingham would like to invite you to visit her website at www.charlottebingham.com

THE LAND OF SUMMER
by Charlotte Bingham

As the eldest of four daughters, American heiress
Emmaline Nesbitt has always understood
that she is obliged to wed. But no proposals
have so far come her way, until at a ball in her
family home she meets Julius, a handsome and
charming Englishman who wastes no time in
proposing to her. Shortly after, Emmaline
sails to England for her wedding.

What awaits her on arrival is a long way from her
expectations. She is brought to a strange house
full of odd guests and eccentric servants – a far
cry from the fine home Julius had promised – as
well as a very different Julius. As the days go by,
her fiancé changes beyond recognition, so much
so that Emmaline believes there is no future to
their relationship. But that is before Julius's past,
and the history of his family and background
make themselves plain to her.

9780553819793

THE ENCHANTED
by Charlotte Bingham

Joint ownership of a small dark chestnut colt from western Ireland brings together a group of very different people . . .

When Kathleen finds a mare in foal, despite the fact that she and her father can barely afford to feed her they take her in. Tragically the mare dies, leaving an orphan which they name The Enchanted. But even as he is growing up among Ireland's lush pastures, Kathleen knows that they will eventually have to sell him, and with him will go her heart . . .

The recently widowed Helena is encouraged by her eccentric friend Millie to take the plunge and buy a share in a horse. Suddenly, both women find themselves involved not just in the fate of the little horse, but of Rory James, his trainer, who has only recently taken over the run-down racing yard.

Luck does not run Rory's way when The Enchanted mysteriously sickens. It seems only Kathleen can help, and so it is that under her care The Enchanted is able to live up to his name and astonishing things start to happen to all those around the little horse . . .

'Charlotte Bingham's devotees will recognise her supreme skill as a storyteller'
Independent on Sunday

9780553817829

GOODNIGHT SWEETHEART
by Charlotte Bingham

Before the Second World War breaks, Chevrons,
the idyllic country house where the Garlands
have lived for centuries, has already been
touched by events in Europe. To the horror of
her family, Katherine, the eldest daughter, has
run off to join the Nazis. On the outbreak of war,
young Caro Garland and her friend Robyn leave
Chevrons to help the war effort. In London, they
are joined by Edwina, a beautiful Irish girl with
such striking looks that she catches the eye of the
future Prime Minister. While Caro and Robyn
join the First Aid Nursing Yeomanry, Edwina
is singled out for undercover work of
the most glamorous nature.

All the girls meet and fall in love but in such
an atmosphere of fleeting pleasure and fatal
acceptance, it would seem that the young will
never find lasting happiness.

'Charlotte Bingham's devotees will recognise her
supreme skill as a storyteller . . . A heartwarming
romance which is full of emotion'
Independent on Sunday

'An engaging, romantic and nostalgic read'
Daily Mail

9780553817812

THE WHITE MARRIAGE
by Charlotte Bingham

Sunny's mundane country life is changed over night when handsome, stylish Gray's Bentley breaks down outside her parents' cottage in Rushington. It seems that he may have fallen in love with her. Although Sunny herself remains unconvinced, her best friend Arietta believes that Sunny is soon to be set on the road to wealth and happiness.

Shortly after meeting Gray for the second time at a local ball, Sunny is invited out by his close friend, the beautiful socialite, Leandra Fortescue, who tells her over lunch that Gray wants to marry her if she will accept certain conditions. Sunny does accept, even as Arietta is leaving Rushington to work in London.

Sunny soon joins Arietta at her cheerfully chaotic lodgings. It is here that she realises that she can find the sort of contentment that has eluded sophisticates such as Gray and Leandra. Here too she meets Hart and, despite being engaged to Gray, falls in love with him, just as Arietta has fallen for his friend, jazz-playing painter, Sam. By chance Arietta comes into a secret about Gray, but is afraid to tell Sunny, and yet not to tell her might ruin her future.

9780553817836

IN DISTANT FIELDS
by Charlotte Bingham

When Kitty is invited to stay with her friend
Partita at Bauders Castle she is sure she must
refuse. Her mother, however, sees it as an
undreamed-of opportunity for her daughter to
escape from the dark presence of her notorious
father, and pawns her engagement ring to enable
Kitty to go. Partita's parents are enchanted
by Kitty and she soon becomes part of their
privileged and glamorous lifestyle.

It seems that the family's grand way of life is
unassailable, but it is not. After one last idyllic
seaside holiday, war is declared. The young
men cannot wait to volunteer, while the girls
go on nursing courses, and the castle becomes
a convalescent home. They are sure that the
war will be over in a few weeks, but once the
wounded start arriving from the Front, the harsh
reality of conflict becomes clear to them all,
none more so than Kitty and Partita.

9780553818048

OUT OF THE BLUE
by Charlotte Bingham

Florence Fontaine has still not recovered from a family tragedy when she discovers a strangely dressed man asleep in her guest cottage at the Old Rectory. Against her better judgement she offers him breakfast, only to rue the day as she finds herself caught up in the resulting drama of his life. Florence's young and beautiful daughter, Amadea, is immediately suspicious of Edward, as he appears to be called, fearing that he might be a fraud.

Against everyone's advice, Florence enlists friends and neighbours to help restore Edward's now wandering mind and discover who he might be. As the mystery unfolds, it becomes apparent that Edward's history is entwined with that of nearby Harlington Hall, but that his real identity is something quite other.

Florence and Amadea become united in their quest, an adventure that takes them into many pasts, not least that of the young man whom they are now dedicated to help. In doing so they are finally able to put tragedy behind them, repair their once disjointed lives, and embrace a new and happy future.

9780553815948